Child of the Mist

Child of the Mist

the Mist

Jeanne Montague

PIATKUS

First published in Great Britain in 1996 by
Judy Piatkus (Publishers) Ltd of
5 Windmill Street, London W1

The moral right of the author has been asserted

A catalogue record for this book is available from the British Library

ISBN 0–7499–0359–7

Set in 11/12 pt Times by
Datix International Limited, Bungay, Suffolk
Printed and bound in Great Britain by
Bookcraft (Bath) Ltd.

Prelude

Wind in her hair. Wind in her face. The taste of salt on her lips. The child stood alone on the edge of the cliff, her skirt whipped back against her thin limbs. It felt clammy, sticking to the bare skin beneath.

Her eyes were closed, the lashes damp and salty, too, the sun a glowing red blob against the blackness of her lids. There was an exaltation within her, a response to the stark wildness of her surroundings.

'The edge is dangerous,' they always said, those doubters who had lost their sense of magic and wonder. 'Chalky, crumbling. Be careful where you tread. It's not safe to go up there. Stay away.'

She could not stay away. It would have been like abandoning a friend. Freedom. Space. The never-ending vault of heaven above – the eternal expanse of sea below. Restless, changing, white-crested.

Gulls wheeled and called close to her head. She had been motionless for so long that they had grown bold. There was noisy activity on the cliff face. Nests had been built in holes and on ledges – homes for greedy hatchlings clamouring to be fed. The child opened her eyes, swaying slightly. She stared down the sheer grey drop to where the Atlantic breakers pounded and smothered the tumbled mass of rocks or hurled themselves against the jagged points which she likened to dragon's teeth.

Mother was afraid that the child would slip and plunge down the three hundred foot drop, dashing her brains out. Mother was fearful of so many things; of the dark, of Father when he was drunk, of the gossiping women, of the debt collector, of the gentry who owned the port.

The child feared little, only her father when the drink was in him, and then more on her mother's account. When sober he was amiable enough, and he had been proud of her when she started school. The teachers were strict, but she did not mind this, avid to learn, and the

1

bullies who tried to victimize her in the playground had soon given up after meeting her bunched fists and flying feet.

'You've got spirit, lass!' the fishermen and miners had said to her when she went to fetch her father from the public bar of the Ship Inn, their tone half deprecating, half admiring.

'She has that,' he had growled into his mug of cider, his speech, like theirs, of so marked a dialect as to be indecipherable to people who were foreign to those parts.

The family were poor. The child was aware of this but only vaguely, having never known anything else. Not as badly off as some; there was always food on the table – bread, cheese, vegetables from the garden, some fish, a bit of meat or bacon sometimes. The cottage was warm in winter with its slate roof and fire banked up with driftwood collected from the shore or fallen branches dragged from the nearby forest. Her clothing was adequate and she was still too young to pine for anything finer. The only irksome thing was having to wear a skirt when she yearned for breeches, like those much-envied lads who swaggered about the harbour, hands thrust deep in their pockets.

But in the fields and woods, on the beach and, above all, atop the towering cliffs, she could hitch up her skirt and tuck it into her drawers, leaving her long skinny legs free for running, jumping, wading and climbing.

Ten was a grand age to be, she had decided. Mother did not worry quite as much as she had done in days gone by, though there was always that strict admonishment every time she left the cottage – to be careful, not to speak to strangers and be sure to be home before dark.

Mindful of this, she checked the sun's position, reassured that there were hours in which to roam. Sure-footed as a chamois, she took the sheep track bordered by sea-pinks and marram grass clinging tenaciously to the sparse soil. She sang as she went, her high, sweet treble blending with the strong wind and the thin, sad wail of a curlew.

Her destination was further inland, but never far from the omnipresent sea whose boom and hiss could be heard over all. The luminous, almost unearthly light, the vibrant colours and movement intoxicated her. She touched the grasses and the soft, feathery tamarisk as she passed, lifting her fingers to her nose and inhaling the heady smell of crushed foliage. For a moment her senses blended into one, no longer separate, just a single awareness of the beauty around her. There seemed to be no time or space, only the eternal present and the larks singing forever in the blue heights.

No conscious thought guided her; she had always been aware, reared so close to nature she was a part of it. Her feet moved over the ground almost of their own volition, carrying her to one of her favourite

2

places – a barrow raised by mysterious people thousands of years before. It stood like a little island above the surrounding land, an enchanted spot, reputed to be haunted by members of the Little People, the piskies.

Scrambling on to it she scanned the view, pretending to be a guard on the lookout for enemies, then, satisfied that the citadel was not about to be attacked, she sat down in the shelter of its earthen rim. Mother had said these ancient tumuli were burial mounds, but to the child this one was like a garden. It was covered with springy turf and here and there stood a furze bush, mixed with bramble, elder and thorn. The fiery, purple-red of heather massed in thick clumps, and a few tapering spikes of foxgloves shone against the vivid green.

She had her dinner in her pocket; the same food her father took to the mines daily – the staple diet of the Cornish workers, the versatile pasty. Though a foreigner, which meant anyone born on the Devon side of the Tamar River, her mother could make them like no one else. The child's mouth watered as she unwrapped the semicircular pie, with its crimped edges (indented by Mother's thumb) and its filling of bacon, potato and turnip.

It was deeply satisfying, and she ate it all. Lying back in the grass, squinting up at the sky, she daydreamed, thinking of the tales she had heard about the Little People. Her father never liked to see a white rabbit near the mine workings as this foretold an accident, neither would he whistle underground, for whistling was intensely disliked by the knockers. These, so it was said, were tiny creatures with the big heads and wizened faces of old men and the bodies of tiny children. They could be heard tap-tapping in the galleries underground. Her father had told her that a wise miner always worked in the direction of that sound, for there the mineral was sure to be rich.

The knockers were hungry sometimes, and woe betide the miner who did not leave them something from his lunch. The child followed this rule with regard to the piskies, and had scattered a few pasty crumbs. Though these were mischievous sprites and got up to all sorts of tricks, they were nothing like as malicious as the spriggans, another branch of fairy folk who lived near the stone circles and rock-strewn cairns. They had a nasty habit of stealing unguarded babies, taking them away and substituting their own brats in a human mother's rocking cradle.

Once, during a harvest supper celebration in one of the farmers' barns, the child had overheard a puzzling conversation concerning herself. 'There's no knowing where that girl came from,' one old woman had said to another. 'She don't look nothing like her parents at all.'

3

'Maybe she's a changeling – left behind by a spriggan,' the other had replied, and they had both cackled unpleasantly. Later she had questioned her mother who had coloured up, her fine eyes sparkling with anger. Clasping her close, she had ordered her to pay no mind to those acid-tongued old busybodies.

The child had obeyed her from then on – defiant if the village children teased her, ready with stinging retorts and hard fists. Gradually she was left alone, and this did not trouble her. She was happy, a solitary roaming over hill and through woodland. What need had she for company?

She jumped up and wandered on, the sun beating down on her head and neck as she wondered if she should go to where the sea was rushing along the shore and into the gullies, or visit the harbour to watch the fishing boats coming in loaded to the gunnels with their fascinating hauls. Then her eyes were drawn to the dark line of woods in the distance and curiosity inched through her. She had never yet ventured within. It was forbidden territory with large notices that read 'Keep Out. Trespassers will be Prosecuted.'

It did not take her long to reach the fence and find a way through. Supple as an eel, there were few barriers able to withstand her if she made up her mind to cross them. Her nostrils tingled with the odour of wild garlic as she slid down a bank and landed in an overgrown glen. Trees were thick on either side, meeting in an arch over her head. Dazzling patches of sunlight shone through the leaves, penetrating the dense shadows. From somewhere came the curious musical call of a young thrush and over and above all, the mournful declaiming of wood pigeons, a sound which coloured life from dawn till dusk throughout the summer months.

So far so good, thought the child, and penetrated deeper. Now she heard the trickle of water and followed it to a small brook gurgling over flat black stones, twisting and tumbling as it fell. She sat down and took off her boots, tying them together by the laces and slinging them over her shoulder. Wading in the stream, she was so intent on the feel of icy water on her ankles and the slippery sensation of pebbles under her feet that she was unaware of alien sounds at first.

Then her head went up, cocked at a listening angle. It came again, clear and distinct – human voices and laughter. A bolt of resentment shot through her. Others had dared enter her domain.

There was a glimmer beyond the trees, and the sound of people splashing about. She waded on again, was almost there, blocked from view by screening bushes. There was nothing for it, she would have to show herself if she wanted to satisfy her curiosity. She stepped out into the glade.

4

The scene was idyllic – a rippling expanse of sage-green water into which the stream plunged, a miniature cascade. Mossy banks, stately trees, beeches, oaks and ash, and a dazzling display of rhododendrons with leathery leaves and large showy flowers in shades of pink and blue.

A bare-legged group were seated on a low wooden bridge, dangling their feet in the pool. The child was immediately on the defensive. They were boys, and not of her own kind. She summed them up in an instant by the clear, confident tones of their voices, the perfect pronunciation without the trace of a rural drawl, the clean white shirts, the velveteen or tweed knickerbockers. Everything about them proclaimed money and privilege.

'I say,' one of them declared, staring across at her. 'Look what the wind's blown in, chaps. It's a girl. What are you doing here, girl?'

Her hackles rose at his condescending tone. It contained mockery, superiority, laced with something which she could not name – only knowing that it made her feel uncomfortable.

His friends (there were two of them), nudged each other and whispered while never taking their eyes from her. All three were big boys, older then her by several years. The one who had addressed her had blond curls worn rather long, framing a lean face.

He beckoned imperiously, saying, 'Come here, girl. Let's have a closer look at you.'

'Why should I?' she demanded, hands on her hips.

His companions laughed, wrestled, tried to push each other into the water. 'We're brigands and this is our camp,' one shouted, red-headed and podgy. 'You're our prisoner.'

'Don't talk daft!' she replied with lofty disdain. 'I'm nothing of the sort. I go where I want. No one tells me what to do.'

The fair-haired boy, who was obviously the leader, was quietly observing her. 'Are you a villager?' he asked, an intense expression in his eyes. 'You don't talk like a villager.'

Now was the time to lie, or rather to embellish the truth. The girl's imagination was a lively one and she had long ago constructed a fictional background for herself.

She left the cover of the bushes and strolled towards them, head held at a haughty angle. 'Of course I'm not a villager.'

'Then who are you?'

'I can't tell you. It would be more than my life's worth. It's a State secret.' This was fun. She almost believed her story. 'My parents are from among the highest in the land but, for reasons I dare not reveal, I was sent here when a baby to be brought up by a miner and his wife.'

The blond boy threw back his mop of curls and gave a sharp yelp of

5

derisive laughter. 'What rot!' he exclaimed, then stood up as she reached the bridge, his tallness making her want to rise on tiptoe in a vain attempt to match it.

'Why should I lie?' She faced him boldly, even carelessly, though her heart was thumping.

'Because you know you shouldn't be here. Can't you read? Didn't you see the notice? What did you come for? A spot of poaching?'

The girl was possessed of a wicked temper, so the adults had said often enough, shaking their heads sagely. Not much self-control, and a sharp tongue for one so young. Maybe the epithet 'changeling' had not been far off the mark. She was not aware of these things as faults. To her they were weapons to use against hostility, and she did not hesitate to employ them now, for it was hostility coupled with downright un-kindness that she sensed coming from the fair boy.

'I'll go where I damn well please,' she shouted indignantly.

'It swears!' He addressed his friends is a slow, insolent drawl. 'Did you hear that? It said damn. For that it deserves a beating, don't you agree?'

The others leapt up, whooping and yelling. 'The prisoner needs a lesson in manners,' the fat one shouted. 'Come on, let's grab her!'

'Stop being stupid!' the girl exclaimed, but her fists were already clenched into tight-knuckled balls. 'You aren't brigands! You're just silly boys!'

'And you're a dirty gypsy. You look like a gypsy. A thieving gypsy. That's what you came for – to steal!'

The fair boy was close to her now. She could see the flush on his cheeks, the fierceness of his green eyes under curling lashes, the pronounced curve of his nose. He was handsome. He spoke with an assured ring to his voice. He smelled different to the village boys, of soap and clean linen. He was upright, proud, fascinating – her enemy.

The insult stung. Gypsies were feared and despised by miners and fisherfolk alike. It was not the first time she had been compared to them. How she longed to be as blond as he was; fair-complexioned and golden-haired, not the owner of a dark tangled mane of curls which would never be tamed, no matter how often it was brushed.

'I'm not a gypsy,' she said forcefully.

'Oh, no? Prove it.' The boy seized her by the arm. The girl was strong but he was stronger. No matter how she pulled, she could not free herself. 'I think you're a witch as well.'

'We could burn a witch,' the thinner of his comrades cried, hopping about eagerly. 'Let's light a fire.'

'No. Chapman wouldn't like us lighting fires. We'll duck her instead. They used to duck witches, didn't they?'

'Why are you being so horrid?' the child demanded, her eyes darting round for a means of escape. 'The forest belongs to everyone, doesn't it? Why shouldn't I play here?'

'It doesn't belong to just anyone! It doesn't! It doesn't! Dirty gypsy!' they choroused, crowding round her – the handsome boy, the fat one, the wiry one with the sharp features of a ferret.

They were a gang – pinching and shoving – with those vicious little assaults of child on child which she had encountered in the playground. But there was something more. She caught a whiff of cruelty, of bloodlust, and the pleasant glade suddenly became a jungle with herself as the prey.

'Let go! Stop it!' She hit back, hearing the resounding smack as her hand connected with the fair boy's face.

'Bloody little bitch!' he snarled, and landed her a backhanded blow that set the trees reeling.

'She's a girl. Let's have a look at her.' There was a strange light in the thin boy's eyes. The girl did not understand what it was, but though she could not define it or give it a name, she felt it as keenly as if she were a grown woman. It threatened in a way she had never met before.

'Good idea.' The fair youth's mouth slanted in a tight smile. 'Come on, girl. Up with your skirt and down with your knickers. Show us what you've got, and we'll show you ours, and maybe we won't duck you after all.'

The child was outraged. Pull up her skirt up in front of boys! Display her bottom! Her face flamed scarlet and she tore herself away.

'Go to hell!' she shrieked.

This galvanised them into action. Three pairs of hands gripped her. She was hauled on to the bridge, held over the edge, then pushed into the water. It wasn't deep but she slipped and went under, rising with her hair streaming, spitting fury. The boys were standing on the bridge, arms linked, roaring with laughter.

'What's going on here?' A harsh male voice silenced them, and the child dragged herself to the bank and stood there, wringing out her skirt, her small face a pointed mask of rage.

'Nothing, Chapman. We caught a trespasser, that's all,' the fair boy answered calmly. 'Thought she deserved to be ducked. Teach her a lesson.'

The gamekeeper, for it was he, stared down at the bedraggled child, a black dog at his heels, gun held in his hand. He towered over her, a grim-faced man in a corduroy jacket and breeches, a collarless shirt, a red neckerchief and muddy brown boots and gaiters. His dog's nose came forward an inch in front of those boots and there was a rumbling snarl from Chapman. The dog sank down belly on the ground, behind

7

wagging propitiatingly from side to side, its feathery underside sweeping the leaves to and fro.

'You shouldn't be here,' Chapman said, bright eyes observant beneath the peak of his cap. 'Had you lost your way?'

'No, sir.' The child was cold, but controlled her shivering limbs lest they think she trembled with fright. 'I just wanted to play.'

'We think she's a gypsy.' The fair boy had resumed his perch on the wooden planking of the bridge, picking up a fishing rod and casting it carelessly into the water.

'I'm not!' she shouted.

'She's no gypsy. I know her family,' the gamekeeper said firmly. He turned back to her. 'I'll take you home, lass. Put your boots on.'

'I can't. They're soaking wet.' She glared at the boys.

'Then you'll have to go as you are.'

This was no hardship, but she stumped off, furious, after firing a final salvo over her shoulder at the ringleader. 'You won't catch anything without proper bait. I could've shown you what to do.' The blond boy scowled at her and muttered something she could not hear.

She and Chapman walked through the trees, leaving the pool behind. There were only bird-calls now, the sound of the keeper's boots clinking on a stone and his terse commands to his dog. They took a different route to that by which she had come, passing pheasant pens and the gallows which Chapman peopled with corpses in various stages of decay swinging between the trees on wires. Moles and weasels, jays, stoats and rats, all strung up by their necks to scare away other marauders.

Would those boys have strung me up, too, if they'd had their way? she wondered, and unconsciously moved closer to Chapman. He represented normality, the kind of person she was accustomed to. He would sometimes drink with her father in the public house, and she had seen him more than once when she walked along at her mother's side. He always tipped his hat.

But there remained an injustice that wrankled. 'What about those boys?' she asked indignantly as they reached the narrow cobbled street leading down to the quay. 'Aren't you going to turn them out of the woods, too?'

He gave a crooked smile, and said, 'No, lass. They have a right to be there – every right in the world.'

Book One

Winds of Change

Chapter 1

The harvest had been gathered early after the long dry spell of an unusually warm summer. Even now when it was almost ended, the sun still hung like a molten disc in a cloudless sky and heat breathed up from the baked earth. The grave-diggers had sweated in their efforts to gouge a hole in the churchyard deep enough to hold the plain elm coffin.

Rank yellow grass and dusty green yews, a dry-stone wall that enclosed the church and grounds. The sea gleamed in the distance, peaceful today, swelling gently as it rolled in under the smile of the calm sky. There was no hint of winter when the heavy thunder of waves and the fierce winds driving them onwards conveyed an immensity of power beyond human comprehension.

Numb with grief, trapped in unreality as she moved, spoke and acted like an automaton, Margaret Helbren stood near the crumbling rim of the grave as the parson mouthed a few final words. The whiteness of his cassock was dazzling. Little beads of sweat bedewed his face. He was uncomfortable and longed to return to the cool cloisters.

Funerals are worse in fine weather, she thought dully. It would have been better had the skies rained down tears. They could have cried my share as I don't seem able to shed them. Why do I feel nothing? What's wrong with me? Even father's sisters are blubbering, and they didn't like my mother.

The church was tiny, fifteenth-century with a square two-stage tower and octagonal broach spire, built when the sea had been further off. Erosion had followed and at times it was half buried in blown sand. Early that morning the sexton had taken his broom to the flag-stoned interior before the ceremony could take place.

The congregation had been small. The inhabitants of the port were mainly nonconformists who attended the Methodist chapel, but the dead woman had been baptised a Protestant. Not for her the hell-fire and brimstone of a religion tailormade for the poor and down-trodden.

But I don't believe in God any more, her daughter thought angrily, watching the clods fall and hearing the heavy thump as they landed on the coffin lid. It's all a pack of lies. There aren't any angels or Gentle Jesus Meek and Mild. If there had been, they wouldn't have let my mother die in agony. It wasn't fair or right! There's no God, no Virgin Mary, no heaven – only this hell existing on earth.

I know that when she died I whispered the news to the bees and fastened a black crepe bow to their skep, but this was out of politeness to them, not because I hoped she'd gone to paradise. Bees sense when their keeper's dead and if I hadn't told them they'd have died themselves.

She did not realise that, along with the shock of bereavement, her lassitude was due to physical causes, only aware that her very bones seemed to be crumbling with fatigue. The sick-nursing had fallen on her, for the two of them had lived alone in Hazel Cottage since Tom Helbren's death eighteen months before. It had been a struggle to keep going on the few shillings a week doled out from the Miners' Benevolent Fund for Widows and Orphans to which Mary Helbren had contributed regularly, defying Tom who thought the money would have been better spent by himself.

Sometimes Bess Penna, local nurse and midwife, had come to help and, towards the end, Aunt Mercy and Aunt Prudence had arrived, tight-lipped and disapproving, piously doing their duty by their late brother's widow. Margaret had, long before, come to the conclusion that they were ill-named, and never more so than during the last weeks of her mother's life.

Doctors were expensive and rarely called out by the poor, but one day a coach bearing the Aubert crest had pulled up at the gate and Lady Julia had stepped down. Margaret had been aware this was an honour, though her ladyship was renowned for her charity work. It had been obvious that word of Mrs Helbren's illness had reached her at Roslan Manor and she had brought food, blankets, and beef-tea for the invalid. More important than this – she had been accompanied by her own physician, Dr Trengrouse.

It was too late, of course. Nothing short of a miracle would have saved Mary, disease of the lungs far advanced, but at least he had prescribed laudanum to take the edge off the pain. Margaret was grateful for that.

Lady Julia had been graciousness itself, shining like a star in that shabby cottage which might look picturesque from the outside but was woefully cramped within – one up, one down – damp and inconvenient. Every drop of water had to be fetched in pails from a communal well. From a child, Margaret had toiled under the burden of a wooden yoke hung from her shoulders, resenting the fact that no man ever helped, too proud to be seen doing women's work.

Aunt Prudence and Aunt Mercy, one skinny, one brawny, always attired in dark garments and ugly bonnets, even now Margaret could see them sniffling into their handkerchiefs on the far side of the grave. She remembered their awe when Lady Julia called, bowing and scraping in a nauseating manner.

Miner's daughter she might be, but Margaret had refused to kowtow. She had been all too conscious of the threadbare mats on the hardwood boards, the cracked paintwork and dingy walls. Horribly humiliated, not so much for herself as for her mother who had lain, shrunken and feverish against the pillows.

Nevertheless Margaret had remembered to be respectful as she had been taught. Her mother had worked as governess in a castle before she set foot in Porthross, and had kept in touch. Occasionally a box of cast-off clothes had arrived which, when altered to fit, had provided them with garments. But contact had suddenly ceased. There had been changes, a new family inheriting the castle, people to whom Mary was unknown.

So Margaret had faced Lady Julia politely, fully aware that they were already under an obligation to Lord Henry. He had allowed them to remain in the cottage though he would have been quite within his rights to have ordered them out, for it was tied, a part of Tom's wages. His lordship was the proprietor of the tin mine where Tom had toiled until that fatal moment when his overstrained heart stopped. No pressure had been brought to bear on his widow, but now Margaret expected to be given notice to quit.

She was sixteen and untrained for anything except domestic work, though she was able to read and write and use a needle. Because of her own background, Mary had encouraged her to speak correctly. Even so, the future looked bleak.

'Wait a minute!' she shouted, suddenly awaking from her thoughts and stopping the grave-diggers.

She bent and scooped up a handful of soil, letting it trickle through her fingers to fall into her mother's last resting place, then threw in the flowers she had gathered in the stillness of dawn when the wind stirred the trees and a blackbird fluted. They grew without restraint in the garden, mixing with herbs and vegetables. Fragrant carnations, fragile scarlet poppies and delicate mauve campions would now lie forever under the sod with Mary Helbren.

She had never been able to devote much time to them, potatoes, cabbages and turnips taking priority, yet she had loved them and Margaret recalled vividly how her mother laboured until all hours on warm nights. Sometimes, when it had been too hot to sleep, the child had lain under the open window and heard her below, singing softly in the dusk. It had been a reassuring sound on which to drift and dream.

Pain throbbed into life. Margaret's throat was dry and her eyes hot with the tears burning behind them. Never more would she listen to that voice, never more feel the touch of her mother's hand, enjoy her warm embrace, or know her love. She was alone.

'You're not alone,' Aunt Mercy insisted when they reached the cottage a little later. There had been no money for funeral meats, so the meagre crowd of mourners had dispersed quickly once the burial was completed.

'I am. I have no family.' Margaret took the cut-steel pins out of her hat, removed it and laid it on the table – her mother's Sunday-best hat which had been skilfully decorated with black grosgrain ribbon. She shook her hair free. It felt uncomfortable skewered close to her head.

'No, no.' Aunt Mercy eased her bulk on to a stool, her protruding eyes under sandy brows travelling round the room. They were hard eyes, the whites shiny, the irises frosty blue. '*We* are your family. Though it's a crying shame Mary didn't do her duty by Tom and give him sons.'

Aunt Prudence nodded. A gaunt person entirely lacking in bodily beauty, she was already rummaging through drawers and boxes. Both women had barely been able to contain their greed until the corpse was underground. Margaret watched sullenly. They'd find precious little among her mother's few possessions. Thanks to their brother and his spendthrift ways.

'She wasn't a proper wife to him,' Aunt Mercy continued, a big-boned woman who supplemented her fisherman husband's income by gathering whelks and kelp from the shore, working in the fish cellars or carrying pickled herrings to market in a trug balanced on her head. 'I never thought it right that you shared her bed instead of her lawful wedded husband.' Receiving no reply, she licked her lips and added, 'I'm gasping for a cup of tea. Right parched I am. Is there anything in the house?'

Margaret shook her head. 'There's no tea, no milk, no bread. Nothing.' Even if there had been she would not have offered it. She paused, then said, 'She didn't want to sleep with him and there was only one bed.'

'You should have slept in the cubby-hole over there.' Aunt Mercy's eyes switched to the curtained ledge low down on one wall, a bed-place usually reserved for children but where Tom had often collapsed after

14

reeling home from the public house. 'It was a shame and a scandal. I always said so. Didn't I, Prudence?'

'You did, sister, you did.' Aunt Prudence was examining the crockery, mouth pursed as she noted chips and cracks. 'And she never contributed a penny-piece. Wouldn't work like the rest of us women. Oh, no. Too proud she was, with her posh way of talking.'

Anger began to bubble up in Margaret, waking the numbness into agonising life. How dare they criticise her mother? 'That's a lie,' she said, her voice stronger now. 'You know very well she sewed for the gentlefolk and trimmed hats for milliners in Penzance.'

Aunt Prudence sniffed contemptuously. She thought herself a cut above the rest, for she was married to a mine foreman. She was intensely houseproud, a keen chapel-goer and a wearisome meddler in other people's affairs, yet she still slaved away with the rest of them when there was a glut around harvest time. It was then the pilchards came into the harbour in their millions, churning the sea to pinkish-red foam.

'Sewing indeed!' she barked. 'She didn't support poor Tom! Are you sure you've nothing to drink in the house? Not even a nip of gin?'

'Nothing.' It was all too much. Though Mary had painstakingly taught Margaret that adults were always in the right and their doings above suspicion, and that she must never, never argue with them under any circumstances and always do as they said, she knew her aunts were in the wrong.

'Mother was ill. Her lungs were bad,' she replied coldly. 'She had that hacking cough. How could she have worked in the canning factory or the seine house? My father was a drunkard. Any money that mother brought in was wasted on booze!'

The shocked expressions on their faces was deeply satisfying. Gaping at her, eyes wide, they were momentarily arrested in badmouthing a dead woman and ransacking her home.

'Of course she didn't sleep with him,' Margaret went on, in passionate defence of her mother. 'He wet himself when he was far gone in drink. What woman in her right mind wants that in her bed? Would you tolerate it? Or seeing good money poured down the drain on ale and cider?'

Aunt Mercy was the first to recover. 'Every man drinks,' she opined with as much dignity as she could muster and this was considerable with her jutting bosom and imposing height. 'It's a sorry state of things if a man can't meet his friends for a pint after he's slogged underground all day. As for the other – he'd always had a weak bladder.'

15

'Rubbish!' Margaret was launched, forgetting her manners. 'There's drinking moderately and drinking to excess. Father drank to excess. He couldn't stop. It was life to him, food if you like. It meant more than me, more than my mother, more than anything. He had to have it, no matter what. Let the bailiff come, let the tallyman call – he didn't care, just as long as he had the price of a jar.'

The two women were alarmed by the sight of this slim, pale girl, dressed, as were they, entirely in black. She was intimidating in her wrath, eyes glowing in that ashen face, ebony hair tumbling across her shoulders and down her back. Only sixteen, yet she looked five years older. They were at a loss to know what to do with her or how to treat her.

She's not one of us – the thought winged between them as if by telepathy. They might quarrel at times, even take opposite sides in family feuds, but at heart they were thick as thieves and ready to band together against any outsider.

They had been suspicious when Tom married the teacher, a stranger from far beyond the border. For two years she had run the little school. Lord Henry, whose father had built it, had continued with the funding and tuition was free. He had sometimes dropped in to see how the children's education was progressing. Then, quite suddenly, Mary Skipton as she then was, had started going out with Tom and in no time at all they were married.

At the ceremony it had been obvious that she was pregnant but no one made any comment if a bride was carrying her groom's child, yet in this case the circumstances were unsettling. Margaret had come into the world five months later and Tom had taken to drink. The sisters linked these events, blaming Mary for it and the infant, too, if blame could be laid at anyone's doorstep.

'Well, I don't know what's to become of you, my girl,' Aunt Mercy said at last. 'You can't stay here, so you better come home with me. I can squeeze you in, I suppose, as our Jim's going off to be a cowman up along Trewiddle Farm. I can get you a job bulking pilchards. You'll earn five shillings a week if you work hard, and that'll do for your bed and board.'

'I'll make my own way, thank you,' Margaret replied, appalled at the thought of living in Aunt Mercy's crowded hovel and working amidst the smell of fish and the oil squeezed from them in giant presses.

Mary and herself had always walked on the other side of the road when they had to pass the factory where donkey carts loaded with the catch from the great nets had pulled up under its ridge roof. Then the pungent cargo would be hefted between its granite pillars to where

16

women toiled to bulk them, building up layer upon layer of pilchards with salt sprinkled between.

Yet her situation was desperate. There was no food in the house, no money either. She had used up the last remaining coins to pay for the funeral. The secondhand dealer would no doubt give her a few pence for the furniture, but this would go to pay off the debts and settle Tom's slate at the Ship Inn, a long overdue account which had shamed her mother so much she was duty-bound to clear it.

She wished her aunts would go, needing to be alone with her grief. It was horrible to see them picking over her mother's belongings like a pair of greedy buzzards. Everywhere Margaret looked there was some reminder of her. The chair where she had sat to peel potatoes, darn Tom's socks or read by candlelight was pulled out from the table, as if waiting to be occupied. The clothes blowing on the washing line included the nightgowns she had worn. The dried flowers in a pottery jar near the windowsill bore silent tribute to her deftness in arranging foliage, and the gleaming leaves on the castor-oil plant were a tribute to her careful tending.

I can't go on without you, Mother, Margaret sobbed inwardly. Why did you have to leave me? I didn't feel like this when Pa died. It was a relief. Just you and me, happy together. No more rows, no more abuse. I'd taken for granted that you hated one another, but sometimes I'd noticed that other families weren't the same. Fathers and mothers who seemed to get on, and children who didn't hide in cupboards when their fathers came home as I did. I hate loud, angry voices.

Distrusting their every move, she followed Prudence and Mercy who, puffing and grumbling, mounted the staircase that corkscrewed up from a door set in the wall beside the fireplace. Awkward stairs with a niche cut into the thickness of the wall for the manoeuvring of coffins. Margaret noticed a fresh scrape where the undertakers had struggled with her mother's.

Three days ago, in the low-ceilinged attic under the eaves, Mary's soul had finally given up the struggle to remain in her diseased body, and Margaret's eyes went to the bed, so unnaturally neat and bare under the frayed patchwork quilt. The sun streamed in at the casement and peace pervaded the room. Just for a second she thought she saw Mary surrounded by a shining halo as she smiled and told her not to worry as all would be well.

'Did she leave any trinkets, bits of jewellery, ribbons or lace?' Aunt Prudence inquired, her long, pointed nose and bony fingers poking into everything. The vision faded abruptly, leaving Margaret bereft.

'Hardly, and what there was she gave to me,' she answered icily. 'It's no use looking, for you won't find anything you can steal.'

'Steal? What d'you mean – steal?' Aunt Prudence cried in outraged indignation.

'You're an ungrateful hussy, that's what you are!' her sister panted. 'You don't deserve decent folk troubling themselves over you. I've offered you a home and you've turned your nose up. What d'you expect? Some prince on a white charger to come along and carry you away? You're a pauper and you might as well get used to the idea. The Helbrens don't owe you nothing, girl.'

'I want nothing from them, expect nothing.' Margaret stood by the bride-chest, the one and only piece of any value. Mary had brought it with her when she married Tom, and being near it brought a modicum of comfort as if it gave out a gentle emanation.

'Neither you should!' Aunt Mercy was wondering if she dare voice the doubts which the whole of the Helbren clan shared. She drew in a deep breath, then said, 'We can't be sure you're one of us. You was born mighty quick after Tom started acourting your mother.'

'What d'you mean?' Margaret drew herself up, her eyes flashing, while out of the past she heard two old women discussing her at a harvest supper. 'Changeling,' they'd said. 'She's a changeling.'

'Never you mind. That's for me to know and you to find out,' Aunt Mercy answered, face blotchy and perspiring, already regretting speaking out of turn. This was a family matter and not to be mouthed abroad. Not that she could be sure of the truth. Tom had never said – never once complained of Mary's coldness towards him.

'I don't know what you're talking about and I think it's time you went. Thank you for your help but I can manage now.' Margaret could endure no more of their hints, barbed remarks and prying.

Their presence was suffocating. They exuded prejudice and hypocrisy, the blinkered attitude forged by a restrictive religion and generations of servitude. Mary had been different, how or why had never been explained to Margaret, but she, too, had always felt apart from the rest.

'Oh, well, if we're not welcome here . . .' Aunt Mercy began, then moved to the door. 'Come along, Prudence. Let's leave the thankless chit to her own devices.'

Margaret did not accompany them. They could let themselves out. She heard their boots clattering on the uncarpeted treads, then the front door slamming behind them. Silence fanned down over the attic. The dormer window was open and the scent of herbs drifted up from the border to spice the air. She collapsed by the bed and, out of habit, reached across the coverlet seeking those wasted hands which she had clasped so often to comfort the patient's suffering. Her fingers encountered space and her sorrow was a deep fathomless pit. She stayed there for a long time, tortured by loss, guilt and regrets, the shadows lengthening and a breeze cooling her brow.

Practical issues impinged on her thoughts. As yet she had not received notification from his lordship's agent and was reasonably certain she could stay in the cottage till this came. She had lost her appetite so the lack of provisions posed no problem. But tomorrow she must find out exactly where she stood and, if she had to leave, visit the secondhand furniture store and put her business in order.

She had no idea where she was to go or how to make a living, and wondered if the date of the next hiring fair was fixed so she could offer herself for employment. As a cook, maybe? She was competent but too young for such a responsible post. Also her youth barred her from applying as a housekeeper. A servant then – though lady's maid would be more to her taste, but again inexperience was against her though she was prepared to lie about her age.

She rose, restless and deeply disturbed, lifting the lid of the bride-chest and reverently handling her mother's things folded within. There was not much. Margaret was wearing the black dress Mary had made, along with the black woollen shawl bought years before when she delivered bonnets to the store in Penzance. There were two white blouses, a couple of pairs of linen drawers and some lawn chemises decorated with broderie anglaise and threaded through with baby ribbon.

In a long cardboard box, Margaret discovered some elbow-length gloves fashioned of the softest kid and fastened with a row of minute pearl buttons. Too fine to be worn by a miner's wife. There was also a fan, a dainty thing with ivory sticks and lace-edged painted panels. She remembered how her mother would show her these treasures as a treat sometimes, though warning her never to speak of them to anyone.

'They'd think I was giving myself airs,' she would sigh wistfully. 'One mustn't get above oneself.'

Margaret found the walnut-inlaid sewing box, another object out of keeping with their lowly lifestyle. It was lined with red silk and fitted with a tray for needles, a thimble, a plump pink satin pin-cushion and a tiny pair of silver scissors with beautifully wrought handles. This section could be removed to show a cavity beneath for storing cottons, buttons, crochet hooks and embroidery threads.

It's mine now, Margaret thought, as is everything here. Once I longed to possess it, but now this is meaningless. Pain welled up, her heart like an open wound within her.

She came across baby clothes wrapped in tissue paper, beautifully

19

hand-stitched with lace whipped to the borders; long gowns, petticoats, back-flannels, bibs and bonnets, worn by one child only –
herself.

Shall I ever have babies of my own? she wondered. Maybe in years
to come when the brown earth lying like a scar over Mother's grave
has been covered by primroses, snowdrops and violets from my planting and a headstone fixed in place. One day when I'm rich, and
married to someone wonderfully kind, handsome and understanding
who'll love me for myself. Not a miner or a fisherman, never that. I
don't intend to become like their wives, worn down by poverty and too
frequent childbearing, little more than a slave.

A sudden knocking below made her start up in alarm. Was it the
debt collector? Or Mr Skinner, the agent, telling her to get out? She
hesitated at the head of the stairs, tempted to pretend she was not
there, but good sense prevailed. Better to know the worst.

The room which had served as kitchen and living space combined
was filled with dusky shadows. Straightening her spine, Margaret
crossed the floor and opened the door. A man stood there, silhouetted
against the sunset glow. Her heart dropped. It was Mr Skinner.

'Miss Helbren?' Skinner did not remove his bowler hat as he would
have done to gentry. A thin, spare man, attired in a brown suit and
stiff-collared shirt, he wore a short, neatly clipped beard, moustache
and side-whiskers. He was extremely conscious of his position as Lord
Henry's agent with a great deal of responsibility.

'Yes, sir.' She refused to bob to him, an omission he was quick to
notice.

His lips tightened and his eyes narrowed. 'I've a message from Lady
Julia. Can you read?'

'Yes, sir.' Damn him and his patronising air, she thought. He
handed her an envelope and she stepped away from the door, adding,
'Won't you come inside?'

Skinner did so, removing his hat and placing it under his arm. He
stood stiffly to attention, back to the empty hearth, while Margaret,
just to prove that she was used to handling mail, found a knife and slid
it under the flap. Inside she found a letter written on crested paper. It
read:

'Dear Miss Helbren,
    Please accept my condolences on the occasion of your sad loss. It
has occurred to me to wonder how you are placed with regard to the
future. I was impressed by the way in which you cared for your sick
mother and, if you are not already suited, I am prepared to offer
you a post at the manor.

As you may be aware, I have recently been blessed with another son and the nursery staff are short-handed. There are already a head nurse, an under nurse and a nurserymaid, but a maid to wait on the nursery is required.

Should this position be of interest, I suggest that you tell Mr Skinner and he will arrange for you to be brought here.'

The letter was signed 'The Marchioness of Harleigh'.

Margaret was astonished. This had come like a bolt from the blue – or an answer to prayer. She did not pause to wonder if she could carry out the duties required, or even if she wanted to. In a single stroke her difficulties were banished. She had been offered work. She would have somewhere to live. She could hold her head high and retain her independence. Those old cats, Aunt Prudence and Aunt Mercy, could go hang!

'I was told to wait for an answer,' Skinner remarked, tapping his foot impatiently as she read the letter through for the third time.

'Just a moment if you please.' Refusing to be indimidated, she was already searching though the dresser drawer for a pencil. There wasn't any paper, so she turned to him. 'Have you anything I can write on?'

He produced a notepad from an inner pocket and tore off a page. She took it and sat down at the kitchen table. Then, using her best copper-plate writing, she made reply, hoping against hope that she was using the correct form of address, recalling how her mother once wrote to the castle folk:

'My Lady Marchioness,
    Thank you for your kindness in remembering me. I would be pleased to accept the post in the nursery, and can come at your convenience.
    I have the honour to remain,
    Your Ladyship's obedient servant,
                                    Margaret Elinor Helbren.'

She folded the note and handed it to Skinner, saying, 'I expect you know what this is about? I've accepted.'

'Good,' he replied. 'That'll please her ladyship. Quite took to you, she did.' He held out a leather drawstring purse. 'She gave me this with instructions to give it to you if you agreed to her proposal. It's an advance on your five pounds a year pay. No doubt you'll need it to kit yourself out and settle bills.'

Margaret took it calmly as if fully expecting this tribute, but beneath her cool exterior she was stunned. Recovering, she asked, 'When d'you want to fetch me?'

His stern face softened a little as he looked at the lovely young girl. She was too thin, of course, and strained. There were dark half-moons under those brilliant eyes. Nursing her mother could not have been easy. Nothing happened in or around Porthross which escaped his notice and he had heard she was a strong, healthy lass who kept to herself and had, moreover, an unsullied reputation.

This was a point in her favour. Mrs Colby, the housekeeper, was strict and did not approve of flighty pieces. They unsettled the other maids and caused problems among the menservants which disturbed Mr Wakefield, the head butler. Nothing and no one was permitted to ruffle these two important backstairs dignitaries on whom the efficient management of Roslan Manor depended.

'I've to come this way again in two days,' Skinner said, replacing his hat. 'Be ready at midday. I don't like to be kept waiting.'

'Thank you, sir. I'll remember that.' Margaret saw him to the door. 'And can I bring a box with me?'

'You can.' He cast an eye round the sticks of furniture. 'I don't suppose you own much.'

'You're right. But what there is has to go. Just as well as I've no-where to store it.'

'Goodbye, Miss Helbren.'

'Goodbye, Mr Skinner.'

Margaret stood on the threshold watching him walk down the path. It was overgrown, the cockle shells which marked its edge strangled by weeds. It doesn't matter any more, she thought. This place is no longer my concern. I'm off to work at the Big House.

Excitement tingled along her nerves, driving back despair. She held the purse to her breasts and her spirits lifted. It contained more money than she had ever seen all at once. She was sure the haberdasher would be able to supply her with stockings, handkerchiefs, all those necessary little items which she intended to purchase so that she might enter service with head held high.

I'm not going there looking like a beggar, she resolved. Then, closing the door behind her, she marched resolutely out of the wicket gate and headed for the harbour. Her destination was the pie shop. For the first time in days she was hungry.

The wind blew fresh from the west on a morning dry after a day of rain, that soft, all-pervading rain that swept in with the tides, the first for some time. September, and all the lovely shades of early autumn were beginning to meld and mingle on cliff and moor and copse. Broad bands of sunlight broke from rifts in the clouds to run in moving radiance over the land.

22

Mr Skinner, driving a smartly turned-out gig, arrived at Hazel Cottage as the clock in the church tower struck twelve. Margaret had been ready since daybreak, the bride-chest tied up with rope, her own immediate things packed in a wicker Pilgrim basket. This had two halves which could be expanded by not fastening the outer one tightly. It was held in place with a leather strap.

Mr Skinner was on the driver's seat, the reins in one hand and a whip in the other, and she did not wish to get off on the wrong foot by putting him to the trouble of climbing down. She opened the door and waved.

He saw her at once. 'Good day, Miss Helbren. Ready then?'

'Yes, sir. Can the boy give me a hand?'

A young lad, no doubt Skinner's helper, jumped off the tailboard at his bidding and ran briskly up the path. He had unruly hair, a freckled face and cheeky grin. He doffed his cap respectfully.

'Right-o, miss. What's to go?'

Impressed by her grave beauty and wanting to display his strength, he heaved up the chest and staggered to the gig. Without a backward glance at the stripped room that had always been her home, Margaret tucked the Pilgrim basket under one arm and closed the door firmly behind her, pocketing the key which would be handed over to Mr Skinner.

No one had come to see her off, though there was little doubt the news had reached the harbour. In such a close community everyone knew everyone else's business. In any case, the man in the furniture shop would have spread the tale of the disposal of her shabby odds and ends. Margaret was glad she was leaving, her one regret being that the distance between herself and Porthross would not be greater. Roslan Manor was no more than three miles away.

Lord Henry owned all the land thereabouts, renting some out to farmers. He also owned the tin and copper mines and a large proportion of the fishing fleet. The Auberts were a powerful family and had been so since the days when their Norman ancestors sailed across the English Channel with William the Conqueror.

Margaret seated herself on one of the corded cushions that softened the benches each side of the gig. The boy sat opposite. 'My name's Jan,' he informed her cheerfully. 'What's yours?'

'This is Miss Helbren and she's a new member of the nursery staff, so keep a polite tongue in your head,' Skinner said sternly without looking round, his eyes fixed firmly on the road and the horse's broad grey haunches moving smoothly up and down with a jingle of harness.

'Yes, Mr Skinner,' Jan replied, but dropped an eyelid in an impudent wink. Margaret could feel her lips twitching in response.

23

Hazel Cottage was one of several at the top of the steep winding street leading from the quayside and Skinner turned off left. The road widened, following a gentle incline at first, then levelling. It became a lane, hedged in to begin with but losing definition as it came out into the open. The sight took Margaret's breath away – heather all about her, spreading like a glorious mantle over the moor. It swirled and tossed in the racing wind, magenta and amethyst and crimson, like a coloured sea.

She closed her eyes and raised her face to the sky, breathing in the honey-sweet scent of it, wonderful, warm in the sun, an elixir to body and spirit. She had cried herself to sleep last night, filled with sorrow and fear of the future, but now hope put forth tentative roots.

'Lonely old spot this, miss,' Jan commented. 'All right now, but you get stuck out here when its misty and it's a different story. We'll be passing the Weeping Maids soon, and I wouldn't like it after dark, I can tell you.'

Throughout her wanderings Margaret had never ventured this way, though she had heard of the circle of stones, twelve in all which, so the story went, were princessess who before time began had been turned to stone by a sorceress. Now she saw them not far away and the light down on her arms rose.

They were spread out in a ring, blue-grey against the heather, taller by far than any princess less than a giantess had any right to be. Sunlight flickered over them and they glistened, ornamented with patches of yellow lichen.

The horse trotted by, ears pricked, the wheels of the gig bowling over the rough path dotted with clumps of couch grass, clover and thrift. Margaret turned her head, following the circle, as mysterious and enthralling as the barrow where she had played as a child. Why had the stones been put there between the earth and the sky? What magical rites celebrated, what pagan gods worshipped?

She was convinced the ring had been marked out for the purpose of ritual, but did not know how she knew, sensitive to otherworldly things. The Weeping Maids commanded respect, their ambience awesome, making her aware of her mortality.

Now the road dipped into a wooded valley, running along beside a river. 'We're almost there,' Skinner said.

Margaret stared ahead intently. The trees thinned, parkland rolled before her and there, so far away it looked like a toy, stood the mighty walls and castellated rooftops of Roslan Manor. Parts were still fortress-like, the rest mostly Tudor with touches of Palladian, a glorified mixture of architectural styles affected at the whims of its owners

24

down the centuries. To Margaret it was a wonderful fairy-tale palace grander than anything her imagination could possibly have conjured.

As they drew nearer she became aware of the scale of the place, a vast frontage with wings on either side, the stonework scrolled and carved and flamboyantly finished. A myriad windows winked, a company of gargoyles grimaced from gutterings, while great statues of kings and knights occupied alcoves placed at regular intervals along the façade. A flight of broad, shallow granite steps swept up to a front door as high as the entrance to a cathedral.

Skinner left the circular gravelled drive and wheeled away to the rear. They passed under an arch leading to a stable block with a grand façade and a central tower where a clock marked the time, topped by a glittering weathercock. A row of outbuildings helped to form a large enclosed square where grooms were busy offsaddling horses and gardeners wheeling in produce.

Several workers touched their hats to Skinner and, as the gig halted, came over to discuss problems pertaining to the estate. A door connected to the main block opened and closed every so often, and each time a smell of cooking wafted out, reminding Margaret she had not eaten that day.

A rider clattered round the corner of the stable, a young man on a superb bay. He handled his mount with ease, drawing her to a halt by the gig. 'Ah, good day, Skinner,' he said, and his voice was authoritative and cultured.

Skinner doffed his bowler. 'Good afternoon, Mr Newark, sir. What can I do for you?'

The young man gentled his fidgety mare, leaning forward to pat the long, black mane. He stared at Skinner from under the peak of his tweed cap. Chestnut curls poked from beneath it, his hair shoulder-length.

'That prize bull – what's his name?' he asked.

'Emperor, sir,' Skinner supplied.

'That's right. I saw him in the last cattle show. Walked off with all the trophies. A fine animal. I've spoken to the marquis and he said to come and see you. My uncle's herd needs fresh blood. He'd like to borrow Emperor to service his cows. Can you arrange this?'

'Certainly, sir. I'll get on to the head cattleman about it. When's a convenient time for him to bring Emperor over to Martock?'

'Middle of next week suit? I'm anxious to get it over and done with before I return to university. Thank you, Skinner. Good day.'

'Good day, sir.'

The young man dug his knees against his mount's sides, but before he turned away he looked directly at Margaret. She knew it was rude to stare, but was unable to help herself, registering broad shoulders under a hacking jacket, fawn riding breeches and dusty brown boots, a face of regular, handsome features, sunbrowned and healthy-looking.

Now he flashed her a wide, white smile and she saw that his eyes were a deep, sapphire blue. Their intent, direct gaze made her suddenly shy. Then he touched his crop to his cap and rode away.

'That's Mr Peter Newark from the next estate,' Jan informed her. 'He's down from Oxford, staying with his uncle, Lord Fenimore.'

'Shut up, Jan, you gasbag. Get on with it,' Skinner reproved and climbed down from the gig.

Jan hopped off the tailboard and gave Margaret his hand as she lifted her skirt and stepped to the cobbles. She was comforted by the feel of his firm, warm fingers, her stomach churning with fear.

People were eyeing her; the outside staff and those who came from the kitchen. She pulled back her shoulders and kept her head high, looking neither to the right or left of her, Pilgrim basket clutched firmly by its strap.

'Come along, Helbren.' Skinner turned in her direction. 'Mrs Colby is waiting.'

He conducted her through a side door and mounted a short flight of stairs. They reached a door and he tweaked his jacket into place and removed his hat, smoothing a hand over his hair. Then he tapped softly.

'Come in,' called a voice.

He stood aside so that Margaret might precede him and she found herself in a large room where a woman was seated at a plain, functional desk, with a drop-leaf writing surface and a forest of pigeonholes filled with papers. Her pen was moving busily over a ledger, but she glanced up as they came in, laid it aside, closed the book with a snap, nodded at Margaret and smiled briefly at him.

'Good afternoon, ma'am. This is Margaret Helbren, the new girl for the nursery,' he said, his voice modulated and respectful.

'Ah, Lady Julia's protégée?' Mrs Colby looked her over, her eyes sharp under level brows.

'That's right,' Margaret answered, gripping her trembling hands together.

The housekeeper was middle-aged, her brown hair scraped back under a small lace-trimmed cap. Because she occupied an envied place at the very top of the servant hierarchy it was in order for her to wear a grey alpaca dress after the noon hour had passed, with a fine black silk apron fastened across the front.

'So, Helbren – and have you ever been in service before?' she asked in a tone that brooked no nonsense.

'No.' Margaret met her eyes without flinching. No one would have guessed she was shaking like an aspen. 'And I do have a Christian name, you know.'

Mrs Colby's brows shot up. 'Here we only use surnames among the staff. If you ever have occasion to speak to me, then you'll address me as ma'am. Is this understood?'

'Yes, ma'am.'

'And you curtsey if you happen to pass her ladyship or other members of the nobility, and never dream of speaking to them. Is this clear?'

'Yes, ma'am.'

'You've a lot to learn, I fear.'

'Yes, ma'am,' Margaret repeated, the inflection in her voice making Mrs Colby throw her a dubious stare.

The girl held herself with a poise and grace unbecoming to a servant. Her pale face was exquisitely formed, and she had the most striking violet eyes, their exact colour dependent on how the light struck them. It fluctuated between smoky amethyst and translucent violet, and the calm way in which those eyes met hers disconcerted the housekeeper.

'You'll not be under my jurisdiction,' she went on. 'Though you'll be answerable to me for your behaviour. Mrs Broom is the head nurse. You are to obey her in everything. Do you understand?'

'Yes, ma'am.'

'We don't encourage followers. You aren't courting, are you?'

'No, ma'am.'

Taking a peep around her Margaret was awed by her surroundings, and this was only the staff quarters. What must the rooms occupied by the family be like? The housekeeper's parlour was spotlessly clean and tidy, used as an office as well as a private sitting room. Here Mrs Colby hired and fired and consulted with the cook, gave orders to the housemaids and laundrywomen, kept the accounts and managed the household expenditure. At meal times she ate with the other upper servants and frequently played hostess to visiting valets and personal maids if the Auberts were entertaining.

The polished floorboards were partly covered by a large square rug, the windows hung with printed cotton curtains, the large circular table in the centre draped in a fringed chenille cloth of a rich glowing red and the mantelpiece festooned with a length of the same material. There was no fire, but the brass fender, coal scuttle, tongs and poker shone. The walls were lined with shelves, and a large cupboard took pride of place, the furniture of good quality which had come from the front of the house.

Margaret had never seen anything so fine, painfully conscious of her down-at-heel boots, and the much-used dress, shawl and hat. She

27

wanted to die when Mrs Colby cast a disparaging glance at the Pilgrim basket.

'Ah, well, you'll do, I suppose,' she concluded without much conviction. 'They're without a still-room maid at present in the nursery. The other one left with a flea in her ear for rudeness to Mrs Broom. Watch your step, Helbren. She rules with a rod of iron and expects everything to be done just so.'

Having concluded the interview, she dimpled at Skinner, saying, 'Take her to the kitchen and introduce her to Mrs Frith. If you care to return here, luncheon will be served shortly.'

'Thank you, Mrs Colby.' They smiled at one another, two of the upper echelon who looked forward to eating in seclusion and exchanging news with Mr Wakefield, far removed from the servants' hall where the others ate.

'Leave your basket in the passage,' Skinner ordered on the way to the kitchen. 'Jan'll take it to your room.'

'And my chest?' Margaret was worried about losing it.

'Is already there.'

The kitchen seemed to be the size of a church, well lit and ventilated by windows facing the square. The cook was sitting in a Windsor chair, a well-built woman wearing a black cotton dress, a white pinafore with straps that crossed over at the back, and a starched cap. Though she took her ease, she kept an army of underlings busy about their various duties. Sleeves rolled up, white aproned and white capped, they worked diligently at the vast deal table with its well-scrubbed surface and plain-turned legs.

It was fitted with a shelf beneath for storing cooking pots and pans, and above it hung a large rectangular frame where utensils were hooked ready for use. Theirs were menial tasks, peeling fruit, cleaning and chopping vegetables, having everything in readiness for Mrs Frith to take centre stage in her own good time, when, like the temperamental artiste she was, she would set about creating delectable concoctions to titillate the palates of the marquis and his family.

The stone-flagged floor was scrupulously clean, as were the lime-washed walls against which dangled burnished copper skillets and other implements. An immense dresser extended from floor to ceiling with a solid wooden back, drawers in its lower part and shelves of graduated widths on which crockery was displayed. An open door led into a scullery where a further battalion were washing dishes in large stone sinks and setting them to dry on wooden draining boards.

The smell of roast meat coiled seductively from the direction of the big black range. A side of beef rotated there, speared by a clockwork device that enabled it to be hung vertically before the open fire and cooked evenly. A hooded screen reflected the heat and caught the fat in a container at its base, though drops missed, hissing and sizzling on the coals.

Margaret thought she might faint with hunger.

'The new girl, Mrs Frith. Her name's Helbren,' Skinner said, fractionally less deferential than when he had spoken to the housekeeper, but not far off.

Mrs Frith nodded, eyes set deep in a plump red face. 'You're nothing to do with me really, girl,' she said, in a fruity voice, 'and don't rightly belong in my kitchen. You're nursery staff. But since you're here you better have something to eat. You're so thin a puff of wind might blow you over. Fetch her some dinner, Berry.'

The girl she addressed darted to the stew pot simmering on the range and ladled some on to a plate. This was put on a side table along with a hunk of bread. A spoon was laid beside it and a chair pulled up.

'Thank you,' Margaret murmured, and the girl gave her a quick smile. Bright-eyed and friendly, she had an oval face and a pert, tiptilted nose covered with a sprinkling of freckles. Russet curls poked rebelliously from beneath the edge of her starched cap.

Skinner had taken his leave, and Margaret was now alone in this strange place surrounded by unfamiliar people. She sat down and ate her way solidly through the delicious, gamey stew.

'It's good,' she murmured to Berry.

'The pot's kept bubbling, topped up with meat and vegetables. That way there's always plenty of soup,' Berry explained, running her hands down her apron.

'I see,' Margaret said.

'You and me are sharing a room,' Berry announced importantly. 'I'll show you where it is. You'll have to change into uniform before you take up their tea.'

'What are the nursery people like?' Despite the hot food, Margaret's stomach still felt hollow.

'Can't tell you much about 'em. I knew Betty Plimmer, the girl you've replaced. She was a good sort.'

'I hear she was dismissed,' Margaret said, as she wiped round the plate with the last of the bread.

Berry smiled mischievously. 'She cheeked Nanny Broom, so they say. Got her ears boxed and was given the sack. Betty had told me Nanny's a proper tartar. We don't have nothing to do with the nursery lot. Never sets eyes on 'em – well, only from a distance when they brings the little 'uns down for prayers or takes 'em out. It's a separate world, the nursery is.'

Mrs Frith looked across at Margaret. 'Have you finished? Good. Now Berry can take you to your room. Come back when you're properly dressed and you'll be shown where things are kept so you can serve nursery tea. Nanny likes it at four o'clock sharp so there's plenty of time to get the children ready for the drawing room.'

'There's nothing much to do for tea, only bread and butter and cake,' Berry explained as they left the back premises which were cut off from the rest of the house by green baize doors.

'Why do the children go to the drawing room?' Margaret was confused by the information pouring in. She had stepped into an alien world with rules she had never dreamed existed.

'It's the only time their parents see 'em, apart from Sunday prayers. Just for a half-hour every day – that's all. What a life Lady Julia has, eh? She can pop out as many babies as she likes and there's plenty of people to look after 'em.'

'I don't think I'd like that,' Margaret answered slowly, following Berry's swishing cotton skirts and the stiffly starched apron bows that spread out like wings at the back of her waist. 'When I have a baby, I'll want to care for it myself.'

Berry shuddered, and looked at her over her shoulder. 'I wouldn't. Nasty, smelly, screaming objects. I should know. My Ma had ten and I was glad to get away from home. By the way, my name's Susan,' she continued as they traversed the linoleum covered backstairs, well out of earshot of superiors.

'And I'm Margaret.'

'Fine. We girls call each other by our given names when the old bitch ain't listening.'

'Mrs Frith?'

'No, she ain't so bad. I'm talking about Mrs Colby. She's a cow, and you've got to be careful the others don't tell on you and get you into her bad books.'

'Surely they wouldn't?'

'Oh no?' Susan stopped, turned and rolled up her eyes. 'Everyone tattle-tales. And you'll have to look out for the footmen, too. They're always trying to take advantage of a girl.'

'What's it like, working here?' Margaret asked as they moved on, still nervous and worried.

Susan paused in the stairs leading to the fourth floor, and shrugged her shoulders. 'As good a place as any, I suppose. Being in service is a dog's life. Who'd do it if they had another way of making money? I've been here three years, and it's not too bad. There's a lot going on. A whole heap of servants, people coming and going in the kitchen, 'specially when there's a big party planned. There's plenty of men about.

Too many, if you ask me. As I've said, you got to be careful and don't give 'em half a chance. Just keep your legs closed and you'll be all right.' For one so young her attitude was alarmingly disenchanted.

The climb to the top of the house seemed to go on for ever. The stairs used by the servants connected with all the rooms occupied by the family in that rabbit warren of a house, and also gave access to their own sleeping apartments. The room Margaret was to share with Susan contained a wardrobe, a chest of drawers, a marble topped washstand with a jug and basin and, beneath it, a chamber pot and pail. Nothing like as fine as Mrs Colby's parlour, but a hundred times better than the attic in Hazel Cottage.

Susan pointed to one of the two narrow beds. 'That's mine,' she declared. 'You can have the other. Keep your clothes in the bottom drawer, and there's space in the wardrobe for hanging things. Mrs Colby said you were to have a dress that belonged to Betty Plimmer, till she has one made for you. It's on the hook behind the door. The privy is out the back. I'll show you where when we go down, but we use the po at night. Ma Colby don't like us wandering about after we've gone up to bed. Don't look so scared. It's strange at first, I know, but you'll get used to it.'

Susan proved to be an outgoing, inquisitive soul who soon had the relevant facts about Margaret's history as they chatted while she unpacked her belongings and tried on the dress. The floral pattern had faded and it was too big at the waist and too small in the bodice, but would have to do for the moment. A white apron, cuffs and collar completed this summer uniform.

'It'll be dark blue come October,' Sarah commented. 'You'll have to wear the cap. It's one of the rules.' She twirled it on her finger before tossing it over. 'A shame to hide that lovely hair, but maybe it's for the best in the long run. You don't want to be noticed by the gentlemen or you'll end up in real trouble.'

'It's unlikely any gentleman will notice me,' Margaret answered, standing before the fly-spotted mirror and adjusting the unbecoming headgear. An image of the horseman in the yard flashed across her mind, and she added, 'Though I saw one this morning as we drove in. He came over from somewhere called Martock. Wants to borrow a bull.'

'Oh, that'll be Mr Newark. Stays with Lord Fenimore at Martock Hall sometimes. Haven't heard anything bad about him, but as for the rest – you'd do well to run a mile from 'em.'

'Why?' Margaret finished adjusting her cap and stood looking at herself in the mirror.

'You're pretty,' Susan observed. 'Don't do no good being pretty

31

round here, though all the girls hope to marry a manservant one day, maybe a butler, if they're lucky. But it's the toffs you've got to avoid.'

'Surely they go after ladies of their own class?'

Susan laughed, seated on the bed and swinging her legs, enjoying a respite. 'They do if they want to get married,' she agreed. 'But we're looked on as fair game. All right for a bit of slap and tickle, then it's "Goodbye darling, it's been nice knowing you!" More than one has left under a cloud since I've been here, put in the family way by a guest or even a relative of his lordship.'

'How awful.'

'I agree. The girl's ruined. She either has to go back to her family in disgrace, or take to the streets. There's nothing else for it. And the man who's to blame gets off scot-free. He may give her some money to keep her mouth shut, but when it's gone she's done for with no one to provide for her and her bantling.'

Margaret shivered. There were unexpected pitfalls of which she must beware. Was it only an hour or two ago that she had left the shelter of Hazel Cottage? She felt she had packed in a year's experience since then.

'You look nice, my dear,' Mrs Frith said, when Margaret presented herself in the kitchen.

'Thank you, ma'am,' she said, her face lighting up with so radiant a smile that Mrs Frith could not help returning it.

She was making pastry on the marble slab at the end of the table. Her sleeves were pushed back displaying a pair of strong arms, her big hands moving so dexterously over the food. Perfect rosettes came into being, carved from the rolled-out dough – little knots and mock leaves to ornament the pie she was fashioning.

'Mother used to make squab pie, but I didn't think the gentry ate it,' Margaret observed, recognising the ingredients.

'Oh, yes, deary. Lord Henry likes plain old Cornish food sometimes. It's a different kettle of fish when he's entertaining, mind.' Mrs Frith sprinkled a little sugar and a handful of currants over the sliced apples, onions and mutton lying on a bed of pastry.

'Mother told me that the Phoenicians introduced the recipe when they came here hundreds of years ago, trading for tin.'

'Did they indeed? Well, I don't know nothing about that. Sounds too far-fetched for me.' Mrs Frith put in a little funnel shaped like a blackbird with opened orange beak to let the steam escape, gave the pie a pastry roof, crimped the edges, and arranged a ribbon pattern.

The kitchen clock chimed half past three. 'Lord love you! Get on your way, girl!' she cried. 'Show her what to do, Berry, then come back

32

here double quick. I needs you to pop over to the dairy and fetch another pound of butter.'

There was a room off the kitchen which Susan said was reserved for the nursery. It was here that Margaret was to collect the dishes to be carried up at meal times. It was plainly furnished with a table, a dresser for plates, jugs, cups and several trays of varying size. Susan took one of these and set about laying it with a golden saffron cake, a plate of homemade biscuits and another of wafer-thin sandwiches.

'These are for the nurses,' she quickly explained. 'The white and brown loaves for the children are already upstairs and you'll cut and butter them as the under nurse tells you.'

'Don't the children have cake?' Margaret picked up the tray. It looked elegant with its fine china cups and saucers standing on an embroidered cloth.

'Oh, yes. They'll have a slice or two from this one – if they've been good. The older ones, that is. Not the baby, of course. Come on, we'd better get going. Follow me.'

They climbed the stairs again, then Susan led the way through another door leading to a different part of the house. Now there was thick carpet under their feet, and a short flight leading upwards, the top barred by a little gate.

'This has to be kept bolted,' Susan whispered as they passed through it, 'in case one of the children escapes and falls down.'

Margaret, whispering too, asked, 'How many are there?'

'Six,' said Susan, pulling a face to indicate disapproval of her ladyship's fecundity. 'Least ways there's six in all but the eldest son is away most of the time, university and that, and the two young ladies are looked after by a governess. She's French and they calls her mam'zelle. Nuisance, as we have to wait on her separately. That leaves a boy and a girl and the baby in the nursery, though they all sleep and have their meals there – 'cept the heir, when he's home, of course. Thinks hisself God Almighty and no mistake, swanning around the place like I don't know what. You won't have much to do with the children. What you got to look out for is Mrs Broom. When she speaks to you, don't forget to give her a bob. All right?'

Margaret tried to gulp down the lump in her throat. The china on the tray clinked faintly in her shaking hands. 'I suppose so,' she answered with an uncertain smile.

'I'll leave you to it or Mrs Frith'll be on the warpath. There's a dinner party tonight and all hell will be let loose in the kitchen. Cheerio, good luck, and I'll see you later.'

Susan gave her a little push, propelling her along the short passage towards the closed door at the end. When she reached it, Margaret stood there for a second, plucking up her courage. She took a deep breath and rapped softly. No one came, so she waited a moment then tapped again.

This time a child's voice called out from the other side of the door. 'Someone's knocking.'

'Stand back, Master Harry. Let me see who it is. I expect it's your tea arrived, don't you?' another voice answered. Then the door swung back and Margaret stepped into her new life.

Chapter 2

Sunlight and warmth, the smell of carbolic soap, baby talc, floor polish, children – and that faintly scorched aroma emitted by freshly laundered garments subjected to a hot flatiron.

A boy stood in the doorway, the glow behind him forming an undeserved halo round his curly head. He wore a white sailor suit with navy-blue edging. A rosy-cheeked young woman in a print dress and enveloping white pinafore held him firmly by the hand.

'It's the new girl!' she exclaimed in broad Cornish to someone out of sight.

'Who's she?' the boy asked, freeing himself and pointing at Margaret, his childish treble dictatorial. 'And where's Plimmer?'

'Now, Master Harry, what has Nanny told you? "Who's she? The cat's mother?" And it's very rude to point. Just you mind your manners,' the young female reproved and stood aside to let Margaret through, adding, 'I'm Doris.'

An older woman came from an inner door. She had kind eyes and an understanding smile. Her dress was made of good quality material, her apron pristine, as was the cap on her smooth brown hair. Margaret responded to her motherly air, that sick, trembling feeling abating a little.

She managed a curtsy, saying, 'My name's Margaret Helbren.'

The boy was still staring at her. His slightly slanting hazel eyes and peaked brows gave him the impudent aspect of a faun. She stared back. He stuck out his tongue, unobserved by the others.

'There's no need to bob to me,' the woman said. 'I'm the under nurse, Thora Dauncey. Your first task is to prepare the bread and butter for the children's tea.'

'I know,' Margaret replied, anxious to appear familiar with her duties. 'Berry told me. One plate of white and one of brown.'

'I don't like brown,' the boy announced loftily. 'And I want jam.'

35

'"Want shall be your master." You'll eat what you're given. And stop showing off, if you please,' Thora rebuked him, then looked at Doris. 'You can stay and help her, but don't hang about. There's that pile of ironing to finish.' Her hand shot out and seized the boy in a vice-like grip. 'Not you, Master Harry. They don't want you plaguing them. Any more of your nonsense and I'll tell Nanny and there won't be any tea for you at all. So you'd better behave.'

'He's a little devil, that one. You have to have eyes in the back of your head when he's about,' Doris said as she led Margaret to a pantry not unlike the room off the kitchen, except this one had a sink for washing crockery and rinsing out small items of clothing. 'Nanny don't trust the laundrymaids with the baby's woollies,' she explained. 'Either me or you has to do 'em. Nappies too, if he has a rash on his backside. Ever so fussy she is.'

Two firm, crusty-topped farmhouse loaves stood on a round wooden breadboard near a butter dish, a pot of strawberry jam and several large plates. 'They has to eat a slice of buttered bread before they can have one with jam on it,' Doris continued as they sliced and spread. 'Master Harry won't get jam today because he's been rude.'

'I didn't realise they'd be treated strictly. I thought they'd have cake for breakfast, dinner and tea, if they asked for it,' Margaret said, the smell of the homemade bread tantalising her nostrils. Never had she seen so much food, served on such china. The ware for the children was bordered with characters from nursery rhymes.

'Oh, no, deary,' Doris replied, eyes wide in her round face. 'They've got to learn manners. How else are they to take their place in posh society? Discipline is all important, so Mrs Broom says. She won't stand for no nonsense. Has 'em from the month, she does, after the midwives go. They're trained in *her* ways, and no mistake. "Spare the rod and spoil the child," she says. They gets a bashing sometimes, I can tell you, when she's got one of her moods on or has taken a drop too much. Fond of her tipple, she is.'

Margaret was astounded. She had no yardstick by which to measure the routine of the nursery. Wait and see, an inner voice told her. You can't judge by a nursemaid's prattling. Maybe Doris doesn't like Mrs Broom. Perhaps she's been told off and bears a grudge. Surely a woman in charge of children can't imbibe, can she? Terrible memories of her father's violence rose up to haunt her. I won't think about it, she resolved. Nothing is going to spoil my first day here.

When the plates were filled Doris led the way into the day nursery. It was so lovely that Margaret's former doubts melted into envy. With such a background as this what might she have made of herself? she wondered, and the iron bit deeper into her soul, a shaft of hard cold steel that had been tempering inside her for years. There was no rhyme or reason to it, but she had always felt she should have been born somewhere better than the poverty of a miner's cottage.

White paintwork and colourful friezes; a solid table and pine wheel-backed chairs, a cretonne-covered couch, two armchairs; a coal fire glowing behind the meshed guard enclosing the hearth, with diapers airing on the high brass rail. There were toys in abundance; a rocking horse, a doll's house, a box of lead soldiers, bricks, tops, books, a miniature theatre and puppets.

Sprigged curtains billowed in the breeze from the barred windows facing a wide view of the rear gardens. Expanse of lawns, ancient stone walls where blue lobelia and snow-on-the-mountain cascaded, the glitter of greenhouse glass from beyond privet hedges, flowers nodding in herbaceous borders, the whole surrounded by sentinel trees.

An atmosphere of good living permeated the room. Its young inmates might suffer harsh discipline and lack contact with their parents, but they would never know hunger or cold. Were it not for precious memories of her mother, Margaret would have gladly exchanged her childhood for theirs.

Doris set the tea things in front of Thora at the head of the table and motioned Margaret to sit at the other end. There was no sign of the nanny.

'She sleeps of an afternoon, does our Mrs Broom. Oh, yes, she's a widow. Some poor bloke took her on once and then snuffed it,' Doris, that mine of information, had already said. 'All the high-ups have a snooze. Mrs Colby'll be sleeping off lunch, and Mr Wakefield, too. I'll have to wake Nanny with a cup of tea shortly. She'll take the children to the drawing room, all posh-like, as if she's the one what's done the work.'

A flaxen-headed tot was seated next to Thora. Her big cornflower blue eyes roamed the company, propped up as she was on a large cushion that enabled her to reach her plate.

'All right, Miss Jane? Nurse will cut your bread into soldiers, shall she? There's a good girl.' Thora folded a napkin into a triangle and tucked a corner under the collar of the toddler's frock. On her other side a baby harnessed in his highchair was happily banging on the apron-shaped tray with a silver-and-coral teething ring.

'Oh, Dauncey, can't you stop William making that dreadful racket?' complained a plump-faced fourteen-year-old with pink bows in her dark brown hair.

'Mind your language, Miss Evelyn. "Racket" indeed. Wherever did you hear that?'

37

'You say it, Dauncey,' put in Harry, pushing his luck.

'That doesn't mean it's for you to copy. And you were young once, Miss Evelyn, just like baby,' Thora reminded tartly. 'Master William is so good. Aren't you, my angel?' she cooed, adjusting the bib beneath his fat little chin.

'He's a bore,' piped another girl pettishly. Two years older than her sister and by far the better looking, it was obvious she was going to be a beauty. 'Why do we still have to eat with the children? Mam'zelle has her meals in the schoolroom. I think Evelyn and I should be allowed to join her. I hate being surrounded by babies. Roderick eats with Mama and Papa when he's down from Oxford. I'll be thankful when I go to finishing school.'

'I think we'll all be glad, Miss Fenella, then we shan't have to look at your miserable face. Cheer up do, or you'll turn the milk,' Thora replied in her crisp way. 'We don't want sour milk in our tea, now do we?'

'I don't care,' Fenella pouted, tossing her honey-blonde ringlets.

' "Don't care was made to care," ' Thora answered crushingly, and concentrated on spooning bread mashed with warm milk into William's rosebud mouth.

'Shall I wet the pot?' Doris asked.

'Yes, and when I've poured, you can pop along and wake Nanny.'

Doris leaned over the fireguard, wrapped a flannel holder round her hand and filled the brown earthenware teapot from the kettle simmering on a trivet above the coals. The exotic smell of scalding Assam blend filled the air. One impression after another crowded Margaret's mind; the children, their nursemaids, the white toy cupboard reflecting the sunlight in a tracery of gold, the rivalry existing between the young Auberts.

Suddenly Harry announced, 'I think Helbren's prettier than Plimmer. She had a face like a camel.'

'You don't know what a camel looks like.' Evelyn pushed back her plate and went into the attack.

'I do. I've two in my Noah's Ark.' His sisters had been given jam and he was raring for a fight.

'Now, now. Be quiet both of you. We don't talk when we're eating, do we?' remonstrated Thora, mopping up William who had spat out a mouthful of pap. 'You know what Nanny says. She won't have argufying in her nursery.'

Evelyn grimaced at Harry. At the mention of Nanny, secretive, conspiritorial looks slid over their faces, enmity forgotten as they united against a mutual foe. Margaret, embarrassed by Harry's remark, was surprised at their reaction. Was the nanny such a formidable person?

Strange undercurrents rippled through the ether, things unspoken of jarring across her nerves.

'Can I have some cake?' asked the irrepressible Harry.

'Certainly not. If you can't have jam, then what makes you think you'd be allowed cake? I really don't know what's got into you this afternoon.'

'He's in love with Helbren,' giggled Evelyn, trying to stifle her laughter in her napkin.

'How d'you know?' Fenella, smiling slyly, was only too willing to torment her brother.

'I'm not. Shut up!' Harry shouted, red in the face.

'Children! Children! Be quiet, all of you!'

'What does "in love" mean?' lisped Jane, round-eyed with wonder at the unusual tea-time rumpus.

'Never you mind. Evelyn's being silly.'

'Evelyn's a silly goose. Goosey, goosey gander,' mocked Harry in an infuriating sing-song.

'Whatever's happening? I've never heard such a row! It sounds like a bear garden in here!'

The loud voice struck across the room like a thunderclap. The noise stopped as abruptly as if a door had slammed shut. The older children sat stiff-backed and still, hands locked in their laps. Even the rebellious Harry was mute. Jane's eyes filled with tears and her mouth quivered. William was the only one unaffected, contentedly chewing on a rusk.

As Mrs Ada Broom advanced towards the table, the others kept their eyes down, with the exception of Margaret who was curious to see this martinet to whom she would now be answerable.

She was a big woman in her late forties, plum-coloured silk skirts rustling, the front protected by a lawn apron edged with ecru lace. Everything about her was big, strong and plain. She had a broad face in which every feature was large, apart from her eyes which were small and pale with colourless lashes. Her gingerish hair was piled high over concealed horsehair pads and adorned with tortoiseshell combs. Their eyes locked, and Margaret met the frosty stare of a woman who resented anyone with the slightest suggestion of beauty.

'Who are you?' Mrs Broom demanded, hands on her hips in a stance that betrayed her working-class origins. Though born in the city she resembled the fishwives who bulked pilchards in the factories in Porthross harbour.

'Margaret Helbren.' There was no hesitation in her answer, no fear either, just coldness.

'The new maid,' Thora supplied. 'Stand up, Helbren, if you please.'

'Ah, yes. Mrs Colby's told me about you.' Mrs Broom walked slowly round her, eyeing her up and down, from the top of her head to the tips of the scuffed shoes poking out from beneath the ill-fitting uniform dress. 'Fisherman's daughter, aren't you? I hope you've had a good wash. Don't want the smell of fish in my nursery.'

She glanced round at her audience with a smirk. The children tittered obligingly. Margaret could feel the hot blood rushing up into her face. 'I'm not a fisherman's daughter. My father was a miner.'

Mrs Broom shrugged her heavy shoulders indifferently. 'Miner, fisherman, it makes no odds. You're one of the villagers. Though you don't talk like them. Why is that?'

'My mother wasn't from these parts.'

'I guessed as much. You lack an accent, though there's a bit of a burr. I'm a Londoner myself. You won't find me talking like a bumpkin. But I don't put on no airs, and I don't expect my nursery staff to neither.' The homely face with its thin-lipped mouth flanked by bulging cheekbones was thrust closer. 'Just you remember that, my girl. No airs, and no followers. If you gets yourself into trouble, then don't come running to me. You'll be out on your ear in a trice. D'you understand?'

The room darkened as a cloud passed across the sun. Aunt Prudence, Aunt Mercy and Mrs Broom, sisters under the skin, narrow-minded bullies disappointed with their lot and taking it out on everyone who swam into their ken. Margaret had thought to leave her unpleasant relatives behind, but it seemed they had pursued her in the guise of the nanny. She did not flinch from Mrs Broom's scorn and sly innuendoes, meeting her eyes with such composure that the nanny looked away.

'You'll not find anything to complain about,' Margaret said levelly, noting that the children were watching her first brush with their nanny, testing her, wondering how far they could push her. 'I've never shirked hard work. You may have heard that I nursed my dying mother. I don't much care for men, so it's unlikely I'll encourage them.'

'Ha! That's what they all say, but they soon change their tune,' Mrs Broom boomed. This startled William who screwed up his face and began to cry. Thelma unbuckled the straps and lifted him from the highchair, patting his back soothingly.

'Time to get them ready,' Mrs Broom commanded. 'Into your clean clothes, children. Go along. No hanging about. You, Helbren, can wash the plates and then take the kitchen ones back to Mrs Frith.'

Margaret inclined her head and stalked regally into the pantry, crocks on a tray. There was only one way to deal with such a woman, and that was to portray indifference and make sure her tasks were carried out meticulously. But the thought of enduring Mrs Broom's tyranny indefinitely cast her into deepest gloom. I won't always be a nurserymaid, she consoled herself as she fetched the kettle and filled the enamelled bowl in the white Belfast sink. Surely there must be a way to better myself?

She swished the soda crystals around to dissolve them and dunked the cups, her thoughts running on. It was lonely in the pantry, but this was a relief. She liked her own company, a solitary by nature. No brothers or sisters, accustomed to roaming the cliffs and fields by herself, and making her own decisions. It would be strange to share a room, stranger still to be part of the nursery, nanny-ruled and child-oriented.

Doris came in, leaving the door ajar. 'D'you want to see them ready to go down?' she whispered. 'Master Harry's in a paddy. He kicked Nanny. He'll get a thrashing come bedtime.'

The two girls peeped through the crack and watched the procession pass. Mrs Broom carried William, Thora followed behind gripping Harry by the hand. He was dragging back, a sulky cherub in a clean white sailor suit. Then came Evelyn and Fenella with Jane in the middle.

'Don't they look sweet? Butter wouldn't melt in their mouths, would it?' Doris remarked wryly. 'No one but us sees the other side of 'em. The muslin the girls are wearing is only for ordinary. You should see them when there's guests. All silk and lace. They looks like princesses.'

'Take those bits of bread and leftovers to the piggery,' snapped Mrs Frith, up to her eyes in dinner preparations and having no time for a fledgling maid. 'It's over the yard,' and she waved a floury hand in the direction of the back door. 'Then you'd better go upstairs. I can't have idle hands cluttering the place. Far too busy. They'll need you to help get the children to bed when they comes up from the drawing room.'

Susan was washing dishes in the scullery sink and the other servants were fully occupied. Feeling out of place and in the way, Margaret slipped out. She drew in a deep breath. Blessed fresh air, blessed solitude.

The yard was deserted, no grooms, no estate workers. It was early evening and those who did not live at the manor had gone home, while the others, apart from the kitchen staff, were having supper in the servants' quarters. She walked across the cobbles, not sure in which direction the piggery lay. Mrs Frith had issued her with a pail of peelings, to which Margaret had added the bread and cake. A wicked waste in her eyes. Had she had her way the unused slices would have been kept in a tin for next time.

The days were still warm but there was an autumnal nip in the air once the sun went down. The leaves were already turning, tipped with brownish gold. Smoke spiralled skywards from behind the high walls of the kitchen garden. The groundsmen had started cleaning up in preparation for winter, lighting bonfires, clearing vegetable plots and adding to the compost heaps.

Did they keep bees? Margaret wondered, and hoped that the old man to whom she had given her hives would take care of the little creatures. She trusted they wouldn't pine, and had been careful to tell them goodbye.

She missed the sea. How long before she felt sand beneath her feet again? According to Susan, the girls employed at Roslan Manor were expected to write home once a week. The letters were then given to Mrs Colby who placed them in a special box on the hall table with the rest of the outgoing mail. There was no one Margaret wanted to write to. The maids and footmen were given a week's holiday per year, but where would she go? To visit her aunts? She shuddered at the idea. Early days, she warned herself. Who knows what may happen?

She was so lost in thought that the sound of hooves did not penetrate until a magnificent black Arabian stallion came charging through the gate. She dropped the bucket. Froze. A huge equestrian head with snapping teeth and wildly rolling eyes loomed over her. The rider yanked in the reins. The beast whinnied and skidded to a halt inches away from her. She could feel its heat, smell the ripe odour rising from its glossy, foam-flecked hide.

The shadow of the horseman blanked out the sky. She looked up, half hoping it was Mr Newark. It wasn't him, yet recognition lit up her brain, but from where? The memory flickered and was gone.

She had the impression of height and good looks. He was bare-headed, the sunset touching his hair with crimson and tracing over the thin face, the proud nose, arched brows and hard eyes. His black jacket fitted his shoulders superbly, and tight white riding breeches displayed his long, muscular thighs. He sat his horse with careless arrogance, every line of him expressing ancient lineage.

'Did Timur nearly mow you down?' he said, his voice loud and confident, his smile mocking. 'He's a vicious brute and you're lucky he didn't bite.'

'Lucky, am I? You should keep him under control,' she answered with quiet fury.

Her anger amused him. 'What's your name?' he asked.

'Why? What is it to you?'

'Tell me your name!'

'Margaret Helbren.'

42

She could feel his eyes boring into her, a slightly puzzled expression on his face. 'Haven't I seen you before? I'm sure I should have remembered someone so damn pretty.'

'I hardly think it likely. I'm working in the nursery, as a maid.' There was a frightening air about him, and this annoyed her. She did not want to feel fear, of him or any other man.

He threw back his head and his laughter rang across the yard. 'Nurserymaid, eh? Wiping my sibling's arses?'

'Who are you?' she grated.

'Roderick, Viscount Stanwood.'

Now she understood. Fenella had mentioned her brother was home from Oxford, and Doris had told her his title. She moved away, intending to head for the pigsty and safety. The company of hogs was preferable to his.

'Excuse me, my lord, I have work to do.' She picked up the bucket purposefully.

'Wait a moment. I haven't given you permission to go.' His voice rose slightly, a predatory glint in his eyes.

'I take my orders from Mrs Colby or Mrs Broom.' Head high, she outfaced him.

'They work for me,' he said, frowning down at her.

'Do they? I was under the impression that Lord Henry and Lady Julia employed the staff.'

He tightened his hands on the reins for the stallion was pawing the cobbles restlessly. 'It's your duty to obey me. How old are you?'

'I don't have to answer that.'

'Yes, you do. I repeat. How old are you?'

'Almost seventeen. My birthday's next month.'

'Old enough, and certainly big enough.' He scrutinised her so insolently that she ached to strike him.

He cocked a foot out of the stirrup and swung down, hitching Timur's rein over a post. He was taller than she had thought, and well built for all his youth.

He had her trapped between himself and the stable wall, an arm braced on either side of her, boxing her in. His hair was gold, with paler streaks, and the eyes regarding her from between thick lashes were pure emerald green. She could smell him, hot from his ride, hot with something else, too, which she could not name, only aware that it put her on guard. She had never seen a gentleman so close before, or any man come to that, save her father.

The memory was unfortunate for it made her shrink away, and Roderick took this as a challenge, more determined than ever to have her. She could not go far, the rough stone wall pressing into her spine.

43

His face came nearer, his smile taunting and an alert expression in his eyes.

Innocent if not ignorant – she had lived too close to the soil not to know about procreation – she was alarmed by his ragged breathing and the hardening of his body. Here was no common lad whose face she could slap. He kept his weight balanced on one hand against the wall and gripped her round the waist with the other.

His lips hovered above hers as she stared up at him. Hovered, came closer as he bent his head. She was conscious of him as a master who should be obeyed in everything by such as her, yet was filled with rebellion. She turned her face aside and brought up her fists to shove against the tough wall of his chest.

Roderick chuckled. 'All right. What is it you want? Presents? Money? Jewellery? Name it and it's yours. I don't usually take a refusal from a servant, but you're different, Maggie – or shall I call you Meg? Worthy of extra attention, though the result will be the same in the end.'

'Let me go,' she snarled. 'I don't want anything from you. I must get back or Mrs Broom will be angry.'

'Mrs Broom can go to hell,' he said, his tone reminding her of his brother, Harry. The same hauteur and belief in his right to have his way at all times.

She had her good name to think of and could not risk giving in to him, having seen how girls were treated if they gave birth to a bastard. Outcasts, universally despised.

Roderick found her defiance refreshing. Usually his victims were afraid to deny him, especially if he threatened to report them to Mrs Colby for slovenly work. This girl, however, acted as if she didn't care, *this girl* with her dark beauty and amazing violet eyes.

Where had he seen her before? In Porthross? A barmaid, perhaps? She didn't look the type to work in a public house. Why, smarten her up a bit, put her in an expensive gown and she'd almost pass as a lady. Who was she? Some gentleman's bly-blow, conceived in a hayloft or in the woods on a moonlit summer night?

'Where d'you come from?' he whispered, ignoring the hands wedged between his chest and her breasts. Then he had a sudden flash of a girl by a pool long ago. He and his friends had called her a gypsy.

In that same instant Margaret recognised him, too. 'So it's you,' she said slowly. 'That bad-mannered boy in the spinney. You haven't improved with the years.'

'And you're the gyspy brat who was trespassing.'

'I didn't know the land belonged to you.'

His hands tightened on her painfully. 'Time for you to be nice to me, Maggie,' he said huskily.

He took her resistance for pretence. It suited him to accept the belief among his peers that girls from the lower orders enjoyed sex, whereas the genteel young ladies they would eventually marry were above the coarse demands of the flesh, physically different from their lowly counterparts.

'Go away!' she shouted. 'Leave me to get on with my work. I'm not going to make love with you, so put that idea right out of your head.'

'Make love?' Roderick said, with a mocking smile. 'That's a rum way of putting it. Love doesn't come into it. Nor will it ever in my dealings with the fair sex. Love weakens a man, makes him vulnerable. What is love anyway? An abberation. When I wed it'll be for money. Someone who'll be a meek wife; obedient, unquestioning, adoring.'

'I pity her. You're a nasty piece of work,' she snapped back.

'Aren't you being rather foolish?' he observed, a hand tracing the side of her averted face. 'Your skin is so beautifully soft. Is it like this all over? Not just your face, but your breasts, thighs, every part of you?'

'You've got a bloody cheek! Get away from me.'

'Will you meet me later?'

'No. Mrs Colby doesn't let us leave our rooms after bedtime.'

He laughed wickedly. 'She'll turn a blind eye if she catches you slipping out to meet me. So will old Nanny Broom.'

'I don't want to meet you. Stand aside, if you please.'

'And if I don't?'

'I'll scream.'

I won't, she thought, even as she issued the challenge. It would be awful if we were found like this. I'd get the blame. She could imagine the contemptuous eyes, the unkind gossip: That new girl, hasn't been there five minutes and she's already making a play for the viscount.

Roderick was enjoying himself hugely, more aroused than he had been for ages. Her refusal fired his lust. Was she frigid? Somehow those eyes, the shape of her face, the movements of her body convinced him that beneath her cool exterior lay a deeply passionate nature. He wanted to explore it, to bring it to the surface. Maybe, he'd even install her in one of the estate cottages and keep her as his mistress. That would be something to tell his fellow students at Balliol, bringing it out quite casually: 'Oh, by the way, chaps, I found this pretty little thing when I was home during the vac. Gorgeous girl, hot as hell. Her thighs fall apart at my touch. She's always ready for rogering. Can't get enough.'

Aloud he said, 'I'll wait for you, Maggie. D'you know the way to my room?'

'I don't want to know.'

'Ask any of the servants. They'll direct you,' Roderick said carelessly, but he was hoping it would not get back to his mother.

Lord Henry, though stern, was a man of the world and prepared to pay off troublesome females if this was the only way to keep their mouths shut, but Lady Julia disapproved of laxity, able to reduce her children to pulp with a few well-chosen words.

But, driven by his appetites, he cupped Margaret's chin in one hand and lowered his mouth to within an inch hers. His breath brushed her lips. She turned her face away, muttering, 'I shan't come to you. I don't even like you.'

'You will, you little idiot!' His voice was rasping, his grip turning to steel. 'And I'm now going to taste pleasures to come.'

'Everything all right, my lord?' A cheerful, masculine voice enquired from behind them.

Roderick dropped his hand, spinning round, face dark with rage. 'What the devil——?'

A lean, wiry man stood at the entrance to one of the outbuildings. He was wearing a dark green jacket with brass buttons, matching breeches and gleaming black gaiters over highly polished boots. He held a peaked cap under one arm. Sherry-gold eyes were regarding Margaret with amusement in their depths, but there was a hard edge about him, too, as his gaze switched back to Roderick.

'Everything is fine, Watson, thank you,' Roderick answered crisply, regaining his composure with lightning speed.

'Right, sir. I've just driven back from Penzance. Lord Henry and Lady Julia have been shopping this afternoon. Dinner will be served soon, but you'll have time to change. Shall I tell a groom to take Timur, sir? Looks as if he could do with a rub down. You don't want him getting a chill, now do you?' He had Roderick's measure, not in the least intimidated, standing his ground.

'Good idea,' Roderick agreed, then lowered his voice, addressing Margaret. 'I'll expect you at eleven o'clock. You'd better be there.' He turned on his heel and strode off.

Watson ran a hand through his short, straight brown hair, his eyes twinkling at Margaret. 'Bothering you, was he? He's a randy blighter. Don't have any truck with him, if you want my advice. I'm Luke, by the by, and I'm the chauffeur. Just as well I was putting the Lanchester to bed and, nosy being my middle name, heard something going on out here and had to take a look. You're new, aren't you?'

46

She was shaking, totally unnerved by the encounter. Meeting Roderick had resurrected that incident from childhood long-buried in her subconscious, when she had first realised there were those who had and those who had not – and that she belonged to the latter. Now he had appeared again, wanting to rob her of the one thing she had managed to keep – her self-respect.

Luke came closer, but not close enough to scare her. His kindness was like balm to her bruised feelings. 'I only arrived today,' she replied, smiling tentatively. 'I'm the nursery still-room maid.'

'Is that so? Well, I guess Mrs Broom'll be wondering where you are and getting herself worked up into the bargain,' Luke said, taking a packet of cigarettes from his pocket, withdrawing one and striking a match on the heel of his boot.

'Oh, dear. I think you're right. I don't want to be late and make a bad impression.'

Luke regarded her through a smoke haze and gave an ironic bow. 'Shall I escort you back to the house, madame?'

'Would you? But first, I've to find the piggery. Mrs Frith won't be pleased if I go back with a full pail.'

'Far be it from me to upset Mrs Frith, a good woman with a magic touch where pastry is concerned.'

He was kind and nice-looking, and Margaret dared to trust him. Somehow she knew he would not try to take advantage, so she followed him to the outhouses. It was twilight now, dusky blue and mysterious. Bats made swooping, noiseless rushes across the lawns and owls screeched in the woods. She was glad of Luke's company, suddenly missing the familiarity of the cottage and her mother's love, plunged into the depths of sorrow.

'What's up?' Luke asked gently, hearing her muffled sob.

'My mother died a few days ago.'

'I'm sorry to hear that. But you'll have some happy memories of her, won't you? I never knew mine, was brought up in an orphanage in Sheffield. Left on the doorstep. Some poor lass's bit of bother. She should have kept her knickers on.' Though he joked, there was pain in his eyes.

'I'm sorry.' Margaret impulsively laid her hand on his.

'Don't be,' he answered, shrugging. 'I never known anything else, an orphanage boy, then apprenticed to a blacksmith and later becoming a mechanic in a car factory. I struck lucky when I had to deliver a a new motor to Lord Henry in London. He offered me a job as chauffeur, and that's what I've been ever since.'

Margaret sniffed and wiped her eyes on a corner of her apron. 'I'm still sorry you didn't have a mother. Yes, I've happy memories of mine, except for the end. She died of lung disease. That's why I'm here. Lady Julia was kind enough to employ me. I had nowhere else to go.'

'Cheer up,' Luke said, grasping her by the elbow and guiding her across the yard to where light shone through the kitchen windows. 'If you need any help, just call on me.'

Susan met her at the door, frowning with worry. 'You was gone a long time,' she scolded, and gave Luke a searching stare. 'What's she doing with you?'

'I showed her where the pigs live, and brought her home safely.' Luke's eyes glinted with amusement, and he looked beyond her into the kitchen. 'Hello there, Mrs Frith. Got a slice of your wonderful pie for a starving man?'

'Come in, you rascal, and stop making so much noise,' Mrs Frith's voice was indulgent. He was obviously one of her favourites. She was sitting in the rocking chair by the fire, a bottle of ale in one hand.

Margaret scurried upstairs and Doris let her into the nursery. She could hear the children splashing about in the bathroom and went to assist. She had not expected to find running water gushing from taps, both hot and cold, and the novelty of a flush toilet fascinated her. At home, she had taken a bath in a galvanised tub placed before the fire, the water drawn from the well and heated in kettles, a laborious procedure which made bathing a chore. The privy had been at the top of the garden. At Roslan Manor, however, engineers had installed pumps and plumbing and heating, and the very latest in sanitation.

There were two bathrooms in the nursery wing; one for the children and one for Mrs Broom. The other nurses were expected to use those allocated to the servants. The same applied to the lavatories, though Margaret was to learn that Doris and Thora cheated, often using Mrs Broom's when she was absent.

Bathtime was hectic; first Jane, then Evelyn, then Harry. The elder girls were allowed to stay up, bathing later. William was already asleep in his crib in the night nursery. Although Margaret was not permitted to wash the children, she was expected to clear up afterwards, fold and put away their clothing, place soiled garments in the linen basket, hang up the towels and turn down the beds.

All the while she was brooding on her brush with Lord Roderick. The last thing she intended to do was go to his room. Though the thought was alarming, she could not help wondering what it would be like if she did and how it would change her life. She would lose her virginity for a start. There was no doubt that his intentions were dishonourable.

If it had been the pleasant young gentleman she had seen that morning, things might have been rather different. He did not look like a seducer and she was sure he would treat her with respect. She smiled at the idea.

Thora brewed cocoa which they drank seated round the table. There was no sign of Mrs Broom. Then Margaret said goodnight, leaving with a list of duties for the morning, the first of which was bringing up breakfast at seven-thirty, after she had attended prayers in the servants' hall. She found Susan waiting for her at the bottom of the nursery stairs, and soon they were undressing in their room.

'You wants to watch that Luke Watson,' Susan warned, sliding down in bed and pulling the covers up to her chin. 'Him in his smart uniform. You should see him driving those cars. Thinks he's the cat's whiskers.'

'He was kind to me, came to my rescue when I was fighting off Lord Roderick,' Margaret answered, flat on her back on the mattress, feeling the sheet against her bare arms, softer than that used at home.

'You what?' Susan bounced up, her hair in two pigtails each side of her face, eyes round in the lamp light.

'He galloped into the yard on that great brute of a horse. Nearly knocked me flying, then he got pushy, wanted me to go to his room tonight.'

'You never said you would?' Susan looked aghast. 'Oh, Margaret, he's trouble with a capital T.'

'I told him I wouldn't, but I'm not sure he believed me.'

Susan subsided, leaned over, lowered the wick and blew out the light, a whiff of paraffin spicing the air. 'Keep out of his way. He's bad,' she said into the dimness.

Margaret did not reply. It was all so alien; the sounds drifting up through the house and in at the window; the hushed voices as servants passed on the stairs carrying out some late order; a dog barking from the direction of the stables; the rustling of the trees outside.

A wave of homesickness swept over her, sending scalding tears to her eyes. She longed to be back in the cottage, but there was no return. No mother to comfort a skinned knee or tale of unfair teasing. She was truly alone in a harsh world.

She lay wide awake long after Susan's gentle snores stirred the stillness. As she watched the patterns flung in squares on the floor by the moonlight, she wondered if Lord Roderick was waiting and getting angry. It was a disturbing thought and when at last she dropped into oblivion she took with her a final image – that of his mocking smile and hard green eyes.

By defying him years ago and again today, she was uncomfortably certain she had made an enemy.

49

Chapter 3

Lady Julia Aubert, nee Templar, was a controller. It was her nature to be so and she carried it off with flair, so subtle in her dealings with people, be they members of staff, acquaintances or her own family, that they were unaware of being manipulated.

She relished her role as Marchioness of Harleigh, had seized the chance to marry Lord Henry, and thrown herself into the part with zest. The youngest of five daughters, she had been bridesmaid to each of her sisters and, after being presented at Court to the ageing Queen Victoria, had netted the bachelor of the season, a handsome and eligible man who had lately inherited the title of marquis.

Seated at her dressing table at Roslan Manor preparing herself for the day, she contemplated her reflection in the triple mirrors and sipped coffee, a habit she had developed when at finishing school in France, the same establishment to which her daughter, Fenella, was to be dispatched in less than a month.

Julia was approaching forty, but appeared younger. Aware that good looks helped one through life enormously, though not classically beautiful she had skilfully developed her assets so most people were left with the impression that she was ravishing. Her hair was blonde, kept in shining condition by the application of camomile and the regular use of an egg yolk whisked in water. Most ladies washed their hair no more than once a month, but Julia liked to have her maid, Boughton, shampoo it every week, even during menstruation, which was unheard of and most unconventional.

Julia *was* unconventional. On the surface she was the perfect wife, supporting her husband in his political career; he was Tory Member of Parliament for Porthross and district. But she had hidden depths which she displayed to no one, not even Roderick, her first and favourite child. She missed him when he was away at Oxford, but there was no need to think of that yet. They had a few more halcyon weeks together. Sometimes she paused to wonder if there was not a hint of incest in their mutual adoration. Even this added a spice to the relationship and she made no attempt to conceal her possessive love, spoiling him outrageously.

Of the six children whom she had carried in her womb and pushed out into the world in that undignified, bloody process which she could only describe as barbaric, Roderick resembled her the most. Physically certainly, flaxen-headed and green-eyed. In temperament? Possibly. She liked to think she knew her son through and through, but had to admit this was not true. Roderick was deep. One never knew what was going on in that devious mind.

Harry was fair, too, but his features were those of his grandfather, the old marquis. Julia had never met her late father-in-law in the flesh, but there were portraits, and photographs aplenty. These had proved him to have been a sportsman as he posed with his guns and the bodies of slaughtered animals. Not only those indigenous to his native land; the tiger skins and snarling, mounted heads adorning the walls proved he had hunted big game in exotic places.

Fenella and Evelyn were a cross between the Auberts and the Templars. Jane was one on her own, a throwback to some former ancestor, while Baby William undoubtedly favoured his father. His eyes were blue, his skin swarthy and his curls dark. He'll be handsome, she thought with satisfaction, if he grows up like Henry. Handsome, debonair and totally incapable of being faithful to any woman for more than five minutes.

She remembered reading in some highly salacious literature which Henry kept hidden in his desk that men thought about sex eleven times an hour, their bodies responding in the customary manner. Where did the writer get his information? she had wondered, but was sure, nonetheless, that it was true of Henry.

'Good morning, m'dear.' As if conjured by her thoughts, her husband came through from the dressing room linking their bedchambers.

He was attired for riding, and her heart did a strange little flip in her chest at the sight of him. Even after more than twenty years he still had the power to move her. Henry Charles George Aubert, a powerfully built man, with thick black hair lightly silvered at the temples, wide cheekbones and an aquiline nose. His upper lip was firm, hinting at impatience with incompetence, but the full lower one spoke of sensuality.

Julia had long ago decided that he oozed sexual attraction from his pores. This had struck her forcibly when she first met him at her coming-out ball, though in those days she did not know what it was. He had thrilled her then, an untried virgin with her head stuffed full of romantic notions which excluded the crude act of copulation. She had been entirely unaware of this until her wedding night.

'I'm well, thank you, my lord,' she replied, formal because Boughton was present.

Julia swivelled on the dressing-table stool to face him and he came across and kissed her cheek. He smelled of shaving soap, cigars and that musky masculine odour all his own. She fought the urge to seize him by the lapels of his riding jacket and pull him down to her, grinding her mouth against his with a passion refined women were not supposed to feel.

Henry smiled and smoothed his moustache with a long brown finger, admiring this woman in her loose, green and silver pegnoir, her hair cascading across her graceful shoulders. Julia was an ideal wife in every respect, extremely presentable, a wonderful hostess and competent manager. She had, after all, been trained to be so, and she rarely bothered him with household details, disputes or bills, keeping within the budget allowed for running Roslan Manor and their elegant London establishment.

She had given him children and he never doubted for one moment they were his. Julia was loyal, unlike some other society ladies who ensured that the first two or three offspring were fathered by their husbands, thus protecting the dynasty, then followed their own inclinations and took lovers. No gentleman ever commented if later additions to the nursery did not resemble him in the least, providing there was no open scandal. Divorce was a terrible disgrace, even the innocent parties ostracized.

What Henry did not know was that Julia had disobeyed the rules in one respect: she had fallen in love with the man she married. Though never betraying this for an instant, not even in the rutting heat of the bed, she had given her heart into his keeping and, over the years, this had received a battering. Even then, she had not complained of his infidelities, keeping her counsel, but never for a moment forgiving or forgetting. Beneath that sweet exterior lay a core of steel: the iron fist in the velvet glove.

The days following Margaret's arrival at the manor were busy and confusing. She would have been lost without Susan and Doris. They took her under their wings, helping her in a dozen ways.

Her tasks consisted of sweeping and dusting the nursery, cleaning the bathrooms, rinsing baby clothes and running up and down with meals from the kitchen. She had little to do with the children, but returned their tentative overtures, helping out with them if called upon to do so.

The resident seamstress altered the two lightweight dresses issued so they fitted reasonably well, and measured her for her winter uniform. She was provided with several sets of collars and cuffs, thick black stockings, underwear and stout sensible shoes. Thus equipped, Margaret performed her chores so efficiently that even the eagle-eyed Mrs Broom could not fault her.

'Well done, Helbren,' she commented on inspecting the night nursery after Margaret had finished, running a critical finger along the high picture rail to make sure no speck of dust had been overlooked. 'Let's hope you keep up this standard.'

'I will, ma'am,' Margaret declared, flushed with exertion, more pleased by this grudging praise than she cared to admit.

She might not like the nanny much, that cold, unbending woman who drove the nursery staff hard, but was happy to think her mother would have been proud of her.

'They tell me you can sew,' Mrs Broom continued, taking one of Jane's frocks from a hanger in the wardrobe. 'See what you can do with this.' There was a triangular tear in the flounced skirt. 'The sewing woman is all very well for plain things, staff uniforms, linen and that, but hopeless when it comes to anything finer.'

'I'll do my best,' Margaret replied, examining the rip. 'I can cut a piece from the hem and back it, drawing a few threads from a seam to use as cotton. But when am I supposed to do this?'

'During the evenings, of course.'

'In my spare time, you mean?' This was a joke. Spare time consisted of one afternoon off a fortnight and Margaret had not been there long enough to merit it.

'If need be, yes.' Mrs Broom looked at her as if she was stupid. 'You can start after tea. If you make a neat job of it, then I've things of my own in need of repair.'

The prospect was daunting, but Margaret had no choice, so when she had washed up and trailed down the several flights of stairs to the kitchen, she fetched her mother's sewing box from the bride-chest and settled by the window with Jane's frock. She gazed out at the filmy clouds sailing in a high, thin sky tinged with crimson. The daylight was fading. Soon she would have to take her work to the table and light one of the lamps.

The workbox stood on the window seat beside her and, when she opened the lid, a delicate scent arose from the lavender bag inside. She hurt as she remembered her mother making it. Before she had left Hazel Cottage, she had uprooted some plants and taken them to the mound of earth beneath which Mary Helbren's body lay. Kneeling beside it, she had used her hands to dig little holes and replant the flowers, puddling them in, as her mother had taught her. She could only hope they would not wilt, and vowed to go there again in the spring with seedlings purchased from her wages.

It was not often she allowed herself to dwell on her loss. To do so reduced her to angry grief. But now, searching in the tidy box for the needle case, thimble and scissors, it was hard to control her feelings.

'Where are you, Mother?' she whispered, blinded by tears. 'Why did you have to die? I need you. There's no one else to turn to.'

'That's a fine sewing box. Where did you get it?' demanded Mrs Broom, her harsh voice jarring across Margaret's thoughts.

She stood just behind her, having a habit of sneaking up quietly. Margaret caught a whiff of gin on her breath and saw that her face was flushed. She had retired to her room after tea while Doris and Thora attended to the children, emerging when they were in bed and the nursery quiet. She was more bedizened than usual, wearing helio-trope silk with lace frills and a black velvet choker with a cameo brooch pinned in the centre.

'It belonged to my mother.' A sob caught in Margaret's throat.

'Oh, yes? Pull the other leg, it's got bells on it,' Mrs Broom sneered. 'Walnut inlaid, with silver scissors? Rather too grand for a fisherman's wife, I should have thought.'

She never spoke of Margaret's parentage without that jeering inton-ation and a slighting reference to fisherfolk.

Margaret's withering stare should have blasted her where she stood. 'Father mined tin, and Mother had worked in a castle before she mar-ried. She was a governess, and the family loved her. This was their parting gift when she left.'

'Hoity-toity! Don't you get uppish with me, miss!' Mrs Broom's mean little eyes narrowed, her thin mouth setting like a rat-trap. 'I suppose you hope to worm your way into a similar position, eh? Well, you might have done if you hadn't been so toffee-nosed. Lord Roderick fancies you.'

'I don't know what you mean,' Margaret said, lowering her eyes to her work, pinning the patch in place.

'No?' Mrs Broom planted herself where Margaret could not avoid seeing her. 'Didn't he nearly run you down the first night you was here? Didn't he order you to go to his room? I know he did, 'cause he said to me that I wasn't to stop you. He'd make it worth my while if I turned a blind eye.'

Margaret met her gaze fearlessly, taking comfort from the feel of her mother's thimble on her finger. 'Ah, so that's it. You were done out of a bribe when I didn't turn up.'

54

Mrs Broom scowled. 'It doesn't do to upset Lord Roderick. He can turn nasty. A person has to keep on the right side of him.'

'Is that why Betty Plimmer was dismissed? Because she wouldn't let him – or because she did and found herself in trouble?'

'I'm not saying nothing more. No one could accuse me of being a blabbermouth. But just you be careful, that's all. And I wants that frock so as Miss Jane can wear it first thing in the morning. D'you hear?'

'Yes, ma'am. It'll be ready.'

'Thora and me are going to join Mr Wakefield and Mrs Colby for a game of cards. That leaves you and Doris to mind the children. Don't get 'em up, unless they wants the lavatory, and don't put up with no fuss. They're in bed and there they should stay. If I find you've been spoiling them, you'll be for it. Understand?'

'Yes, ma'am.'

Mrs Broom rustled out with hardly a stagger, leaving a strong smell of eau de cologne and gin in her wake, an unsavoury combination that turned Margaret's stomach, but her words had been more sickening.

She knew what prostitutes did. There had been a couple of women in Porthross with unsavoury reputations. She had heard her aunts prattling about how they sold themselves for money. Mrs Broom had proposed taking a bribe from Lord Roderick for looking the other way if Margaret went to him. So what did this make her? There must be a name for someone who was party to such matters.

'There is,' said Luke when she asked him next day. 'It's bawd if female, pimp if a man.'

'Have you ever been with a prostitute, Luke?' she asked, leaning against the car he was polishing, one of a fleet of gleaming vehicles belonging to Lord Henry who was enthusiastic about motoring, following the example set by King Edward VII.

Paying particular attention to the brass headlamps out front, he did not look at her. 'That would be telling. Maybe I have, maybe I haven't.'

'Don't be mean,' she grumbled. 'There is so much I need to know. Nobody seems willing to talk about things like that.'

Her time was limited. In fact she had no business being in the coach house now transformed into a garage, Luke's domain where he pampered his lordship's cars. But every day, while the children were in the drawing room, she managed to slip off under the pretext of emptying the pig bucket, enjoying a few minutes of freedom. Sometimes she simply dawdled, admiring the view, talking to the stable cat, whistling at the doves who preened and paraded, toes turned in, on the mossy tiles, but today she needed to consult Luke.

'What are you telling me?' she persisted. 'That Mrs Broom was willing to sell me to Lord Roderick?'

'That's putting it crudely. She wouldn't see it that way, I'm sure,' he said with a crooked grin. 'She'd be most offended.'

'What a hypocrite!' Margaret exclaimed. 'And she's in charge of little children!'

Luke straightened his back, putting down his polishing rag and regarding her with those light brown eyes with laughter lines fanning out from the corners. His shirtsleeves were rolled up above the elbows, showing his tanned forearms with their crisp fuzz. The neck was open over a broad chest, equally sun-browned and hirsute, and a canvas apron covered his breeches, an old pair, not the smart uniform ones.

'Madam isn't aware of her foibles,' he said slowly. 'As far as she's concerned Mrs Broom does a thorough job and runs the nursery like clockwork, never bothering her with problems. The gentry like it that way and don't enquire too deeply about what goes on behind the green doors. She sees her kiddies once a day, and they're smartly turned out, well behaved and polite.'

'She doesn't know Mrs Broom tipples, and sometimes smacks them too hard?' A cloud darkened Margaret's face, a cold feeling of help-lessness holding her enthrall. 'I'll tell her ladyship,' she added with sudden resolution.

'Steady on,' he cautioned, coming over to where she stood, a friend and adviser which was all she required of him, though he wanted to give her more.

'I must do something,' she exclaimed. 'Those poor children.'

'And who is going to listen? You're new, a very lowly member of staff. You're not even allowed to speak with the mistress.'

'Can't you say something? You see her almost every day, don't you?'

He grinned wrily, propping his shoulders against the whitewashed wall and lighting a cigarette. 'What do I do? Say to her, "By the way, madam, your son wants to sleep with the nurserymaid, Mrs Broom will let him for a fee, and she drinks like a fish and knocks the children about." Oh, yes, that would go down well, wouldn't it? She'd be quite likely to tell me to mind my own business and give me the sack. Besides which, I never seen Mrs Broom raise a hand to them. Have you?'

'Not exactly,' she admitted, glancing uneasily at the wide open double doors as if expecting the bulky figure of the nanny to appear. 'She's too clever for that, but I've heard her walloping them, especially Master Harry, and they live in dread of her.'

'Children are tough little beggars,' he vouchsafed, head back, blow-ing smoke towards the rafters. 'They have to be or they'd never survive. Master Harry probably deserves everything he gets, a right limb of

Satan. He tries it on with me, but I let him know where we stand. He likes cars, though, and loves to come down here and tinker with the engines, good as gold then. I'll sound him out, if you like.'

'If I like? Is it down to me then to do something about Mrs Broom's mismanagement?' Her eyes sparked with rage, her hair seemed to spark, too, and Luke thought how desirable she was, in agreement with Lord Roderick on that score, though recognising that his own feelings could easily develop into something deeper.

'Take it slow, sweetheart,' he advised, dropping the butt to the floor and grinding it under his heel. 'Box clever. Don't put the old bitch's back up.'

'Seems like I've already done that.' Margaret picked up the pail and walked out of the door. 'Why doesn't she like me, Luke?'

'Look in the mirror, and then at her ugly mug. There's your answer,' he commented with a farewell wave of his hand. 'I'll see you at the service in the Great Hall tomorrow. Your first, isn't it?'

'That's right. I'm looking forward to viewing Lord Henry and Lady Julia at close quarters.'

No morning began without every servant being expected to arrive promptly for prayers at six-thirty. These were conducted in the servants' hall by Mr Wakefield, but the routine was different on Sunday.

'Lay out your clean dress,' Susan instructed at bedtime that evening. 'You've got to be neat as a new pin.'

An early start, the morning chores performed before breakfast, then upstairs again to change. Margaret had been detailed to help with Jane and Harry. Mrs Broom, very grand in black silk, carried the baby who was swamped by his white lawn dress, a bonnet and pale blue velvet pelisse edged with swan's-down.

He was fretful and Margaret sympathised. He must be most uncomfortable, happiest when he was rolling round the nursery floor clad only in his diaper. It was a mild day yet under his dress he wore a vest, a binder, rubber knickers over his nappy, then woollen ones, a pilch tied down the side with sarsenet ribbon and a voluminous starched petticoat.

There was nothing she could do for him, much as she would have liked to. He was not her responsibility, and she had her work cut out with Jane, who was sulking, and Harry, who had a mischievous glint in his eyes. Resembling a galleon under full sail, Mrs Broom proceeded down the three flight of stairs and into the Great Hall.

'Grrhh!' growled Harry, staring up and challenging the snarling head of a lion, shot by his grandfather on safari in Africa.

'Hush, dear,' warned Thora.

'Why must I hush?'

'You know very well. Don't be naughty,' Thora whispered, then gratefully handed him over to his tutor, Cedric Rigsby, a pale, gaunt young man suffering from acne who had the unenviable task of trying to instill knowledge into the recalcitrant Harry.

The governess, Mademoiselle Ranier, accompanied Evelyn and Fenella, a small, chic lady with the vivacious sparkle of a Parisienne. Raven-haired, with black eyes, she was not exactly a servant nor yet a member of the family. Margaret had heard the maids gossiping about her, saying she was neither fish nor fowl nor good red herring.

The Hall was impressively gloomy and magnificent, with oak panelling and fireplaces at either end carved with the Aubert coat of arms, their hearths wide enough to take logs the size of a man. The roof was timbered and arched like a church, the walls hung with crossed pikes and shields and tattered flags captured by warrior Auberts in battles long ago.

There were portraits of gentlemen in ruffs and ladies in farthingales; landscapes and hunting scenes; the exterior of the house depicted two centuries before. The passage of time was marked by a monumental German clock with figures that moved round, striking little bells to chime the quarters and hours. Full suits of armour stood in corners, faceless and sinister under plumed helmets.

The nursery party were shown to chairs arranged on the left of the oak refectory placed in front of an elaborately chaste screen. A large leather-bound Bible with brass clasps lay open on its surface. Mr Wakefield came in with Mrs Colby, followed by his lordship's valet, the parlourmaids, housemaids and kitchen staff. Luke brought up the rear, looking straight at Margaret and pulling a face as if to say, 'What a farce!' With much shuffling, rustling and whispering, everyone settled on their places.

After a short pause the butler opened a door and Lord Henry stalked in with Lady Julia, accompanied by her maid carrying madam's reticule and prayer book. Lord Roderick trailed behind, sleepy-eyed and bad-tempered.

Julia's tiny, squat-featured pug trotted at her heels, beady eyes alert, tail as tightly curled as a pig's. He had a tendency to roam, till his mistress called him sharply to order. He retreated under her chair from which he peered out moodily, lifting his lip back from pointed teeth in a warning snarl if anyone dared approach.

Margaret glanced at Roderick. He met her eyes and a sneering smile curved his mouth. It was unpleasant, and she turned her gaze to Lord Henry.

Roslan Manor was so vast that the more humble of the back-stairs brigade could go for weeks with barely a glimpse of the master or mistress. Curious about him, she could now look her fill. For a middle-aged man he was remarkably well-preserved, fitting superbly into this grand setting, his features reflecting those of the men in the portraits. His rich voice echoed across the Hall as he started to read a passage from the Bible. Its timbre sent shivers down her spine.

It was a long parable and Harry swung his legs and yawned. Thora placed a firm hand on his knee. Jane behaved much better, watching her father in awe. William had gone to sleep, his little face obscured by his bonnet as he nestled against Mrs Broom's shoulder.

The moment came for prayers. Throats were cleared, chairs scraped back as the staff prepared to kneel. The women's full-skirted posteriors looked like small hills surmounted by stiff white apron bows. Harry was intrigued by the sight, and not only Harry.

The pug, his mistress's attention diverted, trotted round them, sniffing. No one dared move, heads bowed. Margaret, on the end of the row, was aware of him stopping. Turning her head sharply she saw him lift his leg and heard the hiss as a jet of urine shot over her clean skirt. She glared at him and he scampered off, heading back to the shelter of Lady Julia's chair.

There was nothing Margaret could do but endure this crowning insult. Doris had seen what happened, saying as they walked out the door once the service was over, 'I should've warned you. He always does that to one of us. Likes the smell of clean linen, I suppose.'

'Can't you complain to Lady Julia?' Margaret wanted to cry with frustration, aware of the yellow stain on her skirt.

'No. We just wait till we catch him on his own and then kick ten buckets of shite out of the dirty little sod!'

Susan said much the same thing, passing it off with a shrug, but Margaret found it impossible be so philosophical. The action of the pug, they said his name was Coco, seemed to underline her position: anyone could treat her as they pleased – Mrs Broom, Lord Roderick, the dog.

Her birthday passed unnoticed by anyone but her in October. There was a flurry of activity as Harry's trunk was packed. Luke drove him to the station to catch the train which would take him to his father's old public school where he was to become a boarder. Fenella, too, departed for France, chaperoned by Mademoiselle Ranier. Rigby was dismissed, a sad figure moving out of their lives to take up a post elsewhere. A new governess arrived for Evelyn, a jolly girl named Natalie Toner, given to wearing severely tailored costumes, striped blouses, neckties and round straw hats.

Margaret, Doris and Susan formed a band, calling themselves 'The Three Musketeers', united in their aim to stand firm against the

59

bullying of Mrs Colby and Mrs Broom. Thora was popular, and the nurserymaids hoped she would take over one day. But as time went by Margaret realised that their ambition was to find a man with whom they could 'walk out'. Despite their jocular condemnation of the opposite sex, they both wanted to be married some day. Margaret could not share this dream.

The example set by her parents was ever in her mind. The quarrels and arguments still rang in her ears, the grinding poverty, his drunkenness, her mother's despair, her own sensations of being ripped apart by the two of them. Luke was the only one who seemed to understand, streetwise and tough, familiar with the underside of life.

One wintery day in November she managed to escape Mrs Broom, determined to enjoy the leisure due to her. The air was clear, the sky a watery blue, the trees bare, a touch of frost whipping the colour into her cheeks. She was warmly dressed in a brown woollen skirt and jacket, a knitted scarf round her neck and matching beret cocked at an angle on her dark hair. In defiance of Mrs Colby, she wore it down, curling over her shoulders. This was her time. Nothing to do with the housekeeper or the nanny.

So far she had not explored further than the yard. Now she intended to investigate the numerous outbuildings. Like most large country estates, Roslan catered for the wants of the manor. The sheep and cows grazing its meadows provided meat. The fields and gardens supplied fruit and vegetables and fodder. It had its own blacksmith's forge, carpenter's shop, dairy and laundry.

Having wandered round these and taken a short walk through the grounds, she went in search of Luke. It was late afternoon when she stepped into the dimness of the coach house, looking forward to seeing him, yet wary. Though she distrusted men, she was sometimes tormented by strange, pleasurable sensations running through her breasts and between her thighs when she daydreamed of finding the perfect lover. She was afraid of what might happen if she was alone with Luke in an intimate setting, and knew his bedroom was in the loft above.

Roslan Manor had been built in Norman times and was strongly fortified. These defences had last been used in sixteen forty-five when a legendary Lady Aubert had held her house against the Roundheads while her Cavalier husband was away fighting for the ill-fated King Charles I. Now this area, once needed for stabling cattle against siege, was used for storing coaches, gigs, governess carts, and the motor vehicles.

'Ah, there you are. I thought you weren't coming.' Luke heaved his shoulders from the Lanchester against which he had been lounging.

There was no doubt about it, he was certainly a good-looking man. She liked his smart uniform with its shiny buttons. The manner in which his dark breeches and tight boots fitted his well-shaped legs pleased her, too. In all, Luke was a lovesome person and she wondered if Doris and Susan had been right when they said he was smitten with her. A chauffeur's wife? It was a reasonable prospect. She was fond of him, yet knew she could never love him.

'I would have gone stark staring mad if I'd stayed in that nursery a second longer,' she exclaimed.

'You're not happy, are you?' he said quietly. 'What is it you want, Margaret?'

She threw out her arms in despair. 'I don't know. That's half the trouble. I should be content, but I'm not. I don't want to spend my days looking after children.'

He moved a fraction nearer. 'You won't mind your own?'

'I don't know if I want them. They're a tie and I'd like to travel, to see the world, to be independent so no one had the right to tell me what to do.'

'You'd like all this, perhaps?' He made a sweeping gesture that took in the cars, the carriages, the great state coach in which the Auberts appeared at public functions.

'Yes, I would.' Her face glowed and her eyes shone. 'I'd take Lady Julia's place any day.'

'D'you think I don't want to own one of those cars?' he responded on a slightly bitter edge. 'D'you think I like this uniform and doffing my cap to 'em, waiting outside shops for hours while she makes up her mind which hat to buy? We'd all like to be the boss, wouldn't we?'

'Some more than others,' she said, and walked over to the state carriage, admiring its beautiful lines, shiny dark green lacquer, yellow wheels and silk curtains at the windows, the whole slung on massive leather straps. 'Can I look inside?' she asked.

He nodded, opened one of the crested doors, pulled down the iron step and stood back with an ironic bow. Margaret put one foot on it and grasped the sides of the frame, pulling herself up. It was dark inside and had a faintly musty smell, but she was enchanted with the plush upholstery and comfortable seats big enough to serve as beds if need be. Luke demonstrated the smoothly sliding panels opening on little cupboards for the storing of provisions and personal effects.

'Oh, how lovely to be able to travel in such luxury!' she cried. 'Let's pretend I'm a princess in royal robes, and you're my gallant.'

He suddenly leaned across and seized her hands in his, saying, 'I don't want to play games. I've been wanting to ask you. Will you be my young lady? Can we walk out together?'

61

'No,' she said quickly, freeing herself.

'Why not? I want you to marry me,' he urged, his voice gruff. 'I'll look after you. I've never felt like this about anyone before.'

'I can't,' she whispered, and wondered why she was refusing him. He was a fine man and this was probably the best offer she would get.

'What is it, sweetheart? Have I upset you?' He looked so miserable that she was ashamed of herself, though it had never been her intention to give him the wrong idea.

'Of course not.'

His face set in disappointed lines. 'I thought you liked me.'

'I do. It's just that—' she stumbled over the words, shook her head and fell silent.

'Come on. Spit it out. I won't laugh,' he persisted.

'I've always had this feeling that I didn't belong among the villagers. And I don't feel at home with the servants either,' she said slowly, eyes down as her fingers pleated her skirt, fold over fold. 'I hope you don't think I'm foolish, but I want something better.'

'I'd like that too. Why can't we do it together? Me as chauffeur and you as housekeeper in some cushy little billet. Mr and Mrs Luke Watson. What a team!' His pleasant mouth quirked up at the corners.

'You don't understand. I want to be a lady – a *real* lady.'

Luke shook his head. 'You have to be born to it. D'you think some gent'll fall in love with you and marry you? No, my lovely, gentlemen are only interested in girls like you for one thing. You saw what happened with Lord Roderick. No toff is going to take a working-class woman to wife. His kind would turn against him. He'd be an outcast, and you'd be crucified. Everyone would hate you – his lot, and yours.'

'Does it have to be through marriage? I'd rather achieve it by my own efforts. To own a house like this, walk through the rooms and know every stick and stone of it is yours. A husband wouldn't be necessary. It could be done with money.'

'It would take a miracle,' he answered, and moved to go, helping her out of the carriage. 'Meanwhile, I'm here when you need me. We'll still be friends, won't we? But I'm serious when I say I want to marry you.'

'Thank you, Luke. Maybe one day I'll take you up on that, but I simply must try it my way first, though I don't know how. Work for myself? Run a business? Something will turn up, I'm sure of it.'

Christmas was fast approaching, bringing with it an air of bustle and excitement that spread throughout the entire house. It even invaded the privacy of Julia's boudoir, a quiver of anticipation tingling along her nerves.

The children were expected home, Harry having completed his first term at boading school, Fenella leaving France for a month's vacation. Roderick was on his way and would not be returning to Oxford, having obtained a degree in law. He would be with them till he decided what he wanted to do. Maybe he would stay there for good, helping his father with estate management.

They were entertaining a dozen guests for the festivities and the organisation was complicated. Julia had spent an extravagant week in London, shopping in Harrods department store, at Liberty's and numerous exclusive shops, then returning to the country with her purchases. She possessed exquisite taste, using colourful paper and tinsel bows when wrapping presents for her children, Henry and those friends and relatives who would be spending Christmas under their roof. Her own wardrobe had not been neglected and she had treated herself to several expensive and highly fashionable creations from the House of Worth.

Best of all was the knowledge that Henry would be there full-time, playing the host as only he knew how, organising the Boxing Day meet as Master of the Porthross Hunt. No chance for him to slip off for dalliance in any other direction and she had made sure that only devoted couples had been invited to stay, certainly no wanton jades who might lure him from her bed, if only temporarily.

A few days before the saturnalia began, she attended the service on Sunday morning, rising rather late as Henry had been particularly amorous the night before, which she attributed to the risqué lingerie she had bought whilst in London. Dressing quickly, she grabbed Coco under one arm, hurried into the Hall and took her seat.

When the lesson was over and she prepared to kneel for prayers, she inadvertently stepped on Coco's paw. Cheated of sharing her breakfast, he was even more belligerent than usual. A sharp yelp, a snarl and she felt a tug at her skirt and heard an ominous ripping sound.

'Coco!' she hissed angrily. 'Let go!' But when she finally rose a length of fabric trailed down, mauled by his spiteful teeth. 'Oh, you bad dog!' Julia was extremely annoyed. 'Wakefield! Come here! Take him outside immediately.'

'Yes, milady. Certainly, milady,' said the butler, solemn as a judge, fastening the lead to Coco's collar and marching him away.

The footmen looked on, poker-faced but satisfied, tired of madam's pet trying to hump their legs and weary of clearing up the turds he casually dropped whenever he felt like it. The housemaids were jubilant.

Boughton, fussing, was trying to calm her mistress. 'What a pity. It's a nasty scag.'

63

'I can see that, you fool.' Julia forgot to be calm and reasonable. 'It's one of my favourites, too.'

A quiet voice spoke beside her. 'If I could have the dress, madam, I'd mend it so that it would never show.'

Julia swung round. Violet-blue eyes were regarding her levelly. It was the dark slender girl whom she had last seen in a sickroom in Porthross. Mary Helbren's daughter. Julia never forgot a face, a name or an injury. She had offered Margaret work, had observed her at the Sunday services, and listened to progress reports from the housekeeper. She was doing well, apparently, though a touch haughty. Julia had not been surprised, having half expected this.

'There is a seamstress already,' she answered briskly. 'And Boughton is competent.'

'I'd like to do it for you, Lady Julia. Mrs Broom will vouch for my skill with the needle,' Margaret persisted, astounding herself by her daring.

William was crying, the noise distressing his mother who never could bear to hear a child howling. 'Don't trouble Nanny now. She must take the baby upstairs. What a frightful noise he's making. Very well. Boughton, see the dress is delivered to the nursery.'

'Yes, madam. At once,' Boughton promised, one of those people who blame themselves for everything. Now she was feeling responsible for Coco's vile behaviour and threw Margaret a watery-eyed, grateful look.

'Are you ready to leave, my dear?' Henry strolled over to Julia, proffering his arm. 'I told you ages ago you should let me put a bullet in Coco's head. I've never met a more unpleasant brute. Tried to bite me the other day, but I put the boot in pretty smartly. You spoil him. That's the trouble. Give him to me for a few days. I'll soon train him.'

'It's all right, Henry, really.'

Julia slipped her arm through his and they walked from the Hall. She was outwardly calm but angry inside. Not because of the accident. What was a skirt after all? It was the girl who had upset her, the girl whose eyes had betrayed a hunger too deep to be expressed and a determination that challenged even Julia's strong will.

Just for an instant she questioned her wisdom in bringing Mary Helbren's child to live under her roof. This was unsettling, too, for Julia rarely, if ever, had doubts.

Chapter 4

'Hi there, Mater. Everything fine and dandy?' Roderick asked as he breezed into Julia's boudoir. Coco, reinstated, bounced up from the hearth rug, barking hysterically.

'Such slang! Where do you learn it?' she complained happily, hushing the dog and advancing on her son, arms wide open. His lips were cold and tasted of frost, outdoor freshness clinging to his hair. He had just arrived and come straight to find her.

'The Yanks, Mama – such capital fellows. There were several at university. I'd like to visit America. Don't you know anyone there?'

'I do, as it happens. I've a cousin who married a tycoon's daughter.' She drew him closer to the fire crackling in the marble fireplace, its glow mirrored by brass andirons. 'You're freezing. Was the journey frightful?'

'The train was late, and Watson had to hang around in the waiting room. But we got here in record time. That motor's a goer, isn't it? Will Papa let me drive it?'

She shook her head dubiously. 'It's his pride and joy. Nobody touches it except Watson.'

'I'd like one of my own. Saw a super little racer in town. Can I buy it? Go on. Say I may. I'll take you for a spin.' He switched on his most engaging smile, and she saw again the angelic little boy with the golden curls whom she had loved to dress in velvet suits and Vandyke collars. She had tried this with Harry but it was not the same.

'Darling, you'll have to speak to your father,' she replied. 'I can't say yea or nay to that.'

'You can. You're in charge around here.'

'I don't know what you mean?' She fluttered helpless hands, fragile-looking in her peach velvet afternoon gown with its tiered skirt and oval neckline, her hair dressed high on her shapely head.

'Maybe I'm mistaken.' Roderick backtracked. Twenty now and

thinking himself a man of the world, he decided to let her play her games. She managed the old man beautifully.

'Of course you are. Papa's in charge. Always has been and always will be. He's the master of Roslan, and when he dies which, God willing, won't be for years, then you'll take his place. I'm merely his consort.' Julia gave him a stern glance, but could feel herself bubbling with happiness. Her son was home.

'Can I bring Lester to meet you?' Roderick changed the subject.

'Where is he?'

'Wakefield's showing him to his quarters. I'm glad you've put him in the room next to mine. I say, d'you suppose Papa's valet would look after us, too?'

'I'm sure he will. I'll have a word with him. Bring your friend to the drawing room for tea. I'm looking forward to welcoming him.'

That's settled that, Roderick thought smugly. I knew she'd come up trumps. Lester Kealan and he had become inseparable, two of the liveliest undergraduates in Oxford's history. Trouble? Certainly, as their tutors would testify, but managing to sail through the examinations and come out with flying colours. How they had achieved this was little short of miraculous, their social life taking precedence over study. Wild, headstrong, up to any dare or adventure, they drank hard, gambled feverishly and fornicated as if sex had just been invented especially for their benefit.

Mama is blissfully ignorant of this, thank God, he thought, prodding Coco out of the way with his foot and standing, spread-legged, on the Persian rug before the fire, coat tails flipped up as he warmed his thighs. Had she known a half of what we got up to at Oxford she'd have banned Lester. But I must get hold of a car, otherwise we'll be condemned to the dullness of family celebrations, party games and all that rot. Penzance isn't far away and we could easily run down there for a spot of fun, slipping off at night perhaps, when the rest have retired.

He wondered if Peter Newark could borrow his uncle's car. No harm in asking, though he had his doubts. Peter wasn't like him and Lester. He hadn't behaved like a varsity man, too damned serious by half. Not really one of the crowd. Pity that. They were bound to meet now he was staying at Martock Hall – no doubt he'd be at the Boxing Day Hunt.

Newark was off to South America in the New Year, so he'd told them, or somewhere equally grim. No need, of course, the Newark's had plenty of 'tin'. Lord Fenimore had no heirs and was rumoured to favour his youngest nephew. Peter could have had a grand time swanning around playing the gentleman farmer. Why did he want to go to Brazil?

66

Already Roderick could feel gloom settling over him, the restrictions of home like iron chains, stopping him from drinking, gambling and chasing girls. Mama was fine. He could get money out of her, but he was not looking forward to seeing his brothers and sisters, considering them to be an almighty bore. In his eyes Fenella was a conceited minx, Evelyn a nonentity, Jane a spoilt brat, Harry a blundering ass, lacking the subtlety (some might call it low cunning) Roderick himself had mastered at that age, and William scarcely human, a wailing, puking suckling.

He remembered being shocked when his mother announced that she was pregnant again. The ever-present resentment against his father had flared up. How dare he inflict this on her again? Jane had been barely two. His beautiful mother made sick and ill, swelling up like a toad with the new baby growing in her belly. Surely the old devil could have found someone else to hump?

Musing on this brought him back to the subject never far from his thoughts. Even as he smiled down at his mother, he was speculating on the likelihood of new maids having been engaged during his absence.

There was the girl, Margaret. He had not been able to forget her, but she had already refused him once. A nub of anger and baulked desire smouldered inside him. How could she? Haughty little bitch! He didn't particularly want to go down that avenue again, refusal damaging his *amour-propre*. Lester might have better luck with her. Perhaps her attitude had changed. Working under Mrs Broom could be no sinecure. Maybe it had taught her to be grateful for a gentleman's offer.

Boughton sidled in, eyeing him nervously. 'Good afternoon, sir,' she said in her tuneless, nasal voice.

'How are you, Boughton?' he enquired pleasantly. It was as well to keep on the right side of Mama's maid who might be privy to useful information.

Though his love for his mother was the one sincere emotion he possessed, he trusted her no more than she trusted him. Both worked on the principle that all men were venal – women, too.

'I'm well, thank you, sir.' An unattractive flush spread up from Boughton's neck to her cheeks. Then she bobbed to Julia. 'The young person has returned your dress, my lady.'

'Ah, show her in.' Julia nodded graciously and settled herself on the Regency day bed.

The decor of her boudoir was in perfect harmony with the architecture. When she had visited Roslan Manor as Henry's fiancée, she had the good sense to keep her mouth shut, but on the return from the honeymoon had made her opinions known in no uncertain terms.

'This awful overstuffed, pompous furniture will have to go,' she had declared to her smiling bridegroom. 'Did you ever see anything so hideous?'

'Can't say I've taken much notice,' he had confessed, his arm around her waist as they had walked through the rooms. 'Now you come to mention it, the mantelpieces do look rather like Chinese pagodas. But Mama liked that sort of thing and my father let her do what she liked. When she died he couldn't be bothered to make changes.'

Julia remembered yanking aside the thick net curtains shrouding the view. 'Had she no idea at all? It's a beautiful old house but everything inside it jars. Thank heavens she left the Great Hall alone. That's perfect. But as for this tacky bric-a-brac, it will have to be given to the next church fête.'

The despised Victorian Gothic furniture had been removed to the attics, replaced by the Elizabethan, Carolean and eighteenth-century items consigned to the dusty depths by the late, unappreciative marquis and his wife. Roslan bloomed, restored to its former glory, and Julia had reserved some of the finest examples of craftmanship for her own suite of rooms.

The walls and ceiling were tented in pale pink silk, the portières of rose damask, the couch upholstered in a matching fabric. A Meissen shepherd and shepherdess carried out their wooing on the marble overmantel, peering coyly at each other round the ormolu clock. The escritoire was Napoleonic, walnut inlaid with rosewood, supported on slender legs and ball feet. The scent of potpourri wafted from a pair of Cantonese bowls exquisitely painted with Mandarin figures. It was the room of a woman of taste and discernment, and Julia experienced satisfaction every time she relaxed there.

It was here, like a spider in its web, that she schemed and plotted, made out guest lists, decided which invitations to accept and which to refuse, and generally planned her campaigns.

Margaret, stepping gingerly through the door, the gown over her arm, drew in a breath. Unschooled though she was, her soul soared, responding instinctively to such beauty. The room seemed to glow as if sunshine had been trapped within it. Outside, Cornwall lay in the harsh grip of winter, but here one could have been in Italy – fragrant with the scent of olive groves and cypress trees, luxurious beyond measure.

Then she saw Roderick and the illusion shattered. He had an elbow on the overmantel, clad in a casual dove-grey suit with a yellow checkered waistcoat. He seemed taller than ever, his fair hair coiling around his soft collar. Nonchalant, confident, feet crossed at the ankles, his eyes fixed hers, green as a serpent's.

'Come in, Helbren,' Julia said in melliferous accents and gestured for her join them. 'Show me what you've done to my poor, damaged skirt.'

Aware that her knees where shaking, Margaret screwed up her courage and walked across the carpeted floor. She had had a run in with Mrs Broom who had been incensed by her action in the Hall.

'Creeping. That's what you were doing,' she had accused. 'It was disgraceful.'

Margaret had not deigned to reply, performing the additional tasks Mrs Broom deliberately put on her and working far into the night to complete the repair. Making sure she had left nothing undone which the nanny might fault, she had dressed herself with scrupulous attention to detail before setting off for the mistress's room.

Julia examined the mend, a needlewoman herself, adept at embroidery, then looked up, smiling and saying, 'Well done. It's almost invisible. Isn't she clever, Roderick?'

He glanced at it, raised an eyebrow and said, 'Jolly good. What happened, Mama? Did you catch it on a nail?'

'It was Coco getting above himself,' she admitted, handing the dress to Boughton. Then she raised her eyes to Margaret. Their resemblance to her son's was uncanny – the same glittering emerald hue. 'I'd like you to look after my repairs.'

Margaret gulped, then found her voice. 'Very well, my lady. But what about Mrs Broom? I've my work in the nursery.'

Julia's smile deepened as she rested against the cushions. 'I think we can come to some arrangement with Nanny. There's less to do now Master Harry and Miss Fenella are away most of the time. Leave Mrs Broom to me. Off you go now. I'll speak to you later.'

Margaret retreated, mindful of her instructions never to turn her back on her employers. This was not easy to perform, and she did it in crabwise fashion, aware of Roderick watching her. Mind reeling with possibilities, she congratulated herself on the successful outcome of her impetuous action last Sunday.

She had known she was breaking the rules, but it had seemed an opportunity too good to miss. A rumour was going round backstairs that Boughton's old mother was ailing and that she might be forced to leave service and nurse her. Who was going to take her place? Margaret had decided it would be her. She shared this with no one, not even Luke.

*

'Oh, look, Helbren – look! Look!' Jane was transported, her hot little hand clasped in Margaret's as they stepped into the Great Hall.

Early afternoon on Christmas Eve and they were on their way out for the obligatory walk. Doris was hard at it finishing the ironing, and Margaret had been ordered to replace her. Mrs Broom had no intention of venturing into the cold herself. Thora had gone on ahead, pushing William in his large black perambulator, coach-built and splendid, with Harry dragging his heels behind her.

Margaret had deliberately made a detour; the word was that the Hall had been decorated. She wanted to see it even more than Jane, her mother's voice ringing in her ears, telling of Yuletide spent in the castle and the glories thereof. Though Mary Helbren had always endeavoured to make this a special time for her daughter, her resources had been woefully limited.

Margaret remembered the small presents she had received on Christmas morning; handknitted socks; an orange; a penny bar of chocolate. Food was always more plentiful then, though they had gone short for weeks beforehand in order to indulge. But all in all, it had been a time of trial and heartache for, despite her mother's efforts, Tom Helbren had used it as an excuse for drinking to oblivion.

Pig! Margaret thought angrily. Disgusting pig! No, that's an insult to a harmless animal. There's nothing to compare with his brutish behaviour, my dear mother's planning to no avail, Christmas dinner, such as it was, ruined when he fell in the door and collapsed with his head on the table after shouting insults at her.

Now Jane was tugging at Margaret's skirt, eyes round as saucers, and she forgot the past, sharing in the child's delight. The smell of sap seeping from burning logs, the sight of streamers and evergreens festooning the beams, the holly wreaths – and the tree, a rafter-high fir felled by the foresters and dragged in early that morning. The footmen had dressed it with shining glass baubles, cascades of silver beading and spun-glass ornaments. They had clipped tiny metal candle holders into place and showered it with glistening mock snow.

'Look at the parcels,' whispered Jane, staring at the brightly wrapped heap arranged on the floor at the tree's base. 'Are they for me?'

'Oh, no. They're for the estate workers' children. Your father has invited them to tea. I hear there's to be a magician, and Santa Claus will drive up in his sleigh.'

'Pulled by reindeer?' Jane's eyes were growing rounder and rounder.

'Ponies, I expect.'

'Will he have a long white beard and wear a red robe?'

'No doubt he will.' Margaret had been told that Mr Wakefield played this part every year. It was his only venture into acting and Susan said he carried it off superbly.

'Is that food for the children?'

'Yes. Didn't the same thing happen last Christmas?'

'Don't know. Can't remember.'

'Well, you won't miss it this time.'

Trestles stood in readiness against the walls, covered by paper cloths and loaded with cakes, sandwiches, jam tarts, trifle and jelly. The nursery staff had their orders to make sure their charges were ready by three-thirty, to come down and assist their parents in the distribution of this largesse.

'Isn't there one for me?' Jane asked wistfully, pointing to the packages.

'No, dear. You'll hang up your stocking tonight and in the morning you'll find Father Christmas will have filled it,' Margaret explained, feeling an unwarranted shiver of excitement tingling down her spine, though she did not anticipate receiving anything herself.

It was enough that she was a part of the general bustle. The house had been thoroughly cleaned, guestrooms aired, beds made up, fires lit. Mrs Frith resembled a generalissimo organising a military operation. Every pantry and larder were crammed to overflowing. Never in her life had Margaret seen so much food. It was almost obscene. Night and day, for what seemed like weeks, preparations had been in full swing. Every imaginable traditional English dish had passed through Mrs Frith's hands or under her critical eye, plus a few additional ones known only in Cornwall.

Wakefield, that inestimable butler-cum-Santa who also held the keys to the wine cellar, had been issued with a long list. A section of the male staff were detailed to ensure a constant supply of crystal lumps of frozen water from the ice house. Lead-lined mahogany coolers stood in readiness for the champagne. Green bottles of port and vintage wines were dusted off and chilled or warmed according to the dish they were to accompany. The tantalus standing on chiffoniers in dining room, study, library and smoking room had been unlocked, their cut-glass decanters glittering amber, pale gold or pure white from the French brandy, Scottish whisky or gin held in their depths.

Footsteps at the doorway of the Great Hall made Margaret turn. A man was crossing the floor towards her. 'Is Lord Roderick at home?' he asked, smiling in an engaging way.

He brought with him a blast of outdoor cold that clung to his long waterproof cape. His felt hat with a heron's feather tucked in the band gave him a dashing air, like a soldier, perhaps, or someone on an important mission. His features were handsome, but it was his eyes

71

that were so arresting, the extraordinary power of his deep blue eyes that lit up when he smiled.

'I'm not sure,' Margaret said.

She recognised him immediately, and was nonplussed, yet glad that she was wearing her new coat and hat. Its brim, trimmed with a bow and a shot-silk rose, framed her face becomingly and was really too grand for a servant. This was fine, as she did not want him to know she was one.

'He isn't here,' Jane lisped, staring up at him. 'He's gone riding with Lester. I know, 'cause I heard him tell Wakefield.'

'Thank you, young lady.' His lips twitched though he had pulled his face into a serious expression, treating her like one grown-up to another. 'Would you be so kind as to tell him Peter Newark called? I'll try to catch up with him, but let him know anyway. Will you do that for me?'

'Yes. He's my big brother,' Jane said brightly, clinging to Margaret's hand with her free one, the other buried in an ermine muff.

'I'll see he gets the message,' Margaret promised, surprised by Jane's precosity when she was usually shy. For her own part she was aware of feeling unsettled in his presence. He was too masculine, too tall – she felt like a dwarf and this made her stiffen her spine and assume an aloof air.

He gave her a broad, warm smile, and raised his hat. 'Thank you, miss. I'm charmed to have met you. I hope this will happen again.'

'So do I,' she replied, stunned, startled and guilty. He obviously mistook her for a guest. She stared after him as he swung away and strode out of the Hall.

'He a nice man,' pronounced Jane.

'Yes, dear, very nice,' she agreed thoughtfully.

Peter was conscious of a prickle of irritation. He had better things to do than chase around after Roderick. It was high time Uncle John had the telephone installed, though he had to admit he had not seen one at Roslan Manor. Too remote a spot for the cables, maybe, but a nuisance. He could have saved time by calling that selfish blighter.

He stuck a foot in his stirrup and swung up into the saddle. The cold cut like a knife, his mare's breath hung around her in a vaporous cloud, but Peter was glad to be back in Cornwall.

Born in India where his father had been a colonel in the British army, his early days had been euphoric, but then had come boarding school in London. Sometimes he had been shipped back to Bengal for the long holidays, but if not he had gone down to Martock Hall. It was his mother's birthplace, and her brother, a confirmed bachelor, liked nothing better than having members of her family stay with him. Although his parents had eventually retired to England, these regular visits to Martock had continued throughout the time Peter had been studying at Oxford.

'It'll be just you and me for Christmas, boy,' Lord John had said before Peter left in September for his final stint as an undergraduate. 'You're more than welcome.'

'That'll be grand, Uncle,' Peter had answered, as he and that bluff country squire sat smoking on the terrace where peacocks strutted, spreading their elegant tails before their dowdy hens. 'The parents are going to be in France. Stewart's in Dacca, no leave for him till spring, and I wasn't much looking forward to staying in the London house. It hardly seemed worth opening Sandford Orcas.'

'Quite right, my boy. You bundle down here to me. We can do a spot of hunting. Let me know the time of your train and I'll send the car to pick you up.'

The car! Peter frowned as he bobbed his heels against the mare's sides and rode away from Roslan Manor. Roderick had nabbed him in the Ship Inn last night, muttering something about borrowing it. He had wanted Peter to drive, saying, 'Come on, old chap. It'll be a lark. We'll pick up a couple of tarts. What d'you say?'

Peter had promised to think about it, but wished he had given a definite refusal. He had no desire to go whoring with Roderick and Lester. It wasn't his style. No prude, he had had his fair share of amorous encounters, but he respected women, liked them for their intellect as well as their bodies, and did not care for Roderick's attitude. He had never found it necessary to pay for sex and had no intention of starting now; neither did he see the fun in coercing frightened young servant girls.

Ah, well, he thought, I shan't have to put up with Roderick and his like for much longer. Soon I'll be on my way to Liverpool and boarding a steamer, taking the high seas to Rio and then on to Mexico and the United States.

Peter's upbringing had made him a nomad. He liked travelling, different races, cultures and customs a source of endless fascination. His only brother, Stewart, the eldest and heir, had done the right thing, following in their father's footsteps by entering Sandhurst and then serving in the Raj. But despite his mother's desire for him to do the same he had refused.

Peter had a stubborn streak, a quietly forceful man who always got his way when he had made up his mind to do a thing. He wanted to garner as much information about the world as he could, though what he intended to do with it was anyone's guess.

73

He headed towards the open land, on the lookout for Roderick and Lester. The wind was cold and strong, carrying the scents of moor and sea. A robin trilled from the hedge as he passed, and the sheep raised their heads to stare at him, then went back to their search for fodder. He urged his mare into a gallop. The days were short, and the warmth of Martock Hall beckoned. Wanderer he might be, but there were times, like now, when he knew that one day he would put down roots here.

Tonight he would go with Lord John to the little grey church that had sat on the hillside in sun or wind for centuries, and he would remember the temples to Shiva, and the tales his ayah had told him of the pantheon of Indian gods. She had come from Madras, middle-aged, dignified, her skin so dark as to be almost black, speaking English to him in a lyrical voice, the silver in her ears and on her wrists shimmering against the darkness of her oiled hair.

One religion had no precedence over another, he had decided, debating at length with the college dons. The Norman church, with its crucifix, candles, stained glass and singing, the temples with their gods, candles, incense, ornamentation and chanting, all carried a similar message though presented in different ways – the eternal search for the holy grail, the triumph of light over darkness.

He had reached the top field and caught sight of two riders on the far side. He headed towards them, already forming the words of his refusal. He would put it as tactfully as possible. It was not his intention to offend Roderick, in fact he hoped to be invited to the Boxing Day Ball, curious about the beautiful young woman who had been with Jane in the Great Hall. Was she an Aubert cousin? he wondered.

His second sighting of her. He had never forgotten the girl with the violet eyes glimpsed in Mr Skinny's pony-trap last September.

Margaret and Jane darted back the way they had come, through the servants' quarters, using the doorway reserved for the children.

It led to their part of the garden where they could play without disturbing the grown-ups, each having their own plot to excavate or cultivate according to disposition. A swing hung dejectedly from the solid branch of a gnarled apple tree. Mrs Broom did not approve of too much winter exposure, though the daily constitutional was sacrosanct. It gave her the chance to toast her toes and drink tea laced with brandy by the nursery fire.

'Is it going to snow, Helbren? Can I make a snowman? Can I go skating? Can I go tobogganing?' Jane shouted, hopping on her short legs, tightly buttoned into brown leather gaiters, the hem of her calf-length tartan dress showing beneath her velvet top coat, curls buried under a large beret.

For one so young her vocabulary was wide, and Margaret liked to think she had had a hand in this, never too tired to answer questions, read stories aloud or engage in conversation. Out of earshot of Mrs Broom, of course. Though not wanting to bother with them herself, she was fiendishly jealous of anyone else influencing the children.

Now Margaret laughed. 'Hold on! It doesn't often snow in Cornwall. The climate's warmer than other parts of England. Wait and see.'

But she was not so sure. The fields were brushed with frost under the heavy grey sky. Glassy icicles hung from boughs and gutterings. Taking Jane's gloved hand in hers, she led her along the path to the copse beyond the wicket gate. Ahead she could see Thora, with William sitting up in his pram against a pillow, pink cheeks and button nose almost obscured by the fur sewn around his bonnet.

Harry saw them first, groaning loudly, 'Oh, Lord!'

'Mr Newark came,' Jane announced importantly. 'He gave me a message for Roderick, and I said I'd tell him.'

'Did you, dear? How clever of you,' Thora said abstractedly.

'He told me to tell him he was looking for him,' Jane persisted.

'Be quiet, you silly baby,' Harry sneered.

'Be quiet yourself!' Jane retorted.

'Baby!'

'Nasty!'

'Hush, children! That's not the way to carry on. It's Christmas,' Thora said briskly. 'Be kind to your sister, Master Harry.'

He considered himself too adult to play with Jane, treating her in a lofty manner. He was always quoting the 'chaps at school', shocking Thelma and outraging Mrs Broom with his newly acquired language. The nursery atmosphere was more fraught than usual, for Fenella did not want to be there either, dropping French phrases in an irritating manner and having no time for Evelyn, but Natalie Toner took no notice, treating them equally.

Margaret could hear them now, voices high-pitched with excitement, and then they emerged from the woods, carrying bunches of mistletoe. Fenella, eyes sparkling, cheeks flushed, was fulfilling her early promise. When she was eventually presented at Court there would be no shortage of gentlemen wanting to marry her. Evelyn, too, was improving, losing some of her puppy fat, her skin clearer.

Natalie shepherded them along in her breezy way, clad in a tweed bloomer suit and high boots. The servants muttered about her insistence on wearing knickerbockers, but she took no notice. She was an ardent cyclist, supported Mrs Emmeline Pankhurst and the women's suffrage movement, and thought most men were scum.

'You should have worn breeches like me,' she said to the girls. 'So much more convenient than skirts. Beastly, heavy things, always getting muddy round the bottoms and picking up twigs and leaves. As for corsets! Don't even mention the word! Men have a much better time of it than us.'

'Dresses are much prettier,' said Fenella, adding smugly, 'I'm glad I'm not a man.'

'Oh, I don't know. Skirts are a bore on the tennis court.' Evelyn was keen on sport and had set her heart on a bicycle like Natalie's.

'Who wants to rush about getting hot and sweaty playing tennis?' Fenella asked. She had come back from France more argumentative than ever.

'Miss Fenella! That's a common way to talk,' put in Thora, jiggling the pram to pacify the grizzling William. 'Horses sweat, gentlemen perspire, and ladies go all of a glow.'

The girls giggled and Fenella held up the sage-green sprays with their clusters of creamy white berries. 'We found some, though the woodsmen said mistletoe was rare this year. Where shall we hang it?'

'I suppose you want someone to kiss you under it?' remarked Harry, scuffing the ground with the toe of his boot. 'Golly, who'd want to kiss *you*? He'd have to be off his rocker!'

'Beast!' Fenella retorted and went to hit him. He sidestepped neatly.

'Who is it you're after, eh?' he taunted. 'Could it be that smarmy pal of Roderick's? It is, isn't it? You've gone red as a beetroot.'

'I think it's time we got on with our walk,' Thora pronounced firmly. 'Come along, children.'

'That's it. Forward troops! Quick march!' chorused Natalie.

'But we'll have to carry the mistletoe,' wailed Evelyn.

'No we won't. Give it here. We can hide it behind the bushes and come back this way to collect it.' Natalie put her words into action. She should have been a soldier. Margaret could visualise her in uniform and thought what a loss to the army. She'd have made a grand sergeant major.

'I'm cold,' said Harry, who wanted to sneak back to the house and poke about, hoping to discover where Mama had hidden his presents.

'Then get moving. That'll keep the blood circulating.' Thora set an example, striding up the path resolutely, pushing the pram. William was asleep.

Through to the other side of the coppice they tramped, coming out on a ridge that fell steeply down into a valley. An unsheltered spot and

76

the wind was keen. Thora insisted they fill their lungs with deep breaths, saying, 'That'll brush the cobwebs away!'

Margaret stood there, skirt flattened against her thighs with the force, scarf flapping, face aching with cold, staring across the moor towards the Weeping Maids, the shadows deepening, purplish green. The day had never really yielded to the light. It had been necessary to keep the lamps burning indoors, save for a brief spell at noon. Over the rise and down a little way she saw two riders, black figures on black steeds.

Fenella shaded her eyes. 'There's Roderick, and his friend, Lester.'

'So it is.' Natalie looked in their direction. 'Marking out the start of the Boxing Day meet, I shouldn't wonder.'

'I'm riding in it,' Fenella said with a lift of her chin.

'So am I,' Harry insisted. 'Papa says I'm a natural. I'm to be blooded.'

'That's nothing. I was blooded when I was a younger than you are now.' Evelyn refused to be outdone. 'I'll be at the hunt, too.'

'You're afraid of horses,' Harry scoffed.

'No, I'm not.'

'You are so. I've seen you cringe when you offer one an apple on the palm of your hand.'

'That's only because they slobber so much.'

Margaret was hardly conscious of their bickering, eyes riveted on the dark, steadily moving figures, sombre against the stark landscape. She made out Roderick on Timur. It was as if the sight of him had been branded on her brain by that single incident in the stable yard, but his companion was taller even than he, and rode easily as if born to the saddle.

'Don't they look fine,' Fenella enthused, echoing Margaret's thoughts. 'His name's Lord Lester Kealan, and he's heir to an earldom in Ireland.'

'How d'you know he's going to be an earl?' Harry hated her acquiring information before he did. It gave her the edge on him.

'I was introduced to him at dinner last night. You'll meet him this evening. Isn't it wonderful to dine with the adults? That's one good thing about Christmas, though I do wish I didn't have to wear a babyish white dress. I can't wait till I'm eighteen and can let my skirts down and put my hair up.'

'Shall I come to dinner, too?' Jane's round face was solemn, bewildered by these changes in routine.

'No, dear. Not this year. You must go to bed early or Santa Claus won't come.' Thora put an arm round her. 'But you'll be allowed to join in the meal tomorrow night, as a special treat.'

'But I want to stay up. Fenella and Harry are going to. Why can't I?' The tension proved too much for Jane who burst into tears.

'There, there, pet. Don't cry. Here, let nurse wipe your nose. Come along, now. A nice big blow. That's it.'

Lester Kealan. The name had a fine ring to it, Margaret thought, closing her ears to Jane's full-blown temper tantrum. Lord Lester, Irish earl. Would it be possible for her to get a closer look at him while he was a guest in the house? Unlikely, as she was neither a parlour or chambermaid. Her curiosity was immense.

Natalie offered to carry Jane home, pickaback style and, still weeping copiously, she was hoisted into position. They started to retrace their steps, but Margaret lingered, watching the riders turn up across a couple of fields and out through a gate to the tawny moor till they were lost in the vastness of sedge and rush and arching, empty sky.

Mrs Broom was pacing the day nursery, very agitated. 'You've taken your time,' she shouted as Thora and Margaret shepherded the children in.

'It's barely half past two,' Thora answered firmly, refusing to be bullied. 'They'll be able to rest and get changed before welcoming the workers' children.'

'I know that.' Mrs Broom's face was red, her bosom heaving. 'But something's happened.'

Doris, looking up from exchanging the flatiron for the fresh one heating on the hob, pulled her mouth into a warning grimace. Thora saw her and frowned slightly.

'What is it, Nanny?'

'A telegram arrived, and it wasn't for one of the family.' Mrs Broom took William and sat down in the rocking chair with him on her wide lap.

'Who?' Thora asked, unbuttoning Jane's coat and slipping it off.

'It came for Boughton,' Mrs Broom said portentously.

'Mama's maid?' Fenella spoke as if surprised that she had a life outside of Roslan.

'Why?' Harry wanted to know, planting himself on the hearth rug as he had seen his brother and father do. 'Who'd send a telegram to old Boughton?'

'A neighbour sent it. Her ma's been took bad. She's to go home immediately and look after her. Watson's going to drive her to the station. In ever such a state, she is, and the journey will take hours, it being Christmas Eve.'

'But how will Mama manage?' Fenella demanded, grasping the full

78

import of the situation. 'She must have a maid! It's essential that she look her best. The guests will be arriving.'

'There's the rub, Miss Fenella. She wants Helbren to help out, but I've told her its impossible. You've no experience, have you, Helbren?' And Mrs Broom cast her a venomous look.

'How d'you know what I can and can't do?' Anger boiled up in Margaret. Her chance had come, and this ugly, low, vindictive woman wanted to stop her. 'I'll go to her right away.'

'You'll do no such thing.' Mrs Broom handed William to Thora who took him automatically, though staring at Margaret. Doris was staring too, but carried on ironing.

'How are you going to prevent me?' Margaret whirled round and started out into the passage.

Mrs Broom was behind her, a hand clamping on her arm. 'Listen here, my girl,' she growled, voice lowered. 'I can make things mighty difficult for you. I've only to say the wrong word to Mrs Colby or Mr Wakefield. They're particular friends of mine. I needs you here – in my nursery. Who d'you think you are, eh? Sneaking around behind my back, trying to ingratiate yourself with her ladyship. You're a fisherman's brat. The lowest thing that crawls. If he *was* your father, that is. Maybe he wasn't, and your mother a slut.'

Margaret kept her temper, though her fist clenched and she almost smashed it into that mocking face. She became very still, only the fierce light in her eyes betraying her rage. Then she played her ace.

'If you make any trouble I'll tell Lord Henry you drink too much, beat his children and put opium in William's bottle to keep him quiet.'

Mrs Broom's face turned a muddy grey, and her cheeks quivered. 'What are you talking about? Every nurse uses an opiate to soothe babies when they're teething.'

'I agree it can be an effective medicine, but you add it to his milk regularly, not only when he's troubled with his teeth.'

'Rubbish!' the woman shouted. 'As to proving I'm too fond of drink? He'll laugh you to scorn. Everyone enjoys a tipple now and again. And he'll agree with me that children need discipline.'

'They respond far better to kindness and understanding.'

'Poppycock! What d'you know about children?'

'What do *you*, Mrs Broom?'

'I was a nurse before I married Mr Broom and I went back to it when he died. You can't do a thing to me.'

'I can try, and I will if you stand in my way.'

It was a head-on conflict. Had Mrs Broom been sober, her age, experience and authority might have won the day. As it was, she

79

lowered her eyes and said, 'So it's come to this, has it? I've been generous to you, girl. Trained you, worked on you—'

'You treated me like a slave.'

'It's your job to fetch and carry.'

'I've had enough of it. I'm going to Lady Julia and you can't stop me.' With a final, searing glance, Margaret opened the door and went out.

She ran to her room, aware that every moment was vital: Mrs Colby might send one of the other girls to assist Lady Julia. Quietening her mind, she sifted through every scrap of information her mother had once given her concerning the duties of a lady's maid.

What had she to commend her besides sewing? A dress sense, perhaps, though this had barely been given the chance to develop; a knack for dressing hair. Surely this should be enough to start with?

Squaring her shoulders, she tapped lightly on her mistress's door. A voice told her to enter. She walked through into the boudoir.

'Helbren, I want you to lay out my evening gown,' Julia said from the couch. 'Boughton has gone. What a palaver! So inconvenient. I really can't be bothered with it. It's essential that I rest before tackling those hordes of children. You'll find my dresses in the armoire.'

'How shall I know which one to choose, my lady?'

'It's oyster satin, trimmed with coffee lace. You can't miss it.' Julia continued to reel off a list of instructions, ticking each item on her fingers. 'There's a tight schedule today. First this wretched tea party at which I'm obligated to show my face, then I greet my guests who'll be arriving at six o'clock, God and their transport permitting. After this I come back here to dress. This takes an hour. At seven-thirty I go down to the salon to receive them, then dinner follows at eight. We shall be dancing afterwards, so I may not be back till the small hours. During that time you tidy here, wash my underwear and perform minor repairs. You'll then wait up to prepare me for bed.' She paused, then added, 'Unless Lord Henry accompanies me. In which case you'll take your leave.'

'Very well, my lady. Do I keep the fire burning?'

Julia's arched brows shot up to meet her wispy fringe. 'Good heavens, no! The chambermaid will see to that. You're not to get your hands dirty, and will have quite enough to do looking after me.'

'Yes, madam.'

'We'll talk about wages after Christmas, when I've seen what you can do. If you're not satisfactory I'll have to start looking elsewhere, but I've a notion you'll fill the post admirably.'

'Thank you, my lady.'

Julia waved a languid hand. 'I don't want thanks, girl. You'll move into the room down the corridor which was Boughton's. Do it after you've put out my gown and helped me get ready for the trek to the Great Hall.'

'Yes, madam.'

'Now leave me to my nap. Pass that magazine, will you? No, not the *Ladies Journal* – that parish nonsense will do. It's so boring it will soon send me to sleep.'

I'll resent being ordered about by her before long, Margaret thought as she settled Julia, tucking a shawl around her knees. But just for now, this is good, the first rung of the ladder.

When she saw the bedchamber she stood still in amazement. It was like that of a queen – deeply carpeted, panelled in light oak, with walnut furniture and a magnificent bedstead. Turned mahogany posts supported a tester, the whole draped in a snowy fall of lace.

I want it, or something very like, Margaret decided, and went to the wardrobe covering half of one wall. She opened the carved doors and stopped dead. It was lined with clothes, one half given over entirely to evening attire. She feasted her eyes on the glory of silk robes, velvet capes, fur stoles – Valenciennes lace of cobweb delicacy – mantles and over-robes, dinner gowns, ball gowns, opera gowns. They breathed out the sweet emanation of flowers, whispering of fêtes, galas, official engagements in palaces.

To one side were shelves holding shoes suitable for every event: satin slippers with Louis heels and diamanté buckles; day shoes of patent leather with buttoned bars; ankle boots of finest kid; knee-high riding boots; shoes trimmed with pink down. There must have been several dozen pairs of footwear. Higher shelves held hatboxes containing wide-brimmed feathered creations and close-fitting toques.

Margaret was so fascinated she almost forgot her mission. The oyster satin hung apart from the rest, shrouded in layers of tissue paper. She lifted it down, laid it across the quilted bedspread and started to upwrap it. Never had she seen anything more gorgeous. A tiny silk label inside the low back read Worth, Paris. It had obviously never been worn, reserved for this special night to celebrate Christmas.

When it was completely unveiled, she picked it up and held it against herself. The full-length mirror flung back her reflection. Pale face with a flush beneath the cheekbones, great violet-blue eyes. She instinctively knew that the creamy hue was not for her, too soft. Her rich colouring demanded something more vibrant. But the style was flattering, and she pressed the material to her narrow waist, swishing the skirt that fell into a train behind.

I could carry it off, she thought triumphantly. I could wear such a dress and look like a duchess. Oh, God, give me the chance to do so one day.

What next to complete her ladyship's attire? The tallboys gave a clue, the neatly arranged drawers revealing chemises, corsets, *Directoire* knickers and fragile silk stockings. She selected those which she considered suitable for evening wear, relying on instinct and those tales of grandeur told by her mother.

She had just finished when a tap on the outer door announced the arrival of a maid carrying a tray. A footman was in tow, and he swept up Coco by the collar and took him away for a walk. Lady Julia, dreamy-eyed and yawning, drank her tea, then said, 'My hair's ruffled. Can you do something about it, Helbren?'

Into the bedroom and, with her ladyship seated on the dressing-table stool, Margaret did her best to rearrange the curls.

'Good,' Julia said, peering into the hand mirror which Margaret held behind her so she might view the back. 'Now then, five minutes before I come up to dress for dinner, you'll run a bath.'

'Yes, madam. Would you care to glance through the things I've prepared? I hope I've made the right choice.'

Julia strolled across to the bed. 'Boughton couldn't have made a better selection. By the way, I've spoken with Mrs Colby and henceforth you'll take your meals in her parlour, along with the butler and the visiting personal servants.'

'Yes, madam.' Margaret bobbed, but was panicking inside. What would they make of her, those sophisticated valets and maids used to travelling with their masters and mistresses? And Mrs Colby with her gimlet sharp eyes and friendship with Mrs Broom?

She suddenly realised this post might have its drawbacks and that she would need to use her wits to avoid ruining the opportunity. When Julia had gone down to the Great Hall, a footman arrived to help her move into Broughton's old room.

'Gone up in the world, have you?' he remarked jovially as he and Jan carried the bride-chest between them.

'I always knew it wouldn't take you long,' the boy piped, cheeky as ever.

'It'll be hard work, Helbren,' the footman continued, hatchet-faced but amiable, admiring her with twinkling brown eyes. 'She'll keep you on the trot till all hours, will her ladyship.'

'I can deal with that,' she answered, Pilgrim basket in her arms, staring at her new quarters with growing satisfaction.

A light room, with a brass bedstead and floral curtains, it was far superior to the one she had shared with Susan. There was no time to unpack. The charity tea was over, the presents distributed, the entertainment done, the Hall cleared as if the conjurer had indeed waved a magic wand.

Wheels crunched on the drive as carriages and limousines started to arrive, disgorging passengers where the line of footmen waited to carry in luggage. The marquis and his marchioness stood at the top of the steps to welcome their visitors.

It's begun, Margaret thought, as she ran her ladyship's bath, and I *will* succeed.

Chapter 5

'Welcome back, Lady Fenella.'

'Thank you, Helbren. Where's Mama?' Fenella's eyes swept the drawing room of 21 Upper Grosvenor Street, the Auberts' town house, with balconies overlooking Hyde Park.

'She'll be here directly. At the moment she's in conference with Mrs Colby,' Margaret replied.

'Discussing the preparations for my ball?' Fenella asked, incapable of thinking of anyone but herself.

'Exactly. Shall I ring for refreshments? Would you like to go to your room?'

'I've had lunch, and I'll wait here for Mama. I'm actually glad to be home for once. I'm being "brought out"! Isn't it just the most exciting thing that can happen to a girl?'

'I should imagine it must be,' Margaret agreed drily, then she chuckled. 'It's certainly causing mayhem. I've never known her ladyship in such a flurry.'

'Oh, dear! I can't wait! Just think, Helbren – I shall curtsy to King Edward and Queen Alexandra in the drawing room at Buckingham Palace! Then the ball, and the most handsome and wonderful men in London besieging me with offers of marriage!'

Fenella danced round the room, ringlets coiling from beneath her flower-wreathed hat, still a child in the eyes of polite society. Not till she was eighteen and 'out' would her hair be put up and her skirts touch the ground. This longed-for birthday was in a month's time when the rituals essential for her to attain womanhood would be carried out with pomp and ceremony in accordance with tradition.

Yes, she's a beauty, Margaret decided. The Auberts won't have much trouble getting her off their hands. Not so Evelyn, a plain dumpling with a rebellious streak, very earnest and something of a bluestocking, much influenced by Natalie Toner. She was due to attend the French school which her sister had now left, but there were ominous rumblings. Evelyn was refusing to go. At sixteen she was amazingly determined and clear-sighted as to which direction her future lay, wanting to attend university, willing to study to this end and unstinting in her admiration of the Suffragettes.

Not my problem, Margaret told herself, yet since that memorable Christmas a year and a half ago, she had kept in contact with the nursery. Thora and Doris had reported regularly, though it was not easy for them to meet, every moment of Margaret's time taken up with Lady Julia.

She had been touched to learn that she had made a favourable impression on the children and relieved when Mrs Broom left under a cloud and Thora took over. Margaret liked to think she had been instrumental in the woman's dismissal, reporting her misdeeds to Lady Julia, unable to rest easy thinking of Jane and William left to her tender mercies.

She caught sight of herself in one of the several Venetian mirrors hanging against the primrose and white striped wallpaper, and paused to take a longer look. She had become accustomed to this opulent showpiece of a room with its rococo Regency splendour. This and similar gorgeous places had become the norm. Yet sometimes it seemed as if she moved through a stage set, wearing fancy dress, not quite recognising the miner's daughter who had once roamed barefoot on the cliffs.

Her slim form was neatly arrayed in a grey-blue costume of fine alpaca; long skirt with a tight waist that belled out at the hem, a waisted jacket worn over a white blouse, the lacy jabot falling from the high collar. A quiet, modest outfit befitting such an important member of staff. Mrs Colby and Mr Wakefield were almost too friendly these days, currying favour.

Now she was going with her mistress to Regent Street and the big stores, driven by Luke, and although she would carry Julia's handbag and any small purchases, she saw herself more as a companion than a servant. Yes, she thought, it's time I paid a visit to my aunts. I want to see their faces when I turn up on the doorstep, obviously doing well for myself.

'Where *is* Mama?' Fenella came to rest beside her, fretting impatiently, tapping her foot in its little kid shoe. 'I need to see her. Every single item of my wardobe is just too terribly babyish, all those boring white frocks with pink sashes.'

'She's aware of this,' Margaret soothed. 'A shopping expedition is planned.' Then she added warningly, 'but don't imagine for one moment she's about to encourage you into black velvet.'

'I know that,' Fenella pouted, wandering to the French windows that gave on to the balcony. Sunlight poured through them, echoed in the yellow damask drapes. 'It's so silly! I want a black gown above all things. I wore one at a masquerade ball at the academy – went as Lucretia Borgia and everyone said I looked stunning. But then, the French are so much more liberal, aren't they? Because of the Revolution, I suppose. Perhaps we should have a revolution in England. Where are we shopping? At Dickens and Jones?'

'Undoubtedly.'

'In those gloriously smart hat shops in the Burlington Aracade?'

'I expect so.'

'And my gown for the presentation? It has to be white slipper satin, you know, and I'll have elbow-length gloves and ostrich feathers in my hair.'

'You'll settle for this, instead of black velvet?' Margaret's reply was a touch acerbic. This spoiled chit had no idea of life's downside. 'There's a modiste in Bond Street who's popular with the débutantes and their mamas. Don't worry, Lady Fenella. I'm sure your mother has everything in hand.'

She had, rustling in a few moments later, a silk stole draped across the shoulders of her grosgrain gown, a huge hat topping her magnificently dressed hair. 'There you are, darling,' she enthused, bearing down on her eldest daughter and enveloping her in a perfumed embrace. 'How was school? Is dear Madame Dubois in good health? I really must visit her when next we're in Paris. Evelyn is looking forward so much to entering her academy.'

Margaret let this pass. It was nothing to do with her. Though she agreed with Natalie that women, even the privileged ones, had a raw deal, it was not her place to comment on Lady Julia's wayward child. She was playing a waiting game, content in her position for the moment, educating herself and learning about the mores and manners of high society, gaining knowledge day by day and squirreling it away.

She had accompanied Julia to house parties at stately homes, hobnobbed with the servants of dukes and duchesses, spent a summer at the Aubert villa in fashionable Brighton, and travelled to a Scottish castle in the grouse shooting season. There was talk of a trip to the Riviera.

Luke was in the quiet, tree-shaded street, guarding Lord Henry's latest acquisition, a maroon Marchand limousine. The sun sparkled on the brass carriage lamps, radiator and horn, and the clean grey tyres with bright red-spoked wheels. He clicked his heels and saluted, then opened the rear door for Julia who deftly managed her enormous hat. Fenella jumped in unaided and bounced on the sprung seat, momentarily forgetting her almost-eighteen status.

Solemn as a judge, he merely said, 'Morning, Helbren,' as Margaret followed them inside.

She nodded, equally formal. 'Good day, Watson.'

They were still friends, though by now he had accepted that she was not interested in a closer relationship. She had one afternoon off a week and an evening now and again. Should these coincide with his free time, they might stroll in the park together or attend an entertainment, though his taste differed from hers. He liked burlesque and picture shows; she was stirred by classical music, enraptured when waiting on Julia in the marquis's box at The Royal Opera House, Covent Garden or concerts at the Albert Hall. But Luke taught her valuable lessons about London, and she was able to find her way around, fearlessly entering the horse-drawn buses, haggling with hansom cab drivers over fares, shopping in the lively markets in which the city abounded. The country girl was becoming a cosmopolitan.

Though it was barely two o'clock the West End was crowded, and when they reached Regent Street vehicles lined the kerbs outside the palace-like stores with broad, showy windows displaying the most splendid articles for sale. Though many of the smaller establishments had been taken over by emporiums catering for every requirement, there still remained individual linen drapers, lace warehouses, plumassiers, milliners, boot and shoemakers, glovers, stocking and corset shops, and a manufacturer of umbrellas and parasols.

Julia was intent on an orgy of spending. It was not every day a daughter was presented at Court. (Henry had muttered a fervent, Thank God, glooming over the bills.) But she had been looking forward to it for years, the thought of this event compensating for the pain when she had given birth to female offspring. Now her hour had come and she was going to milk every drop of pleasure from it.

Fenella had to be fully equipped, as did her mother. With so much entertaining, balls, a visit to Royal Ascot, picnics, *fêtes champetres* and charity galas at which Fenella simply must be seen, she would be chaperoned by Julia attired in the height of fashion. The girl was on the marriage market and the Auberts were honour-bound to support her, their wealth and rank a lure to a prospective husband and his family. Competition was fierce.

'It's not so very different from the villagers at home,' Margaret remarked to Luke as they waited in the cobbled square where the modiste had her smart boutique, its hanging flower baskets and bow windows of dimpled glass giving it an alluringly foreign ambience.

Julia and Fenella had disappeared through the green painted door more than an hour since.

'How so?' As there was no one about, Luke relaxed his usually alert pose in the driver's seat and stretched his legs. 'I'd give anything for a smoke,' he complained. 'It's forbidden on duty.'

'Farmers are fussy when their girls come of age. Suitable husbands have to be found,' Margaret went on, longing to take off her shoes and ease her aching feet. Julia was nothing if not demanding on shopping sprees. 'And if they're seeking wives, the candidates have to prove they are strong and healthy, good breeders who'll be able to produce sons and work in the fields and dairy, take part in haymaking, wring a chicken's neck and slaughter a pig if need be. No one gets married for love. That's frowned on, just like it is among the nobs. Land is of prime consideration or livestock, probably both, and if it's a fisherman, then he'll choose a girl whose father owns a boat. I wouldn't have stood a chance, for we had nothing.'

'I want to marry for love,' Luke said, turning to give her a meaningful look from under his peaked cap. 'Don't you?'

'I can't imagine ever falling for a bloke,' she answered testily. 'I think I'll wind up an old maid.'

'You won't,' he teased. 'Not a girl like you.'

'Ha! Blokes are nothing but trouble.' Her eyes were a dark, stormy colour, shaded by her hat brim. 'My mother married a drunk. I'll not go down that road.'

The style of presentation gown and material selected and Fenella's measurements taken, mother and daughter returned to the car. The next stop was the Burlington Arcade, a covered promenade leading from Piccadilly into Cork Street. It contained a double line of small shops which sold nothing but luxuries; embroidered shoes, silver-mounted whips, fancy garters, filigree flounces, scent bottles, brocaded sashes, frivolous falbalas of all descriptions.

'Oh, look at those jewelled dog collars,' Julia exclaimed, and her eyes glistened with tears. 'I could have bought one for poor darling Coco had he not died.'

The sudden and mysterious ailment which had carried Coco off had never been explained, but there was a rumour among the staff that someone had lost patience with his unpleasant habits and added a lethal dose of rat poison to his food. He had been buried in a corner of the grounds reserved for family pets, mourned by no one but his mistress who had ordered a headstone to mark the spot.

Fenella hurried from side to side of the arcade, not knowing which treasure to look at first. They paused at a tobacconist's shop, its window filled with boxes of cigars, Turkish cigarettes and Meerschaum pipes, and Roderick suddenly materialised from within.

'Good afternoon, Mama. Home from France then, Fenella? Jolly good!' he cried, removing his hat with a heart-melting grin.

Margaret could feel her skin creeping and withdrew to the back of the group, but then she noticed the man accompanying him. He inclined his head and smiled at her, impossibly handsome, tall, strongly built, with a sun-bronzed skin and piercing grey eyes. He was clean-shaven, but his sideburns were long, as was his curling black hair.

She recognised him at once. He had been riding on the moors on that never-to-be-forgotten Christmas Eve when her life had changed dramatically, and she had glimpsed him again on several occasions when he was visiting Roslan – Roderick's bosom companion. But this was the first time he had acknowledged her. She was aware of a strange sensation in the pit of her stomach as his eyes lingered on her.

It meant nothing to Lester, a natural reaction to a pretty woman. Earl's heir he might be, but he was also an adventurer, coming from a long line of reckless rogues who had always exerted a powerful attraction over women. It was as if every sexually exciting characteristic of his forebears had been gathered together and emphasised in Lester Kealan.

'Lester, how well you look,' Julia said brightly.

'Thank you, Lady Julia,' he answered, and lifted her gloved hand to his lips, not touching, merely hovering over it, then he switched his attention to Fenella who became even more animated, bedazzled by his charm.

'I didn't know you intended to shop, Roderick.' Julia always used a faintly hectoring tone when addressing him, calculated to make him feel guilty. 'You could have escorted us.'

'Dearest Mama, Lester and I had a little shopping to do on our own account,' he answered blandly, judging her mood to a turn. 'When one has been out of the country for over a year, one simply has to visit the old haunts and see what's about.'

He glanced at Lester who responded with a lift of one curving dark eyebrow. The tobacconist was an accomodating man who allowed the rooms above to be used by streetwalkers. The young men had come out of the shop lighter in purse but relieved of their frustrations. Roderick stuffed down his guilt. It had given him quite a shock to find his mother there, and for one paralysing moment he had thought she had found out about the whore they had just shared.

'I'll expect you to dine with us tonight, Lester,' Julia insisted. 'Then you and Roderick can render a full account of your travels on the Continent. He's told me nothing yet.'

'But, Mama, I've only been in London a couple of days,' Roderick protested. 'Give a chap a chance.'

'Blame me for the delay, dear lady,' Lester purred in that beguiling voice with its soft brogue. 'I refused to let Roderick go until I'd shown him the family seat in County Wicklow. There was horse-racing on the Curragh which we simply had to see, and that's how we came to catch a later ferry.'

'I forgive you,' she said magnanimously. 'Though I consider it rather naughty. I missed my boy.'

'I sent you picture postcards, Mater, and wrote,' Roderick went on, holding out his arm to her as they strolled through the arcade.

'Not often enough. How d'you think I felt, trapped in England while you were off doing goodness knows what in France and Germany and Italy?' Julia tucked her hand possessively into the crook of his elbow.

Fenella walked along at Lester's side, remembering her dignity and acting grown-up, airing her French. Margaret was alone, her eyes fixed on the arrogant set of his shoulders, seeing how he slowed his loose, rangy stride to accommodate the girl. His hair flowed from under the brim of his rakishly tilted fedora, coiling into loose rings. To her dismay Margaret discovered that she wanted to touch him. She lagged behind, putting as much space between them as she could.

'Lady Julia, may I hope you'll forgive my misdemeanour and permit me to take you to tea at the Ritz Hotel?' Lester murmured as they reached Cork Street. 'I'd be most awfully grateful if you would.'

'Oh, Mama, can we go?' begged Fenella, in a state of frenzy engendered by his close proximity, forgetting to behave with the decorum expected of a genteel young lady.

'Fenella, be quiet,' Julia reproved, pretended to consider, then said graciously, 'Thank you, Lester. That will be delightful. Shall you hail a cab?'

'I have my own car. It's on the other side of the street. I'll fetch it,' Lester offered.

'Do you drive?' Fenella breathed admiringly.

'I do. Every man will be driving soon, carriages a thing of the past,' he assured her. 'Though the horse will be with us for ever. A noble beast to be sure. You're a first-rate rider, if I remember correctly.'

'The Boxing Day Hunt, ages ago. I was a child then, but I've never forgotten.'

'Neither have I, Lady Fenella.'

'Shall we be going?' Julia suggested, considering this conversation had gone on long enough. There were bigger fish in the sea for her

90

daughter than an impoverished Irish lord, all charismatic charm and no substance. 'Helbren,' she called over her shoulder. 'Tell Watson to return you to Grosvenor Street. Prepare the blue chiffon for tonight, and take the sapphires from the jewel-case. Oh, and inform Lord Henry of my whereabouts, should he enquire.'

'Yes, my lady,' Margaret answered crisply, though she burned with shame that Lester should hear her addressed in this way.

Just before she turned to retrace her steps, his eyes met hers and he smiled a little regretfully. Had he wanted her to go along, too? This was ridiculous and she pulled herself together sharply. He couldn't possibly be interested in her, could he? She tried to put him from her thoughts, but found herself dwelling on him, even when Luke left the Marchand in a side street and took her to a corner café for tea and currant buns.

The last diner had been served, satisfied customers lingering over port and cigars, no one ever in a hurry to leave the Warwick.

'Home from home,' an enthusiastic admirer had called it, and this had been repeated in more than one notable guide to London's restaurants and hotels.

'Home from home, and I guess that's right,' Lillian Glynn said to herself as, cash-box under one arm, she hitched up her silk skirts and mounted the curving Georgian staircase that gave an uninterrupted view of the foyer with its reception area, black and white tiled floor, and spiky aspidistras in ornate jardinières.

A smile lifted her generous coral lips as she sashayed across the deep-pile carpet leading to her own room, that inner sanctum where few were permitted to enter. Biddy had switched on the electric lamps with their opaque glass shades and drawn the sumptuous balled and fringed curtains across the bay windows. She hung about, awaiting her mistress's instructions, a strange little humpbacked creature whom Lillian had rescued from the gutter, unintentionally earning her life-long loyalty.

'You off to bed, ma'am?' Biddy had been with her ten years but had never lost her Cockney vowels and intonation.

'No, not yet.' They had this conversation most nights. 'I feel wide awake, and I'm expecting Lord Lester. He's dining out, but he likes a chat and a nightcap. You get off. I can manage. Jenkins will lock up later.'

When Biddy had limped away, Lillian went to the table and took up a squat black bottle of stout. She unscrewed the cap and poured the contents into a tumbler, the creamy froth rising to the top. It had a scent like damp leaves. She bore it and the cash-box to the writing desk. A silver chatelaine dangled from her waist, its chains holding several keys of varying sizes. One fitted the box, another the desk and, sitting before it, she became completely absorbed in counting the day's takings.

Placing the coins in bags, she stashed them in a drawer, ready for transference to the bank next day. Then she drew an account book towards her and opened it. Incomings and outgoings were neatly recorded, every business transaction concerning the hotel carefully entered. Dipping a pen in the brass inkwell, she paused thoughtfully for a moment before adding the latest amount to a neat column on the left side. On the right she wrote the expenditure in a firm hand, replaced the book and locked the desk.

She sighed, well pleased. The Warwick was going from strength to strength, its reputation for comfort and superb cuisine unrivalled, the toil and heartbreak of her early life amply rewarded.

'Why don't you put your feet up now, Lily?' some of her intimates often said. 'Take it easy. You deserve it.'

She always shook her head, answering, 'I'm in the habit of working. Wouldn't know what to do with myself if I wasn't. Can't put customers off. I always remember the bad times when I was skint, and hate saying no if there's the likelihood of turning a coin.'

'Glutton for punishment, that's you, Lil.'

There were not many people left who called her by those old sobriquets – Lily, Lil, Liz. She had been born plain Lily Browne of Wapping Stairs, later becoming Lilybelle Lucerne, dancer and singer, but had put that behind her long ago. People had short memories and for ages she had been known as Mrs Lillian Glynn, proprietress of the Warwick Hotel, Conduit Street, Mayfair.

After draining her glass and opening another bottle, she sat back and admired her bedroom, never tired of looking at it. To her it was the symbol of achievement, representing years of struggle. Though, when she took it over, the refurbishment of the hotel had been left to interior designers, here she had followed her fancy. Copying ideas from ladies' magazines and buying pieces from department stores, she had fulfilled the dreams of the starving urchin from the East End, who had slipped up West sometimes, pressing her nose to the plate-glass windows.

These shops had seemed like Aladdin's cave to her, filled with wonders, and she had promised herself that one day, she didn't know how, she'd swan in and order whatever took her eye. She had kept that promise.

A tester bed dominated the room, lavishly hung with plum-coloured curtains, a gold-embroidered quilt spread over its width and a heap of velvet cushions piled against the inlaid headboard. It was matched by a monumental dressing table and an equally gargantuan wardrobe. The carpet was crimson, the wallpaper an exotic pattern of birds of paradise and tiger lilies from the William Morris studios. Framed photographs adorned the walls, mostly of Lillian in her stage days with a nipped in waist and daring décolletté, though there were several of other performers, signed, 'With love to Lilybelle.'

The hearth had copper fire irons, the empty grate concealed behind a widespread Japanese fan decorated with chrysanthemums against a backdrop of snow-capped Mount Fiji. A chiming malachite clock upheld by Spelter figurines occupied the centre of the mantelpiece, flanked by Staffordshire china dogs and a pair of elegant Spode vases. Several small tables held conch shells, domed glass cases of waxed fruit, and alabaster hands steepled in prayer.

It was as if the outmoded Victorian vogue for an overabundance of florid ornaments had found a resting place in Lillian's domain. Whenever she was depressed she went out and bought herself something, possessions symbolising success and security. Fortunately she had a good eye and was a quick learner, picking knowledgeable people's brains, or else her room might have resembled a pawnbroker's shop. As it was the whole delightful hodgepodge managed to appear harmonious.

Lilybelle Lucerne was dead, Lillian Glynn very much alive.

'Here's to you,' she said, toasting her reflection.

It was one of her better nights, she decided, tilting her head and regarding herself critically. 'Why, in this subdued light I might pass for twenty-five. There are a few crow's feet, and little wrinkles round my mouth, but these add character.'

She picked up a hare's foot from where it lay on the Brussels duchesse set protecting the highly polished surface of the dressing table, dipped it in rouge and touched it to her cheeks. Her amber eyes immediately seemed brighter. Cosmetics were wonderful inventions, she mused. Of course one had to use a feathery touch. Only the demimonde painted blatantly. Real ladies merely pinched their cheeks and rubbed their lips to give added colour. Women of Lillian's age and station could get away with make-up, especially if, like herself, they had learned the art of applying it.

She sipped the stout and touched a hand to her red hair. Once this had been natural, a nimbus shining amidst the dross of her existence, so bright that men had wanted to warm their hands at its flame. Now it owed that coppery glow to the regular application of henna.

I'm not grey yet, she thought, leaning closer and subjecting the roots to close scrutiny, not a single silver thread. Some woman start to get a few by the time they reach thirty-five, but I've been lucky so far.

'You was born lucky, Lil. Got the luck of the devil!' she could hear Gran saying from the dim and distant past. Poor soul, dead these twenty years now. She'd relied on Gran, her world falling apart the day she died, the only mother she had ever known, her real one dying in childbirth when Lillian was twelve months old.

As for her father? God only knew who he had happened to be. Some sailor maybe, docking briefly in the Port of London and seeking solace in a whore's arms? Perhaps a Paddy fresh from Dublin, navvying on building sites? Lillian had no idea of the identity of whoever had impregnated her mother during some loveless incident involving animal lust and a monetary transaction.

Where she came from had hardly mattered. Bastards were commonplace, as were poverty, misery and a short life span: Gran had brought up a large family of her own besides various illegitimate offspring belonging to her daughters.

'Crips, you gals,' she would exclaim in weary exasperation each time one of them admitted to being in trouble. 'Up the duff again? Sloppin' out another babby! Won't you never learn?'

Lillian remembered her as an old woman in a moth-eaten shawl, realising with a shock that she could have been little more than forty when she died, constitution ruined by working long hours in a match factory. Lethal, they were, and Lillian had avoided them like the plague. No wonder her mother had gone on the game. As a child, Lillian had managed to get work collecting the glasses in a public house, bringing home her meagre wages to help out. But once the stabilizing influence of Gran had gone and the family broken up, she too had considered taking the slippery slope to damnation by becoming a prostitute.

I didn't though, she ruminated, as the stout went down, taking the edge off the pain lurking inside her at all times. Went on the bloody stage instead, though that's almost as good as.

A talent had manifested itself, surfacing from among the genes bequeathed by some unknown ancestor. She had a natural ear for music, could dance like a sprite and sing like a nightingale, possessing the right balance of brazen cheek, greed and theatricality necessary to raise her from entertaining pub riffraff to an audition at a music hall. From there, by way of sleeping with the manager, she had climbed steadily towards her goal.

It had been a gruelling slog – touring the provinces, playing in second-rate theatres to rowdy audiences, staying in seedy lodging houses with flea-infested beds, fighting off the advances of fellow artistes, lecherous members of the public, or opportunist landlords. But she had done it by the time she was twenty, ending up as a star at the Prince's in the heart of London's theatre-land.

She had loved being loved, the cheers of the crowd the sweetest of sounds as she curtsied and kissed her hands to them – their adulation repaying her tenfold for the humiliations, the endurance, the sheer dogged determination needed to claw her way to the top of a dodgy profession.

Down in the hall of the hotel the front door bell clanged. That would be Lord Lester. A quick visit to the kitchen to assure herself that the staff were clearing away dinner and laying up the breakfast trays before going to bed, and she would join that young dandy. Lillian tucked a stray curl into place, drew in a breath so that her ribs rose beneath her tight stays and pushed her breasts high, squared her beautiful shoulders and swept from the room in a whisper of purple flounced skirts.

A footman showed Lester and Roderick into Lillian's parlour and left them after pouring two snifters of brandy. 'Sit down,' Lester said, waving a hand towards a leather upholstered wingchair. 'That was a champion meal. Please convey my compliments to your Mama's chef.'

'I will, but I must say I envy you.' Roderick looked round the cosy room, furnished with overstuffed sofas and heavy draperies in ecclesiastical colours. 'What a capital hotel this is. More like a private house. How long are you staying in London?'

Lester lowered his agile body into the opposite chair and crossed one knee over the other. 'Thought I'd hang on a bit. Take a look around. Certainly be here for Fenella's coming-out ball.'

'Are you looking for an heiress? I certainly am,' Roderick said, bending forward so that Lester could hold a match to his cigar.

'A wife? Don't know if I want to take on the snaffle.' Lester's eyes slitted as he watched the blue smoke rising to the decorated frieze, picked out in green and red, with traces of gold leaf.

Roderick lifted his shoulders in a shrug under his faultlessly tailored evening jacket. 'Who does? But the family line has to continue, doesn't it? And it's down to me as heir apparent to do my duty and wed some suitable filly.'

'God, it sounds awful!' Lester said with a grimace. 'Why are the débutantes always so grim, while chorus girls and trollops set a man's blood racing?'

'What about lady's maids?' Roderick suggested craftily. 'I saw you this afternoon, giving Mama's the eye.'

'I presume you're referring to that girl you've told me about, the one you lust after. What's her name?' An eyebrow shot up, a thin smile lifting Lester's lips.

95

'Margaret Helbren. Very prim and proper, I wanted to give her a roll in the hay a while back, but she wasn't having any.' There was a vicious gleam in Roderick's eyes. 'As a matter of fact, it started long before that. I caught her trespassing once, when we were nippers.'

'You wanted her when you were a boy, and you've gone on wanting her ever since. Is that it? Refused you, did she?' Lester put down his glass, linked his hands behind his head and studied the ceiling.

Roderick scowled, lower lip rolled out sullenly. 'Bloody gypsy. That's what I called her the first time, and my opinion hasn't changed. I was fishing with friends in Colt Spinney, and she came strolling along as if she had a perfect right to be on my land. We threatened to duck her if she didn't take down her drawers and show us her wares.'

'Charming behaviour, calculated to endear you to a young girl.' Lester's sarcasm coiled round the roon. 'I hope you did better the second time.'

'Damn it, I didn't realise it was her till I'd started to mess around, trying to kiss her and get a feel of her breasts. You know how it is.'

'Do I?'

'Oh, come off it, Lester! You're no saint. Bloody hell! I've seen you in action often enough.'

Lester looked at him coolly, saying, 'I've found gentleness by far the best route to success with women. Never had to resort to force.'

'Smooth blighter,' Roderick growled, then grinned suddenly. 'I'll bet you couldn't seduce the icy Miss Helbren.'

'You do? How much are you willing to gamble?' Lester's swarthy face seemed even more saturnine under the soft light of the wall lamps.

'Three hundred guineas.'

'Make it five and you're on.'

'Done!'

They leaned over and slapped their palms together, sealing the wager.

'And how long am I given to achieve this?' Lester asked, reaching for the decanter and topping up their glasses.

'Let's say the night of Fenella's ball. And I want to watch,' Roderick stated, running the tip of his tongue over his lips, his body betraying the excitement engendered by this idea.

Lester threw back his head and laughed loudly. 'Right. After the ball it is.' Then he sobered, his eyes darkening to pewter. 'It won't prove a hardship. She's beautiful.'

'And a virgin.'

'How can you be sure?' Lester was sceptical.

Roderick tapped the side of his high-bridged nose. 'I've been sounding out the servants. Apparently, she's as pure as the proverbial snow. Watson has tried but failed. She hasn't any followers.'

96

'Intriguing.' Lester settled back in his chair, holding the glass between his narrow hands and viewing the rich golden liquid reflectively. 'I might make her my mistress.'

'And while you'll be having all the fun, I shall be stuck with some shapeless maiden who'll be expecting marriage before she opens her legs. It's only fair I should enjoy Maggie by proxy, as it were. On my wedding night, I'll remember you rogering her as I hump my plain wife, hoping to get her in foal pretty damn' quick.'

'Who is in foal? One of your mares? This sounds interesting,' Lillian remarked as she glided into the room. 'Could it be a future Derby winner?'

Roderick and Lester jumped to their feet, well-bred young men who had been taught never to remain seated while a female was standing, unless, of course, she happened to be a servant or shop assistant. Lillian fitted into neither category, regal, rather intimidating, her fashionable gown sparkling with sequins and beadwork, her hair dressed in that high, full style so much in vogue.

'I was talking about my prospective bride,' Roderick replied brightly, wondering if there was any truth in the gossip that Lillian had been willing to give her favours in exchange for advancement.

She was still a fine woman, and though his appetite had been temporarily appeased in the room above the tobacconist's shop earlier, he could feel a stirring in his groin at the possibility of bedding her, dreaming of being dominated by an older woman from a lower class, as he had been by his nanny, Mrs Broom's predecessor. She had introduced him to sexual pleasure, coarse, common and bold, playing with his young body at bathtime, tucking him into bed with her sometimes where this exciting game continued. Big breasts, wide hips, firm, experienced hands.

Even now the smell of unwashed linen and female sweat roused him. He would lurk in corridors and beneath stairs to catch a glimpse of the maids – white aprons, ankles in black stockings. The memory of such sights provided him with fantasies for solitary fulfillment.

'You're engaged? Are congratulations in order?' Lillian's voice returned him to the present.

'Oh, no, not yet, but I suspect I may be by the end of the Season. Essential to produce a son, you see.'

'Of course.' Lillian's dimples deepened and she waved a gracious hand, adding, 'Please be seated, gentlemen,' then settled herself on the chesterfield. Lester handed her a glass of brandy.

Just for a moment Lillian contemplated the wisdom of drinking this on top of stout, but the thought was a fleeting one. She could hold her liquor with any man, keeping a perfectly clear head. Only sometimes,

97

in that dead time between two o'clock and dawn, did it occur to her that she might be dependent on it. When morning came she could shrug this off, lace her first cup of tea with spirits and resume the mantle of responsibility.

Now she was at that stage of inebriation when it seemed she could perform any feat, confidence at full stretch. It was perfectly logical that she should be seated in her parlour entertaining members of the aristocracy. Handsome young savages, both of them, so charming, with not the slightest hint of snobbery. She was fully aware of Roderick's need, and toyed with the notion of satisfying it.

'And you, Lord Lester?' she said vivaciously, while speculating on how he would be between the sheets. 'Are you seeking a bride?'

He subjected her to the full force of his smile, white teeth gleaming between finely chiselled lips. 'I think not. I've more adventuring to do before I settle down.'

She chuckled, and reached out to touch his arm with lazy intimacy. 'Are you trying to tell me marriage will make any difference? Gentlemen don't "settle down", do they? I understand that matrimony doesn't change their way of life – they still drink, gamble, keep mistresses in love nests tucked away in some secluded spot.'

'That's hardly fair,' Roderick answered, adopting his most winsome manner. He had been a frequent visitor to the Warwick since their return from Europe, finding the free and easy atmosphere most convivial. 'Dash it all, a fellow is entitled to some fun, surely?'

Lillian merely smiled. She knew these elegant gentlemen inside out, had seen it all. The Stage Door Johnnies in their tailored evening suits, opera capes and top hats; once they had haunted her dressing room bearing bouquets, jewels, invitations to dinner at the Café Royal. Then there had been the middle-aged roués with reputations to preserve, polititians, princes, magistrates, influential figures in the Government. Their attentions had been more discreet, overtures usually carried out by an intermediary, but all, young and old, had only one goal when it came down to it – that of getting a girl on her back.

'What do their wives do for fun?' she asked, though keeping her tone jocular. It wouldn't do to let them suspect she favoured emancipation and that major threat to male security which they looked upon with as much terror as castration – votes for women.

'Oh, there are a hundred things, I'm sure. Mama keeps busy, especially now, with Fenella about to enter society.' Roderick was not in the least introspective and never bothered to look further than his immediate wants. It did not cross his mind to wonder if females were happy with their lot.

'I expect you're right,' Lillian conceded, thinking what fools men were. Then she changed the direction of the conversation. 'Are you staying the night, Lord Roderick? There's a spare room in Lord Lester's suite.'

'No, I'll get a growler home. Mama is complaining that I'm not spending enough time with her.' Lester rose, Lillian with him. She tugged at the worsted bell rope hanging by the fireplace.

Within seconds a footman appeared at the door. 'Tell Jenkins to fetch a cab, Talbot,' she ordered. 'And have Lord Roderick's hat and cloak ready in the hall.'

'Yes, madam,' he said, bowing, and she registered how fine he looked in his knee-breeches and jacket. There was something about a uniform that had instant appeal, even that of a manservant.

He had only been there a week, young, strong and virile. Lillian always selected her staff with care, particularly the men, engaging them for their height, breadth of shoulder and the shape of their calves, so important in formal wear. By two o'clock in the afternoon each day they were silk-stockinged and pumped in full black livery piped with silver, their stately mien adding a dash of style to the Warwick Hotel.

Lester walked Roderick to the door, and when he returned gave Lillian a steady stare before saying, 'Do you have any objection to my bringing a young woman to the restaurant for dinner? She's not of my class, you understand. I couldn't very well be seen in public with her elsewhere.'

With a slither of silk on silk, she lifted her legs and stretched them on the settee, the tip of a satin shoe peeping from beneath the hem. 'Gentleman can dine here with women if they wish, but I'm warning you, this isn't a bawdyhouse. I can't afford any scandal which might result in loss of trade.'

'But if we slipped upstairs later, would you look the other way?' Lester insisted, leaning over her and holding a match to the Abdullah she had inserted in a long jade holder.

'I'd not object, providing you're discreet,' she answered, admiring him through the smoke haze, the warmth of good Almanac tingling along her veins, making her feel reckless and desirous.

'I promise to be careful,' he went on, smiling down into her eyes, his own so steel bright and unblinking they seemed almost hypnotic.

'Is she beautiful?'

'Oh, yes.'

'I'd like to meet her. Let me know when you're expecting her and I'll get Chef to prepare something special,' she said, responding to his maleness, almost envying the girl, though too sensible to get involved with this swashbuckling Irish lord.

It would be fatally easy to fall in love with him, but she recognised the type. They were anathema to her – the kiss of death. Her first love had been like Lester, tall, dark and suave. He had made her pregnant and a bungling backstreet abortionist had brought about a termination that had left her barren. Later there had been another, younger, wilder, even more devastatingly attractive. When their passionate affair ended in disaster she had considered suicide, but had married on the rebound instead.

Lillian shuddered inwardly as she remembered these mistakes brought about by her obsessions with unsuitable partners. No, Lester and his kind were not for her, though she never doubted she could have him if she wanted. Two hopeless love affairs and an awful marriage to a neurotic comedian who beat her if her act was more popular than his had taught her a salutory lesson. In the end another wife had turned up. Not only had he been an abuser, he was also a bigamist.

Where love failed, kindness had triumphed in the large, genial shape of her last long-term lover, an elderly hotelier whose needs had been undemanding and who, when he died, had left her the Warwick. The hotel was like the child she would never have – her pride and joy. No man would be permitted to undermine that.

But she was a hot-blooded woman who had experienced the pleasures of the senses and these could not be denied. No potentially dangerous gentleman for her, however, and when Lester had gone up to his suite, she retired to her room, saying to Talbot, en route, 'Bring up that bottle of brandy in fifteen minutes.'

'Yes, madam,' he answered, watching her as she mounted the stairs, her hips swaying provocatively.

She was sitting in bed when she called for him to enter, amused to see him standing nervously just inside the door. 'Your brandy, madam.'

'Thank you, Talbot.' She threw him a radiant smile, and he was dazzled by this vision in the black lace robe, her white shoulders and upper breasts bare, the flaming hair tumbling about her face.

She patted the side of the bed. 'Sit down. Have a drink.'

'I'm on duty, madam,' he stammered, petrified.

She giggled and bent forward so that he could look straight down the deep valley between her lush breasts. 'I'm the boss, remember? What I say goes. Now, sit down.'

He gingerly lowered himself on to the coverlet, comparing the grandeur of this room with his own humble lodgings, an attic at the top of the house shared with two waiters. He sipped the brandy. It burned its way down his throat and settled in his belly.

'How old are you, Talbot?' She knew very well, having conducted his interview herself.

'Nineteen?'

'And you've been in service a long time?' She rested a hand on his satin-breeched knee.

Talbot swallowed hard, imagining the mockery of the other men if this got out. His experience was limited to a fumble or two with servant-girls, completely unsatisfactory as, in his excitement, he had suffered premature ejaculation. This woman was amazing, a lady in his eyes. That she should have singled him out was almost unbelievable.

'I started as a boot-boy when I was twelve,' he muttered, blushing as he wished his breeches were not quite so tight and revealing. 'Then worked my way up.'

'And your ambition?' She was enjoying herself immensely, feasting her eyes on his boyish face, correctly assessing his torment and hugging to herself the knowledge that she was about to make his dreams come true.

'To be a butler.'

'Ah, well now, Talbot, we'll have to see what we can do about that, shan't we?' She pushed back the coverlet. Her robe was open down the front, alabaster flesh exposed, breasts, belly, thighs, the dark triangle between. She held out her arms to him.

Talbot groaned and went into them. Lillian closed her eyes, tasting his young mouth, his young flesh – this was how she took her pleasure these days. No love, no commitment, no pain.

Chapter 6

Margaret's feet skimmed over the scalding pavement. She hated the feel of shoes and stockings and all the trappings imprisoning her body, and would have given almost anything for sand under her soles in place of tarmac, cliffs rearing high instead of stone buildings and gulls replacing the endless conclave of pigeons.

London sweltered under a semi-tropical May. The newspapers reported that it resembled Italy and predicted a change in world climate. Some had even gloomily prophesied the melting of the Polar ice caps and universal flooding. The 'End of the World' sects thought the Day of Judgement was nigh. The citizens of London in general relished the heat after a freezing, blustery start to the year. On Sundays and in the evenings, they turned out in their thousands to stroll in the parks, sit under the trees and listen to brass bands, tempers so much improved that their children scampered about happily without being slapped or lectured.

Margaret slowed her pace when she passed between the scrolled ironwork gates of Hyde Park. She took off her hat, pulled out her hairpins and gave her head a vigorous shake that brought her curls tumbling down. Apart from removing her jacket and slinging it over one shoulder, this was as far as she dare go. Even appearing in public in her blouse caused stares, but she was past caring.

There was a week to go before Fenella's big day, and the house was in an uproar. Most of the chaos was caused by Fenella herself, a bundle of nerves and near hysteria. It's not long now, thank God, Margaret thought, sauntering along, face raised to the cloudless sky, much more of this and that girl would have a breakdown. And the rest of us with her, all ending up in the madhouse. If I see another dressmaker or milliner or hairdresser, I'll scream!

She felt sorry for Mrs Colby and Mr Wakefield; in their hands lay the complicated organisation of the ball. Mrs Frith had been given her

102

orders concerning the buffet and the kitchen staff were working like galley slaves. Every morning Mrs Frith left the house at five-thirty to take a hackney to Covent Garden Market in order to consult with bakers, butchers, fishmongers, florists and vintners. Fresh produce was essential, and some would be shipped up from the Roslan Manor greenhouses.

To add to her problems, more than a dozen important guests from far away would be staying at Upper Grosvenor Street, necessitating menus for several days. Mrs Colby was halfway demented as Lady Julia ordered rooms to be prepared for Lord and Lady This, and the Duke and Duchess of That, then changed her mind several times over and generally caused confusion.

It was little short of miraculous that Margaret had been granted a free afternoon. Fortunately, Fenella's great-great-aunt had arrived from Scotland, a tyrannical dame in a crinoline purchased in the eighteen-sixties, who had demanded to be taken to lunch at the Clarendon Hotel. Margaret's services had been dispensed with, once she had helped Julia to dress. No doubt she would pay for it later by being expected to stay up half the night.

Now she headed for the Serpentine Lake, clutching a paper bag filled with bread crumbs for the ducks. It still amazed her to find so many oases in the heart of the metropolis. Not only St James's Park and Hyde Park, but small, tree-filled areas surrounded by spiked railings for the use of those who resided in the stately squares, and lovely gardens glimpsed through arches. Further out, but no more than a bus ride away, were wide heaths, once the haunts of highwaymen, but now places where the workers and their families relaxed on Bank Holidays.

Energy tingled through her. Reared so close to the earth, the deprivation of sunshine and clear air affected her physically and depressed her mentally. She hummed to the music drifting from the bandstand where instruments gleamed and the conductor in full dress uniform commanded his troupe, beating time with a baton held in a white-gloved hand.

Hyde Park was the meeting place for king and coster alike. Guardsmen in scarlet coats escorted maidservants, dashing blades in white flannels and striped blazers ogled the girls, young ladies minced along escorted by duennas, dogs romped and barked, and children bowled hoops or played ball under the watchful eyes of nannies. Margaret rejoiced in it, smiling at chubby babies in high perambulators and nodding to their nursemaids.

The sun painted shadows on the man-made lake. Families were picnicking on its banks, and Margaret regretted not having a companion. It would have been grand had Susan been able to come along, but she was now a parlourmaid and on duty. Margaret stood at the edge, throwing crusts to the cob and pen who drifted over, a clutch of fluffy chocolate-brown cygnets in their wake.

'Looks fun, doesn't it?' said a voice at her side and she swung round to see Lester. He nodded towards the hired craft sculling across the lake's tranquil surface. He was dressed in a casual cream linen suit and polka-dot tie, and removed his panama hat as he spoke. 'Good afternoon, Miss Helbren.'

Margaret could feel her face flaming, the shock of his sudden appearance and the way he addressed her as 'Miss' robbing her of speech, then, 'Good afternoon, sir,' she managed to say.

'On your own? No Lady Julia?' He leaned easily on his silver-topped walking cane, subjecting her to the scrutiny of his grey eyes, so pale in contrast to the olive-skinned face.

'I'm alone. That's one advantage of being a working girl. I don't need a chaperone,' she replied, then could have bitten off her tongue for drawing attention to the class distinction. She had not meant to do this, but everything seemed to be coming out wrong. 'I like to watch the ducks,' she ended lamely.

'Lucky old ducks,' he murmured, then suddenly straightened. 'I say, would you do me the honour of coming out in one of those boats?'

'Oh, sir, I couldn't.' She had never felt more flustered, alternately hot and cold, a dozen possibilities chasing themselves around in her mind.

'Why not?' He was cool, amused, but not mocking.

'Well, it's not done, is it? You being who you are – and me,' she trailed off helplessly.

'My dear Miss Helbren, do the rules apply here? Let's pretend they don't, shall we? Supposing I was just an ordinary chap, what would you do?'

'I'd probably give you a right ticking off for being so saucy,' she sparked at him. 'You might even get your ears boxed into the bargain.'

His loud laughter made heads turn. 'You'd assume I was trying to pick you up, is that it?'

'What else would a man be doing, speaking to a girl he doesn't know?' Despite herself, Margaret responded to his ease of manner, managing to get a grip on her emotions.

'Supposing, like me, he was feeling lonely and wanted someone to share this lovely afternoon?' His candid eyes met hers, and she felt that concentrated gaze, that warm communion. A great silence seemed to weigh on the scene. It was as if they were alone where the lake shone and glittered.

'I'm sure you need never be lonely, sir,' she ventured, and was about to add a rider to the effect that a hundred more suitable women would jump at the chance of being with him, when the thought suddenly struck her: Why not me?

'You're wrong there, Miss Helbren. I'm often alone, and like my own company.'

'I understand. I spent much time by myself when I lived at home.'

'And where was that?'

'I come from Cornwall – Porthross to be exact.'

'Indeed? You don't have a Cornish accent.'

'My mother wasn't a local woman. She was born in Bristol.'

She was not sure how it happened, but he offered her his arm and she took it, the material smooth under her fingers, the muscles beneath iron-hard. She walked with him towards the wooden pier where rowing boats rocked gently at their moorings and an attendant waited to take money and issue tickets.

Nothing had ever felt more natural and right.

After an exchange of coins, Lester stepped into one of the boats, laid his cane on the bottom and held out his hand to her. It was as if a spark of electricity crackled at his touch. She could feel it coursing down to her core and exploding in an exquisite pain. She stumbled. The boat rocked. His grip tightened, moving from hand to wrist, thumb pressed against the throbbing pulse. An arm clipped her waist and she was lifted and settled on a flat plush-covered pad. He sat opposite. He removed his jacket, loosened his tie, rolled up his shirt-sleeves and picked up the oars. The attendant cast off.

Lester smiled at her and she lost some of her awe. With his head bare, shirt open at the neck, forearms naked, he looked almost, but not quite, like a common man. This was how it must be to 'walk out' with a suitor. The maids were always talking about it, whispering and giggling, wanting to have a sweetheart they could call their own.

Lester braced his feet as he leaned into the oars and soon the boat glided into the centre of the lake, its bow pointing towards the bridge. Margaret rested against the cane back of the seat, placing her hat beside her, glad that she had worn her embroidered muslin blouse and lace-trimmed linen skirt in a sugared-almond shade. At least she did not look like a servant.

'You certainly know how to row,' she remarked conversationally, after cudgelling her brains to find an opening gambit.

'I was in the team at Oxford and have entered for the Royal Henley Regatta. It's a three-day event and really an excuse for a party. You should come along.'

This was like a dash of cold water. The light went out of her eyes.

'Oh, yes! Fat chance!' she muttered. 'If I do, I'll be shoved into the background, running errands for Lady Julia.'

He sobered at the resentment in her voice. 'You don't like your position? Doesn't she treat you well?'

'No, and yes.' She was afraid to express herself too strongly. He had Roderick's ear and could be a tale-bearer. 'I'm lucky to be where I am, I suppose, and she's kind. Let's me have her unwanted clothes, and I've a room to myself. I travel with her, see life, but make no mistake, I'm never allowed to step over the mark or forget that I'm only there to work.'

'That's the way of things,' he reminded gently. 'Some of us are born with a silver spoon in our mouth, and we do hold a tremendous re-sponsibility. We run the country and keep the wheels of government turning.'

Her eyes fastened on his. 'You don't, do you?'

'Not yet, but one day I'll take over the earldom and then things will change drastically. Gone will be the days of wine and roses. I'll be imprisoned in an old manor house in the heart of the Wicklow Mountains, looking after my tenants, listening to their complaints, harvesting the land.'

But even as he spoke he was wondering if indeed there would be anything left by the time he inherited, Treleen Towers mortgaged almost beyond redeeming. His father, like himself, was a gambler, a womaniser and man of the turf, spending too much money at the races or in the gaming clubs and whorehouses of Dublin.

'You'll make a fine landlord, I'm sure,' she said, wanting to think well of him and banish Susan's warning voice that echoed in her head, telling her to beware of the young bloods.

His eyes sparkled, the grey transformed to silver. 'Thanks for that vote of confidence.' He steered the craft to a curve in the bank, shaded by a weeping willow, let its nose bump against the mud and shipped the oars in a shower of diamond drops. 'I should have brought along a hamper and a bottle of bubbly. Never mind. Next time.'

'Next time? D'you think we're going to make a habit of this?'

'I sincerely hope so.'

'Now look here,' she began, abandoning her relaxed pose. 'Let's get a few things straight. I may not like it much but I don't want to lose my job.'

Dark brows shot up towards the errant lock of blue-black hair falling over his brow. 'And why should you do that, Margaret? I may call you Margaret, mayn't I?'

'How do you know my name? Well, really! I've never – in all my life

106

– never met anyone – such downright cheek—' Her speech had disintegrated into stutters.

'No need to get excited,' he said softly. 'It wasn't difficult, not to someone as determined as myself.'

'Why did you want to know?' She gave a small, defeated gesture.

'Because you're the loveliest girl I've ever seen.'

Lester spoke sincerely. He was always sincere with the woman he was currently wooing, even though this time the main aim was to win a bet. Just for the moment Margaret meant everything to him, filling his horizon. He was going to say more when something about her stopped him. It was the girl herself, pretty, beautiful even, with her mass of tangled hair.

Roderick had called her a gypsy. Maybe she was, but Lester thought it more likely she had Celtic blood. Blue eyes ringed with thick black lashes, raven hair, a creamy skin. He had seen and enjoyed them in Ireland. He was caught by her air of vulnerability, and sensed there had been tragedy in her life, and he saw more – a glimmer of passionate sensuality that promised much.

The willow locked them into greenish gloom, as if they were under the sea. Sounds drifted from the distance, the shrill laughter of children, the band playing a selection from light operas, the carolling of birds, the gurgle and swish of the water slapping against the hull.

Margaret's breath shortened, turmoil in her blood, that aching need manifesting, goose-bumps stippling her skin. She was afraid, staring raptly at him, hoping against all hope that he would not tempt her into doing something she would regret. She had withstood Luke, but that had not been hard. The emotion she felt for Lester was entirely different, compelling, threatening to get out of control.

'Margaret.' Her nerves tingled as he spoke her name, softly, caressingly. She could not move, as fascinated as a rabbit before a snake as he shifted over to sit beside her. 'Margaret, my dear, if heaven should be like this, then I don't mind dying.'

She was rigid, knees locked together, hands clenched in her lap. Had it been Luke speaking or anyone else, she would have told them not to be so silly. Not so this man. With his wonderful voice as seductive as silk, his endearing understanding and dazzling personality, he made her want to believe that love could conquer all, the social gulf between them easily bridged.

'You talk like a poet,' she sighed, still rigid, grabbing on to her reserve like a lifeline.

'I read poetry, but can't write it,' he said, and idly picked up one of the tresses that lay on her shoulder and, as if of its own volition, the hair curled round his finger.

Her heart was pounding, resolution melting under the onslaught of desire and dreams. She had heard of chorus girls marrying dukes, so why shouldn't it be possible for an earl to wed a lady's maid? I could play the part to perfection, she told herself. I've learned a lot from Lady Julia. People often mistake me for one of her relatives, never guessing I'm nothing more than her dogsbody.

'We'd better be getting back,' she said, though she wanted to stay there more than anything on earth. 'I musn't be late. Lady Julia will expect me to unlace her stays so she can enjoy a siesta. There's a busy night ahead. The American Ambassador and his wife are coming to dinner.'

'I know. I've been invited.' He took her hand in his, her slim fingers laced with his browner, more powerful ones. They were warm and dry and she yearned to feel them caressing her skin.

Very gently he drew her against him in the leafy green bower. She hardly dared breathe, aware of their hearts beating so close together, tempted to yield to the delicious feeling of being protected and defended. A tingle started at the base of her spine as one long finger slowly traced the line of her chin, her throat and finally hovered over the peak of her breast. Then his hand dropped away.

'You're right,' he said huskily. 'It's best if we return. I can't trust myself and I respect you too much to do anything we might both regret. But tell me I can see you again.'

She looked into his eyes, and said, 'I'd like that very much.'

'I'll take you out one night.'

She retreated into hauteur. 'It's impossible.'

'No, it isn't.' He was eager, almost pleading with her to agree. 'No one need know. I promise it will be above board, no strings, just companions, you and I.'

This touched her deeply. To be his comrade was the greatest inducement of all. He would not try to storm the ramparts of her virtue. They could enjoy each other's company, share mutual interests in a quiet, peaceful, uncomplicated way.

'I love opera,' she said, very aware that his arm was still holding her.

'So do I. We'll go to one next week. What night will you be free?'

Her forehead rucked in perplexity. 'I can't be sure. Lady Julia wants me on call most of the time. I'll have to let you know.'

'Good. Can't you fake sickness or something? Surely, you can get away to meet your friend for one evening at least?' The strength of his hand at her waist was a persuasive argument.

'I'll try,' she whispered. 'Am I really your friend?'

'Of course. I feel that I can trust you. Is that so?'

'Oh, yes.' She closed her eyes, seeing behind the lids the image of his brows, the shape of his cheek, the hair curling against it.

Soft as a conspirator he said, 'Come, kiss me, friend.'

She was not prepared for that. From him friend was a more moving word than lover. She could not answer, but he did not want her to talk.

His mouth was gentle, the touch of closed, smooth lips, a light kiss in no way alarming, leaving her hungry for more. He put her from him firmly and returned to his own seat, slipping the oars into the rowlocks. The leaves parted and the boat slid into open water. The interlude was over, but for Margaret it had only begun.

He escorted her to the park gates, every inch the gentleman and she watched him as he strode down the street swinging his cane, feasting her eyes on his tall, elegant figure until he turned the corner and she could see him no more.

'How did it go? Come on. I want a blow-by-blow account,' Roderick demanded when he and Lester were ensconced in the smoking room late that night. 'Did you get the chance to touch her up?'

'Don't be crude,' Lester chided, taking a cigar from his gold case, piercing it and lighting it carefully. 'I took her boating on the Serpentine.'

'You did what? Rather public, wasn't it?' Roderick eased himself down in a deep armchair, whisky to hand. He had spent the evening being charming to his mother's guests, given no chance for a report on Lester's progress with Margaret.

'The park was full of plebeians,' Lester announced. 'No one from our circle. Anyway, the lake isn't without its private nooks.'

'Did you roger her? I've done it in a boat before now. There was that jolly waitress at Oxford – Gertie or somesuch name. D'you remember her? Biggest breasts I've ever seen – a married woman, naturally. We very nearly fell into the water.'

Lester experienced a spasm of irritation. Roderick lacked finesse. 'We agreed she'd be deflowered on the night of the ball,' he reminded icily. 'Why rush an enjoyable experience? Little Miss Helbren is a delightful girl. I could become quite attached to her.'

'I say, steady on, old lad. That's going it a bit strong, isn't it? You can't get fond of a servant. It won't do at all.' Roderick was genuinely shocked.

'These bloody distinctions,' Lester growled, a sombre expression in his eyes. 'She's unfortunately betwixt and between. Kicking against the pricks, yet unable to do anything about it. There's good breeding somewhere along the line, and it shows.'

'Good Lord, I thought this was a prank. You aren't getting serious about her, are you?' Roderick eyed him, worried.

'There's no point. Nothing can possibly come of it.' Lester's voice was hard, his eyes, too, yet in their depths was a restless anger.

'Are you meeting her again? It'll have to be done under cover.'

'I'm taking her to see *La Traviata*. She shares my love of opera.'

Roderick's fair brows shot up. 'Covent Garden? Have you taken leave of your senses? You'll be recognised.'

Lester's lips curved into a wry smile. 'Don't worry. We'll go up in the gallery. I'll wear an ordinary suit instead of evening dress, and no one will be any the wiser. I've done this before. It's refreshing to sit with genuine opera lovers rather than those who only go there to be seen and haven't the slightest idea what's taking place on the stage.'

'There are times when I can't understand you,' Roderick commented, one slim black leg hung over the arm of his chair, foot swaying. 'Anyway, how is the delectable Maggie going to get time off? Mama needs her most nights.'

'This is where you come in. Invite her out to dinner on Wednesday. Make it early. That will give Margaret time to slip off and meet me.'

'But how do we know Mama will agree?' Roderick said glumly. 'She's in a most frightful wax at the moment, and Great-great-auntie being here doesn't help. Terrible old hag! She stinks.'

'All the more reason for your mother to go with you and enjoy herself. You can do it. She thinks the sun shines out of your backside.'

'I'll give it a go. But why should I help you win the bloody bet?' Drink tended to make Roderick truculent.

Lester levelled him a steely look. 'You don't have to, but I rather imagine you want the seduction of Margaret Helbren as much as I, enjoying it second-hand, as it were.'

'I do. Have no doubt about it. It'll be well worth the money to watch you humping that stuck-up bitch.'

The bench seat was hard, with precious little leg room. It was hot and crowded, but Margaret was in paradise. The top tier of Covent Garden Opera House – up in the gods – the realm of the dedicated *aficionado*. Only those short of money but with a passion for opera were prepared to queue for hours at the red double doors in a side alley abutting the theatre, enduring rain or blistering heat in order to climb dozens of stone stairs and lose themselves in the heady rapture of music drama.

Below in the Grand Tier, the Dress Circle, Stalls and boxes the audience were entirely different. Margaret had been among them on several occasions, entering by the magnificent foyer and crimson-carpeted staircase, seated at the back of the Aubert box, depressed by high society's lack of appreciation. It was as much as they could do to keep quiet once the curtain went up, the ladies longing for the interval when they could preen and flirt, flutter their fans and gossip, while the men could not wait to make it to the crush room to smoke, drink and indulge in sporting talk. But in the gallery she was among fellow spirits.

Lester had been waiting for her in his car at the corner of Upper Grosvenor Street, his valet detailed to keep places in the queue till they arrived. As soon as the doors opened, they had rushed headlong up the stairs, fighting to be among the first to reach the top and grab the best seats in the centre of the front row, a wooden barrier with an iron rail the only protection from a dizzying drop into the pit.

'Chocolates?' Lester said, placing a large, beribboned box on her lap.

'Oh, thank you!' It was too much. Tears filled her eyes. To be seated with him, thigh pressed to thigh, her hand clasped in his, the excitement, the buzz of anticipation, friendly smiling faces, the common bond of music. I've never been this happy before, she thought.

The orchestra was tuning up, oboe players practising their trills, a flautist tossing off a few scintillating arpeggios, the throb of a bass drum. The tension grew. Suddenly the conductor appeared, weaving his way towards the rostrum amidst a spattering of applause. He raised his arms, the house lights dimmed and the first, hushed, poignant notes whispered out, high and faint, played by violins.

The curtain rose on the glittering ballroom scene of Act One, and Margaret became entirely absorbed in the sad story of the courtesan, Violetta, and her heart-rending choice between the handsome young man she loved and her rich protector. Pathetic Violetta, living at a hectic pace though riddled with consumption.

When the curtain finally came down there was a moment's silence, followed by thunderous clapping and cheering. Margaret wept into her handkerchief. The death scene had affected her deeply.

'Violetta so much wanted to live – and it was cruel how they separated her from her beloved Alfredo – poor woman, a victim of fate,' she sobbed.

'There, there, don't cry. It's only a story,' Lester soothed, guiding her down the stairs, still weeping. 'I expect by now the heroine is knocking back a glass of wine in her dressing room.'

'But the music is so beautiful. I can't bear it. It tears me apart.'

It had indeed touched a nerve. Her own unhappiness welled up, that never-ending longing for her mother, the memories of the black days of her childhood with the everlasting rows, her sense of displacement

111

– a servant, yet wanting more. She could easily empathise with Violetta. And Lester seemed to know this without her having to speak of it. There had only been one other person who had treated her as an equal, and that was Peter Newark, but he had vanished, gone abroad, so Susan had said when Margaret enquired.

They stepped out into the warm evening air. A sickle moon hung high over London, and Lester kept an arm round her. 'I've a gramophone and records in my rooms, if you'd like to hear more,' he suggested, helping her into the car. 'You're not expected yet, are you?'

'I have to help Lady Julia prepare for bed,' she sniffed, dabbing her eyes, her mind still resounding with Verdi's tragic music and the soprano's thrilling voice. She clutched the chocolate-box – his gift to her. I'll keep it for ever, she vowed to herself, as a reminder of this evening.

'She won't be home for a while. Roderick's taking her to the theatre and then the Café Royal.'

'How d'you know?'

'He told me. Isn't it lucky for us?'

'Yes, very.'

It was impossible to think coherently. The power of the music and the excitement of being with Lester intoxicated her. The afflictions of her life melted away and her heart sang in sheer thankfulness for this unexpected joy.

'You'll come to my hotel?' He spoke as if her answer meant everything to him.

'Is it quite proper?' Margaret looked at him and did not care if she was breaking the rules.

'Oh, yes. The Warwick is run by a most respectable lady. I have my own suite. Your reputation won't suffer.'

'All right, just for a short while, but you will take me to Upper Grosvenor Street?'

'Cinderella, I promise you'll be back before the clock strikes twelve, the car turns into a pumpkin and myself into a frog.' He laughed openly, throwing back his head and taking the balmy air in his long throat.

They cruised through the town, caught from time to time in the headlamps of other vehicles. Piccadilly was busier than at noon, people idling along the pavements or riding in hansom cabs, leaving the Leicester Square theatres, making for the cafés and clubs. The gaslamps, haloed with yellowish light, cast a glow on the huge feathered headdresses of ladies escorted by gentlemen in silk hats and crimson-lined evening capes. Pairs of policemen walked with measured tread, hands clasped behind their backs, truncheons dangling from leather belts, heads protected by domed helmets.

A gang of rowdy, top-hatted young men were gathered round a stall, attracted by the smell of frying sausages and hot coffee, rubbing shoulders with burly workmen and street-cleaners. Prostitutes lurked in doorways, soliciting business. Beggars tugged at coat-sleeves with their whining hard-luck stories. Buskers performed on banjos, penny-whistles and spoons, caps open hopefully at their feet. Ragged old women stood on street corners with trays of matches for sale. Urchins dodged among the adults, waiting for the chance to dip into pockets. The nightlife of London was in full swing.

Lester eventually pulled up outside a large house in a row of other large houses. The frontage was impressive, Doric columns supporting a shell-shaped arch, with tall sash windows on each side. It consisted of three storeys, with the addition of a basement below and attics in the roof. He led Margaret up four wide steps to a front door with light streaming through coloured-glass panels.

'Don't be nervous, little thing,' he said, and touched her cheek. 'This isn't Bluebeard's Castle, nor yet some sinister opium den that profits from the white-slave traffic.'

'I'm not nervous,' she lied.

He pushed open the door and they were met by a retainer in black livery. 'Good evening, Jenkins,' Lester said, allowing Margaret to precede him.

'Good evening, my lord,' Jenkins answered solemnly.

'Send a bottle of champagne and a plate of sandwiches to my rooms,' Lester ordered as he took the keys Jenkins unhooked from a row behind the reception desk.

'Ham, or cheese and tomato, my lord?'

'Both. Oh, and if my man Radley arrives, tell him I'm not to be disturbed. I'll be going out again later and he can go up to the apartment then.'

'Very good, sir.'

'And how was the opera, Lord Lester?' a female voice addressed him, and Margaret turned to see a beautiful woman coming out of a well-lit room across the hall.

'An excellent performance, Lillian,' he answered lightly, then added, 'May I introduce Miss Helbren? Margaret, this is my long-suffering landlady, Mrs Glynn.'

'How do you do?' Margaret said, impressed by this elegant creature, envying her panache.

'Pleased to meet you, I'm sure,' Lillian answered with a reassuring smile.

'Miss Helbren and I are about to listen to recordings of arias from the opera. I hope this won't inconvenience anyone.'

Is this the young woman he was speaking of the other night? Lillian wondered, curiosity aroused. A shop girl? A maidservant? She doesn't look working-class and could pass as gentry. Even her accent is convincing.

'My dear sir, you know we keep late hours here. Your music won't disturb us, will it, Jenkins?'

'No, madam.'

Margaret was impressed by the size and grandeur of the hotel, gripping the polished handrail topping the wrought-iron banisters as she went upstairs with Lester. Thick carpets, an atmosphere of comfort, not extravagant but conveying an aura of luxury. She was glad she had worn an ivory crêpe de Chine and chiffon gown of simple, flowing design. Lady Julia, toying for a while with the arty fashions favoured by the Aesthetic Movement, had now discarded them. Thus Margaret had obtained a whole new wardrobe when her ladyship returned to more traditional garments.

A pedimented cedarwood door led into Lester's suite. 'It has everything I need,' he explained, hand on the porcelain light switch, the sitting room springing into being. 'This splendid parlour, a bedroom, a guestroom, a bathroom and a room for my valet. What more could a bachelor want?'

'What indeed?' she said with an attempt at nonchalance, as if being alone in a man's apartment was an everyday occurrence.

A tap on the door, and a young footman entered, holding a silver salver on which stood two champagne flutes and a plate wrapped in a napkin. In his other hand he carried an ice bucket in which a bottle was plunged to its neck.

'Thank you, Talbot,' Lester said and dismissed him, adding as the door closed, 'Sit down, my dear. Remove that delicious bit of nonsense you call a hat. "My house is your house", as they say in Spain.'

He took the bottle from the bucket, gripped it between his knees and drew the cork with hardly a pop. Margaret had never before drunk champagne, the bubbles tickling her nose. It was deliciously cool. 'Just like fizzy lemonade,' she pronounced.

He grinned, put down his glass and went over to the gramophone standing on a side-table. He cranked up the mechanism with a handle protruding from its panelled oak case, then selected a record from among several lying on a shelf. Soon she was reliving the music of *La Traviata* by courtesy of the nickel-plated horn.

He refilled her glass and settled down on the deeply cushioned couch beside her, resting his head against the back. He closed his eyes. 'Beautiful, isn't it? Adelena Patti. Such a glorious voice. Italian but born in Madrid, you know.'

114

The singer could have hailed from Timbuctoo for all Margaret cared, wanting nothing but to drown in the sounds. I've reached my goal, she thought in wonderment, the champagne doing its work. I've succeeded. Mother would be proud of me. The wine helped her forget that her mother would not have been proud of her being there alone with a handsome young man.

The music stopped and Lester turned over the record, then returned to her, plate in hand. 'Would you care for a snack?'

She shook her head. 'I don't need food. I could listen to this for hours.'

'So could I, but I'm hungry as a hunter.' He took a bite at a sandwich and smiled at her.

Margaret lost her concentration. His face had sobered, eyes storm-grey and she stared, fascinated, at the tiny scar at the corner of his right eye. The mark was less than half an inch, the result of a scrap perhaps. Lester laid aside the plate, and brought her close to him, holding her round the shoulders.

'I've enjoyed tonight more than I can say. Can I see you tomorrow?'

She shook her head. 'There's a full day ahead, every moment filled by Lady Julia.'

'It's gathering momentum, this presentation business. How tiresome. I, for one, shall be glad when Fenella's "out" and her ball in progress.' Little do you know why, he thought, projecting to that night when he would surely win his wager.

'What will happen after? Will you leave London?' She glanced sadly at him, shrinking from an empty future. This was only their second encounter, but he already dominated her thoughts.

'I haven't any plans.' He touched her lower lip with his thumb, stroking it slowly, thinking she was like a flower ready to open for him as if he was the sun.

Her mouth burned, strange impulses making her want to draw his fingers into the warm wetness, lick them, suck them, feel the texture of his skin with her tongue, taste it. This was the only food she required. She nestled her head into his chest, breathing in the now familiar scent of him. He nuzzled her throat and hair, and her arms stretched round his neck, fingers playing with the curls at his nape.

'Dammit!' he grunted when the jarring hiss of the needle stuck in a groove drew his attention to the gramophone.

Maybe it's a timely interruption, he thought. Jesus, how can I wait till the ball? It would be child's play to take her now. My bed is waiting in the next room.

His groin ached, passion pounding for release. He had deliberately put a curb on his lust, avoiding the whores, determined to let the

115

tension build till he possessed Margaret. He believed she really was a virgin. Untried, innocent, and this roused him to the point of pain, for he was the one who was going to turn her from a girl to a woman through the agency of love and sex.

'But you're not offering her love, are you?' said the voice of his good angel. 'She'll love you, and suffer. Is this what you want?'

'Do you really care, just as long as you spend yourself between her thighs?' put in his evil daemon.

Lester took the record from the turntable and returned it to its brown-paper wrapper. He was half tempted to call the whole thing off. Why was he playing this cruel game? He could easily drive her to Grosvenor Street without more ado and pick up a prostitute on the way home. It would be better that way. All right, so he'd lose five hundred guineas, but if he continued she would pay an incalculable price.

His good angel, sitting on his right shoulder, argued with the bad one on his left. 'Leave her alone,' it said. 'Make some excuse not to see her again.'

'What's the matter? Getting soft?' taunted the bad one. 'Go on! Get her knickers off. She's very bedworthy, and just about asking for it. Think of the money. You'll lose face with Roderick, too.'

The bad angel won. It nearly always did.

Margaret was sitting where he had left her on the couch. He went back to her and said, 'Are you going to let me kiss you?' The onus was now on her.

'I don't think I'd be very good at it.' She was overcome with shyness, rendered gauche and awkward.

'You were wonderful the other day.'

'That was a friendship kiss. I haven't had any experience of the other kind.'

'That's good. I want to be the first.'

He put his hands under her elbows and raised her up, opening his jacket and drawing her inside, feeling her shiver at the contact with his body through his lawn shirt. She held back, afraid of the rush of feeling that weakened her kness and reduced her to jelly.

'We shouldn't. I must go home.' She looked up at him with fear and longing, aware of how tall he was, her brow only just reaching his collar bone.

'Don't be afraid. I won't hurt you.'

He eased her head back and pressed his lips to the smooth white column of her throat. She released her breath in a low moan and trembled as his hand coasted lightly over her breasts then moved up again to support her under the arms.

116

She wanted to cry, 'Don't stop!' Wanted him to unbutton her dress and the fragile chemise and rub his thumbs over her nipples.

I've the instincts of a whore, she thought, aghast. No, that's not right. Susan says whores don't enjoy it, and only do it for the money, poor cows. Then what does this make me? A mad woman filled with unnatural cravings? I must be, for Susan says that respectable women aren't supposed to enjoy caresses, only permitting the intimate act to please their husbands and produce children.

Her lids fluttered opened and she watched him gravely, not wanting to miss a moment. Her whole body was tingling with anticipation. Ecstasy shook her to the marrow as his mouth closed on hers. He moistened her lips with the tip of his tongue, holding her face and tracing the outer edges of her mouth. Her breath escaped in a gasp and she opened her lips under his. They stood, open mouth to open mouth, his left hand at the back of her head, his right arm round her waist holding her to him.

She felt his slippery, fleshy tongue tangling with hers, sweet as honey to the taste, and herself growing warm and liquid and flowing into him, pressing herself close, feeling the bough of his male organ hard and high against her thigh. There was a low, humming vibration in her ears, her need building up to a breathtaking madness. She kissed him back, her tongue with its newly discovered joys moving into and around his mouth, as if it was an extension of his, not separate. She wanted that kiss to never end.

Lester's blood throbbed, her young unspoilt sexuality stopping his breath. It was as if he was experiencing his own first time which had happened – he barely remembered when – years ago now. Dreams long discarded in the harsh reality of life, when he had believed that one expressed one's adoration of the beloved through the body, every touch, each caress a statement of that perfect love. But now all he sought were pleasures of the flesh. He did not want the complication and pain of love, concentrating on the gratification of lust in the most varied ways possible.

He was hard, needful, having difficulty controlling his hands so that he did not alarm her. With an effort, he merely stroked the flushed swell of her cheekbone and stared into her eyes which seemed so much older than her face. But she clung, would not let him go, grinding her breasts into his chest, her hips into his. He knew she did not realise how dangerous it was to open herself to him in this way.

'Kiss me again,' she pleaded, and her hair had fallen down across his arm.

'In a while, sweetheart. I want to look at you.' His voice was harsh with desire, but he was thinking, Roderick, you bastard!

117

Her hands explored his face as if her eyes were sightless, and moved to his hair, fingers buried in the thickness of it. She wanted to familiarise herself with every part of him, to be with him each moment of every day until they were old, old people. To live with him, sleep with him, wake in the morning with him beside her, and give birth to his children, miniature replicas of themselves. Her heart felt as if it would shatter with happiness too great to be borne.

Lester was at the point where he would either have to take her to bed or drive her home. 'Come along, Cinders,' he said quietly. 'It's nearly midnight. Pin your hair up. Get your hat on. We're going.'

'Must we?' She leaned into him, caution fled, willing to stay if he asked her and damn the consequences.

'Yes, we must.' He kissed her again, lightly this time, but still holding her breasts in the cups of his hands as if they were holy objects.

Jenkins was sitting in the leather-hooded porter's chair. He creaked to his feet as they came downstairs. 'Good night, sir. Good night, miss.'

The drive through the warm, scented darkness, the streets quieter now and Margaret leaned with her head on his shoulder, her hand in the bend of his elbow. Why do we ever have to reach the house? she thought. I could go on driving with him through eternity.

The car halted in a patch of darkness beyond a street lamp. He turned in his seat and kissed her, then said, 'Good night, darling.'

Dizzy and light-headed, she asked, 'When shall I see you again?'

'That very much depends on you, or rather your employer. You can leave a message at the hotel. Make it soon.'

'I will, oh, yes – I will.'

Hands clinging, fingertips touching, a final kiss. Then the motor chugged away and Margaret walked on air to the servants' entrance down the basement steps. The usual feeling of annoyance at having to use a different door to the family did not matter tonight. Nothing mattered but that Lester loved her. He had not said so, not in so many words, but Margaret knew. She was sure he was shy, covering up his true feelings. Of course there would be troubles ahead. An alliance such as theirs was bound to cause a scandal, but she was convinced they could weather it together.

She let herself into the quiet kitchen where the range glowed and the pots and pans stood ready for breakfast. The tabby cat seated on the rag-rug, paws folded neatly, glanced at her with slanting golden eyes. The clock over the mantelpiece struck twelve times.

Margaret laughed aloud as she slipped through the door that connected with the backstairs. If she was Cinderella, then surely Lester was Prince Charming? A fairy-tale was about to come true.

Chapter 7

Julia was supremely happy as she took the floor on her husband's arm, opening the ball with a waltz. Never had Henry looked more distinguished, and never had she felt more beautiful, successful and sure of herself. This was the crowning achievement of their lives together. Just for a moment, with everyone nodding and smiling and murmuring congratulations, any troubles that had gone before were of little consequence.

A kaleidoscope of colour swept past her as she whirled to the strains of *The Merry Widow Waltz*. The glorious ballroom with its marble pillars, Wedgwood-blue medallioned ceiling and crystal chandeliers was the acme of perfection. And the couples that now joined their host and hostess on the polished parquet were from among the highest in the land – titled, wealthy, sure of their place in the scheme of things. The lights scintillated on medals, on tiaras, and priceless jewels adorning throats, arms and fingers. Expensive distillations from the perfumeries of France mingled with the pungent odours breathed out by great swathes of carnations, roses, lilies and jasmine delivered from Cornwall.

It seemed only yesterday that Julia had appeared at her own coming-out ball when she had first set eyes on Henry Aubert and fallen irrevocably in love. As they dipped and swayed at their daughter's celebration party, his white-gloved hand pressed lightly below her shoulder blades, the other clasped with hers, so she was remembering how she had chafed under the edict that if one danced twice with the same partner then one was considered 'fast'.

She had wanted to dance every dance with Henry, very cool to any other young man who requested she do him the honour of allowing him to partner her in the polka or cotillion. A love match? On her part, at any rate. She had pestered her parents until they finally gave their consent, though they had had a prince in mind for her.

Banishment to the Continent for six months had not changed her mind. She had mooned about Cannes, and written to Henry every single day. On her return, their betrothal had been announced.

She smiled up into his angular face, seeing the grey sprinkling his dark moustache, the haughty patrician nose and that firm mouth. Still devastatingly handsome, mature, knowledgeable, a sportsman who kept his body in shape. Kind and generous, too, respected by staff and tenants alike. She pressed a little closer, wanting to rest her head against his chest, but this would not have been considered proper even though they were approaching their twenty-second wedding anniversary.

She had been lucky to have married the man she loved, but from the early days had known she was not the only woman to respond to his strong attraction. Henry had enjoyed his fair share of cocottes and, though jealousy had torn her to shreds, she had never reproached him.

As he had once shamefacedly confessed when one of his indiscretions had come to light, 'They are my gardens. I need my beautiful little gardens.'

No gardens tonight. None of those women who fascinated him, people of little standing, sad creatures who had fallen under his spell. She might have found it in her heart to pity them, if that organ had not been calcified by his infidelities. So she despised them instead. They amounted to nothing, insignificant insects. When it came down to rock bottom, Henry was hers. It was she who had given him legitimate children. Even so, she had never forgiven those whose love for him had also borne fruit.

'Doesn't Fenella look enchanting, my dear?' he said, bending close, his breath tickling her ear pleasantly. 'I'm so proud of her, and of you, her lovely mother.'

'Thank you, Henry,' she murmured. 'I only wish Evelyn had half her charm. No matter. She is still young. Plenty of time to change her attitude. All this nonsense about education. What do girls want with university? A year or two in Paris is what she needs.'

It was a glorious night, the stars hanging low in an indigo-velvet sky. The great house had been designed for such occasions early in the previous century by a fashionable rakehell of an Aubert who had often entertained the Prince Regent within its walls, offering His Royal Highness an abundance of food, wine and women. His descendants had kept it in prime condition, their town house where they resided for the Season, their ladies playing hostess, their unmarried daughters paraded at lavish soirées where they were put on display like so much merchandise.

Margaret's feelings were mixed as she stood on an upper gallery and looked down at the scene. Part of her longed to join in, the other part hugged her secret close like a miser brooding over his treasure. She was meeting Lester when the ball was over.

Sixty feet of shining oak floor stripped bare of carpet, lined with banquettes and gilt chairs set at intervals along the walls or in little conversation groups around small circular tables. The dancers drifted, seeming weightless, the pastel shades of the women's gowns delicate as sweetpeas, the black and white uniformity of their partners' evening suits making a pattern of light and darkness.

The visiting débutantes sat with their chaperones, clad in pure white like vestal virgins. If a man wished to dance with one of them, he bowed to the lady in charge and, if she approved, his name was entered on the little pink card the girl wore attached to her wrist. When his turn came, he led her away, returning her punctilliously as soon as the music stopped.

Margaret could see Fenella waltzing with a subaltern in very slim-fitting blue trousers and a scarlet coat ornamented with much gold fogging. His moustache was waxed into sharp points, and she was laughing up into his face with an expression of almost drooling admiration which would get her far with the opposite sex.

All day Margaret had witnessed her being the centre of attention: the presentation, followed by the hectic preparations for the ball. Fenella still wore white, but no longer of childish cut. This gown was taffeta, tiny-waisted, the skirt flaring out, the neckline low and garlanded with pale pink roses. The frilled hem brushed the floor, its short train hooked up by a tiny loop attached to her little finger when dancing. She wore kid gloves to above the elbow, and her hair was swept up into a twist topped by a diamond-studded band. Her every ambition had been fulfilled save one: that of receiving a proposal of marriage, but it certainly looked as if she would not have to wait long for that.

'I wish I was old,' whispered Jane, small face earnest as she gripped the gallery rail, nose wedged between the gingerbread scrollwork as she stared at her envied older sister. 'I want to wear a dress like that and dance with a soldier.'

'You will, deary. You'll be the belle of the ball one day,' Thora promised, one hand resting on the child's shoulder, the other clasping William's fingers. Both were in their nightclothes, having been permitted to slip down from the nursery to witness the revels.

'Which is more than can ever be said for us,' Margaret remarked.

'Ah well, that's the way of the world.' Thora shrugged and picked up William, setting him astride her hip. 'Can you see, lovey? Later on

121

Nanny'll sneak up some of the fancy food, shall she? Would you like that?'

'Good job Harry isn't here.' Margaret rested her elbows on the rail and leaned over. She had just caught sight of Lester coming out of the card room with Roderick and walking towards a gaggle of simpering maidens who were glancing at them over the edges of their fans.

'Her ladyship knows her business, and dispatched that trouble-maker to stay with Lady Rossiter and her boys. He can run around to his heart's content at their place down in Devon.' Thora prepared to take the children upstairs. It was long past their bedtime. She followed the direction of Margaret's fixed stare, eyebrows lifting.

'Are you coming? I'll brew some tea, if you like. It's going to be a long night for you. I shouldn't think Lady Julia will be ready to retire before two.'

Margaret dragged her eyes away from Lester. She smiled faintly at Thora. 'I've been told to stay on duty. She'll send a footman if she wants me to fetch anything for her.'

'Right, but don't forget, I'll be there if you need me. Too much noise going on to settle. These big parties always upset routine. The staff have been on the go since six this morning and they won't see their beds much before dawn, not by the time everything is cleared up. Come along, children!' And with a final uneasy glance at Margaret, Thora swept her charges away.

Margaret, half hidden behind a pillar, watched the gaiety below, hearing laughter, the high voices of the ladies counterpointed by the deeper tones of the gentlemen and the music of the orchestra on a dais at one end of the ballroom. Beyond, framed by an arch, was an ante-room where supper had been laid out. To the right of this was the drawing room and an enormous conservatory with a carp pond, a fountain and hundreds of exotic plants.

At one time she might have been consumed with jealousy of the damsels in their modish gowns, but not any more. She could watch Lester dancing with this one or that and feel nothing but compassion for the girls. None of them stood a chance with him. She might be wearing a plain dress and no ornaments, but it was she whom he wanted. She who had been with him the night before in his rooms at the Warwick Hotel and on other nights, too, listening to music, drinking champagne and exchanging passionate kisses and caresses.

Just to think of this made her breasts tingle and a coil tighten in her womb. But we've done nothing wrong, she thought. He's never stepped over the bounds of decency. He wouldn't. He's said so. It's me who urges him to go further and who wants to take the ultimate step which will make me his.

I know he'll not let me down. I trust him. We love each other so much that I'm sure he's about to suggest he take me to Ireland and introduce me to his family. They won't know I'm a servant. We can make up some story. Ireland is miles away over the sea – almost a foreign country.

The young ladies in the ballroom might fancy their chances, but she would be in his arms when it was over. They had arranged it, Lester saying as he held her close when they parted last night, 'I'll wait for you at our usual spot.'

'It may be very late,' she had warned, feeling his fingers playing up and down her spine through the thin material of her blouse.

'That doesn't matter. I'll be in the car.'

The anticipation was acute. Maybe tonight they would become one. Maybe he'd suggest they elope. Lester was capable of anything. Now and again, in the midst of the heady excitement of being in love, the cool voice of reason struggled to be heard. Had she not sworn that no man should divert her from her determination to become an independent woman? What of the advice of Susan who had warned her never to yield to a man above her station?

The rules don't apply to Lester and me, she argued with herself. The famous star-crossed lovers of history never listened to reason, did they? Romeo and Juliet for example. Did they stop loving one another because their families opposed them? No, indeed. They were willing to die.

The mundane intruded into her romantic revery. Lady Julia ordered her to fetch a fresh handkerchief. She took it down to the conservatory where her mistress rested between dancing. Lester and Roderick were seated beside her on a green cast-iron Coalbrookdale rustic bench. Neither stood when Margaret appeared. Lester did not even look in her direction. Just for a second, her spirit plummeted, the difference in status yawning like a chasm.

She was dismissed and returned disconsolately to the gallery, but was eager to make excuses for him. Of course he couldn't acknowledge her. No doubt he longed to sweep her into the dance, but was unable to as yet. In a year's time, perhaps less, she would take her rightful place at his side, but for the moment this was their precious secret.

Supper was served, followed by more dancing. The débutantes were escorted home at midnight, but older friends and guests who were staying at the house lingered to drink more champagne or disperse to the card tables. Couples who had plighted their troth after last year's presentations wandered into the moonlit garden, chaperones following at a discreet distance.

'Lord, love us! Ain't they ever going to bed?' Susan complained,

123

passing Margaret on the backstairs, a tray of glasses in her hands. 'My feet are killing me! You off duty, then?'

Margaret shook her head. 'Not till her ladyship says so. I may be lucky if Lord Henry wants to be alone with her. Then I'll get my marching orders.'

'Quite likely, I should say,' Susan opined sagely. 'He ain't been hitting the plonk too hard, so I guess he'll want his oats. Disgusting at his age, but there you are. That's men for you.'

'Not all men,' Margaret ventured, standing on the stair above her and looking down into her face.

'Oh? You an expert on men all of a sudden? What you been up to, eh?' Susan shot her a sharp glance.

Margaret permitted herself an enigmatic smile and did not answer. She wanted to confide in Susan, but did not quite dare. She could just imagine what she would say – things she wouldn't want to hear.

Unable to worm more out of her, Susan whisked away, and Margaret went to her room to make certain everything was ready for her escape. She would give herself a few moments to change out of her working clothes, then leave the house and hurry to where Lester would be waiting to embrace her.

Around a quarter past two a stirring below told her Lady Julia was on her way. Hearty good nights were being exchanged on stairways and in corridors. Margaret took up her position near the dressing table, hairbrush in hand, ready to administer the one hundred strokes necessary to keep her ladyship's locks in mint condition. The boudoir door opened and closed.

'Helbren, you can go now,' Julia said as she wandered into the bedroom, dropping her fan and beaded bag on to a chair and beginning to let down her hair. Her face was flushed and her eyes sparkled. 'I shan't want to be wakened till noon. Order a tray to be brought up then.'

'Yes, my lady. Good night.' Margaret dipped a curtsy, standing back so that Lord Henry could pass through the door. 'Good night, my lord.'

He gave her a smiling, quizzical look, in high good humour, and she was struck by his similarity to Roderick. Not in colouring, but in posture and build. Aristocrats to the bone – and so was Lester.

There was still a good deal of activity downstairs and Margaret had to wait her chance to leave unobserved. Mr Wakefield and Mrs Colby, tired and irritable, harassed the weary maids and footmen. Tables had to be cleared, china and glassware washed and put away, silver returned to the butler's pantry, spare food distributed among the staff or placed in Mrs Frith's larder, flowers removed or freshened, chairs stacked and floors polished, the Turkey carpets unrolled across the ballroom floor. Maids were lifting the damask tablecloths, shaking them free of crumbs in the garden and folding them into laundry baskets along with soiled serviettes.

The terraces were swept, the conservatory mopped, ashtrays emptied in the smoking room, green topped card tables brushed. Then the breakfast room was prepared for the first meal of the day. With any luck, the staff might snatch a couple of hours' sleep before daybreak when the chores began all over again.

Margaret stepped out into the dewy freshness, a hush holding London in thrall. Her feet made little sound on the pavement as she hurried round the corner, her heart leaping as she saw the bulky outline of Lester's car.

'You're early,' he whispered against her lips.

'Lord Henry is sleeping with her ladyship.'

She slid across the leather seat beside him, her daily existence fading like a mirage. This was reality. Now she was herself, dressed in silk, fragrant with attar of roses from a perfume spray Lady Julia had thrown away. And her lover was with her, sweetly attentive, one hand on the steering wheel, the other touching hers. They passed Hyde Park, thick-dark and sinister, but instead of taking the road towards the hotel, Lester turned the car in another direction.

'Where are we going?' Margaret asked eagerly, sitting up and adjusting her feathered headband.

Lester was full of surprises. He might take her to an all-night coffee stall in Soho, to the Embankment to watch the twin rows of lamps reflected in the dark, swift-flowing Thames, the faint night mist picked out with pin stars of light, or pause outside the bulky fortress guarding the city, the Tower of London with its grey walls and bastions and perhaps a tiny square of gold high up in a turret.

'I want you to meet some friends of mine,' he said levelly, eyes on the road. 'They have a house in Chelsea.'

Margaret was too overwhelmed to question further. This confirmed her hopes. He wanted to introduce her to his friends. Therefore this meant that he was not in the least ashamed of their association. Confidence tingled through her to the tips of her toes. Her destiny was being fulfilled. It was as if the car moved not over tarmac but through the sky, a chariot bearing her onwards towards a brilliant future.

She did not recognise this part of town – a place of wide streets where some of the large houses were divided into maisonettes, and eventually Lester braked, handed her out and escorted her towards one of them. They entered a porch and from there a spacious, mosaic-tiled hall. She followed him down a short passage to another door. He produced a key, opened it and ushered her inside.

A sweet smell pervaded the air. He switched on a light. They were in a lobby, the walls pattered in dark red-flocked wallpaper studded with fleur-de-lis. Lester stood looking round, expressing puzzlement, then called out. 'Hello! Is anyone there? Have you gone to bed?'

Margaret traced the source of the smell which reminded her of church. Incense smouldered in a brass chafing dish, tendrils of bluish smoke weaving towards the ceiling decorated with frescoes of vine leaves and bunches of purple gapes. It was as if she had stepped into a story from *The Arabian Night's Entertainment*, the decor a curious mixture of medieval and oriental; drapes and damascene brasswear, divans heaped with tapestry cushions, Persian rugs in jewel hues on walls and floors, wrought-iron *objets d'art*, drawings, carvings, paintings and pots.

Lester, frowning, searched the rooms leading from it, returning to say, as he ran a hand through his hair, 'Dammit, they're out. They promised to be back. I suppose they've been delayed. Artists, you know, hopeless timekeepers. They get interested in something – a new piece of sculpture in somebody's studio, a poetry reading, or simply talking endlessly over a bottle of wine.' He paused in front of her and took her hands in his. 'I'm terribly sorry, Margaret.'

'Don't worry,' she reassured him hastily. 'It doesn't matter. We're together, that's what counts.'

'Bless you. You're so understanding.' He drew her towards him and she went into his arms, clasping him tightly round the waist. 'I could look in the kitchen. See if they've anything to drink, or maybe you'd like some coffee?'

'There's no need. I just want to be with you.' She felt exhausted suddenly. It had been a hard day. She loosened her cloak and sat down on a couch by the empty fireplace.

Lester found some brandy and poured two glasses. He came to her quickly and knelt on the rug at her feet, turning her hand palm-upwards and placing kisses there, running his lips from her wrist to the inside of her elbow. He let her go and handed her a glass. They drank in silence, then he looked up at her, the dim, pinkish light planing his cheekbones and the deep hollows of his eyes, throwing the lashes into relief.

'There's something I want to ask you?'

'Yes?' Whatever it was, Margaret was willing to give it to him, sipping the brandy out of politeness, wanting only to be held again.

'I shall be visiting Ireland soon.'

'Yes?' she repeated, a catch in her breath. Was this the invitation she

126

had dreamed about? Somehow her glass was empty and he had refilled it.

He cradled his head in her lap, rubbing his cheek against the dark green silk covering her knee, and his hand slipped down to fondle her ankle, tracing the bar of her satin shoe, the smoothness of her stockings. The brandy was making her giddy. She struggled not to build her hopes too high, but it was impossible.

'Would you come with me?'

She could not believe he had spoken these words. 'To Ireland?' she echoed.

'To my home. I'd like you to see it.'

'But I couldn't do that – not unless—' She stopped then tried again. 'Should I be travelling as a servant or guest?'

'Supposing I said – as my fiancée?'

'Are you serious?' She leaned down to him, her dark hair falling towards his face, her life hingeing on his reply.

He fought down the thrust of desire, breathing hard, forcing himself to drink slowly. He answered her question with another. 'Would I lie to my dearest friend?'

Margaret closed her eyes. It had come, the moment for which she had been praying. She said the first thing that came into her mind. 'I'll have to leave service.'

'Of course, but not yet, darling. Just for a while we'll keep our secret. This makes it all the more special.'

She felt the sudden chill as he moved, and opened her eyes. He was standing there, looking down into her face intently. More handsome than ever. Her man. Soon to be her husband. She saw the cleft in his chin, the swarthy skin, the little scar, the long black hair and that hungry, hungry mouth.

He held out his hand and raised her up. 'We have the apartment to ourselves. Let me show you the rest of it.' It was as if he was daring her to embark on a great adventure.

Dim lighting, exotic sights and odours. Another room – a bedchamber like an Arab tent – draped in silk, in embroideries, in woven rugs. A vast divan, wider and longer than any bed she had ever seen. Its headboard was inlaid with mother-of-pearl, its coverlet of matched jaguar pelts. She saw the sudden shock of her own face reflected in a mirror hung between the draperies nearby. I'm dreaming, she thought. I'll wake up in my room in Grosvenor Street, or maybe even in Hazel Cottage, finding that the last two years have been a fantasy.

Lester took off his jacket, threw it down and turned to her. His fingers brushed the tendrils of hair from her forehead softly. His lips followed his touch, closing her eyelids with little tender kisses, hands caressing her expertly, her arms, her shoulders, her back. Desire quivered along her nerves and penetrated her brain, robbing her of coherent thought.

'I want you,' she moaned against his lips.

'I know. And I want you.' He unbuttoned the fastening of her bodice and slipped a hand inside, fingers working their way past the barrier of her lawn chemise and touching her breasts. Pleasure shot through her. There was a looseness in her limbs, and she relaxed, sighing, falling against him as if sinking into warm, dark water.

The bed was at her back, and he eased her on to it, kissing her throat, her exposed breasts. 'Take off your clothes,' he begged, and there was an irresistible note of urgency and need in his voice. 'I want to see you naked.'

No one had seen her naked since she was a child. Not even her mother. Slowly she undressed, the brandy fumes making her head spin. Everything came off, gown, petticoat, and lace-trimmed drawers. She leaned over to unbutton her shoes, slip off her garters and peel down her stockings.

'No. Leave them,' he commanded and he was like a stranger, his eyes burning with a gemlike flame, the line of his lips taut.

She paused, questioning, a shadow darkening her happiness. Lester looked at her without speaking, then he smiled and the tension passed. 'You have such lovely legs,' he explained. 'I enjoy the feel of silk covering them.'

I must learn the ways of men, she thought. I'm so ignorant. She lay there motionless and exposed, yet excited by doing something she knew was absolutely forbidden between a couple who were not man and wife. It was as if she could see Aunt Mercy and Aunt Prudence and hear their strident voices shouting, 'Hussy!'

But I'm not a hussy, she protested inwardly, I'm in love and he is to be my husband. There's no sin in anticipating this, is there?

Lester stripped rapidly in the subdued light and she watched him, fascinated, but at the same time terrified, recalling old wives' tale about what men actually did to women, horrific stories of pain and bleeding and injury. Without his clothing he looked alien, hairy, large and powerful, very male. Where was the gentle friend who had taught her about music and woven magic tales of the Irish leprechauns? He moved closer and excitement and fear were making her feel sick. But the die was cast. She looked into his eyes and realised there was no retreat.

Then there was more than mere looking, hands smoothing her silk-covered calves, muscular arms holding her, chest hair brushing her breasts, long, strong legs winding round hers, a knee insinuated between her thighs, and that large stiff phallus pressing against her belly.

Shyness swamped her. 'Turn out the lamp,' she whispered.

'I want to watch you,' he growled. 'Don't struggle. It will only hurt for a moment, I promise.'

A fiery current ran beneath her skin, a knowledge passed down through the race memory of women. This was not strange to her, instinct overcoming reluctance and the astonishment of remembering how men were really made. She wanted more kisses, more melting caresses, but Lester was impatient now, spreading her legs, rearing above her, pushing against the barrier of membrane sealing her secret self. She cried out, her love for him making her cling to his shoulders, wanting to unite her flesh with his, waiting for that supreme moment when she would be carried into the realms of bliss.

He was like an athlete straining over the last hurdle, breath laboured, sweat pouring from him, head back, his face contorted. The hymen ruptured, he achieved his goal, his movements furious, plunging and ploughing. Margaret sobbed, raised her hips to meet that invasion, pain superseded by the beginning of pleasure. She felt his struggles, heard him groan before collapsing on her, his weight pressing her into the feather mattress.

'You're disappointed,' he panted. 'It's not unusual, the first time. I'll teach you about your body's needs. Don't worry. We'll do it again in a while. You'll enjoy it, I promise you.'

He cuddled her, smiling vaguely, eyes closed. She was aware of anti-climax. Her loins burned with an unsatisfied ache, and her insides smarted. But it was not long before he roused, eager to guide her along the pathways of passion, using his tongue and fingers to bring her to a thunderous conclusion.

In the aftermath she lay there adoring him. She would have died for him if need be, and waited breathlessly for him to say those words of love she longed to hear. They did not come. He merely smiled, then dropped a light kiss on the tip of her nose, got out of bed and started to dress.

She stretched luxuriantly, arms wide, no longer embarrassed by her nakedness. 'Where are you going?'

'I must return you to Lady Julia.'

'When can I see you again?' She sat up, wild-haired and wild-eyed. In spite of their agreement to hide their love, she had been half hoping he would throw caution to the winds and keep her with him.

'Soon. Come to the hotel.'

'But your friends?'

He glanced at her as he shrugged his shoulders into his waistcoat. 'Which ones?'

'The people who live here. The artists. You said you wanted them to meet me.'

'Oh, yes, so I did. I'll arrange it for another time.'

She gathered up her clothes, catching sight of herself in the mirror. Surely, she must look different after what had just taken place? She stood there nude, cupping her breasts in her hands, examining her face, expecting to see a rosy glow. It was said that one could tell when a woman was pregnant by the light in her eyes, the bloom on her skin. So why shouldn't the same thing happen when a girl had made love with the man she adored, had felt him penetrate her intimate places and bring her to the peak of pleasure?

When she was dressed, she paused at the door of the bedchamber, looking round for a final time. It was here that she had lost her virginity. Now she was a woman, with a woman's responsibilites, foremost of which was care of her man and the children with which they might be blessed. Not yet, but in the fullness of time.

In the room on the other side of the two-way mirror, Roderick slumped in a chair, having just experienced the most acute sexual enjoyment he had ever known. The mating couple had provided a stimulating show, Lester hung like a stallion, filled with enviable vigour, and Margaret the epitome of half-frightened but eager-to-learn virginity.

Supine and relaxed, still stroking his now flaccid member, he watched her dressing, every aspect of her beautiful body revealed to his lusting gaze. A wide smile spread over his face. Little did she guess that she had been pleasuring two men at the same time.

Five hundreds guineas was a small price to pay for such a thrill.

Lillian gave Talbot a smacking kiss on the cheek and dismissed him from her bed. 'Off you go, Joe. The dining room will be open in half an hour. Mr Grist will tell you off if you're late on parade.'

'He's only the head waiter. You're in charge,' he grumbled, swinging his legs over the side of the mattress and reaching for his trousers.

'I know, but it doesn't do to upset the staff. Now get going. I've a hotel to run.'

She rested among the plump pillows and smiled at him indulgently, a voluptuary who knew precisely what she wanted and how to get it. No man visited her bed twice if he did not satisfy her. Joe, inexperienced and fumbling at the start had quickly learned what to do. She had been patient with him. Not only was he personable, well endowed and a prime physical specimen but had a lost, boyish look which appealed to the mother in her.

'You can come back later,' she announced, and eased her magnificent shoulders into a black silk pegnoir.

'Yes, ma'am,' Joe said, standing in his braces and shirtsleeves. His hair stood up in spikes, making him look about twelve.

He could hardly believe his good fortune. Not only had he landed himself a job with a future, but the boss wanted him to bed her. What a woman! Beautiful, generous, introducing him to erotic delights he had never dreamed existed. She was fascinating, barbaric, almost pagan in her demands, and he had already felt the edge of her trenchant tongue. No one took advantage of Mrs Lillian Glynn. Joe had quickly discovered there were certain limits beyond which he dare not venture. Whereas a more fly character would have tried it on, Joe was a simple lad who was fast developing a doglike devotion to his dominating mistress.

'Send Biddy to me,' Lillian ordered, pouring herself a stiff gin and drawing on a cigarette. 'Time to prepare for the fray.'

'Many in tonight?' Joe was wondering about tips. Most of Lillian's customers were open-handed and he wanted to buy her a present. He sat on the bed to lace up his shoes.

'A fair few. Some of my favourites, so that's all right.'

'Other men you fancy?' Joe knew this to be unwise but could not stop, a hot lump of jealousy lodged in the region of his chest.

Lillian glanced at him in the mirror, busy pinning up her thick hair. Beneath the negligé, Joe could see the fancy red satin stays that drove him demented. Trimmed with black lace, they squeezed her figure into an hourglass shape, pushing her opulent breasts so high they almost spilled over the top. Long black and gilt suspenders stretched down over her thighs, attached to stockings so dark they resembled greyish mist. Joe could feel himself hardening again.

'Other men? That would be telling,' Lillian teased, noting the discomfort she was putting him through. It was flattering in the extreme to rouse a young man to a frenzy of almost uncontrollable lust. She relented, beckoning him over and caressing his chest through the gap in his shirt. 'Don't worry, love,' she murmured. 'I could have had them if I'd wanted, but I chose you, didn't I?'

With that impetuosity and need which she found so stimulating, he snatched her up against him and covered her mouth with his. She responded with an ardour of her own, then broke away to say, 'Not now, darling. It's time we were both getting ready to face the public.'

When he had gone she attended to her make-up for the second time that day. Having a lover was all very well, but it was time-consuming. Yet she could not resist sending for him in the afternoons, at that hour when she usually rested. Her maid limped in and, 'Wipe that disapproving look off your face, Biddy,' Lillian said sharply. Biddy fussed over her like a mother hen, jealous of her position as confidant.

'He's nothing but a boy.' Grumbling, she shook out the crimson gown and spread it over the bed, adding two underskirts in moiré silk, fluffy and flared and frilly, which, like the dress, were cut plain and tight-fitting round the hips with an immense amount of frou-frou from the knees down.

'So? And what has that to do with anything?' Lillian's arched brows drew together, eyes flashing warningly. Biddy was voicing her own deep-seated doubts and it was annoying.

'It's not dignified in a woman of your age.' The maid expressed her concern by giving an extra shake to the garments.

'Stuff that! Just keep your long nose out of my business. Lace me up and stop your jaw!'

Lillian clung to the bedpost while Biddy heaved at the back-lacing. Though fashion decreed large hips and bosom, it also demanded a distinctly diminutive waist. The American artist, Dana Gibson, had set the pose and this had spread to England. Everyone wanted to copy the Gibson Girl look, the chest carried forward, the shoulders down, the waist long in front and short behind.

'Phew!' Lillian's breath came out in a rush as Biddy gave an extra hard tug.

She stepped into her lace-trimmed knickers and stood relatively still while the petticoats were adjusted, followed by the gown. When her toilette was completed, her hair piled into fat, sausage-shaped curls kept in place with combs and velvet bows, Lillian admired her image in the pier glass while Biddy added a final spray of perfume.

'What d'you mean by "a woman of my age?"' she demanded, flicking open a painted fan with ivory sticks and prinking at herself over the edge, making big, alluring eyes.

'Nothing, deary.' Biddy, having had her say, was prepared to let her off lightly. 'That Talbot's a lucky chap.'

'He is. I agree. I'm too good for any man.' And Lillian swept to the door in a swish of skirts and a cloud of *Jicki*.

The dining room was full by the time she arrived and she stood in the doorway for an instant, making her entrance as if she was still treading the boards at the theatre. A chorus of male voices greeted her, and she smiled graciously as she made her way between the tables.

It had once been a salon, richly ornamented with plaster swagging, arches surmounted by gilded Cupids, and a ceiling with painted panels depicting the gods on Mount Olympus. A pink-veined fireplace stood at one end, but the Warwick had been modernised, central heating installed. A telephone hung on the wall by the reception desk and could be used by arrangement. Such an establishment suited raffish gentlemen down to the ground, though Lillian did not permit prostitutes to hire rooms. Any flashy tarts who appeared at the front door wanting accommodation were turned away smartly by the watchful Jenkins. But it was a different matter if a resident wished to entertain a female in his suite – but quietly, no rowdy parties were permitted.

Lillian spotted Lester at once, and saw he was accompanied by Miss Margaret Helbren, his frequent guest of late. Try as she might, she had been unable to find out anything about her. He was being annoyingly vague, and she had fared no better with Roderick who simply looked smug when she broached the subject.

The girl had a vulnerable air and the way in which she followed Lester with adoring eyes boded ill. Lillian knew him of old, long before he went abroad with Roderick. Her role as hotel proprietress enabled her to keep a finger on the pulse of upper-class activities. Gentlemen confided in her when in their cups and she tapped into the very efficient grapevine that was existent among the servants, too.

Thus she had heard how Lester had taken the social scene by storm when he left university, a most sought-after spare man for country house parties, able to dance, appreciate music and get a difficult horse across country. Several married ladies had fallen for him, and it was rumoured that those distinctive grey eyes had turned up in a couple of nurseries where they did not rightly belong. This, along with gambling debts and other inconveniences, had necessitated his retirement to Europe for a year.

Since his return he had kept a low profile, and his name had not been romantically linked with anyone important. Lillian sauntered over to his table. The men rose, she seated herself and they resumed their chairs. They had already dined and Lester ordered another bottle of wine.

'Good health,' Lillian said, toasting him over the rim of her glass. She nodded to Margaret. 'And to you, my dear. You're becoming quite a regular visitor.'

'She enjoys the food,' put in Roderick, grinning across at Lester. 'Ain't that so?'

Lillian, watching them, did not like what she saw. There was something definitely shady going on. 'I'll tell Chef. He may even invent a

133

new dish and name it after you,' she answered coolly, slanting a smile at Margaret. 'Have you been in London long, Miss Helbren?'

She was giving her a lead, though it was her rule never to probe into the affairs of her guests. The Warwick was noted for its discretion. Her benefactor had been a retired butler who understood the ways and tastes of the wealthy. He had bought this splendid eighteenth-century house, engaged a French cook, and set about providing for a select clientele.

Lillian had met him backstage and they had formed a firm friendship. An elderly bachelor, she had satisfied his need to be punished in order to attain sexual completion. In return, he had taught her about the hotel business and named her as his heir. She had been sad when he died, and honoured his memory.

Margaret raised her eyes to meet Lillian's, more confident now that she was Lester's mistress. It gave her a position of sorts. 'I've been here some time, Mrs Glynn, though my birthplace is Cornwall.'

'I've never visited there, but I hear the coastline is spectacular,' Lillian said, wanting to ask more but Margaret retreated into her shell, so she changed the subject, addressing Lester, 'Will you be going to Henley this year?'

'Wouldn't miss it for anything,' he replied, a waiter leaping forward to hold a match to his cigar. 'Though I'm expected in Ireland,' and he smiled at Margaret, the expression on his face beautifully lit and shadowed by the table lamp with its apricot silk shade.

She smiled back, radiating happiness. These people did not know she would be going with him – no one knew. The dining room hummed with talk, gentlemen eating, drinking, chatting with friends: some had ladies with them, not their wives, she presumed. Yet it was as if she and Lester were already on the deck of the ferry, salt spray in their faces, his arms round her as they crossed the Irish Sea. Only he stood out with diamond brightness, Lester, her lover and mentor on whom she relied. He was her lodestar, her *raison d'être*.

Then her attention sharpened as a man paused at their table. 'Hello, Lester. Good evening, Roderick – and Mrs Glynn,' he said.

'Peter Newark, by all that's holy! How are you?' Lester stood up, seized him by the hand and shook it vigorously. 'Where the deuce have you been hiding yourself?'

'In Rio, then Mexico and finally New York. Got into London this morning.'

'Sit down and tell all.'

Margaret remembered him instantly, though he had matured, chestnut-bearded, tanned and strikingly handsome. His eyes lit up as they met hers, but before he could speak again Lester introduced her.

'Miss Helbren, my sometime companion.'

Peter shot him a hard stare, then switched his eyes back to her. They were like sapphires, clear and penetrating. 'How d'you do, Miss Helbren?' he said steadily, then added, 'Haven't we met before?'

'In the Great Hall of Roslan Manor. It was on Christmas Eve.' She was fearfully embarrassed but struggled to brazen it out. What must he think of her? Lester's cavalier introduction had cut her to the quick. Casual companion? Is that all she was?

Peter was surprised and angered, disappointed, too, but covered it well, adept at hiding his feelings. Through all his adventures, amatory and otherwise, and there had been several, he had never forgotten her. Some nights, for no apparent reason, he had seen her eyes against a tropical sky dusted with stars and wondered about her. Was she well? Was she married? Above all – just *who* was she?

'I remember,' he said quietly. 'Little Jane was with you. Not so little now, I suppose.'

'Have either of you gentlemen a cigarette?' Lillian interrupted, sensitive to disturbing ripples in the air. Each leaned forward with a flourish of gold cases. She accepted one from Peter, her fingers afire with jewelled rings. 'It's good to have you back. Are you staying in England long?' she said.

To her way of thinking, he would be a far better suitor for Margaret than Lester. In the past he had sometimes taken rooms at the Warwick, and was doing so again. Lillian liked him. He had not forgotten her during his absence, and an array of postcards from faraway places were propped on the mantelpiece in her parlour. He was forthright in speech and had a down-to-earth manner, yet retained refinement and sensitivity. A cool, steady man who, to Lillian's knowledge, never lost his temper, never broke his word or did a mean hand's turn.

'I've no definite plans, as yet.' He treated her with as much respect as if she was a titled lady.

'What were you doing in America?' Roderick asked, snapping his fingers at Joe who was passing, tray balanced aloft. 'Fetch me a whisky and soda. D'you want one, Peter?'

'No, thanks. I was seeing the lay of the land,' he answered crisply. 'I've business contacts there.'

'Commerce, d'you mean? Why are you bothering with that? It's no occupation for a gentleman. Doesn't your Papa give you a big enough allowance?'

'Strange as it may seem, I rather like working.'

'Good God! The man's mad! Who'd want to toil when there are so many jollier ways of passing the time?' Roderick was drunk and spoiling for an argument.

'Some of us have no choice,' Lillian observed, looking across at Margaret who had grown quiet.

Lillian wondered if she was a working girl. Her hands, though soft-skinned, did not have that delicate, useless look of ladies of leisure. They were practical hands, like Lillian's own.

'I've American relatives,' Roderick said, squinting at Peter through half-closed lids. 'We're off to the South of France soon to meet up with 'em. They're on a Grand Tour or somesuch rubbish. Are you coming, Lester? Mater would like that. Seems she's taken quite a shine to you.'

'I'll think about it,' Lester replied slowly, leaning back in his chair, legs stretched out under the table, his foot brushing against Margaret's.

'Oh, do come! It'll be a tremendous caper. Remember what a good time we had in *La Belle France?* And my American cousins sound sports, by all accounts.'

'When are you going?'

'After Henley. Can't possibly miss that, can we?'

'You're on. But you'll have to foot the bill. I'm pushed for cash.'

'Oh? I thought you'd come into money lately.' Roderick formed his hands into the shape of eyeglasses, leaned his elbows on the table and studied him through them. 'Didn't I hear you'd won a wager to the tune of five hundred guineas?'

'Did you? I wonder who started that rumour?' Lester responded calmly.

'I thought you were going to Ireland,' Margaret burst out, unable to hide her alarm. If they went to France, she would have to travel with Lady Julia. How could she bear to see Lester, day after day, without betraying herself?

He gave her a cool smile. 'I can do that later in the year. This is too good a chance to miss. Don't you agree?'

Lillian saw the tightening of Margaret's lips and the pain in her eyes as if she had received an unexpected wound and the blood was welling. What was going on between them? And what part was that young rakehell, Roderick, playing in it?

Time to send out the scouts, she decided and certainly time to call in a few favours.

Peter, too, was aware of warning bells. When Margaret slipped away to the ladies room, he made an excuse about being tired from the journey, said goodnight and followed, catching her in the passage. She started, the colour mounting to her cheeks. The corridor was deserted, but she did not fear him; her feelng was one of shame. For some

136

inexplicable reason she wanted to look well in his eyes, and cursed herself for her foolishness. This man meant nothing to her, his good opinion even less.

'Mr Newark?' she looked at him questioningly, eyebrows raised.

'Miss Helbren.' He did not move aside, merely remaining where he was, looking down at her in a considering way.

He could smell her perfume, and the faint honeysuckle fragrance of her hair, and saw the soft curves of her face, and those large, beautiful violet eyes. His heart contracted within him, and he longed to hold her, not entirely in desire, more to shield her from harm.

'What is it you want?' She was nervously certain that he required something from her.

'Nothing. I'm here to give you a friendly warning, that's all.'

'A warning?' she repeated, her heart fluttering like a caged bird under her silk bodice.

'Yes. Be careful of Lester and Roderick. They're not exactly trustworthy.'

'That's an awful thing to say. I thought they were friends of yours.' She found it easier to whip up anger than listen to his words which found an echo somewhere deep inside her.

'Acquaintances, not friends. I can count my real friends on the fingers of one hand.' His penetrating gaze bored into her and the stillness of him was unnerving. Margaret had the urge to tell him everything, as if he was her confessor.

'I don't think this is anything to do with you,' she said stiffly. 'And suggest you mind your own business.'

He gave a lopsided smile, arms folded across his chest as he lounged against the wall. 'You're right, but I find it hard to stand by and watch a cad take advantage of you.'

'How dare you?' she hissed. 'Who says he's doing that? You don't know anything about it.'

'I know something about him,' he pointed out, ice cool. 'We were at Oxford together. Lester has always been selfish, and is a noted philanderer.'

'You're wrong, Mr Newark. One day soon you'll see just how wrong.' She was close to him, ready to push past, but his hand on her arm restrained her.

'I'd hate to see you come a cropper. Be careful, Miss Helbren.'

'Oh, I will, sir, I can assure you of that. Careful of men like you who betray friendships. Lester is a fine, honourable man and I'm proud to know him.'

Just for a moment they stood there, eyes locked, and she read something in his that astonished her. Concern? Admiration? It was

137

impossible to tell. Then she dragged her arm free and rushed away without a backward glance.

Peter sighed and shook his head, then walked slowly through the hall and mounted the stairs to his room. He was certain of one thing: there was no way he was going to stand by and watch Lester ruin her life.

Book Two

Wheel of Fortune

Chapter 8

It's strange how much smaller everything has become since I was last here, Margaret mused, as the car rattled along the cobbled main street of Porthross.

In reality, nothing had changed. There was the same briny smell spicing the air, the same sparkle on the water lapping the quay, the same hot sunshine. Yet it seemed to have shrunk, closed in, only the horseshoe-shaped harbour retaining its grand sweep. Luke drew the vehicle to a standstill outside a terrace house.

'This it?' he asked, cocking an eye at her.

'Thanks. I'd better get it over with,' she answered, pulling a face. 'You're lucky not to have any relatives.'

He grinned and patted her shoulder. 'Good luck.'

Already lace curtains were twitching at windows up and down the row, the Marchand causing a ripple of interest. Children skipping on the paving slabs abandoned their game and began to gather as Margaret lifted her skirt in one hand and stepped out.

'This your car, missus?' they shouted, hopping about like monkeys in their hobnailed boots. Luke shuddered as small sticky fingers left imprints on the shiny varnish.

The children were shabby but adequately dressed, the boys in knickerbockers and jumpers, the girls in cotton frocks and grubby pinafores. They had round, brown faces and bright eyes. These were not from cots where the standard of living was low. Their fathers were men with steady jobs, like Aunt Prudence's husband, the mine foreman.

Margaret opened her reticule and distributed sweets from a paper bag. They grabbed them eagerly, though one impudent lad piped up at Luke, 'Got a spare Woodbine, mister?'

'No, I haven't! And you shouldn't be smoking,' Luke said sternly, still seated at the wheel. But there was a twinkle in his eye as he looked at Margaret and added, 'I'll be back to pick you up. How long d'you want?'

'Give me an hour. That will be quite sufficient,' she replied and, as he drove off, knocked on the front door. Normally the back entrance was used, but she was more "company" than "family" now, and guessed she would be received in the parlour.

The cottage, like its fellows, was built of local stone with a grey slate roof. Margaret knew Aunt Prudence would have seen the car arrive, spying from an upper casement, but was deliberately keeping her waiting. She bit her lip in vexation and put up a hand to straighten her straw Breton sailor hat, aware that she looked out of place. The children were knotted into a group, staring at her, cheeks bulging, mouths smeared. Everything had gone quiet, except for the screech of seagulls wheeling and diving.

Then the door swung open and time did a backward flip as she stared into Aunt Prudence's cadaverous face and flinty eyes. 'I got your note,' she announced grimly. 'Decided to grace us with a visit, have you? You'd best come in. Don't want the whole street gawking.'

The door led directly into the parlour. It was cramped, its dimensions made even smaller by Aunt Mercy's bulk. If Aunt Prudence had grown more scrawny, her sister was bigger than ever. She occupied an upright chair and, like Aunt Prudence, was wearing her best dress. Apparently their niece was now considered to be a person of importance.

'How are you, Aunts?' Margaret began, not knowing where to start and regretting writing a letter saying she was coming to see them.

'I'm well, thank you, except for the rheumatics in my knees,' Aunt Prudence said, her hands folded primly at her waist.

'And I gets rather short of breath going upstairs these days,' Aunt Mercy put in, little eyes staring out from between rolls of fat. "Course, I've always worked hard. Never had it easy, like some. We've both toiled and moiled. Isn't that so, Prudence?'

'It is indeed, Mercy, but that's the way of the Christian. Meek and hard-working, following the example of Our Lord.'

They've not changed, Margaret thought with a sinking heart. Simply grown older and more set in their ways.

The parlour was dingy, with a horsehair sofa, squat armchairs with the springs gone, an ugly table and cheap ornaments. Over the fireplace was a print depicting a rock in the middle of a stormy sea, where a young woman (obviously a repentant sinner) in a white calico dress with draperies of symbolic scarlet clung to a graveyard cross. Her face was raised heavenwards, bathed in redeeming light. It was titled *Saved!*.

The room had a musty, unused smell. Margaret would have

142

preferred to be invited into the kitchen where there was a modicum of warmth and homeliness. No chance of that by the look of things. They were determined to keep her at arm's length.

Greetings over, silence fell, thickened, emphasising the impenetrable barrier between them, and in desperation Margaret took two gift-wrapped packages from her bag. She handed one to Aunt Mercy and the other to Aunt Prudence, saying, 'I didn't know what you'd like, but bought these in one of the London department stores.'

Aunt Prudence sniffed down her long nose, handling her present with her fingertips as if it might be contaminated by the wickedness of the city. 'Did you indeed? Department stores? What are those, pray?'

'Huge shops, Aunt, where one can buy almost anything.'

Aunt Prudence sniffed again. 'Really? I think I'll stick to the one on the corner of our street.'

There followed a rending of paper as they undid their gifts. Inside were artistically decorated tins containing biscuits. 'Very nice, I'm sure,' said Aunt Mercy grudgingly.

'Useful to keep things in when you've eaten the biscuits,' Margaret explained eagerly, trying her hardest to make contact. 'They're splendid as button-boxes.'

'Rather fancy, aren't they?' Aunt Prudence objected. 'And I like eating homemade food, not things bought from a store. You don't know what's in 'em.'

So much for my attempt at peacemaking, Margaret thought in a surge of exasperation.

Aunt Prudence set her tin on the table and said, 'You'd better sit down, I suppose, unless you're afraid of creasing your skirt.' And she glanced disparagingly at Margaret's floral-printed muslin dress. 'You're looking mighty grand.'

'Oh, this . . .' Margaret gestured towards it, then sat gingerly on the edge of a chair and began to work her fingers out of her gloves. 'It's my afternoon off, you see. I'm Lady Julia's personal maid now.'

'So we gathered. Didn't we, Mercy?' Aunt Prudence sat opposite, back ramrod stiff. 'You may not've been in touch with us, but we've heard tell what's been going on.'

Margaret could feel the blood rushing into her cheeks. What had they heard? Nothing about her and Lester, surely? This was impossible. But she glanced guiltily at the Fallen Woman in the print. Was Margaret, too, lost in the storm-tossed waters of depravity?

She calmed herself, concentrating on her true reason for visiting them: the need to show how well she had done. It was almost as if she was vindicating her mother. 'Then you know I've been her ladyship's maid for nearly two years,' she said. 'I go all over the place with her. We're visiting the South of France, after Henley Regatta.'

Two pairs of cold eyes considered her. 'France, eh?' Aunt Prudence's lips pursed, and Margaret could almost read her thoughts. France, that wicked place of lax morals and frivolity. Anywhere even vaguely termed 'abroad' meant sin to this repressed Cornishwoman.

Margaret yielded to the temptation to give her something scandalous to chew over when she had gone. 'We'll visit Monte Carlo. Have you heard of it? All the aristocrats go there to gamble at the casinos. Even King Edward used to spend time at Monty before he came to the throne. Probably still does sometimes.'

There. Put that in your pipe and smoke it! she thought with savage satisfaction. Her aunts rustled and snorted. They exchanged I-told-you-so glances.

'You'll enjoy this traipsing about, I dare say,' Aunt Mercy announced. 'You're your mother's daughter all right.'

'It's hard work,' Margaret said, ignoring that last remark. 'Her ladyship needs looking after every moment of the day and night. I care for her clothes, iron them, wash them, get stains out of them, pack everything when we're going on journeys, and even act as her hairdresser.'

'But the rewards are worthwhile?' Aunt Prudence stared pointedly at her dress. 'You didn't buy that on a servant's pay.'

'I'm supplied with suitable clothing, and Lady Julia lets me have things she no longer requires.' Margaret was appalled by their blatant hostility.

'Are you courting yet?'

'No,' she lied, thinking, if only they knew. It was on the tip of her tongue to tell about her engagement to Lester.

Not yet, she told herself firmly. He's said I'm to say nothing to anyone. No one knows, not even Luke or Susan, though I've a feeling they suspect something. They treat me differently lately, in a guarded way.

'What about that fellow in the car?' Aunt Mercy eased her vast hips and the chair groaned in protest.

'That's Luke Watson, his lordship's chauffeur. He'll collect me in a short while.' Margaret wished it was now, finding the atmosphere claustrophobic.

She wondered uneasily if they could sense she was no longer a virgin, and longed for Lester, a hollow ache inside her. She had not seen him for a week. He had remained in London with Roderick, while Lord and Lady Aubert returned to Roslan Manor prior to their departure for Europe. The younger children were to remain in Cornwall

144

in the care of Natalie and Thora, but Fenella would accompany her parents abroad, with Mademoiselle Rainier as chaperone.

The clock on the overmantel ticked steadily but the hands seemed stuck. I've got to get away from here, Margaret panicked. It was a mistake to come.

'Has anyone been seeing to Mama's grave?' she asked.

'Did you ask that someone should?' Aunt Prudence replied frostily.

'No,' Margaret admitted, eyes cast down. 'I visited there in February and paid the undertaker to organise a headstone. I hope he's done it. I'll call into the churchyard on my way back.' She cudgelled her brain for topics of conversation and came up with, 'How's Uncle Daniel?'

'Suffering from his chest, but carrying on,' Aunt Prudence replied. 'Some of us have to keep the nuts and bolts of life together.'

'And Uncle Jonus?'

'Fishing, as usual. We scrape a living, with the Lord's help,' Aunt Mercy answered piously. 'D'you go to church, girl?'

'We have daily service.'

'I'm glad to hear it,' Aunt Prudence intoned, but dubiously as if Margaret's immortal soul was already beyond saving. 'I hope this carries on when you get to Popish France.'

Margaret chose to let this pass, asking, 'How are my cousins?'

'Doing well for themselves,' Aunt Mercy said firmly. 'Jim's head cowman at Trewiddle Farm now. Jack's gone down the mine, and our Belinda's getting married come September. Ever such a steady young man. They'll live with his parents and she'll help out with the livestock, then he'll take over one day.'

'My Elias is a lay preacher.' Aunt Prudence's voice rang with pride. 'He's had the call, and may become a missionary, preaching among the heathen in Africa and suchlike.'

'Are they happy?'

'Happy? They're doing their duty.' Aunt Prudence flashed her a severe glance. 'We're not put on this earth to be happy.'

This was more than Margaret could stomach. 'Aren't we? If the Lord is supposed to be a god of love, then why wouldn't He want His creatures to enjoy life?'

Prudence's mouth dropped open. Aunt Mercy shifted her bulk, glancing hesitantly at her sister. Aunt Prudence recovered first. 'It's not for us to question what our Maker does or does not want. Our instructions are clearly laid out in the Bible, and our preachers are His mouthpieces.'

Margaret leapt up. 'If only I could make you see!' she cried. 'There's so much out there, so many marvels you've never even dreamed of.

145

The ocean, for example. You've lived by it all your lives, but have you ever stopped to drink in its beauty and power? Have you looked at the stars and wondered about the universe?'

'Never had time for such nonsense,' Aunt Prudence barked, watching her warily. 'Too much to do, too many children to look after and a man to feed.'

Margaret's eyes shone and she moved closer to her. 'Oh, Aunt, think, feel, experience! Your life is a prison of your own making.'

'You're talking rubbish.' Aunt Prudence glared at her. 'If this is what mixing with "carriage-folk" has done to you, then you'd have been better off in the seining factory.'

Margaret shook her head, doubting she would ever be able to reach them, but making one last effort. 'I've discovered music. Have you ever really listened to it?'

'We sing hymns in chapel.'

'I don't mean hymns. I've been to concerts and the opera house.' She fumbled for expression, recalled the lucid way in which Lester had spoken of it. 'Genius, talent, call it what you will,' she went on. 'Certain people seem inspired to produce beautiful sounds.'

'I don't know nothing about that,' Aunt Prudence said huffily. 'Any road, how're we to get to concerts and the like, out here in the country?'

'I'll help you buy a gramophone,' Margaret offered earnestly.

'I won't have one of those new-fangled machines in my house. Devil's work, if you ask me. You've been in the wrong company, my girl. Too free and easy with the high-ups. Seems like it's gone to your head.'

'I'm sorry for you,' Margaret said quietly, picking up her gloves and handbag. 'You're missing so much.'

The aunts rose too. 'You going then?' Aunt Prudence asked with undisguised relief.

'Let me know the date of Belinda's marriage and I'll send her a present.' Margaret was relieved to be leaving yet upset because she was as much an orphan as Luke. She had nothing in common with these people.

The Marchand was parked outside, its motor running, and Margaret climbed inside. Luke released the handbrake and they were off. Down to the bottom of the hill, a turn on the quayside and the long climb back the way they had come, every move watched by an interested audience to whom the internal combustion engine was an innovation, viewed with suspicion and not to be trusted. It had taken them years to accept the railway train; the horseless carriage would take even longer.

146

'How did it go?' Luke enquired without looking at her.

'As I expected, though I'd hoped otherwise.' His kind voice brought tears to the surface. 'I'm an outsider, always have been, always will. We're as different as chalk from cheese. Can you take me to the cemetery, please?'

'Anything you say, princess. Your wish is my command.'

Luke drove along the cliff road to where the church stood. He stopped and, by a tacit agreement, got out of the car, positioned himself against the low wall and pulled out a pack of cigarettes, prepared to wait while she made her solitary pilgrimage.

Margaret stood with him for a moment, looking across to where the rock-bound coast stretched away, throwing out great, black towering projections that met the flowing tide. She had missed the age-old song of the sea, and entered the churchyard by the lych gate, thinking of the people who lay there, sleeping their last sleep, lulled by the endless echoes of the waves as they rolled in to break at the foot of the headland.

I must see Lester, she thought. How many days do I have to endure without him? Four, five? If only he was here with me! We'll visit when we're man and wife, to drink in the beauty of the earth, sky and sea.

A mason had carried out her instructions, placing a grey stone at the head of the mound, bearing the inscription: Mary Joyce Helbren. 1864–1903. Rest in Peace.

With a pang she noticed that her father's grave, not far away, had been kept in order by loving hands. Those of his sisters no doubt, that hateful pair of crones who behaved spitefully towards the despised wife, even after she was dead.

Margaret sank to her knees on the dry soil beneath a shady sycamore. To her surprise she found the flowers she had planted were flourishing. Someone had kept them watered. Certainly not Aunt Prudence or Aunt Mercy. She plucked out a couple of weeds that had dared show their heads, then sat on, deep in thought.

She believed that her mother knew about Lester. Though impatient with organised religion, the feeling of that spiritual presence could not be denied. Mary's shade did not condemn her; it seemed to understand. Had she loved Tom as ardently? Somehow Margaret found this hard to believe. Was it possible there had been another lover, someone to whom her mother had given herself, body and soul?

She lingered where the sunlight made a shadow pattern of shifting leaves, and the disagreeable meeting with her aunts faded. Almost asleep, she suddenly became aware of a figure on the other side of the path. A woman was bending over a tiny grave, the earth still brown and fresh. She wore mourning black, and was arranging foxgloves and granny-bonnets in a jar. Tears glistened on her cheeks, but when she looked up and saw Margaret watching her, she smiled and came over.

'Are you Mary Helbren's child?' she asked timidly, a young woman though her face was lined, brownish smudges beneath her eyes.

'That's right.'

'I knew your Ma. She was my teacher. I hope you don't mind, but I took the liberty of weeding her grave. She was very kind to me at school, had a way with her, making lessons interesting.'

'So it was you who kept the plants fresh? Thank you.' It was a comfort to know someone else had esteemed her mother. 'I'm not always here, you see. I travel with my mistress.'

'I know. You're Lady Julia's maid. You look very like your Ma.'

'Do I?' Margaret said, pleased. 'I miss her terribly, even now.'

'They say that time heals, but I've only just buried my babby,' the woman murmured. 'One morning I went to lift him from his crib and he was dead. The doctor can't explain it. My husband's drinking worse'n he was afore. We've four girls, but this were the boy he wanted. Folk look at me sideways, thinking I smothered the child. As if I would harm my own!'

Margaret reached out to her. 'People can be cruel. I'm so sorry.'

The woman lifted the hem of her skirt and wiped her tears. 'I'll go on keeping her grave tidy, when I come to see to his. She was a real lady, despite what they said about her.'

Margaret stiffened, some of the good feeling evaporating. 'What did they say?'

'Nothing I ever believed, miss. You know how they like to gossip.' The woman seemed to shrink into herself, as if she had spoken out of turn.

'Tell me, please. What was it they said?' The bright day seemed to have darkened.

'Oh, this and that, miss. That Tom Helbren married a bad 'un – damaged goods, was how they put it, but I never, never agreed with 'em. I told 'em straight – she wouldn't never do anything shameful.'

Margaret turned away, leaving the woman standing by Mary's grave, her simple act of kindness marred by the suspicions her words had aroused. She recalled her mother's isolation, and her own, which she had attributed to the fact that neither of them worked in the factory or attended the chapel. Was there something more? All those hints dropped by the aunts. What had happened in Porthross years ago?

'You look better,' Luke remarked as he helped her into the car.

'Do I? It must be the air up here.' Margaret could not explain. He was her friend but it was hard to voice the sadness within her, the

148

uncertainty and doubts. 'I've one more visit to make. Will you drive me to the Weeping Maids?'

'What d'you want with those old stones?' Luke gave her a sideways glance. 'They say witches dance there when the moon's full.'

'I need to go.' Margaret's chin set in that mulish way which he recognised. It was no use arguing with her.

The Marchand bumped over the rough track, while Luke swore and fretted about the suspension. 'Stop here,' Margaret said. 'We'll walk the rest of the way.'

' "We"?' he grumbled. 'Who said anything about me wanting to come?' But he got out and trudged along beside her.

By a strange optical illusion those huge grey lumps seemed to advance to meet them. It was as if the twelve enchanted princesses were regarding them, immemorial, brooding and sinister.

Margaret passed between them till she was standing in the middle of the circle. The sunshine dispelled the awesomeness, but not the mystery. She was aware of Luke on the periphery, watching her, then she closed her eyes and raised her face to the heavens, arms outstretched, wishing she was skyclad.

How wonderful to be married on such sacred ground. To exchange vows, hands linked by garlands of flowers. Lester and I will make love when we come here, she vowed, and offered up a prayer to any ancient deity who might be listening.

'*Make him love me for ever. Let our marriage take place soon. Don't let anything spoil it.*'

This was the most important thing in her life, never mind what might have happened to her mother in the past. It was the future that mattered. She thought she felt the earth vibrate beneath her feet in response to her plea.

'Are you ready?' Luke said, his voice rousing her from her trance. 'Time we were off.'

She shook herself, eyes misted with visions. 'I'm ready.'

'What is it you want from the stones?' he asked, the wind ruffling his brown hair, his face anxious. 'What's happening to you, Margaret? The servants are talking.'

'Let them talk,' she answered, feeling languorous and heavy, as she did after mating with Lester.

'Look here, sweetheart,' he went on, his hand on her arm. 'Be careful. You're getting yourself into deep waters.'

This was the second man who had warned her lately, but she smiled dreamily. 'Don't worry, Luke. Everything is fine. I'm happy. Please be happy for me.'

*

149

'I feel like a day out on the river. Which of you gentlemen is going to take me to Henley?' Lillian demanded, hands planted firmly on her hips as she regarded her diners.

'It's a damn fine event. On a par with Eton and Harrow cricket matches,' someone shouted.

'An important fixture in the sporting world, don't-cher-know?' added another. 'The one-mile Challenge Cup and the Diamond Challenge Sculls are coveted trophies and attract the world's best oarsmen.'

'Let's make up a party. I'll hire a launch,' exclaimed one stout, elderly gentleman whom Lillian knew to be a baron.

'And I'll provide the picnic hampers. What d'you say to that, Sir Percy?' she cried triumphantly.

Excitement reigned, each man trying to outdo the other with offers of help. Lillian watched them, a cynical smile playing about her lips. She had them eating out of her hand, no matter their rank and importance.

She had deliberately chosen to make her pronouncement on a night when Lester was dining elsewhere. It was part of her plan to discover his intentions towards Margaret. He would be competing, and if everything was above board she was bound to be there, Henley an important item on the social calendar, providing the excuse for a huge outdoor gathering where the gentry could eat, drink and flirt. Less formal than Ascot, the main attractions were the parties on houseboats, the sumptuous food and the dazzling firework displays.

'Will you join us, Mr Newark?' she asked, strolling over to the table where he sat and occupying a chair.

'I find these occasions rather a bore,' he answered, while the waiter brought another glass. 'I'd sooner enjoy the river quietly, without a glorified shindig. But yes, count me in, Mrs Glynn.'

'Lord Lester will be rowing,' Lillian said craftily, while Peter poured red wine for her. 'I wonder if Miss Helbren will cheer him on. D'you know anything about her?'

'No, I don't. I saw her a couple of times at Roslan Manor and assumed she was a family friend. But if that's the case then why is she meeting Lester unchaperoned?'

He sat back, regarding Lillian with those piercing blue eyes, and trying not to betray too much interest in Margaret. Seeing her again had made it even more difficult to banish her from his mind. He was appalled to think she was having an affair with a man like Lester, and this seemed highly likely. His conversation with her had disturbed him deeply.

Lillian was almost as curious about Peter as she was about Margaret. At his request she had accommodated him in a double bedroom with en suite bathroom. He did not have much luggage or a valet, yet was not short of money, prompt with his rent, generous with tips and lodging no complaints about his laundry bill.

A singularly busy and studious person, he was always prepared to pass the time of day with her or Jenkins. She heard the typewriter clacking in his room far into the night, and his wastepaper basket was often filled with screwed-up sheets.

Now he leaned his elbows on the table and steepled his fingers together, studying her over them. 'I expect you're wondering what I do.'

'I never pry,' she began, cigarette to her lips.

'Of course not –' he struck a match for her and held it to the tip – 'but I'll tell you anyway. I'm writing a book, a collection of stories from all over the world. The hotel industry in particular fascinates me. I'm interested in what makes people tick, how they operate, what they expect when travelling. I envy you.'

'Me?' She pressed a hand to the lace covering her breasts.

'Yes, indeed. You have this knowledge at your command. You actually run a hotel, know what goes on in the kitchens, cater for a variety of tastes, have an astute awareness of customers' requirements and handle them in masterly fashion. Perhaps I'll write a book about *you*, Mrs Glynn.'

'That's most flattering, I'm sure.' Lillian was quite thrown by this. It strengthened her opinion that he would be a useful to have around in a crisis.

Not that she fancied him, perfectly happy with Joe, but she wanted him as a friend. There were times when it was necessary to have a few stalwarts handy. For some reason she could not fathom, she had the feeling that someone, somewhere was going to need her assistance soon. Lillian was given to presentiments which usually proved accurate.

She shrugged this off with a smile. 'Right then, if you're so eager to learn you can help me and Chef get the picnic ready. Bring your notebook. Looks like we'll be catering for upward of twenty.'

Over the next few days Peter found himself involved belowstairs. Lillian was no token manageress, she knew everything there was to know about buying foodstuff, the cost, what amounts were needed. No one overcharged Lillian Glynn or sold her shoddy merchandise.

The excitement of the proposed outing reverberated through the kitchen. Besides the ordinary catering, Monsieur Philippe, the *chef de cuisine*, monumental in build, easily upset, fiery tempered and dripping culinary talent, concentrated on the contents of the wicker picnic hampers. Peter, seated in a corner out of the way, observed and scribbled, while Philippe and Lillian debated and argued, fell out,

151

made it up, slammed in and out, turned their wrath on suppliers and eventually produced a magnificent spread.

The trouble started at the onset when Lillian waved her copy of Mrs Beeton's *Book of Household Management* in Philippe's face and then insisted, 'She says here that for a large picnic we'll need six pounds of fresh salmon, cucumbers, watercress, a leg of lamb, eight pounds of beef, an ox tongue in aspic, a dish of cold veal in jelly, a large chicken pie, salad and dressing, fruit tarts, a dozen cheesecakes, biscuits, rolls and butter, Cheddar and Stilton cheese, and twelve punnets of strawberries.'

'Bah!' Philippe exclaimed with a look of supreme contempt on his melancholy Gascon features. 'That's so *English*, madame! And what do the English know about cooking? Nothing! *Absolument!*'

'It's English people who'll be eating it. English people having an English picnic on an English river, in case you've forgotten!' she shouted back, digging in her heels.

'Very well, madame. Poison them. Give them severe afflictions of the stomach if that is your desire,' he answered loftily. 'I can always take my art elsewhere.'

'And what is that supposed to mean? Are you handing in your resignation?' Lillian had not enjoyed herself so much for a long time. She poured out a glass of his best claret, ignoring his glare.

'If I'm not appreciated here, I regret I have no alternative.'

'Bullshit!' Lillian exclaimed coarsely. 'You won't leave. You'll not find anyone else who'll agree to your outrageous wage demands. Only a fool like me.' She pushed the bottle towards him over the bare surface of the pine table. 'Have a drink, and let's get on with it.'

The lines each side of Philippe's thick lips deepened and he gave a dramatic sigh, followed by an expressive shrug of his shoulders. 'Very well, madame, but only if I make the mayonnaise sauce my way – never mind Mrs Beeton. What does a woman, and an Englishwoman at that, know about sauces?'

'You may make it, monsieur.'

'And perhaps one of my special puddings, instead of fruit tart? And am I permitted to add a *soupçon* of garlic to the salad?' he enquired with heavy sarcasm.

'You can, but don't push it,' she cautioned. 'Some people object to the lingering after-effect.'

'*Mon Dieu!*' he muttered, eyes and hands lifted to the ceiling as if beseeching help from heaven. 'Don't they realise garlic gives the breath a wonderfully sensual odour?'

Equally elaborate preparations were being made by Mrs Frith in the

152

kitchen of 21 Upper Grosvenor Street. This was to be the last big event before Lord and Lady Aubert went abroad, one final effort and then the cook and her assistants could retire to Roslan Manor for the rest of the summer with only the children to cater for. A caretaker and his wife would be left in charge of the town house as was customary.

Julia was well pleased with the results of Mrs Frith's work when the food was presented on damask-covered tables on the deck of the houseboat Henry had rented. It was gay with bunting, striped awnings and tubs of vivid geraniums, and had been towed into place near a landing stage not far from the marquee under whose canvas a band would play for dancing in the evening.

The start of the regatta and one of those marvellous summer days only found in England: scorching sunshine, cloudless blue skies, and that lush green foliage never seen in arid countries. The river was crowded, the banks too, where an explosion of tents had sprung up like mushrooms between the boathouses, brightly coloured pennants streaming from their poles in the light breeze. Craft of all kind bobbed on the water: steamers, punts, canoes and skiffs in a variety of shapes and sizes, some fitted with a sail to take advantage of the wind.

'Oh, Mama, isn't it heavenly?' Fenella enthused, thrilled by the sight of so many dashing young men in white trousers and club blazers, sporting peaked caps or straw boaters. Anything seemed acceptable in this free and easy atmosphere.

They were everywhere – on the bank, performing at the oars, leaning over the rails of launches, chatting with the girls, exchanging greetings with acquaintances. In this extravaganza of socialising and high spirits the chaperones relaxed their vigilance, allowing their charges to go punting with friends.

Fenella longed to go, for she and her mother had been preparing for this for ages, making several visits to the milliner and dressmaker, and selecting the right parasols and fans for each outfit. Even her eagerness to look at the men did not make her forget to raise her sunshade. A pale complexion was considered far more attractive than freckled or tanned skin.

'It is rather pleasant,' Julia agreed, seated in a deck chair in the shade.

Luke had driven the family down to Henley, though the footmen had gone earlier in a hired omnibus taking the hampers, cutlery, glass and china. Margaret and Mademoiselle Rainier had journeyed in another car, the Frenchwoman chattering all the way, while Margaret wanted to be quiet and think about Lester, brooding on how she could endure being in his company yet unable to acknowledge their intimacy. With any luck, he would be spending time with fellow oarsmen.

But at last the moment came when he joined the Auberts for lunch. She stood behind Julia's chair meekly as befitted a servant, her dress of soft faille in a pale sand colour, tightly fitting over the bodice, with the skirt close about the hips to flare to the ground. With it she wore a hat made of wheat straw, trimmed by a dark band with trailing ribbons.

Even so, there was no way she could be mistaken for a guest, any more than Mademoiselle Rainier. Julia saw to that, exercising her power and keeping them both on the trot running quite unnecessary errands.

Footmen in special liveries were waiting at table. Chairs had been arranged under an awning, and while their superiors sat down at the main tables, Margaret and Mademoiselle took their places further along the deck.

Margaret pushed the food about her plate with her fork, while Mademoiselle ate with a Continental appreciation of suberbly cooked cuisine. 'You are not hungry, *non?*' she asked, observing Margaret with bird-bright eyes.

She shook her head. 'Not very.'

'You seem worried, *chérie*. I would like us to be friends. My name is Anna. And you are Margaret, *n'est ce pas?*

She was very like a perky bird, always optimistic, never depressed, dismissing troubles with a philosophical Gallic shrug. Margaret wondered how someone so worldly would have dealt with Lester. She suspected she'd have had nothing to do with him, or at the very least demanded a large settlement before she consented to become his mistress. Margaret tried to console herself by thinking: This is different. I am to be his wife.

She pasted a false smile on her face and said, 'It seems we shall be spending time in each other's company, Anna. Both here and in France.'

'Indeed yes.' Anna impulsively patted her hand. 'Two Babes in the Wood, lost among the aristos. We should look after one another. That girl is a trial. My own *chère* Mama would have taken a stick to her bare derrière long ago.' She nodded to where Fenella was chattering animatedly, seated between Roderick and Lester.

Lillian stood on the deck of a launch steaming up the river. It was a noisy, cumbersome craft, with Sir Percy in a blue reefer and yachting cap tugging at the whistle to clear a passage, much to the annoyance of other sailors, and trying to teach the helmsman his job at the same time.

She had borrowed his field glasses, training them on the houseboats,

154

looking for one called the *River Queen*. Her informants had told her this was the craft hired by Roderick's family, and where Roderick was Lester would also be and, *if* he was playing the game, which she very much doubted, Margaret should be somewhere in the vicinity.

She suddenly saw it, moored on the opposite bank. 'Can we stop here, Sir Percy?' she trilled.

'Certainly, m'dear,' he shouted back, forming his hands into a megaphone and bellowing to the master, 'Drop anchor, cap'n!'

The engines slowed, the vessel anchored, and Sir Percy went round commanding his servants as if he was an admiral and they his crew. Luncheon appeared, but Lillian remained at her post, the scene on the *River Queen* magnified through the powerful lenses.

She saw Lester almost at once, seated at table with Roderick. They were surrounded on all sides by women, an older one, whom she presumed to be Roderick's mother, and a younger version, probably his sister. There were several others of varying ages, leaning forward in their chairs, listening raptly to something Lester was saying, amidst laughter and the flirtatious language of the fan. Lester lounged at his ease and appeared to be basking in this admiration. But where was Margaret?

She swept the deck with the glasses and found her at last, at a table set apart from the rest. Lillian focused the lenses for a clearer view. Margaret was with a sallow-skinned little woman, both of them plainly dressed. Obviously members of staff. This was proved when the older lady gestured imperiously and Margaret went to her, head bowed, face pale and set. Roderick did not deign to look at her.

She's a maid or companion, Lillian concluded, and that bloody rogue is stringing her along. I knew he was up to something devious. Felt it in my water.

She lowered the glasses, dying to corner Peter and talk about this, but Sir Percy and his cronies were present throughout luncheon. Afterwards she wanted to be by herself, suddenly weary. It was as if in Margaret she had glimpsed herself as she had once been, naive and hopelessly in love with a handsome, ruthless gentleman.

She occupied a carpet-covered campaign chair, unable to shake off that tiredness and drop in spirits. Peter was standing not far away, staring at the *River Queen* through the binoculars.

'Bring over a bottle of bubbly, Peter,' she said. They were on Christian name terms by now. 'I want to talk to you.'

He turned his head and raised an eyebrow in her direction. 'How much have you had to drink today?'

155

'Hardly anything. Just a few nips of gin before we left, to get me in the party spirit.'

'And wine with lunch, champagne to follow, then brandy with the coffee,' he reminded. 'I don't know where you put it. I should be flat on my back.'

'I've hollow legs,' she joked, and he sat beside her after filling two crystal flutes.

'Did you see her through the glasses?' she asked, knowing he had.

His panama was tipped forward over his eyes as he lay back in a folding chair, white-trousered legs crossed at the ankles, his feet in canvas deck shoes resting on a stool, giving the impression of being indolently relaxed and uncaring.

'Who?' he grunted.

'You know who. Margaret Helbren, of course.'

'I saw her. Looks like she's Lady Julia's maid.'

'Lady Julia? Is she Roderick's mother?'

'Yes.'

'So we've established that Margaret's a servant. What is Lester up to, d'you suppose?'

He pushed back his hat and opened his eyes and there was so much anger in their depths that she froze. 'You know as well as I. He's probably seduced her, and will go on using her while he finds it amusing.'

'He's a bastard!' Lillian snapped.

'Undoubtedly.' There was a bad taste in Peter's mouth that had nothing to do with the meal they had just enjoyed. 'Though I suppose there's the outside chance he may be sincere.'

'Towards little Miss Helbren!' Lillian's finely arched brows shot up. 'I don't think so. Even if he were in love with her, which I very much doubt, he'll never marry out of his class.'

'I would,' Peter said bluntly.

'Would you?' Lillian cast him a questioning look. 'Really, truly?'

'Yes. I don't set great store by this stupid system of ours. If I fell in love and the girl loved me in return, then I'd marry her and let the devil take the rest.'

Lillian's eyes searched his, and her tense expression relaxed. 'D'you know, I almost believe you're speaking the truth,' she said wonderingly.

Peter laughed without mirth. 'My dear lady, don't sound so surprised. There are a few honest fellows left, you know.'

'I've yet to meet one,' she scoffed, and, as she moved, her lace frills rustled like the plumage of an agitated bird.

Peter gave a crooked smile and, rising and returning to the rail, scrutinised the scene on the houseboat's deck for some time. The line of his mouth was hard, his broad shoulders rigid, and his hands clenched tightly round the field glasses through which he stared.

Chapter 9

'But I shan't be able to see you,' Margaret complained, leaning over Lester, propped up on one elbow, her fingers circling the hard male nipples and tracing patterns in his black chest hair.

'On the contrary, you'll see me frequently,' he said with an indulgent chuckle. 'We'll be living in each other's pockets.'

'Not like this. Not alone,' she persisted, pressing her breasts against him, that gnawing hunger appeased only when she lay in his arms.

'I'm sure you'll be able to sneak into my hotel room sometimes,' he answered, stifling a yawn.

She bounced up into a sitting position, tossing the tousled hair from her face. 'I'm tired of sneaking about. When are we going to come out into the open?'

'Aren't you happy? I thought you loved me,' he said, with sulky mouth and reproachful eyes.

She was instantly contrite, guilty for having hurt his feelings. 'I *do* love you, and I *am* happy. I've never felt like this before. But I'm greedy. I want more of you. Need to be with you every second. D'you realise we've never spent a whole night together?'

He stroked her curls affectionately. 'You worry too much. Take each day as it comes. Everything will work out for the best.'

'Will it?' Her eyes were huge in the subdued light, filled with the questions and fears she was too nervous to voice.

'Trust me,' he murmured and, to silence her, pulled her down and covered her mouth with his.

'I do,' she averred, surfacing from that deep kiss. 'I'm sorry to harp on, but I need to know how you feel about me.'

'I want you,' he growled low in his throat, holding her so that she lay on top of him, thighs parallel with his.

Her breath shortened and that exquisite ache grew inside her. They had just made love, but she wanted to repeat it. She felt whole when their bodies were joined, but, 'Is that all?' she whispered into his neck.

He pressed her face closer, stared up at the draped tester above their heads and grimaced. 'I love you,' he said.

He put her from him, threw aside the coverlets and swung his legs to the floor. Her hand came out, clasping his arm possessively. 'Don't go,' she begged.

'I was dressing when you unexpectedly arrived. Now I must get on or I'll be late for an important engagement. Really, darling, it would be more convenient if you could let me know when you're coming.' The hard glint in his eyes made her uncomfortable.

'It's not possible. My hours are erratic,' she protested, sitting up and hugging her raised knees. 'And these past few days have been so busy. I've only just finished Lady Julia's packing and wasn't sure if I'd be able to get away tonight.'

'I understand, but please be careful from now on. I don't want any embarrassing scenes when we get to France.'

This smarted like salt on her raw emotions, but she pushed down the humiliation and hurt, telling herself that as his Chosen One she was happy to obey him. She watched him move about the bedroom, a magnificent specimen of naked male, wide shoulders tapering to a narrow waist, flat stomach, lean hips, long thighs and muscular legs. His skin was unblemished and tanned, not even the genital area covered when he swam and dried out in the sun, an art he had perfected under Mediterranean skies and practised in England, weather permitting.

A shiver danced over her nerves as she let her gaze slide to the strong, sinewy hands that had such intimate knowledge of her body. She fought back the flood of longing and tried to concentrate on practical matters. The next time she saw him they would be boarding a train, he in a first-class carriage and herself travelling third with Anna and the valets.

Lester picked up a handbell. Radley appeared almost immediately. 'You rang, my lord?'

'Hurry. I must get dressed.'

'Yes, sir. Of course, sir.'

Radley glanced towards the bed without a flicker of expression on his foxy face. Small-built and dapper, his brownish hair was slicked back with Macassar oil. He was very conscious of his position as valet to a titled gentleman, but Margaret resented the vulpine gleam in his eyes whenever he looked her way. He was altogether too familiar. She was mortified because Lester had called him in. It was not right for a servant to see his master's future wife unclothed.

Though they had crossed paths in Lester's rooms, he had never

159

before caught her in bed. Lester must trust him, she thought, or he'd not have allowed this. She pulled the sheet up about her shoulders and wondered how she was to dress with Radley hanging about.

She had arrived at the Warwick after preparing Julia for a farewell dinner party at Lady Rossiter's mansion. Margaret marvelled at her mistress's stamina. She breezed through a full diary without the slightest suggestion of exhaustion. And it would be an early start in the morning to catch the seven-forty train for Dover.

As soon as the front door had closed behind Julia and Henry, Margaret had snatched up her hat and rushed out to find a cab, impelled by the need to see Lester. It had almost seemed he had been avoiding her since Henley and the pain was too much to bear. Once, she would have been overjoyed at the prospect of foreign travel, but now this was another obstacle preventing her from being in his arms.

He stood there impatiently while Radley fussed with the fastening of his bow-tie. 'Get a move on, man!' he snarled.

He was already a stranger. Margaret found his custom-tailored evening suit another barrier. When they were both naked and entwined, it was easier to forget. Now he was as far removed from her as the moon and stars, anticipating meeting friends with whom she could have no contact. He looped a white silk scarf round his neck, slung his opera cloak over one shoulder and picked up his top hat and cane.

He raised an eyebrow in a sharply quizzical arch and said to her, 'Aren't you ready yet, my dear?'

Stung into action, she dragged the bed curtain across with a jangle of brass rings, and fumbled for her scattered articles of clothing. 'I shan't be a moment,' she called from behind it.

'I can't wait, I'm afraid. Radley will order you a hackney. I'll see you later.' And he was gone.

Margaret heard him glumly, the good feeling engendered by love-making evaporating. 'See you later' was one of his favourite phrases, which meant everything, or nothing at all. It let him off the hook. No need to make a firm arrangement. It might be hours or days till the fancy moved him to have her again. Such disloyal thoughts shamed her and she threw up a dozen reasons for his casual behaviour.

She could hear Radley moving about, tidying away the debris. He went into the bathroom and the gurgle of water followed by splashes indicated that he had pulled out the plug and was now cleaning the tub. She took the opportunity of his absence to finish putting on her clothes. Finally she went to the dressing table and stood in front of the mirror, adjusting her hat.

Radley came up behind her. 'Shall I get a cab?' he asked.

'No, thank you.'

'Suit yourself.' Radley shrugged, dropping any pretence of respect which he adopted when his master was there. 'We'll be travelling together tomorrow.'

'Yes.' Magaret did not want to be reminded of this fact.

'I'll enjoy that.' He leered at her, and she had never seen anything more unpleasant and threatening.

'Mademoiselle Rainier will be with me,' she reminded, giving him a steely glance, then grabbed up her purse, ready to leave.

'The French trollop,' he sneered, and sprawled in one of the chairs, helping himself to a cigar from the silver box on the table.

'Don't call her that!' Margaret's voice rose. 'She's not a trollop.'

'And neither are you, I suppose?' Radley regarded her with coldly speculative eyes.

'If you don't stop this I'll tell Lord Lester. And you shouldn't be smoking his cigars.' She was fuming. This was the last straw, to be subjected to the insults of such a vile creature.

'D'you really think he'd care?'

She was halfway to the door, but stopped and spun round. 'Don't be ridiculous!'

Radley rose and edged towards her, staring at her breasts that rose and fell rapidly with her agitated breathing. 'He wouldn't give a tinker's cuss. Neither would he care he if I was to hump you, right here and now. He'd laugh, would the master, probably give me a tip for taking you off his hands. None of the tarts last long with him. "Variety is the spice of life, Radley," he sometimes says to me.'

'You're a bloody liar. Get away from me,' Margaret shouted, and yanked the door open, but even as she fled down the passage his mocking laughter pursued her.

'I don't know how long I'll be away,' Peter said, coming down the stairs, a valise in his hand.

'We'll keep your room.' Lillian glanced over at him as she stood in the reception desk, sorting mail.

'Might as well get on with my mission,' he answered, pausing in front of it, putting down his luggage and scrutinising a train timetable he had taken from his pocket.

'Of mercy?' Her eyes were clear and frank under the sooty lashes. They understood one another perfectly.

'You could call it that. I feel the need to go south.'

'Not the Riviera, by any chance?'

'How did you guess? You must be psychic.'

'Mustn't I just! In need of a holiday, are you?' Lillian perused the letters as if she had no interest in Peter's doings. In reality they had sat

161

long together lately, mulling over what was to be done about Margaret and Lester.

'Not necessarily. There are a few hotels I want to visit, the kitchens in particular. Monsieur Philippe has been kind enough to give me letters of introduction.' Peter rested his elbow on the counter and took out his cigarettes. 'And there are places I can stay in Monty.'

'Not with the Auberts?' She accepted one and slipped it into holder.

'I think not. I'll watch from a distance. But, as we've agreed, someone needs to keep an eye on Miss Helbren. I'm in the ideal position to do so.'

'Not so much her as *him*,' Lillian stated emphatically. 'I wouldn't trust him as far as I could throw him.'

'Maybe we're wrong,' he said slowly, a frown creasing his brow. 'Supposing he really does care for her and intends to do the decent thing?'

'You don't believe that any more that I do. She's in service, as we found out at Henley. He's not the sort of gent to marry a commoner, unless, of course, she happened to be frightfully rich, and then he'd despise her and make her life hell.'

'You haven't any time for him, have you?' Peter found the page he wanted and marked the next train to Dover.

'Have *you*?' Her eyes were hard. Gone were the days when she had found Lester attractive.

He grinned at her wrily. 'No.'

'Well, then – I told you last night how upset she was when she passed me on the stairs. She didn't even see me, and he had left earlier.'

'You'd make a wonderful spy. The Secret Service could use you.'

'You're not so bad yourself. Keep me informed.'

'Don't worry.' Peter crushed out his Rothmans in the brass ashtray. 'That sounds like my hackney. Goodbye, Lillian, and don't overdo it. You're looking tired.'

'Don't say that, dear!' she exclaimed, strolling to the door with him. 'When people tell you you're looking tired, what they really mean is you're looking old.'

'Not you, dear lady.' He raised her hand to his lips and bowed gallantly. 'You will never age.'

'God, but you're a darling man!' She twinkled up at him. 'What a pity you're in love with someone else.'

'In love!' His brow shot up in a quizzical arch. 'What makes you think that?'

'Oh, nothing – nothing at all. Watch your back, Peter. Don't take any risks. Send me a postcard.' She patted his arm as he slung his bag into the waiting cab and climbed in after it.

*

162

'D'you think there'll ever be a Channel Tunnel?' Luke asked Merther, Henry's valet, a gentleman's gentleman of the old school who had served his lordship for years.

'I sincerely hope not,' Merther answered, looking up from the newspaper he was reading, pince-nez on his beaky nose. 'All lovers of England feel that this little "silver streak" with its stormy waves and rocky shores is blessed by Providence, her very isolation being her natural strength and glory.'

'Quite right,' Radley piped up, trying to catch Anna's eye as she sat on the moquette-covered carriage seat opposite him. 'Don't want to make it easier for a lot of dirty foreigners to get in, do we?'

Anna continued to stare out at the countryside flashing past the train windows, refusing to rise to the bait. Margaret, however, glared at him.

'I'd not go that far,' Merther replied, a calm, stately man who never appeared to let anything perturb him. 'Our European friends and their trade links are important to us.'

'Surely a tunnel would make us weak, open to invasion and surprise in time of war?' Luke pushed his bowler to the back of his head, one of the rare occasions when he was not wearing his chauffeur's uniform. His check suit and canary-yellow waistcoat added a certain élan to his appearance. He had been included on the trip as Henry intended to hire an automobile when they reached Cannes.

'That's right,' Radley agreed, leaning forward a little. He, Merther and Roderick's man, Carew, were attired in sober black as usual, on duty most of the time. 'They could creep up on us.'

'And think of the disasters that might happen. Supposing the tunnel collapsed with all that weight of water over it? People trapped inside. It would be horrible!' Carew was younger than the other valets, a fresh-faced boy and Roderick was his first master.

'Have you been on the ferry before?' Luke asked him, smiling.

'No, Mr Watson.' Carew spoke to him respectfully, conscious that he was a very junior member of staff.

'Well, wait till you've experienced the old *mal de mer*, my lad. It might make you change your mind.'

Margaret was hardly listening, aware of the rocking motion of the speeding train, glad of the respite after the mayhem of getting Lady Julia's considerable amount of baggage to the station and stowed in the luggage van. Her own modest requirements filled a suitcase resting in the netting rack above her head. She was glad Anna was beside her, and relieved that Luke was there. Her last meeting with Radley had unnerved her. It was disconcerting to think she would be forced to travel across France with him, that poisonous individual who knew far too much about her and Lester.

Julia had ordered in a quantity of seasickness preventatives, making sure Margaret was well dosed before they embarked. The last thing she wanted was an incapacitated maid. Once her mistress was seated comfortably in the saloon reserved for élite passengers, Margaret fled to the deck, the wind tugging at her hair as she leaned over the taffrail and watched the cliffs of Dover disappearing into the distance.

'You are sad to be leaving home, but I am looking forward to seeing mine,' Anna said, dark eyes sparkling. 'Indeed I am fortunate to be with this family again. While Fenella was at the academy I worked in another household, but was so happy when Lady Julia asked me to return as her daughter's chaperone.'

'Is this your ambition? To work for the aristocracy?'

'Only for a while. I am betrothed to Etienne Masselin, who is apprenticed to his uncle. He has served five of the seven years required to qualify him as a baker – not only of bread, but of the finest *pâtisserie*.' She formed her thumb and first finger into a ring and kissed them, then held them in the air. 'Exquisite! You've never tasted anything like it.'

'You're in love with him?' This romantic state occupied a large proportion of Margaret's thoughts these days.

Anna gave a wise smile. 'Ah, love, *chérie*. What is that, eh? We respect one another. We are from the same stock and have the same expectations. Etienne is older than me. He will make an excellent spouse. I shall marry him when the time is ripe. Meanwhile I work, to add to my dot.'

'How sensible,' Margaret said, the wistful note in her voice making Anna look at her closely.

'What is it? You're troubled. I have felt this lately. Is it concerning a man? Watson, maybe?'

But Margaret kept her counsel; even this amiable woman was not to be let into the secret. She forced herself not to follow Lester with her eyes where he strolled with Roderick, their laughter drifting across the deck, and kept well out his way when they arrived at Calais. Despite the delay caused by customs, there was time to breakfast before taking the train to Paris.

There were further hold-ups when they reached the capital, Julia becoming extremely annoyed when a *gendarme* asked her to hand over her keys and then proceeded to rifle her carefully packed trunks.

'What d'you expect to find in there, my man,' she demanded in French, her command of the language formidable, her sarcasm cutting. 'A hidden cache of cigars? Oh, yes, I smoke them regularly! Or perhaps I might be smuggling weapons? Do I look like a gunrunner?'

The station was crowded, and there were legions of voracious hotel touters ready to pounce on the belongings of new arrivals and carry them off to the omnibuses attached to the establishments that employed them. The Aubert valets fended them off, everyone shouting and gesticulating.

Margaret stayed close to Anna and Luke, confused by the rush of people, the strange languages, the shrill engine whistles, the hiss of steam, the harsh shouts of guards and porters, the barked commands of the station master. Pungent smells assailed her nostrils; sweat and cooking; perfumes; smoke and dust; the overall odour of inadequate drains which she soon discovered pervaded not only Paris but wherever she went in France.

Conveyances waited to take the English party to the St James Hotel in the Rue St Honore. There could have been no better guide than Anna, who excitedly pointed out landmarks as she and Margaret bowled through the busy streets. Just for the moment they were free of men, riding in a two-seater hansom, the valets and Luke following in another carriage, in charge of the mountain of baggage.

Henry had insisted on a motorised cab, piling his family and Lester inside and rushing ahead so that they arrived at the hotel before the servants. There he was greeted by an army of waiters, headed by the manager who ushered him to his suite on the second floor. Margaret was sent up when she arrived a little later, impressed by the size and grandeur of the hotel. She was almost swamped by the wealth of sumptuous detail in the foyer with its high, fanciful *trompe l'oeil* ceiling and columned walls, hothouse palms in china pots, vases and statues and mirrors that reflected the scene over and over.

'Splendid, isn't it?' Anna remarked as she led her confidently up the magnificent staircase covered in fern-green carpet. 'The Auberts always stay here when in Paris.' They stopped outside a double cedarwood door with elaborate brass fittings. 'This is their suite,' she continued, and rapped lightly on the panelling. It was opened almost at once by Merther.

'Are we to have our usual rooms?' Anna asked, sweeping past him.

'Yes, Mademoiselle.'

'I'll take you there later,' Anna promised as they walked through an anteroom and entered a beautifully appointed salon. 'Now I must find Lady Fenella and see what she has planned for this afternoon.'

'Her ladyship is waiting for you, Helbren,' Merther said, and pointed towards a further door.

'It's marvellous to be here again!' Julia carolled as Margaret went in. She was preparing to change out of her travelling costume. 'You'll have to learn to speak the native tongue. Mademoiselle Rainier will teach you.'

165

'Yes, my lady.'

'Run a bath. I feel absolutely filthy. After lunch I intend to do a little shopping.'

Margaret had no time to do more than remove her hat and jacket. She resented being hustled as she walked over thick blue carpet that matched the floral wallpaper. The paintwork was white, the door panels covered in the same paper as the walls. Some were of glass hung with lace curtains, a style which she was to later recognise as typically French. The enormous bed was canopied with yards of cream silk, the furniture heavily carved and ornate, of the period when the country was ruled by the bourgeois king, Louis-Philippe.

The rich brocades, the shimmering damasks aroused in her a longing that almost amounted to sickness. This was a foreign, exotic world and she coveted it.

The luxurious marble bathroom added to her envy. She leaned over the tub, twisted the gold-plated taps and watched the steaming water cascade on to the smooth ceramic bottom. And all the time her thoughts were running: Where was Lester's room? What was he doing now? Would he be strolling down the boulevards later? Oh, Lester, Lester! Why aren't we on our honeymoon and occupying the bridal suite?

'Is it ready?' Julia appeared, wearing an ivory-satin pegnoir.

'Very nearly, madam.'

Margaret poured in a generous measure of scented oil. Pushing up her sleeve she sat on the edge of the tub and reached down, stirring the oil around with her hand. The water was hot and delicious. This should be for my use, she thought angrily. She spun the taps and the flow immediately stopped.

She stood behind Julia and helped her out of her robe, admiring her smooth white skin and well-preserved body. For a women who had borne six children, her figure was remarkably slim and taut. Julia stepped into the bath and sank down with a sigh, inclined to chat.

'That's better. One gets so terribly hot and dusty on trains. We could have taken the Calais-Mediterranean Express, but we like to break our journey. It will be worth it when we reach the Riviera. Such a beautiful coast and so many fascinating persons to meet, though it's quieter this time of the year. In the spring one simply can't move for people, some of them quite common, lured by the casinos. There are numerous invalids enjoying the temperate climate – people with chest complaints and arthritis. It can be quite depressing. You may go and start unpacking, Helbren. Lay out my white lawn dress and leghorn hat. One has to watch one's complexion in the strong sun.'

If only this was all I had to worry about, Margaret reflected,

166

retreating to the bedroom. Perhaps one day it will be. I shall say to Lester, 'Darling, I'm sure I can see a freckle on my nose. Look.'

And he will reply, using it as an excuse to hold me close, 'What nonsense! Your nose is beautiful. I adore your nose.'

She caught a glimpse of him at lunchtime. The Auberts occupied a table in the large dining room, the walls lustrous with different types of wood and hung with a series of watercolours of Versailles in rose-wood frames. On a small stage at the far end, a quintette played Mozart.

There were a multitude of round tables, sparkling with glass and silver where guests of a dozen nationalities talked vivaciously in little, exclusive groups. The maître d', a bulky, dignified black-clad figure with a drooping walrus moustache, hovered solicitously as Henry ordered.

Margaret and Anna sat in an area designated to governesses and companions and, when lunch was over, Anna took up her duties with Fenella and Margaret continued finding the items Julia would need for their overnight stay.

The fact that Julia had not invited her to go shopping emphasised her status. She was entirely dependent on another's whim, her mistress giving no thought to whether she might have enjoyed visiting the stores in this exciting city. As it was she felt isolated in the apartment, hearing distant voices speaking in an alien tongue. Merther and Carew were somewhere about, and probably Radley, but she had no desire to converse with either of them. Lester had a bedroom there, but though she lingered in the salon in the hope of seeing him, it seemed that he, too, was exploring Paris.

Her own room was further down the corridor and shared with Anna. Work done for the time being she retired there to take the opportunity to wash and change. Carefully dusting herself with sweet-scented talc on emergence from the bathroom, she wondered why she was bothering. It would be unlikely she and Lester would meet that night. She ached for him, standing before the mirror in the pretty room with its matching twin bedsteads, cupping her naked breasts in her hands and pretending they were his, desire blossoming, spreading, culminating between her thighs.

He had awakened her passion, shown her how to indulge it and now it gave her no peace. Tears sprang into her eyes. I wish I'd never met him! she stormed, but knew it wasn't true. Curse him though she might in moments of rage and frustration, she was thankful from the bottom of her heart that he was her lover, albeit a frequently absent one.

She changed into a clean dress on the offchance of seeing him and, when Lady Julia returned, resumed her duties. And he was there, taking tea with the Auberts on the balcony overlooking the tree-lined avenue while they entered into a lively discussion on fashion, politics, the wonder of the Paris shops, their plans for the evening.

Fenella was in raptures, as if she had never before visited the city, but this times it was without the restrictions imposed by Madame Dubois and the academy. The only time the pupils had been allowed out was in a crocodile when they were taken to view the Louvre or some equally boring institution. Now she could go with her parents and tonight there was the promise of seats at the opera house, followed by supper at some wildly smart and extravagant restaurant.

'You'll come with us?' Julia enquired of her son, graciously pouring tea from a silver pot set on a little cane table covered with an exquisitely worked lace cloth.

'I think not, Mater, if you'll excuse me. Lester and I want to look up a couple of friends in Montmartre.'

'Must you go there, dear? Isn't that where artists and other undesirables reside?' She pretended to be shocked.

'Leave the boy be,' Henry chided good-humouredly, amused to play at paterfamilias. 'I can recall being a young man in Paris myself. The Latin Quarter is filled with writers and painters and I don't know what else. Stimulating talk in street cafés, a host of pretty girls to ogle. Very *vie de Bohème*, my dear. Just like the opera by that Italian fellow – what's-his-name?'

'Puccini,' Lester said.

'That's right, my boy – sentimental twaddle. Give me a rousing military band any day.'

Margaret listened and watched and suffered. Lester did not once look her way. It was a relief when Julia sent her to the bedroom to lay out her evening gown.

When everyone had finally departed, the women splendid in silks and jewels, the men distinguished in formal black suits, cloaks and toppers, Anna came looking for her. She, too, was dressed for outdoors.

'I've arranged to see Etienne,' she said, and her cheeks were flushed, her eyes bright. 'Would you like to come?'

Margaret shook her head. 'No, thank you. I don't fancy the idea of playing gooseberry.'

'Silly girl,' Anna chuckled. 'It won't be a bout of unbridled passion. His parents will be there and we shall go to a very respectable café. You'd be most welcome.'

'I'm tired. I'll rest till her ladyship comes back.'

In reality, Margaret was still hoping Lester would make some excuse and come to her. He had said that Roderick was *au fait* with the situation and willing to help them, but her distrust of the Aubert heir still lingered.

The hours crawled by on leaden feet and Margaret tortured herself by imagining what he might be doing in Montmartre. He had told her about his visits to that quarter of Paris where the Bohemians held sway, artists, men of letters and talented women, too, who set conventions aside. An area of smoky dives, *estaminets* haunted by the demi-monde, gambling dens – and females everywhere, models, actresses, dancers, and ladies looking for lower-class lovers.

Margaret paced the room, wringing her hands in anguish as her quick imagination threw up one obscene vision after another. Somehow she got through the evening and was dismissed when Henry and Julia came in. She was carrying a huge bouquet and he flourished a bottle of champagne. It was Margaret's cue to absent herself. Anna was back by that time and wanted to chatter about Etienne. Margaret listened when they were in bed. It provided a diversion from her agonised speculations. Roderick and Lester were still out.

Anna slept at last but Margaret lay awake, hearing the hours strike, and it was not till the room lightened to a pale, smuggy grey that she finally heard the muffled sounds of laughter and voices in the corridor outside. He was back, and sleep overwhelmed her, sweeping her away to merciful oblivion.

Margaret had decided to keep a diary. She had started when they left London, and now found it gave her something to do as the train rattled towards the coast. Seated with the journal propped on her knee, she took up her fountain pen and began to write.

'The Auberts decided not to stay in Paris for a second day, and this morning we left by the nine-forty train for Marseilles. I saw Lester from a distance. He looked tired. I'm tired, too. Here I am, imprisoned with the valets, Luke and Anna. They tell me it is a long journey, occupying some fourteen or fifteen hours and exceedingly tedious, though we are promised a break at Lyons.'

'Keeping yourself busy?' said a voice from across the carriage. 'You'll not have much time for scribbling when we get to Monty.'

Margaret looked up and met Radley's predatory gaze. She did not bother to answer. His smirk told her he was aware and rejoicing in her unhappiness. He knew what his master had done last night, what time he had come back to the hotel and the state he was in. Radley, of the low-grade lusts, who probably understood Lester better than she could ever hope to.

'It won't be all work,' Luke chipped in, sensitive to her feelings. He was nobody's fool and, though it hurt him, had known for some weeks that she was having an affair with the Irish lord. 'We shall have time to ourselves and I'll show you the sights.' He turned to Radley, saying, 'Care for a game of cards?'

Margaret sank back in her seat and closed her book. She had the feeling that Radley would try to read what she was writing. Her diary was too personal for his eyes, or indeed for anyone's save her own, and even then she was wondering whether to score through some of her passionate outpourings regarding Lester.

They approached Lyons through spectacular scenery, crossing a fine bridge with the great city stretching out on each side and numerous smaller ones spanning the river. The Auberts had booked a suite in advance in another palatial hotel. The same routine followed but with a difference: Margaret had a room to herself.

She sat by the window as everything fell into silence and sleep. It was getting steadily hotter the further south they went. The sweat pooled in her armpits and dripped from beneath her breasts. She kept the netting across the windows, warned of mosquitoes – a slight hazard in Lyons but it was wise to get into the habit before they reached their destination. Her mind was alert. She had managed to doze on the train. She sat so still that it was as if she was performing a secret magic, concentrating every iota of her will on Lester.

He came to her out of the night, as the moon sailed serenely over the sky and a fragile violet mist hung over the river, dusted with gold from the bridge illuminations. She started at his tap on her door.

'Who is it?' she whispered, her body telling her it was him, her mind warning it might be Radley chancing his luck.

'Hush, darling. Let me in. I want to see you,' he replied, his smooth, silky baritone voice wrapping itself round her heart.

She did not speak. Having waited days for this moment, her limbs felt leaden. She had thought she had been emotionally prepared. Now she knew she was not. Slowly she turned the key, reached for the door handle and pushed down on it. Lester stepped inside.

He was in his shirtsleeves, his legs encased in slim black trousers. He reached for her and she fell against him, almost sobbing at the feel of his hands skimming across her back, at the dear familiarity of his chest crushing her breasts. The smell of him intoxicated her, brandy and cigars, hair pomade and shaving soap. Desperately lonely, sad and afraid, every emotion within her fused and focused into desire. Nothing else mattered.

The room was dimly lit, and he swung her up and laid her on the bed, pushing up her nightgown, fumbling with his fly buttons. He took her without saying anything, and Margaret was so grateful to have him there that she accepted this without question.

Next day on the train she wrote, 'He loves me. I know he does. I was beginning to doubt, but not after last night. He was so sweet to me, held me lovingly, told me not to worry. I must trust him, he said. I will. Lester, my dear one, I promise that I will.'

Now she could take heed of the passing scene, revitalised, surprising Anna by her wit and observations. The Frenchwoman could not know that Margaret's skin was still tingling from Lester's caresses, her mouth bruised by his kisses. 'Till next time,' he had whispered against her lips as he left at dawn.

'The scenery much resembles the Rhine,' Merther proclaimed in his pompous way, a walking guidebook, even more knowledgeable than the Baedecker with which Margaret had equipped herself. He peered out of the window and continued, ignoring Radley's rude yawns. 'It has the same high cliffs, richly wooded promontories, historic and baronial castles and picturesque chateaux.'

'Spare us the lecture, Mr Merther,' Radley said crudely. 'It fair puts a chap off his cards.'

Merther's upper lip curled superciliously. 'The young lady is interested, even if you aren't. To continue, my dear Miss Helbren – the land is full of ancient sites, especially near Marseilles, at Avignon and Arles. Here we shall see many old Roman settlements and ruins.'

With her mind freed and her body satisfied by Lester's visit to her bed, Margaret was able to appreciate the country as they passed swiftly through. The rich, dark earth spawned a wide variety of products that made a continuous change in the appearance of the landscape, from the wheat-growing fields to the vine, and thence to that of the olive. Terrace upon terrace lined the hills and rocky knolls. Every inch of ground seemed to be cultivated.

And the heat increased.

This was most noticeable when the train stopped briefly. Then stepping out of the carriage was like opening an oven door, blasts of hot air coming in waves. Margaret almost gagged when she used the lavatory at one of the stations. It was exceedingly dirty, shared by both sexes, vastly inferior to the toilet facilities on the train.

It was midnight when they reached Marseilles, too late to appreciate the station with its courtyard and garden, orange trees and flowering myrtles. Margaret was so weary by the time she had settled Julia into the Regina Hotel that she fell across her bed without bothering to undress, sleeping at once, hardly pausing to wonder if Lester might take it into his head to join her.

On Henry's whim they remained in Marseilles for two days. Margaret shared Julia's relief at the welcome break from railroads, and her mistress made a point of including her in sightseeing trips.

'You can carry my bag and the guidebook, Helbren, and any small souvenirs I may purchase. I mustn't forget to buy postcards. I've so many to send. You can address them for me. Buy some yourself and post them to friends. I see no reason why you shouldn't benefit from travel, do you?'

'No, my lady.' Margaret picked up the articles indicated and prepared to follow her mistress to the waiting carriage.

'Do you like working for me?' Julia said suddenly, her green eyes sharp as needles.

'Yes, madam.' This question caught Margaret off balance.

'You don't feel in any way resentful of Fenella or myself?' Julia glanced in one of the several mirrors that lined the corridor and tweaked the stiffened organza brim of her flowery hat.

Margaret was tempted to tell the truth, but, 'Resentful? No. Should I be?' she countered, and realised that she did not much care for this woman, suspecting that beneath the genteel exterior lay depths few could plumb.

Julia gave a bright smile. 'You'd be an ingrate if you were, Helbren. Have I not offered you the chance to better yourself? A lot of girls would give their eyeteeth to be in your position.'

'Yes, my lady. Thank you, my lady.' I, too, can be insincere, Margaret thought. I'll play the game your way for now, but you're in for a shock when Lester announces our engagement.

Marseilles was magnificently situated, the greatest port in the Mediterranean. Margaret rejoiced in the hot sun, the sky of a blue seldom seen at home, matching the cobalt waters. Her Cornish blood quickened at this close proximity to the sea. She longed to bathe and then laze on the sandy beaches, and gazed entranced at the vegetation lining the road as they passed in an open calash – palm trees and cacti and aloes, and strange-looking plants with which she was unfamiliar. The air was spiced with the scent of orange trees.

Julia insisted they went on a tour of the parks and monuments.

'Do we have to drag round any more sites?' Fenella moaned after an hour, her face bright pink, little beads of sweat dewing her upper lip. 'I'm tired. My feet ache, and I want an ice cream.'

'In a while, dear. I've ordered our driver to take us to the docks. Papa is down there already. Do stop whinging. You can be very tiresome, Fenella.'

To the docks they went, catching up with the gentlemen who were standing on the quay viewing the vessels which ranged from stately Orient liners to Sicilian feluccas. The latter were closely packed, their enormous masts and sails, their swarthy red-capped crews giving them the raffish appearance of pirate ships.

172

'Aren't they delightful?' Fenella gushed, forgetting to whine. 'I like the South of France, the boys are so handsome. Just look at those sailors! D'you think they're buccaneers?'

Julia frowned sternly at one young rascal who was staring impudently across at Fenella. He had dark, velvety eyes, a bronzed skin, and a slim, supple body.

'My dear girl, nothing so exciting, I'm afraid,' she said acidly. 'Their job is to get cargoes of fruit to the Marseilles market.' She slipped her hand into the crook of Henry's arm. 'Have you seen enough? I suggest we ascend to the Cordiere Gardens which, I understand, command a wonderful view of the city.'

She was indefatigable, too much even for the gentlemen, though they had to admit that the windy heights provided a spectacular vista, the harbour and docks set in a grand amphitheatre of sun-bleached hills. A few miles away, like dark jewels in the shining sea, were several small islands.

'On one of those, I'm not sure which, stands the celebrated Chateau d'If, immortalised by Alexandre Dumas in his novel *The Count of Monte Cristo*,' Lester observed, the warm breeze lifting his hair. His skin was already browner from exposure to the strong sun, contrasting dramatically with his white linen suit. The dark glasses he wore gave him a strangely sinister appearance. It was impossible to read his eyes through them.

'There, Fenella. One learns something every day, doesn't one?' exclaimed her mother from behind the blue veil which she had draped from her hat, a lacy parasol hardly enough protection. 'You can't still find sightseeing boring, surely?'

'No, Mama,' Fenella agreed, hoping to be allowed to return to where the feluccas were anchored. 'But it is awfully hot.'

'We'll go back to the hotel for luncheon, and then take a siesta, but there's more to see first.'

Ignoring her daughter's protests, she turned her attention to the ancient church of Notre Dame de la Garde with its high pinnacle topped by a colossal figure of the Virgin Mary, gazing out to sea and guarding those who sailed. By the time they had passed through the public gardens and crossed the dock basin in a ferry boat in order to visit the Byzantine church of St Nazaire, Margaret had had more than enough. Only the fact that Lester was present made it bearable. She could watch him, listen to the cadenzes of his voice and console herself by remembering the last time they had made love.

The next day was Sunday and, to her astonishment, he called for her in the morning while the family were at church. 'I can't leave,' she protested, knowing nothing would have stopped her.

'Sure, you can. They'll be lunching with a *comte* and his lady. You'll not be needed for ages,' he insisted, his even white teeth flashing in the dark wedge of his face. 'Come on, darling.'

He hailed a cab and within a short while they were in the town. The whole place was like a great fair, everyone bent on fun and pleasure; hucksters' stalls, marionettes, bazaars, open-air concerts and theatres. Margaret clung to his arm, hot, excited, enjoying herself hugely. He bought her candy and tried his skill at the rifle range, winning her a doll.

'She's lovely,' Margaret sighed, holding her treasure on her lap when they sat in a crowded café where old men played dominoes, young studs took up stances at the billard table, and others buried their noses in copies of *Le Figaro*. 'I never had a doll when I was little.'

'Didn't you?' There was a musing quality in his voice, and his usually hard grey eyes were softer.

'I shall call her Mignonette,' she decided, touching the golden curls made of human hair, the pink satin dress, the tiny kid shoes.

'You didn't have much of a childhood, did you?' he said, and clicked his fingers at a passing waiter. '*Café au lait*, and a glass of brandy.'

'It doesn't matter now.' She stared at him, eyes shining with love. 'You are so kind to me—'

'Hush, don't say that.' He placed a finger over her lips.

'But you are,' she insisted. 'And I'm eternally grateful. You entering my life has been like a miracle. Sometimes I want to pinch myself to make sure I'm awake.'

'You make me sound like a holy saint,' he said gruffly. 'I'm far from that.'

She sat the doll on a spare chair and leaned closer to him, winding her fingers in his. They were anonymous in this café. No one knew them. They could have been a boy and girl from the same class. Ordinary sweethearts. Ordinary lovers. It gave her an intoxicating sense of freedom.

'I don't expect you to be perfect,' she whispered. 'We all have faults.'

He kept his face averted and the sombre look lingering there at all times settled over his features. 'You mustn't think so highly of me.'

She sat back, baffled. 'Why not? I love you, Lester. Nothing can alter that. Don't you want me to love you?'

He selected a cigarette, tapped it on the gold case, and slowly lit it. This was a device he had thought up long ago as a delaying tactic to give himself time to think. He blew the smoke through his nostrils. Then he took her hand and kissed it, his breath tickling the flesh.

'That's an odd question. Love is love, I suppose. One can't order or control it.'

174

His touch was hypnotic and she slipped into complacency, without realising he was adept at evading issues, never giving a direct answer to a question. In the smoky atmosphere, filled with foreign voices, the tock of cues against balls, the click of dominoes accompanied by a waltz played on a concertina, she was content to listen as he whispered in her ear. He spoke of what delights he would give her with his kisses and embraces, using secret little erotic words, one hand caressing her back, the other holding her hand.

Limp with love, she allowed him to lull her, and when they walked through the streets he had an arm about her waist, while she clutched the doll to her breast as if it was their baby.

The hotel was deserted. Luncheon over, the staff were either sleeping or at the fair. No one saw Lester slip into Margaret's room. The shutters were drawn over the window, fingers of sunlight working their way through the slats. Dimness, heat – the seering heat of passion. They stripped and he sank to his knees before her, drawing her close, covering her body with kisses. Margaret yielded herself up to his experienced lovemaking. He was her man, almost her husband, nothing could come between them now.

Chapter 10

'This is a fairy-tale world, divorced from reality,' Margaret wrote in her diary. 'I never knew such places existed. My aunts wouldn't believe it, though if they did they'd condemn Cannes as a sink of iniquity. I'm utterly bewitched by it. To think there are those who live their lives through without ever experiencing such colour, scent and sight. My father, for example, who spent his entire life grubbing about under the earth like a mole. It must have been worse for my mother, condemned to endure Porthross, for she had mixed with people who must have visited the Riviera. She knew there was far more than a poverty-stricken existence in a Cornish fishing village. She wanted it for me. And I have it, in a roundabout way. I'm here and, if all goes according to plan, I'll be spending a part of every year in these beauty spots when I'm married to Lester.'

She was on the little iron balcony of her bedroom in the Hotel Windsor, bathed in the glow of the setting sun, great fans of crimson, purple, green and apricot sweeping across the heavens. The sea shone far below, transformed into a lake of fire. The perfume of roses and jasmine wafted up, sensual, evocative, seducing her from scholarly jottings on the flora and fauna to heated recollections of passion.

A Chopin *Nocturne* swelled from further along the corridor, adding an extra touch of romance. The hotel manager had thoughtfully provided pianofortes in most rooms, as well as two in the downstairs salon. This had foiled Fenella's plot to wriggle out of practising. Julia put a stop to such shirking. To be able to play was an asset to any young lady. Gentlemen went to pieces at the sight of a pretty woman seated at a piano, the muted light of a candelabra touching her features while her hands moved delicately over the keys.

But this was not Fenella performing. It was too skilled. Under Lester's guidance, Margaret had learned to recognise quality playing. She paused to listen, but then continued to write.

176

'We've been here for two days, and the Auberts' American relatives are expecting us in Monte Carlo the day after tomorrow. Luke tells me that Lord Henry has already rented a car, so it's back to work for him. I suppose the rest of us will go by train.' Without realising it she pressed more heavily on the pen, the words inky and forceful as she added, 'Sometimes I feel as if I'm about to explode. There's so much boiling inside me.'

She stopped and reached for the doll, little pale bisque-headed Mignonette of the pink-painted cheeks and rosebud mouth, the lips slightly parted to show pearly teeth. Her lids had fringed lashes that opened and closed over lifelike blue eyes. Glass jewels flashed in her pierced ears. Twenty-two inches tall, she had a jointed composition body that enabled her limbs to be placed in several positions. Whenever Margaret looked at her she was reminded of that perfect afternoon in Marseilles.

She lifted her, feeling her lightness, admiring her clothes which were miniature replicas of a child's garments. 'When Lester and I have a daughter, I shan't give you to her,' Margaret promised solemnly. 'Maybe I'll let her play with you on special occasions, but you'll always be mine.'

Was it possible she would know the rapture of giving birth to his baby? Margaret never doubted it, as certain as she was of the earth spinning on its axis, the sun rising at dawn and Julia insisting that everyone improve their education by another bout of sightseeing.

Already that incorrigible tourist had made them stroll in the Hesperides Gardens and along the promenade. Margaret's duties now included that of secretary. She addressed and attached postage stamps to innumerable picture postcards. A few were her own, for she did not forget Susan and Thora.

Wherever they went Julia made a beeline for the gift shops, rooting through the cards and emerging with a stack. Margaret hoped this would lessen when they reached Monte Carlo. It was planned as their final stop, though Julia, the restless one, had been talking in a disquieting fashion of crossing the border into Italy.

'We're visiting Grasse in the morning, Helbren,' she said later, performing the nightly routine of patting cold cream into the fine lines near her eyes. 'That's where the most exquisite scents are created. I expect to come away with a few samples. There's nothing to compare with French perfume.'

Margaret nodded, concentrating on running the silver-backed brush over Julia's hair, but inside she was wishing Lester would buy her some, though she would only be able to use it when with him. Perfume was for prostitutes and great ladies. Maids were forbidden to wear anything stronger than lavender water, and only when off duty.

'Say you don't feel well,' Lester prompted when she managed to escape. He was waiting for her in the corridor. 'I've a much better idea than trailing round the flower farms.'

'What is it?' Margaret glanced about nervously but the passage was empty. It was well after midnight. Most guests had retired.

'Wait and see.' He grinned down at her wickedly, eyes and teeth gleaming in the glow of wall lights shielded behind peach silk shades.

It seemed he was challenging her to embark on a reckless adventure, and everything dark and dangerous within her responded. Why not go? she thought. I'm sick of being Lady Julia's slave.

'All right,' she whispered, and he wrapped her in an embrace she could not fully enjoy, too frightened someone might catch them.

'Can I come into your room?' he murmured, running his tongue round the velvety rim of her ear, sending shivers down her spine.

'I'm sharing with Anna.'

'That's a pity. I need you tonight.'

This is awful, she thought. I don't like these clandestine meetings, though they seem to arouse him. I'll be so glad when we no longer have to hide. But her misgivings melted when he kissed her demandingly, and all she wanted was his strong body, any time, anywhere, under any circumstances.

Julia was displeased when Margaret told her she was unwell and asked if she might stay behind. 'I've been sick all night, my lady,' she added. 'And have to keep running to the lavatory.'

'This is most inconvenient,' Julia snapped crossly, then turned to Anna. 'You'll take on Helbren's duties. Fenella will just have to put up with going where I go, instead of wandering off with you.'

'It is no problem, madame,' Anna said brightly, more concerned about Margaret, saying later, 'Go back to bed, *chérie*. Take nothing but a few sips of boiled water. The English often suffer with upset stomachs in this heat.'

Feeling a liar and a fraud, two conditions alien to her nature, Margaret sat in her room listening to the sounds of their departure. After a while she changed her clothes, tiptoed out and went down the grand staircase, having arranged to meet Lester at the back of the hotel. Wearing a frilly white lawn dress and confident that she was as suitably attired as any lady tourist, she sauntered out into the dazzling sunlight sliced across by the black shadows of buildings.

He was seated in an open-topped car, tinted glasses pushed back on his forehead, the engine running as he smoked a cigarette and drummed on the steering wheel with impatient fingers.

'I hired it especially,' he explained, throwing open the passenger door. She slid into the seat, the leather upholstery scalding her thighs through the flimsy skirt.

'Where are we going?' She snatched off her hat and shook down her hair, thinking, I might as well be hung for a sheep as a lamb. I'm done for if anyone who knows Lady Julia sees us.

'To paradise,' he shouted, laughing as he accelerated.

The car shot forward, and she lifted her face to the sun. This was her treat and she intended to enjoy it to the full. It was exhilarating to dash through the town in this expensive racing model.

'People are looking at us,' she cried above the roar of the engine. 'I expect they're wondering why we're unchaperoned.'

'They'll dimiss us as mad. Every Continental thinks we're a crazy race of eccentrics.'

'Perhaps they'll assume we're married.'

'Maybe they will. This is the Land of Illusion.'

They left the higher ground occupied by a series of fine establishments like the Windsor that catered for titled guests, and wound down through dusty streets, coming at last to the esplanade, a generous road lined with feathery fronded palm trees. It had the sea on one side and a row of hotels on the other. Margaret expected Lester to stop, but he drove straight on.

They cruised passed shops and cafés and villas with cool green shutters nestling among trees and gardens. Vines swarmed over and around the pillars and trelliswork. Carriages rolled by, carrying gentleman in Panama hats and ladies sheltering under veils and sunshades. A couple of rowdy young automobilists hooted in salute as Lester's car left them standing.

The sands were dotted with bathing tents and thronged with people; children splashing in the sea, nannies on the alert, mothers attended by servants and reclining on cushions beneath canvas awnings or enormous round fibre-thatched umbrellas. Sporting gentlemen ventured in, wearing dark woollen swimsuits, and a few daring young ladies paddled in the shallows in knee-length dresses and long voluminous bloomers, their hair concealed by frilly-edged bathing caps.

The sea was studded with white-rigged yachts, dingies and motorboats. Margaret had a sudden inspiration. 'You're taking me sailing, aren't you?' she said.

'Wrong,' he answered crisply, slanting her a smile.

'Oh, Lester. Don't be so infuriating!'

The traffic lessened, the area they were now passing through even more select. Mansions glistened white, glimpsed between wrought-iron gates surrounded by blue gum and eucalyptus trees that overhung high walls.

179

'Can't you smell it?' Lester asked abruptly.

'What? The flowers? The sea?'

'The smell of money,' he said, a grim smile playing about his lips. 'The sweetest smell on earth. The Riviera reeks of it, my dear. Wait till we hit Monte Carlo, though there it's mixed with another odour, the stink of despair and death. The suicide rate is high.'

She shivered and the brilliant scene dimmed fractionally. 'Why?'

'Gambling fever. It can become an obsession, so don't go to the casino and risk your wages, will you?' His eyes were filled with mockery, his mouth twisted into that cruel smile she feared and detested.

'I've no intention of doing anything so foolish,' she said primly, hurt when he burst into a gale of laughter.

'That's what they all say, those who fall under the spell of the Côte d'Azur.'

'I think it's quite wonderful,' she protested weakly, ashamed of her ignorance when he knew so much.

'There's nothing wrong with the place itself. It's the mob who come here that ruin it. The Riviera can be disgusting with its greed, vulgarity, appalling snobbishness and bad taste.'

'But I thought only the best people visited it.'

'So they do, but there are a lot of hangers-on, a festering crowd of crooks and profiteers, pimps and whores, parasites and frauds. Worst of all are those dreary souls Lady Julia loves to cultivate – deposed royalty living on their wits.'

'Why did you come if you dislike it so much?'

'Did I say I didn't like it? Decadence has a certain sick fascination. Like death, the Coast of Futility always wins in the end. Besides, I had nothing else to do, and Roderick is paying. Any journey is exciting, and I suffer from the incurable disease of wanderlust.'

Margaret's optimism took a dive. He sounded so bitter and cynical, discontent and unhappiness festering inside him. Her basic desire was to nurture, but there were times when he was so prickly it was impossible to reach him, and best to remain silent until the mood passed.

The coastal road opened out, the sea on their right. On the other side the lower slopes of rugged hills rose at the back of the town, bright with houses, stuccoed in pink, yellow and white, half smothered in masses of burgundy bougainvillaea. These were interspersed with olive trees, whose sombre, silver-tinted foliage and gnarled, twisted trunks convinced Margaret as nothing else that she was in a foreign country.

In a while the road dipped and Lester steered the car to a grass verge above a sheltered cove. He braked and sat staring at the ever-changing

180

movement of the sea. Margaret waited, hardly daring to disturb his reverie. Then he suddenly hauled her into his arms and kissed her.

'Help me unload.'

The rear seat housed a wicker basket which he swung up and hoisted over one arm. Margaret, carrying towels, rugs and cushions, followed him down a steep pathway to the shore. Lester had already removed his shoes and socks, tie off, shirt unbuttoned, jacket hooked over one shoulder.

'There's no one else here,' she exclaimed when he came to rest near a jagged pile of rocks.

'It's a private beach belonging to a friend of mine. Let's set up camp.' He lifted the hamper lid, took out a bottle of champagne and sank it in a shady rock-pool.

'I haven't brought a bathing dress,' she protested, alarmed as he started to strip.

'Neither have I.' He stepped out of his trousers and stood there naked, stretching his arms above his head, legs spread wide to balance his weight. 'Don't be shy. We won't be disturbed. Didn't I tell you I was taking you to paradise? Adam and Eve in the Garden of Eden.'

Without waiting for her, he padded down to the water's edge and was soon waist deep, then plunged in and struck out vigorously. Margaret hesitated. She had bathed nude in Cornwall, but had known the area, confident that she would be unobserved. Lester did not seem to care whether he was seen or not. And, more important, whether *she* was seen.

'Damn him,' she muttered. 'I suppose he thinks I'm too shy. I'll show him!' And she peeled off her clothes without giving herself time to lose her nerve.

The scalding rays played over her skin as she folded her garments and laid them in a pile on the spread blanket. She shivered with delight as her body woke to the overwhelming need for pleasure. Lester was right. He always was. This was the best possible way to be, mother-naked in the sun and sea. She ran across the sand to join him. It burned the soles of her feet and when she reached the water its white-crested wavelets lapped her ankles like a tepid bath.

She opened her arms wide, wanting to embrace the glorious Mediterranean. It was nothing like the surging seas of home, harsh and cold, battering the Cornish coast. It typified the South where most things could be put off till tomorrow, interwoven with a dark sensuality rooted in basic passions.

She went in deeper, the water creeping over her thighs, her belly, higher to lip her breasts. Lester dived, came up under her, clasped her wet bare body to his, tiny droplets spangling his skin. They played in the sea, indulging the child within, indulging the adult who could not resist the strong sexual attraction surging between them. They could have been the only persons alive, with nothing but the sound of waves and gulls to break the silence.

His eyes were no longer grey, reflecting the sea shades of greens and blues. Margaret, sure she was losing her mind as his hands caressed her, stared into them. They mirrored her desire, an ocean in which she wanted to drown. His hair was slick with water, strained back from his face, the cheekbones more prominent, the lips more red and sensual.

The waves swept round and between them, and though they were pressed so close, she could feel the tickling sensation of impudent watery fingers exploring her core. His face came closer, out of focus, and she tipped back her head and closed her eyes as he captured her lips, his own tasting of salt, cool, refreshing. Then, still kissing her, he swung her up with an arm beneath her buttocks, the other under her shoulders, and carried her to where they would be screened by rocks.

Love in the open air, love with the sand sticking to her wet skin when, in the throes of ecstasy, they rolled off the blanket. Afterwards, they lay prone under the noonday sun, and Margaret longed for this moment to last for ever. He moved, fumbling for his cigarette case. Soon she inhaled the sweet odour of Turkish tobacco. Too idle to stir a muscle, one arm flung over her eyes to shield them from the blinding glare, she heard the creak of the hamper.

'Time for lunch,' he said, his voice low and rich, holding almost the purr of a satisfied tom-cat. 'I'm always hungry after making love.'

It was too abrupt a switch from bliss to everyday, but Margaret sat up and accepted the caviare, pâté and bread-sticks he offered. Two champagne glasses held the sparkling pale gold wine. He toasted her, smiling, 'To you, darling. My pagan queen.'

Later, he fashioned a wreath of sea-pinks and set it on her hair, amusing himself by adorning her body with tiny shells, placing two larger ones over her nipples and another to cover her pubis. 'Now you are respectable,' he teased, lying beside her, sandy thighs pressed to hers, his hair a dusky mane about his smiling face.

'I wouldn't like to appear in public,' she giggled: the champagne bottle was empty. 'Whatever would Lady Julia say?'

'She'd be green with envy. You're very beautiful.' He sobered, his smile tinged with sadness.

'And I'm yours,' she whispered, her arms slipping round his neck to pull him down to her. 'Never forget that. I belong to you, Lester.'

'No one has the right to own another human being.'

'Not owning, darling – I'll be your companion and helpmate till the day I die. Your wife.'

182

He paused, seemed about to say something, then changed his mind. He thrust his hands into her hair, gripping it harshly as he said, 'No more talk. Let's do it again.'

'Are you better, Helbren?' Julia asked suspiciously as she took in Margaret's glowing cheeks and bright eyes. 'I must say you've a healthy colour. A person might be justified in thinking you'd been outside.'

'I did go for a walk, my lady. Haven't you often spoken of the benefits of fresh air? I took your advice.'

I'm becoming adept at telling half-truths, Margaret reflected, though she had been concerned on her return when she reached her bedroom and looked in her mirror. Her face and body were kissed by the sun as well as Lester, and she had the radiance of a woman who has recently been satisfied by the man she loves.

'You've made a quite remarkable recovery, but are somewhat flushed. I hope you don't go down with sunstroke,' Julia said sceptically, settling herself on the chaise longue positioned where she could catch the breeze stirring the lace curtains. 'You may press my emerald satin evening gown. We shall be dining out. You'll have packing to get on with.'

Some of Margaret's happiness dissipated. She was slapped back into place again. Be patient, she lectured herself. It won't be long now. One day soon I'll have a maid to do my bidding, and I swear to treat her well. She'll be a competent, motherly body, plain, of course. I'm not having any attractive girls on the staff. It's not that I don't trust Lester, but it's better to be on the safe side.

Margaret ordered a smoothing iron to be sent up. It was large, heavy and heated by the lump of charcoal smouldering inside. The emerald satin was creased and had to be pressed carefully. The sweat ran in rivulets down Margaret's face and soaked through the back of her cotton dress. After pulling the bodice undone and blowing down it to cool her breasts, she took up a ribbon and tied back her hair. The late afternoon was stifling, and her skin tingling from earlier exposure.

Perhaps Lester could buy a villa with their own private cove. Not at once, of course. He'd have to wait until the expenses of the wedding had been met and they had set up house in London or Ireland. She was rather vague about this. In usual circumstances the bride's father paid the bills, but she wasn't sure what would happen in her case. Presumably the onus would fall on Lester, with help from his family. These were joyous speculations, and before she knew it her work was completed.

The windows of the second-floor suite looked out on the gravelled drive that swept into a circle in front of the hotel. Margaret idled on the veranda, wondering if Lester might be anywhere about. The wind rustled the palms. Spray shot into the air from the central fountain where, at the feet of a statue of Venus Aphrodite, four stone lions ejected water from their opened mouths. The Windsor was quiet, but soon it would begin to stir in preparation for the evening's entertainment.

Everything seemed suspended in the heat quivering over the surface of the drive. The hotel was like an enchanted palace in a legend, and Margaret fell under its spell, caught up in that not quite sane, otherworldly sensation brought about by tiredness and emotional stress.

Why am I here? She wondered. Why did I meet Lester? There were times when their conversations went deep. He had studied philosophy and expounded theories as possible answers to many mysteries. Perhaps he's right, she thought dreamily, and there's truth in the Eastern belief in reincarnation. Perhaps everything is pre-ordained.

He had given her a small suede-bound copy of *The Rubáiyát of Omar Khayyám*. Now she opened it at the poem with the lines:

'The Moving Finger writes; and, having writ,
Moves on: nor all thy Piety nor Wit
Shall lure it back to cancel half a Line,
Nor all thy Tears wash out a Word of it.'

Karma, Lester had said. Destiny. Sometimes he had spoken with a fatalism that alarmed her; it was as if he wished to hand over responsibility for his actions to a higher power. But she had learned a great deal from him, that unpredictable, clever man who had not yet found his forte and settled at anything worthwhile.

A sudden commotion drew her attention to the scene below. A huge, gleaming silver monster of a car came purring up the drive from the direction of the gates. Its hood was folded back and a large man wearing goggles, a cap and voluminous dust coat was at the wheel in place of the uniformed chauffeur who occupied the seat beside him. Three ladies were in the rear, clad in hats and veils and capes.

As the vehicle stopped, the manager appeared at the top of the marble steps, a troop of footmen and pageboys behind him as he descended with hands stretched. These were obviously persons of importance. The big man climbed down, and the chauffeur assisted the ladies. The manager snapped his fingers and a servant helped the gentleman out of his overcoat. The ladies, too, shed their coverings, emerging like gorgeous butterflies from cocoons. One was mature, the others young and vivacious.

'You've arrived in one piece, Uncle Edward,' Roderick shouted, hurrying down the steps with Lester following. 'I received your message. Thanks for telephoning.'

'Thought I'd give Henry and Julia a surprise, my boy.' The big man clapped him on the shoulder. 'We'll stay the night and go back to Monty by motor in the morning. The girls gave me no peace. They are dying to meet you.' He held out his hands to his daughters, beaming with pride. 'Come here, my darlings. Let me present Lord Roderick, Viscount Stanwood. Roderick, may I introduce my daughters, Lady India and Lady Fay?'

They stepped forward, accompanied by their mother who immediately swept Roderick into an embrace and kissed him. They dipped into curtsies like a pair of animated dolls. Roderick bowed, smiled and said, 'I'm delighted. I'd like to present my friend, Lord Lester of Treleen Towers, County Wicklow, Ireland.'

Margaret stood transfixed on the balcony. A premonition chilled the sweat on her skin. The girls voices reached her – loud, bright, with a fascinating American accent. Dressed in frothy white blouses, striped skirts and boaters and wearing rather too much jewellery for that time of day, they moved with a swinging freedom; confident, sure of themselves, everything she was not.

She pressed her hands to her heart, unable to look away or go inside, the book of poems falling to the floor.

Roderick was playing the host till his parents surfaced from their siesta. They started to walk towards the steps, still talking, still laughing. The big man and his stout, noisy wife followed the fawning manager. Roderick had offered his arm to the shorter of the girls, but Lester was still standing by the Rolls-Royce, his dark head bent towards the other who gazed up at him with wide eyes, as if she had just witnessed a holy miracle.

As the days passed, Margaret conceived a deep loathing for Monte Carlo. She was invaded by a kind of languorous depression, a devitalising melancholy. Everything had changed. It was as if she had become invisible to Lester.

The Auberts were staying at the Hotel Metropole, guests in the palatial apartment of Lord Edward Culverhay (Teddy to his American wife who gloried in being addressed as Lady Ethel). This meant that Margaret could not avoid seeing Roderick paying court to Fay while Lester devoted himself to India. They played tennis, went boating, swimming, dancing and to concerts. And the girls' chaperone was worse than useless, never where she should be, more interested in gobbling down pastries than caring for her charges.

Each day Margaret put on a show, neatly dressed and respectful,

185

answering Julia's call, walking into the suite as if she hadn't a care in the world, though breaking up inside. She had struck up a friendship with Ethel's maid, a coloured woman named Crissie who opined that Fay and India were spoilt rotten.

Julia was having a wonderful time. She had not seen her cousin Edward for years. He had only visited home once since marrying Ethel, the daughter of a self-made man who had made a fortune in the steel industry in Chicago. A millionaire, he had refused to settle for less than a title for his only child. Edward had been available, matters arranged through a lady go-between who made a comfortable living from bringing together rich American girls and insolvent, though blue-blooded English gentlemen.

It had not mattered to Carl Vintner that his future son-in-law was the younger son of an impoverished baronet. He had wanted grandchildren whom he would provide with silver rattles stamped with heraldic crests, who would take precedence over him in doorways and later despise him for his bourgeois manners.

Ethel got her title and Edward slipped neatly into the role of a man of substance. When Carl Vintner died, his property, business interests, stock and vast wealth went to Ethel.

She might be vulgar in clothes and speech, but she held the purse strings and called the tune. Julia considered this to be an admirable arrangement and could gloss over the fact that neither Ethel or her daughters would ever acquire the panache of the English nobilty which had taken eight hundred years of selective breeding to produce. No amount of money could buy this.

Nevertheless, Ethel was generous and an Anglophile, her admiration of Julia boundless. Edward and she had not expected theirs to be a romantic alliance. She was eminently sensible and accepted the deal, fond of him in her own way. While he, easy-going and lazy, let her rule the roost and was besotted with his daughters. They were the jewels in his crown.

The casino was the most popular haunt in Monte Carlo, a magnet for those who could afford villas or hotels there, and for the drifters who came in by train daily to try their luck. Julia and Emily enjoyed a flutter, keeping their bets within reason, yet losses which would have seriously embarrassed gamblers of moderate means were a mere bagatelle to them.

One afternoon Margaret went there with Julia, passing through the flower-filled gardens and entering the dazzling concert room. There was nothing to pay. Plush-liveried servants handed them into chairs. Margaret sat with Crissie behind their mistresses. The huge, high-ceilinged hall was gilded and brocaded, offering every show of luxury, the decor predominantly Moorish.

'Sure is grand,' Crissie whispered in her husky voice, 'but I've seen more fancy places in New York and Miami. You should come visit.'

'How can I do that?' Though she was not far from an open window, Margaret could feel waves of heat breaking over her. She wondered if she was about to faint. 'It won't be possible unless Lord and Lady Aubert decide to stay with your master and mistress.'

Crissie shook her black curly head. 'They won't be doing that – not yet awhiles at least. Didn't you know that Lord Edward and Lady Ethel are going to England?'

'The girls, too?'

'Course. He won't be parted from his precious babies.'

Black specks swirled before Margaret's eyes and, just for a second, it seemed she lost consciousness. The orchestra was playing but she was not aware, everything blurred. Then her attention sharpened as, above the sound of strings, she heard India's laughter and saw her entering on Lester's arm.

Moving in a daze of misery, Margaret trailed after Julia when she and Ethel decided to play the tables. She was struck by the contrasting silence as they followed the stream of people through a handsome series of antechambers to the gambling saloons. Everyone spoke in whispers. There was a solemnity about it, similar to that felt in church. The large, spacious rooms contained no furniture except the long tables and chairs used for play. The blinds and curtains were closely drawn, excluding the blue skies, as if those so earnestly engaged preferred dim, artificial light.

Croupiers ruled, pasty-skinned, hard-eyed, spinning the ivory balls and raking in the piles of money. The Auberts and Culverhays made for tables further up where higher stakes were placed.

'Trente et quarante is perhaps a little more favourable to players than roulette,' Henry remarked.

'It depends very much on the shuffling of the cards,' Edward replied, puffing on a large cigar. 'I don't know that I trust those fellows.'

'Now stop shilly shallying, Teddy. Don't be an old meany,' Ethel commanded, seizing the chairs which two men had just vacated, their rueful expressions indicating that they were wiped out.

Henry stood behind his wife, watching and advising in hushed tones as the gold and notes were laid on the green baize surface, either for or against the numbers backed turning up. Lester and India were at the next table, and Margaret recalled his words at Cannes when he had professed to despise gamblers, yet now he seemed as obsessed as any of those he had condemned.

'Lend me some money, Papa!' India sang out, and Edward obligingly peeled notes from his wallet and handed them over.

Margaret longed to sit down, but this was impossible. The hot, smoky atmosphere caught in her throat, the scene sickening her. Cadaverous elderly women; others beautiful and reckless, evidently hired to act as decoys; yet more, well bred and inexperienced, pale and unhappy-looking. The men were hardened and ruthless. Even the young ones showed symptoms of the disease, feverishly clutching their winnings or silently counting their losses.

I must get out of this horrible place! Margaret thought, eyes returning constantly to Lester, seated close to India, oblivious to everything except the play.

He's as much a victim as any of the others. A dark tide of anger raced through her. What a hypocrite! It's a different story when he has money to burn. *Her* money, no doubt. Why, he's no better than those sleek-headed, dapper-suited gigolos fawning over the rich old women.

'I need air,' she whispered to Crissie, and without waiting to tell Julia, just managed to reach the garden before collapsing on a stone bench.

She was unable to control her tears, terrible harsh sobs tearing up from her very guts. All the worries and fears that had beset her since meeting Lester swamped her in a black cloud, restimulating the trauma of her mother's death and back, back, far earlier than that. She felt totally abandoned, reverting to the frightened child crouching in a dark cupboard when she heard her drunken father's slurring voice as he lurched into the cottage.

A shadow fell across her and for a fleeting moment she thought it was Lester, but, 'What's the matter, Miss Helbren?' Peter said.

Seeing him added to her disorientation. Was he real or a figment of her imagination? She could not speak for the racking sobs. He sat beside her and gave her a large white handkerchief, letting her cry it out. Slowly the storm spent itself.

'Why are you here?' she gasped, sniffing and wiping her eyes.

'To look after you.'

'But – but I thought you were in England. This is absolutely ridiculous. You can't be serious. Have you come to stay with the Auberts?'

'No. As I said, my main concern is you.'

He meant it! She could not grasp this reality. 'Why should you bother?' she asked, looking at him, her lashes black spikes, clotted with tears.

He wanted to kiss them away, to close her lids with kisses and bring her peace. No woman had ever made him feel like this. Usually he shared light-hearted relationships, fun while they lasted, doing no harm, but this was totally different. He accepted it, did not question it, was thankful for it, although it was grief.

188

He knew he must tread carefully. She was so fragile, and never more so than now. 'I care what happens to you,' he said gently.

This brought a fresh flood of tears. 'I'm sorry,' she sobbed.

'For what?'

He longed to put his arms round her, hold her against his chest, change her tears to laughter. She looked broken, her face red and streaked. Her hat was off and her hair had come unpinned, tendrils sticking to her wet cheeks. He had never wanted her more, unsure which was the stronger emotion, desire or compassion.

'For crying. It's nothing – really.'

'Look here, Margaret – I'm going to call you that and you must call me Peter – I know your position. I saw you at Henley. You've got yourself in a right old mess, haven't you?'

She dabbed her face, and ventured a glance at his profile turned towards her as his long-lashed eyes contemplated the dazzling blooms in the flower beds. Strong nose, a firm jaw, clean-shaven now: it made him look younger. His hair was glossy, sun-lightened on top, darker at the roots. He was dressed entirely in white, straw hat on the seat beside him, leaner than she remembered, body honed yet powerful.

'A mess? Maybe, if to fall in love is a mess,' she sighed. It was a relief that he knew the truth. 'I'd like to leave – now – at once, but I've no money for the fare and need my job with Lady Julia.'

'I'll help you out, if you like. I can lend you money.' Peter braced one arm along the back of the bench behind her. This was as far as he dare go, knowing she would bolt like a startled hare were he to venture more.

'Oh, no! I couldn't accept. I won't be indebted to anyone. Thank you all the same.' Her chin lifted, and the pride of her wrung his heart, while the beauty of her, emphasised by her distress, went straight to his loins.

He had delayed in Paris, then gone on to Cannes and Monte Carlo, keeping away from areas which the Auberts might frequent. Travelling alone, he had succeeded in keeping Margaret and Lester under surveillance. Bilingual, he had made enquiries about Lester at the casino and in less salubrious gambling houses, learning that he was in debt. There were always shady individuals willing to sell information.

Meanwhile, he had not been idle in his intentions to invade the kitchens, making friends with various hotel managers, including that of his own. Postcards had been sent regularly to Lillian, containing cryptic messages that intelligent woman would no doubt decipher.

He knew about the Americans, had observed Lester's attentions to one of the daughters and heard the rumours flying round that inbred and close-knit community. Putting two and two together had not been

189

difficult and he had waited his chance to speak to Margaret. Disaster loomed, and he wanted to be there when it happened.

To catch her on the rebound? Maybe. Ignoble, perhaps, but he didn't think so. There was far more to his interest in her than the mere satisfaction of lust.

'He doesn't love you,' he said. It was best to be brutal, to make her admit to the truth. At once he realised he had spoken too soon.

'How do you know?' She twisted away from him angrily. 'I told you once before to keep out of my business.'

'Can't you see that you've been mistaken?' Ignoring her rage, his eyes fixed hers – lovely eyes, tear-washed violet. He yearned to taste the salt of her tears, to run his tongue over her cheeks and into her mouth.

'I'll do nothing till I hear it from his own lips. Lester must tell me himself if he no longer wants me. He asked me to be his fiancée and I accepted.'

This news shook Peter. He had not anticipated a proposal. His eyes narrowed and his face grew stern. 'This is more serious than I supposed.'

'Doesn't that prove his love?' She should have felt triumphant but the doubts were multiplying.

'It proves he was determined to have you. I presume you are his mistress?'

'You're so rude!' she blazed, and he admired her even more, stubborn, loyal, infuriating. 'He is my first, my only lover. I think of him as my husband.'

His mouth turned down at the corners. 'Well, Margaret, if I were a betting man I'd wager that he doesn't think of you as his wife. If so, then he intends to be a bigamist.'

She sat there frozen, while the sunshine poured down on the garden, blazing on the domes and minarets of the casino. 'I don't understand,' she whispered at last through stiff lips.

He lost patience, his control snapping, wanting to shake sense into her, then make love to her so passionately that she would forget her unhappiness – forget that she had ever been in anyone else's arms but his.

'Can't you see what he's up to?' he shouted. 'He's wooing India Culverhay. Do you really believe he wants to marry you when he spends so much time with her? Only a halfwit could be so stupid. Isn't it obvious? Yours is a hole-in-the-corner affair. He meets you in secret, uses you like a whore, but keeps it from his own kind and is in hot pursuit of an heiress.'

'He's not ashamed of me. Roderick knows.' His harsh words sent the blood to her face, but even now she clung to the tattered remnants of illusion.

He gave an exasperated snort. 'Roderick is a prize rat. He makes a habit of seducing his mother's maidservants and anyone else he can get his hands on. I shouldn't be surprised if he wasn't at the bottom of it all. He and Lester are thick as thieves.'

'I can't listen to any more of this.' She rose unsteadily, and he put out a hand to support her as he got to his feet. She pulled her arm away as if his fingers at been dipped in acid.

'I'm staying at the Hotel Byron. Leave a message there if you need me.' Peter had never felt more helpless, and it galled him. Usually he could work his way round most situations, but there was nothing more he could do for her just now.

She was trying to tidy her hair, searching for the pins. He pulled a comb from his pocket and helped her. His hands were trembling, the urge to bury his face in that fragrant silky mass almost uncontrollable. She pulled away, wound it into a coil, fixed it securely, replaced her hat and handed back his comb.

'Thank you for your help, sir. I shan't be bothering you again. I'm sure Lester will explain when I see him.'

'Of course. He'll be full of plausible excuses.' He threw out his arms in an angry gesture. 'Have it your own way. I hope, for your sake, that you can prove me wrong.'

She gave him a long look, her eyes huge under the brim of her hat and then turned away.

You're lying, he said to himself as he stood there glumly, watching her walk past the fountain to the casino's entrance. You don't want him to marry her. You want her as your own, to cherish, to spoil and indulge – and, don't pretend your motives are selfless – to take to bed.

Then he clapped on his hat, whistled up a cab and went into town where he spent the remainder of the afternoon in a gymnasium working off his frustration by knocking the stuffing out of a punch bag and wishing it was Lester.

Though she was angry with him, Margaret could not get Peter Newark's words out of her head. They revolved there inexorably – *Lester doesn't love you. He's courting India Culverhay. You're an idiot to believe him.*

After what seemed an endless period she was able to escape to her room during the evening, there to fling herself on the bed, watching the sunset make patterns on the ceiling, her eyes wide and tearless. Half-formed plans were considered and discarded.

Should she hand in her notice and leave Lady Julia's service when

191

they got back to London? If what Peter said was true, her position would be untenable – India there, and Lester dancing attendance. But where could she go and who would employ her? And, more than this, how could she survive the barren wasteland of loss and the destruction of her dreams?

A knock on the door roused her. 'Who is it?' she croaked groggily.

'Lester.'

'Go away.'

'You don't mean that. Let me in.'

'All right, but we've got to talk.' She got up and unlocked the door.

The sight of him shook her resolution and magnified her pain. He had changed from the white linen suit he had been wearing at the casino, now in dove-grey cotton trousers and a striped shirt – no jacket, tie or waistcoat. Casual attire, such as a man wears when lounging in his den, away from ladies before whom he must always be formally clad.

The thought flashed through her mind that she never had, never would belong in this category. He might have treated her courteously at times but never in the way he treated India. This was unfair, for the American girl, though entitled through her father's connections to be called 'Lady' did not behave like one.

His face was serious, eyes alert. 'What's the matter? You look angry. I warned you not to make any scenes.'

This was too much. He had her by the elbows but she pulled away, turning her back on him. 'I'm not making a scene. But neither am I made of stone. You and India. Do you love her?'

'No.' He came up behind her, put his arms over her shoulders and drew her back against him, his hands sliding across her chest to cup a breast in either hand.

'What then? Do you like her?' She willed herself not to respond.

'Not particularly.' Slowly, he turned her, so that she stood with her breasts pressed to his chest. One hand went down to her buttocks, holding her hips firmly against his groin.

'Then why – why are you always with her?'

'I'm duty-bound to help the Auberts. They've been generous to me and Roderick's my friend. He wants to marry Fay. It'll be in his best interest to do so.'

'And you? Will it be in your best interest to marry India?' How can I be so cold, so logical? she wondered, her mind in control, her body frigid.

He gave a light laugh, looking at her in that charming, almost apologetic way she had once found so endearing. 'Darling, you're always talking about marriage. It's not important.'

192

She put up her hands and forged a space between them, terribly aware of his overpowering physical presence, afraid she might weaken. 'It is to me. Are you telling me that you're not courting India?'

'It's you who are presuming so.'

'She's coming to England, I hear.'

'That's true. The girls have never visited there. Their doting papa wants them to see the country of his birth. What's wrong with that?'

Despair invaded her, even though hope struggled pathetically for existence. 'So it's nothing more than a friendly visit?'

'Not entirely. I think Roderick will propose to Fay and be accepted. No doubt the marriage will be arranged, and he'll try to angle a visit to the States during the engagement.'

'And you?' I'm cross-questioning him, she thought wearily. He'll hate this but I don't care.

'I'd like to go with him. It's a place I've always wanted to explore.'

Dear God, she thought, Peter was right after all. 'What about me?' Her voice was barely a whisper.

'Sweetheart, I'm here now, aren't I? There's no need to worry about the future. It's all supposition at the moment.'

He moved towards the bed, his hand linked with hers. Her stumbling feet followed him, that awful pain fading momentarily. Her eyes were sore with weeping, and she longed for the comfort of his arms, to lie down with him and forget for a while.

'Oh, Lester–Lester—' she murmured, the strength draining out of her.

'Hush, sweetheart. There – don't cry any more. We're going home soon. I, for one, have had enough of the Riviera. We can be private in London, like we were before. I've kept on my rooms at the Warwick Hotel.'

Then she did what she had never thought she would have the strength to do. She stood resolutely by the side of the bed instead of falling into its depths.

'No, Lester,' she said firmly.

He looked up at her, his black brows forming into a scowl. 'What d'you mean?'

'It's not good enough. You promised to take me to Ireland as your fiancée. I can't go on this way.'

'Margaret – be reasonable.' He sat up and took her lifeless hands in his. 'We're so right together. Give me time.'

He pulled her to him between his spread thighs and she had never wanted anything so much as to yield to him. It would be so easy to surrender, but she had been called a fool by a man she respected, even though he roused her wrath. It had made her think. Maybe she was too lenient, grabbing at any scraps of affection Lester threw her way.

'I've given you time. Now I need a commitment. If you can't or won't give it, then it's over between us.'

He gave her a long, considering look, his eyes unreadable, and he was angry, unaccustomed to frustration. India was a virtuous girl. No chance of bedding her, and he needed a woman. If Margaret wouldn't oblige, then he'd have to go to a prostitute. He was disappointed, for her adoration was flattering and her sexuality stimulating. He saw no reason why she should not continue as his mistress.

'Over, my dear? You can't be serious,' he said coaxingly.

'I am. I've never been more serious about anything. Please leave now.'

She turned her back on him, going to the window and staring unseeingly at the darkening sky. She heard his soft footfalls behind her and still held herself steady, refusing to turn her head though every nerve within her was screaming for her to do so.

'I'll go for now, darling, if that's what you really want.' His breath lifted the wisps of hair at the nape of her neck, his lips lightly caressing the skin. 'We'll talk again when you're in a better frame of mind, eh? I won't give you up without a fight. Sweet dreams, little thing.'

She knew he had gone by the sudden cessation of warmth and the soft click of the door. Slowly she slid down the wall, down, down until she was sitting on the carpet, her legs refusing to uphold her.

'Oh, God,' she moaned, hand pressed against her mouth like a child struggling not to cry. 'What have I done?'

What use was pride against the torture?

'Damn you, Peter Newark!' she hissed. 'Damn all men! Damn, damn, damn!'

Chapter 11

It was not until after they docked at Dover that Margaret realised she had not had a period for weeks.

At first she tried to convince herself it was due to the change of climate, then thought she had somehow miscounted, but alarmed calculations and hurried totting up of days on her fingers had brought no relief. There was no getting away from it. She was in the worst predicament that could befall an unmarried woman.

A few days later she experienced nausea as soon as she lifted her head from the pillow in the morning and her breasts felt swollen and sore, the nipples painful, the blue veins more prominent against the pale skin. Concealing her sickness and working twice as hard to prove to all and sundry that she had never felt better, she knew she must see a doctor.

To make matters worse the American girls visiting Upper Grosvenor Street were in an overexcited state bordering on the hysterical, transported hither and yon to concerts, balls, dinner parties – fêted everywhere they went. Margaret could not avoid seeing them or hearing their shrill shrieks, endless chatter and giggles which also infected Fenella and, it seemed, their mamas. Even Anna was caught up in the frenzy, engaged to put a polish on their French as their accents left much to be desired. The coffee-coloured Crissie liked to gossip about these goings-on. She was convinced Fay's engagement to Roderick would be announced before they left for Roslan Manor, and had even suggested that India was anticipating a proposal from Lester.

'It's a lie!' Margaret shouted, forgetting to stay calm, moods fluctuating like a barometer.

'How can you say that?' Crissie's luminous black eyes brimmed with curiousity. 'You know something I don't?'

'He doesn't seem to be the marrying kind.' Margaret, face flaming, busied herself with a heap of Julia's ironing.

'Ha! You got it wrong,' Crissie said forcefully, tossing her white-capped head and whisking about the laundry room in her crisp blue skirt. 'I knows them fine gentlemen to a fault, honey. They can't hide nothing from me. I'll admit he's a dandy, handsome as they come, but he's after her money, sure thing, and she's fallen for him, more's the pity.'

Dear God, what am I going to do? Margaret thought, then stiffened her spine and told herself that Lester would stand by her. He'd not let her down. Peter would be forced to eat his words. She made up her mind to inform her lover once her condition had been confirmed. They would have to marry quickly, missing out on the grand wedding she had planned, but no matter.

Run off her feet installing Julia in the town house, helping with the guests and sorting through the clothing required for the trip to Cornwall, two more weeks passed before she had the opportunity to consult a doctor. Then, finally, on a rainy afternoon, she visited one in Pimlico who could not possibly know her or her employers, and he said after examining her, 'Good news, Mrs Helbren. You can start preparing for a happy event. Next March, by my reckoning.'

She had worn her mother's wedding ring, hoping he would attribute her shyness to the natural modesty of a young, respectable married woman. She promised to engage him for the confinement, agreed to return to his consulting room for check-ups and gave a false address, then left, resolving never to set eyes on him again.

Her immediate reaction was one of bowel-churning terror. She took a bus to the Warwick Hotel, ran up the stairs and entered Lester's suite without knocking.

Her heart did a backward flip at seeing him. He was so handsome in his quilted smoking jacket, sitting by the fire and reading a newspaper. He did not bother to get up, looking at her warily.

'Margaret! What are you doing here?'

'I'm pregnant.'

'What d'you mean, you're pregnant?' His brows swooped down into the blackest scowl she had ever seen.

'Just that. I'm having a baby.' She was shaking like a leaf, sick to the stomach, but determined.

He sank back in the wing chair, laid the paper aside and reached for the whisky tot on the sofa table. 'A baby, eh?' He raised the glass and swirled the amber contents before tipping back his head and swallowing it. 'That was careless of you. And who is the father, or don't you know?'

Margaret's mouth dropped open. She was speechless. Disbelief cushioned the shock, then, 'Don't joke about something as important as this,' she said, taking a step towards him.

196

He looked up at her, eyes cold and grey as the North Sea. 'I'm not joking.'

'I don't believe I've just heard that,' she gasped. 'It's *your* baby.'

'Is it?' He took a Havana from the cigar box and carefully clipped off the end.

'You know it is!'

'How do I know? You've been particularly pally with Lord Henry's chauffeur. What is it Shakespeare said? "It's a wise father that knows his own child." I've met a number of cuckoos who've been born into élite nests, certainly not sired by their mothers' husbands.'

'Sired by you, perhaps?' she lashed out.

'Perhaps.' Playing for time as usual, Lester lit his cigar.

From outside the windows came the clip-clop of hooves and the hiss of carriage wheels on wet tarmac. A paperboy was shouting the headlines from the latest editions, and the Warwick was a hive of activity. Footsteps on the stairs, cheerful voices, the clatter of pans from the distance, rich cooking smells creeping up from the kitchen.

The sun was lower, the September light as nothing compared to the South of France. It had been raining, portent of the long winter ahead, and dusk was coming sooner than usual, the London skies pewter. That sombre colour wound round Margaret's soul like a shroud.

She stood behind his chair, resting her hands on the high back, the plumes of fragrant smoke rising, so reminiscent of other times she had spent with him. Unable to resist, she touched his hair. 'I don't care what you've done in the past, Lester. It's now that matters. You and me and our baby. When shall we be married?'

She felt him grow still and tense. 'Married? I don't remember saying anything about marriage.' His words fell like drops of ice, freshly chilled.

'You did.' She stood before him now, looking down into that expressionless face where only the eyes burned with cold fire. 'You said you'd take me to Ireland.'

He shrugged. 'So I may have, but as my mistress, nothing more.'

She could feel the energy draining out of her as if the carpet was sucking it greedily through the soles of her shoes. 'Your fiancée. I was going to be your wife.'

He shook his head. 'I'm sorry, Margaret. You must have misunderstood me.'

'You took me to the opera, taught me about music and poetry. I was your friend, remember?'

'You can still be my friend. All you have to do is behave sensibly about this.'

197

'But I'm having your baby,' she repeated, brain foggy. Even now she could not quite believe his perfidy. Had she done so she might have lost her mind.

'*If* it is my baby, which I doubt. We've not been alone together since that unfortunate argument in Monty when you behaved so unreasonably.'

'It happened before that. Don't make excuses, Lester. You know I'm telling the truth.'

'Do I?' he said, coldly and calmly.

She sank to her knees by his side, clasping his thigh, nails digging into the flesh through the black barathea trousers. 'You've got to believe me. I've never been with anyone else. I love you.'

'And Luke Watson?' His lips lifted in a thin smile.

'He's always been kind to me, but nothing more. I swear it,' she insisted, dry-eyed though every dream she had cherished was crumbling to dust.

Lester's mind was working rapidly. The last thing he wanted at the moment was an open scandal. India was almost netted. He had played that particular fish with the greatest skill and delicacy, knowing he had to please Lord Edward and persuade him to deliver his darling daughter and her considerable fortune into his keeping, and in the most binding way possible.

'Why not get rid of it?' he suggested, attempting to soften the blow by running a caressing hand down her cheek.

'You want me to kill our baby?' She jerked away, the nightmare closing in about her, dreadful, unmentionable things looming out of the dusk. 'You really want me to destroy it and risk my life in the process? And even if I were to agree to something so wicked, I have no money to pay an abortionist.'

'I can borrow it. Roderick's an easy touch, or –' and his smile was sardonic – 'I can tap India for a loan, providing she doesn't get wind of its purpose.'

'She'd lend you money?'

He leaned closer, using the old, familiar magic of his fingertips, touching her lips, her throat, her breasts. 'She'll do anything for me, except make love before marriage. She's a virgin and determined to hang on to her maidenhead, using it as a kind of collateral. She's a girl of strong principles and opinions, but I can tame her.'

'In spite of what you told me, you're going to marry her, aren't you?' Margaret said dully.

'Yes, but if you're a good girl and do as I say, then it needn't make that much difference to our relationship.'

'You're mad.'

'No. Practical. I shall keep a mistress and it might as well be you. But first you have to remove this bit of bother.'

'And if I want to have the child?'

He sighed, and shook his head. 'If you insist on that, you'll get married to some suitable fellow who can bring it up as his. Watson would be an ideal choice. He's fond of you, isn't he? I might even take him on as my chauffeur. That would be convenient, for then you and I could meet whenever we wanted. He'll have to be broad-minded about the arrangement but I'm sure money will talk. It always does.'

'You're a blackguard!'

'I'm a realist. Will you do as I say?'

'You expect me to come to a decision – just like that? I'll have to think about it.'

'Fine. Let me know what you decide and I'll get the cash. You can use it to bring about a miscarriage or as a dowry. Please yourself. If you agree to becoming Mrs Watson, I'll talk to him.'

'Supposing I go to India and Lord Edward and tell them what's happened?' She stared up at him with wild eyes, feeling herself to be tottering on the edge of an abyss.

'Then, my dear, I will deny your accusation. They'll take my word against yours. You'll be dismissed and never see me again. Nor will you receive any money. You'll be out on your own. It's up to you.'

'That's blackmail.'

'Tut, tut! What a nasty word. I prefer to call it common sense.' He stretched out his arms and tried to gather her on to his lap. 'As you're here, we may as well make the most of it. You always make me feel most incredibly horny. I'm rather tired of India's flirting. She leads me on and then doesn't come up with the goods. Not like you, darling. You've never denied me yet.'

'There's a first time for everything,' Margaret said icily, and pushed him away.

He shrugged. 'You're leaving?'

'Yes.'

'And the money?'

'I'll let you know.'

'So this may not be goodbye, Margaret?' He rose, came across and trapped her, an arm resting each side of the doorframe.

Abortion or marriage to Luke. Lester had given her two alternatives, to kill her baby or marry a man she did not love. Either course was untenable. But even now, and this was the most degrading part of it, with all his villainy and callousness, the thought of losing Lester crucified her.

'Goodbye,' she whispered, as he let her out of the door.

'It needn't be goodbye. The choice is yours.'

Lillian, watching from the hall, saw Margaret run down the stairs as if the hounds of hell were after her. Her face was ashen, her eyes unseeing. A repeat performance, Lillian thought, remembering the evening before they left for France. The course of true love certainly isn't running smooth.

'Is something wrong, Miss Helbren?' she asked, stepping in front of her.

Margaret slowed to a halt, almost incoherent. 'No – no!'

'Are you sure?'

She shook her head and escaped through the front door, aware of Lillian's voice behind her. 'I'd be glad to help in any way. Don't forget.'

Numb inside, Margaret went about her tasks mechanically. Even Julia noticed, saying as she picked up her wrap prior to leaving for the theatre, 'What is the matter with you lately, Helbren? You're so abstracted one might be forgiven for thinking you're in love. Is it Watson, by any chance?'

'No, my lady. There's no one.'

'It better not be you Helbren's mooning after,' Julia said sternly to Roderick when she managed a quiet moment with him during the interval. Her green eyes stabbed his fiercely.

'Good God, Mama! Give me credit for some sense. It's Lester.'

'I'm glad to hear it and hope you're telling the truth for once.'

'Don't worry, Mama. I've spoken to Uncle Edward and he's given me permission to propose to Fay. I'll pop the question after supper tonight.'

'Splendid. An American connection will be most useful for the family. Make sure you behave till the knot is tied. We don't want any hiccups.'

Margaret spent the entire evening in a torment of indecision and finally reached a stage of desperation when she no longer cared what happened to her or the baby. When the doctor had pronounced her pregnant, she had allowed herself a fleeting moment of joy, imagining Lester being pleased, still dreaming of happy-ever-after. The harsh reality of his rejection was the cruellest blow life had dealt her. Useless to tell herself that she was spineless and pathetic. The man had cast a spell over her, binding her to him with emotional ropes as strong as steel.

Next day, Luke came to see her, choosing a time when he knew she would be alone. 'Lord Lester's told me you're in trouble,' he said, his craggy face serious. 'He put forward a proposal, so I suppose it's his baby.'

'Yes.'

'Seems like you and me are to wed. How d'you feel about this?'

'I don't know.' She stood there like a pallid ghost, all the light gone from her.

'I'm willing, if you are. I've always loved you, Margaret. We'll make a go of it, you'll see.' He came towards her eagerly, handsome in his uniform, the sort of honest, hard-working fellow any girl would be proud to marry. 'I promise I'll treat the kiddie as my own.'

'You know Lord Lester wants you to become his chauffeur?'

'He talked about it.'

'Did he also say I'm to continue as his mistress?'

Luke's face darkened and he shook his head. 'I'm sure you're mistaken.'

'I'm not. We'll get housed, and he'll expect to visit my bed whenever he fancies.'

'Let's cross that bridge when we come to it,' he answered, blind to anything except the dazzling carrot Lester had dangled before him: the chance to help Margaret, coupled with a better job and a higher salary. He took her cold hands in his. 'Please say yes, sweetheart. What else can you do, apart from try to get rid of it? That's dangerous, Margaret. You may be injured – or worse. I don't want harm to come to you.'

'He doesn't care,' she said freeing herself and twisting her fingers together. She had lost weight and they seemed almost transparent, a faint halo shining round the nails.

'He's treated you badly, but you shouldn't have believed him,' Luke said grimly.

'He said he'd marry me.'

'His sort don't marry girls like you.' Luke had never raised his voice to her before, and Margaret was stunned by the change in him.

Already jealousy was spreading its venom. Is this what married life will be like? she wondered sadly. Will he become violent towards me because of the hurt every time he looks at the child and remembers who fathered it?

'Don't be angry, Luke. I told him I wanted time to think about it,' she faltered. 'He had no right to discuss it with you. I must see him again – talk to him.'

'You'll try to change his mind? He won't alter, you know. He's dead set on Lady India and her money.' Luke looked older, the lines etched more deeply at the sides of his mouth.

She wrote a note to Lester and had Luke deliver it, then waited for his reply. It came before dinner. He agreed to meet her after ten and gave her the address of the house in Chelsea where they had first made

201

love. Margaret sought out one of the scullery-maids. Rumour had it among the servants that she had found herself in difficulties earlier in the year and had visited a midwife in Soho, returning wretchedly ill but trouble-free.

'I want to talk to you, Bridget,' Margaret began, catching her in the dim passageway between the servants' hall and the backstairs.

'What's up? Mrs Colby been going on? I ain't done nothing.' Bridget was a pallid, mouselike girl with dull brown hair.

'It's nothing to do with Mrs Colby,' Margaret began, then stopped, not sure how to go on. She tried again, 'I have a friend who needs help.'

'Yes?' Bridget stood there immobile, tiny mousy paws folded over her grubby apron, head at a listening angle.

'I hear that you were in a delicate condition a while back and went to a woman for aid.'

'Maybe I did, then maybe I didn't. Who's asking?' Defensive, hostile, pink-rimmed eyes stared at Margaret.

'My friend. You don't know her. All I want is an address. It won't involve you and I'll make it worth your while.'

'I can't do that. I promised,' Bridget replied, fidgeting from one foot to the other. 'Took all me savings, it did, and the bloke what got me in trouble wouldn't pay up. Bloody sod! Said he'd see me right, he did, but when push came to shove, he was off like greased lightning.'

'Then you could use some cash. Here.' Gold coins flashed on her outspread palm. Bridget scooped them up, and Margaret retreated with an address scribbled on a scrap of paper. She would try once more to soften Lester's heart, but if this failed . . .

That night she took a hackney to Chelsea. It was a journey steeped in memories. The start of their affair, and Lester had been beside her in his car, offering her the world on a silver platter, or so she had imagined. Oh, he still wanted her, but on his own terms. It was a bitter pill to swallow.

The front door opened at her touch and Margaret let herself into the tiled hall. As before, the house seemed deserted but well tended, lit by fringed and beaded lamps, luxurious in its overstated way. Her own white face with huge anxious eyes startled her as she passed a mirror in a gilt frame. Her nerves quivered and the longing for Lester was like a fever in the blood.

I'll do whatever he wants, she decided as she stood outside the door leading to the apartment in which she had surrendered to him. I'll wed Luke if he insists. I can't stand this any more.

Footsteps within and her pulse raced. He was there! He'd smile at her, tell her he'd changed his mind and would marry her after all. Oh,

God, let him say this! Then he'd take her to bed and soothe away her pain. The door swung open and the words of greeting died on her lips.

'Hello, Maggie,' said Roderick. 'Who's been a naughty girl then?'

'Why are you here?' She glared up into his face and wanted to kill.

'I often visit. Didn't he tell you? Come in.'

Was Lester inside? She had to find out, so entered the lobby, nostrils responding to the pervading perfume comprised of Turkish coffee mingled with ambergris, musk and dried roses.

'Where is he?' Warning prickles ran down her spine. There was something dreadfully wrong.

'He sent his apologies and asked me to come instead.' He sat on the arm of a chair, never taking his eyes from her. 'Aren't I a good substitute?'

'No, you're not.' She turned back to the door. 'Tell him to let me know when it's convenient for him to see me.'

'Can't do that, sweetie. He told me to give you this and say he'll contact you when the dust has settled.' He held out a purse as he rose to his feet. 'It's down to you how you decide to spend it. An abortion or a wedding. Take your pick.'

I'm dreaming, Margaret tried to convince herself. I'll wake to find Lester sleeping beside me. I'll hold him close and cry a little, so relieved to find I'd been having a nightmare. In her bag was the address she had bought from Bridget. Somewhere, waiting outside the Café Royal, the opera house, or a mansion where a select dinner party was in progress, Lester waited in one of the Aubert cars, thinking about her, no doubt praying that she would marry him. A diabolical dream, the whole thing.

The walls appeared to be closing in on her, that floating, dizzy faintness making the room rock. Roderick guided her to a sofa and fetched a glass of water. She sipped it, then leaned her head against the padded back and shut her eyes.

'It could have been worse, you know.' His voice seemed to come from a great distance. 'Some chaps don't give a fig if their tarts find themselves in brat. At least Lester's making provision for you.'

Her lids snapped open and she subjected him to the full blast of her rage. 'And so he bloody well should!'

'Why didn't you take precautions?'

'Oh, so I'm to blame, am I? I don't know a thing about preventing conception. Does he? If so, he should have seen to it. It didn't matter to him. He was quite content to roger me, never mind the consequences.'

'And you to let him.'

'He led me to believe he loved me and intended marriage.'

203

Roderick laughed and said, 'My dear girl, nothing was further from his thoughts. He didn't want to get married, that is not until India came along. It was me who was looking for an heiress, and he's come to the conclusion it's a great idea. The end of his financial problems. No more debts, no more vulgar creditors calling at his lodgings or being blacklisted at his club. He'll be able to gamble to his heart's content and live like a king.'

'He doesn't love her?' This brought a shed of cold comfort.

'Lester loves no one except himself.'

'I pity her.'

'Don't waste your sympathy. She's hard-headed. So is Fay. I shall have to watch my step with her, but I can handle it – worth the effort, to marry a million-dollar princess.'

She crumpled suddenly, sinking her face in her hands. 'I never wanted to fall in love. I had ambitions and was well on the way to achieving them. Why didn't he leave me alone?'

He leaned over her, and his voice was low, silky, almost lewd. 'D'you really want to know?'

There was something infinitely disturbing in his tone. She looked up and the expression on his face made her start. 'Yes. But what has it to do with you?'

'Everything,' he said, and held out his hand to raise her. Her flesh crept in contact with his, but he did not loosen his hold, hurrying her down the corridor, past the room she had occupied with Lester, and into the one next to it.

It was small and sparsely funished. A narrow bed, a standard lamp, an armchair placed before a curtained recess. Roderick urged her closer, then twitched the drape aside. She found herself looking through a window on to the massive, ornate divan she had shared with Lester.

Her eyes widened in astonishment. A naked woman lay there in an attitude of complete abandon, black hair splayed across the pillow, her legs spead. An obese, sweating, bearded man knelt between her thighs. He was wearing nothing but his shirt. The woman was moaning. He was panting, moving his hips rapidly back and forth. His thrusts became frenzied, the woman squealed and writhed.

'Remember the mirror near the bed? It's a trick one. You were beautiful to watch, Maggie. I've seen every inch of you, heard your cries as Lester entered you, your gasps, your love words when you started to enjoy it.' Roderick's voice was thick with excitement.

'You saw us?' she whispered, the colour rushing up into her cheeks.

'That's why he brought you here. He'd been wooing you carefully, for I'd bet him five hundred guineas he wouldn't be able to seduce you.'

'And he won.'

'He certainly did.'

'The bastard!'

'Go on. You enjoyed it.'

Roderick stood behind her. She could feel the heat of his body pressing into her back. His arm clamped round her, holding her tightly. He lowered his head, nibbling at her neck.

'Stop it,' she ground out.

'I want you, Maggie. D'you know what I did while I watched Lester humping you?'

'I don't want to know.'

'I was satisfying myself with my hand. Like this—'

'You're disgusting! And Lester knew you were there?'

'It was part of the bargain.'

'What is this place?'

'A high-class bordello that caters for every fancy.'

'You are both vile! Vile! Monsters!'

She fought free, too angry to feel grief. A bet. That's all it had meant to Lester. The winning of a wager. A cruel game organised with Roderick. How they must have laughed at her expense.

Roderick made a grab at her but she dodged under his arm, pelted along the passage and into the hall. The front door resisted for a moment, but she tugged at it with more than human strength. Down the steps, out into the night. The drizzle had become a steady downpour but she was not aware. She ran on like a deer fleeing from the huntsmen, only pausing when she could no longer draw breath, a stitch clawing at her side. By that time she had put several streets between herself, the house and Roderick.

Panting heavily, she leaned against the wall under a gas-lamp. Rain streamed from the polluted skies, mingling with the tears flowing down her cheeks. Her skirt was soggy to the knees, her hat bedraggled. She clutched her handbag, undid the catch and fumbled inside. The yellow light fell on the piece of paper purchased from Bridget.

She must destroy the child, sickened by the thought of it growing in the warm darkness of her womb, conceived through deception, not love, as she had once believed. It must be removed, then she would be able to think clearly, better able to make decisions about her future.

She memorised the address, returned the paper to her bag, attempted to tidy herself, then pulled on her gloves. Whatever she had to do, and she never doubted it would be unpleasant, it was vital she keep up a semblance of dignity. It was all she had left. Walking towards the main road, she hailed a hansom.

'Where to, miss?' The cabby's bewhiskered face looked down cheerfully from his perch, the rain dripping from the brim of his bowler and cascading across his mackintosh cape.

'Nelson Place, Soho,' she answered clearly, finding the step and hauling herself up and inside. It smelled musty, of stale cigars, cheap perfume and damp. Her uncertain stomach heaved. She clapped a hand to her mouth and fought the urge to vomit.

Skid of hooves and rain spraying under iron-bound wheels. It sounded like the sea – Cornwall, Monte Carlo – those beaches formed vivid pictures in the dark. Lights flashed. The traffic thickened. They were in theatre-land, all the careless gaiety of Leicester Square. The nightlife of London which she had once shared with Lester. And now the unthinkable had happened. He did not love her, and she was about to murder his child.

The vehicle swayed to a halt. 'Here you are, miss,' said the cabby. 'Mind how you go. It's a dirty night.'

The steaming horse and drenched carriage moved away, leaving her standing outside a door. It was one in a small, shabby row, with identical houses on the other side of a cobbled street. Margaret could see no gleam at the sash windows. Perhaps the woman was out. It was the moment of truth. She could either knock on the door, or turn away and go home.

With a tightening in her throat and weakness in her knees, Margaret lifted the knocker and brought it down hard. Nothing happened for a while, then she heard a shuffling from within and a voice said, 'Who is it?'

'You've been recommended by a friend.'

'How do I know you ain't a copper's nark?'

'I'm not. I've money.' Margaret lifted her purse and shook it. Coins clinked faintly.

There was the sound of a bolt being drawn and then the door opened. A thin woman stood in front of her, the dingy hallway lit by a spluttering, unshielded gas-jet.

'Come in, quick!' she muttered.

Margaret stepped past her. The woman lost no time in bolting the door. The place reeked of cats. They were everywhere; on the stairs, in corners, their slanting yellow eyes watchful. Big fat cats, small skinny cats – unfriendly, vicious cats, or so Margaret imagined in her high-strung state.

'I'm in trouble,' she began, a nervous smile masking her disgust.

The woman lifted her bony shoulders in a shrug, the odour of dirty

206

clothing joining that of the felines. 'You wouldn't be here if you weren't,' she answered laconically. 'It'll cost you ten pounds, and I wants it before we starts. I don't want no comeback. You'll have to get out as soon as it's done. Understand?'

Margaret nodded, and pulled out her money. She had been too upset to count the amount Lester had given her, but it was more than the woman demanded. She tried to keep her purse hidden, doling out the sovereigns.

The woman checked them carefully, even bit on several to make certain they were not counterfeit, then, 'Come with me,' she said.

Margaret kept close behind her as they descended a flight of dark stairs leading into the basement kitchen. There were newspapers spread on the cracked, dun-coloured linoleum, and a further army of cats. Some of them came across to rub round the woman's fusty skirts, backs arched, tails fluffed up. The walls were filthy. The place stank of boiled cabbage and kippers, overlaid with cats' urine. A kettle steamed on the grease-blackened gas stove and a heap of dirty dishes cluttered the stone sink. The tap dripped constantly, with a nerve jangling *ping*, *ping*, as the drops hit a chipped enamel bowl.

Newspapers also covered the surface of a large wooden table. This was bare, the only clear spot in the kitchen. It had evidently been used not long before. There was another odour, too. That of blood. As Margaret ventured further in she almost knocked over a pail of water in which floated a red-haloed sponge.

The woman turned up the central gaslight hanging above the table. 'Take your coat off, drop your drawers and get up,' she ordered.

'On there?' Margaret stared at the newspapers, the dirt, the cats.

'Where else? What did you expect? The operating theatre at Guy's Hospital? They wouldn't help you. Only the stinking rich can bribe Harley Street doctors to do it. And they do. Make no bones about it. Their daughters get themselves up the spout same as everyone else, but it's all hush-hush. Sometimes they're sent abroad to have the baby and it's adopted.'

'You know a lot about it.' With shaking hands Margaret took off her hat and coat, lifted her muddied skirts and unfastened her cambric knickers.

The woman tossed the clothes across an armchair by the stove. A large tabby stalked over and sniffed fastidiously before settling down on them. Margaret could hear his deep throated thrumming as he kneaded the fabric.

'I was a nurse. I worked in some of them big houses. I knows what goes on. It's one law for them and another for the likes of us. I suppose it was a toff done this to you?'

207

'Yes.' Margaret felt like a child in the presence of a harsh teacher. The room was clammy and cold. She rubbed her arms with her hands.

'You'll bleed. Have you brought any clouts?' The woman looked at her indifferently.

'No.'

'D'you live far away? Get a cab home and go to bed. If you feel hot and feverish or start bleeding badly, send for a doctor, but don't mention me. If you do, you'll be sorry. My man's useful with his fists. Get on the table.'

'Oh, God, help me,' Margaret whispered, doing as she was told.

'Lie on your back,' the woman said. 'Get your petticoats out the way, open your legs and lift up your knees.'

She pushed the pail nearer with her foot, then took up what looked like a long crochet hook. 'What are you going to do?' Margaret cried, trembling so much that her naked thighs shook.

'Just you shut your eyes and leave the rest to me. You don't want this baby, do you?'

Margaret gripped the sides of the table. Ungentle fingers on her pubis, the feel of something cold, metallic probing her entrance. Her nerve broke. She shrank from that deadly foreign object, sat up, pushed the woman away, got off the table.

'I can't—' She grabbed up her clothes and her bag.

'It's your funeral,' the woman replied, uncaring. 'But don't come back to me in a few weeks' time and want it done. It'll be too late by then.'

'I won't.' Never, never, Margaret vowed, struggling into her coat and running up the stairs. Never enter that terrible house again, or face the woman and her cats. She must see Luke. Tell him to put up the bans. Anything rather than allow that witch to touch her.

Somehow she made it back to Grosvenor Street and, at last, entered the safety of her own room. For a while she did nothing but sit on the edge of the bed, shivering. She was soaked to the skin. In a while she raised enough energy to run a bath, then wrapped herself in her dressing gown.

The room was warm. For the sake of their visitors, Henry had ordered the mighty boiler in the basement to be stoked higher than usual. The Americans were accustomed to efficient heating. Margaret rubbed her hair dry, her thoughts turned inwards, a deep, black well of contemplation swallowing her up. She pressed her hands to her flat belly, wondering about its tiny occupant. Had she stayed on that ghastly table, it would have been dead by now, and so might she.

'You had a narrow escape, baby. We both did,' she addressed it, and

208

suddenly a strange and lovely feeling swept over her, as if radiating from the foetus itself.

Baby. My baby. No one else's. It couldn't be blamed for its conception, poor little thing. A tiny being utterly dependent on me for life, sustenance and love. It's incredible.

She felt precious and holy and of incalculable value.

Her mother must have felt the same when she was carrying her. Needing to be near her, Margaret opened the bride-chest and took out the baby clothes. She would use them for her own infant.

She examined the garments, then laid them aside. Her diary lay there, neglected of late, but she determined to carry on with it, gaining relief by writing down her experiences and emotions. The chest was lined with silk and as she went to replace the contents her fingers caught in it. She was upset by the damage, wondering if it was possible to mend it. As she looked closer, she saw something wedged between the lining and the wood. It was a cheap red exercise book, like those used in schools. On the front was written her mother's maiden name – Mary Joyce Skipton.

Margaret sat on the floor and started to read. By the time she came to the end of the narrative she knew there was no way she could marry Luke Watson.

It was all there: Mary's Skipton's early life in Bristol as the only child of elderly parents who had been of the class known as 'shabby genteel', their deaths leaving her practically penniless, and her first position as governess at the castle. She had been happy there, but circumstances had changed for the owners, and she had obtained a job teaching in the school in Porthross. Then she had met Lord Henry Aubert.

'The villagers are unfriendly, they treat me like a foreigner,' she had written. 'But he is so kind. We walk together sometimes and talk of literature, history and travel. It is as if we are close friends.'

They became more than friends. Margaret's heart went out to her mother as she recognised every sign. The relationship had developed along similar lines to hers and Lester's. Tom Helbren came into the story. He admired Mary, asked her to go out with him, but was refused. Then matters took a more serious turn.

'Lady Julia suspects about us. I'm sure of it, though Henry thinks otherwise. I met her today at the Harvest Festival service. The look in her eyes was frightening. I'm certain she hates me.'

Not long after came the entry which said, 'I am with child. I've told Henry and he is very angry. There's nothing he can do for me and suggests that I marry Tom Helbren to save my reputation. I feel that I'll never recover from this blow. I thought he loved me and wanted us

209

to run off together. It seems that he lied, though I find it hard to believe ill of him. I thought him an honourable gentleman who would never go back on his word.'

The room was so still that Margaret fancied she could hear the blood racing through her veins. Lord Henry was her father, not Tom Helbren. Somehow she was not surprised. But did Lady Julia know?

She turned the pages, skimming over them frantically, seeking answers to questions that had long puzzled her. 'Today Tom and I were married in Porthross. The Methodist Chapel, though I've never been of their faith. What else can I do? I have no money, no friends, nowhere to go.'

There had followed a description of their life in the cottage, and Margaret's birth. 'A baby girl was born to me in the early hours of this morning. I thought I should die of the pain. No one had warned me it would be like that. But my daughter is adorable. She looks like Henry. I'm calling her Margaret Elinor.'

There were many blank pages and intermittent entries, and the final ones must have been written shortly before Mary took to her bed. 'But marrying Tom was the biggest mistake of all. I couldn't bear him to touch me, and he began to drink. He loved me, and I should never have let him believe I cared for him. I didn't, only as a friend. I've never loved anyone but Henry. Tom's sisters guessed, I think, the virtuous Mercy and Prudence. They've never attempted to hide their dislike. Margaret has been my only comfort, my beautiful little girl, though I'm afraid for her. She's dark, and has Henry's eyes, and as she's grown older the Aubert characteristics are strong in her. No one has ever called attention to it, but I'm convinced Lady Julia suspects, though from the moment I married Tom, I've never seen Henry again, only from afar.'

Margaret leapt to her feet and ran to the looking glass, hands to her face. Did she resemble the Auberts? Fenella, Evelyn, Jane, Harry and William. And, horror of horrors – Roderick! They were her half-brothers and sisters. And Lady Julia *did* know. She was convinced of it, and so did Lord Henry. She replaced the book and dressed very slowly and calmly, preparing herself. Then she sat down and waited.

It was gone three o'clock in the morning when the bell rang. Composed and cold, Margaret entered Julia's boudoir. Their eyes locked. Julia calmly continued to unfasten her jewellery.

'What is it?' she asked, laying her necklace and bracelets on the cut-glass trinket tray. 'You look as if you've seen a ghost.'

'I have. The ghost of my mother's past. The ghost of old sins, Lady Julia, and one woman's terrible vengeance.'

210

'Don't talk nonsense. You sound like one of those penny-dreadfuls the maids read. Unlace me.'

'No. We need to talk, you and me.'

'Do we indeed? Well, I shall be the judge of that. I'll talk to you when I decide, and not before. You forget yourself, Helbren. You're my servant.'

'Not any more.'

'What d'you mean?'

'I'm leaving.'

'I knew there was something amiss.' Julia plumped down on the stool and started to unpin her hair, watching Margaret in the mirror. 'Are you in trouble?'

'Do you mean, am I expecting a baby? Yes, I am. It's Lord Lester's, but it could have been your son's. And you would have let it happen, wouldn't you? Or would even your twisted jealousy have baulked at incest?'

Julia remained unruffled. 'Explain yourself.'

'Do you deny Lord Henry is my father?'

'I neither deny nor confirm it. Leave the room at once.'

'You can't avoid the truth, not this time.' Margaret stood over her, powerful in her wrath, no longer intimidated. 'My mother kept a diary. I've just read it. There she states she was his mistress before she married. I'm their love child. You knew it all along. Why did you visit her when she was dying? Was it to gloat?'

Julia calmly unhooked the pendant diamonds from her ears and laid them in the plush-lined jewel-case. 'She was finished. I was alive. She had lost Henry. I had kept him. She had a bastard. I had born his legitimate children. It was as simple as that.'

'So even on her deathbed you couldn't leave her in peace. How cruel, Lady Julia. How despicable.'

A flush stole across Julia's cheekbones and her eyes were like chips of green ice. 'What do you know about it? I've endured years of humiliation because of Henry and his women. Oh, yes, she wasn't the only one. But he was fond of her, too fond. It had to stop. I threatened to leave him. He abandoned her. As for you, his bastard – I watched your progress from afar, but he never referred to you. Men have short memories, you know, especially when it is something they want to forget.'

'Why did you employ me?'

'Her death wasn't enough. You were the walking proof of his infidelity. You had to be punished.'

'It wasn't my fault. I didn't ask to be born.'

'It was just possible he might have come across you in the village,

211

remembered Mary, fostered some sentimental notion of acknowledging you. Men are such foolish creatures. It was safer if you were under my eye.'

'He knew. Every time I attended you, he must have thought, "She's my daughter."'

Julia's laughter was as brittle as glass. 'I don't imagine so. Henry is too full of his own concerns. Like most men, he doesn't want anything to upset the domestic status quo. Quarrels bother him, so do tears. He prefers to bury his head in the sand.'

'It satisfied you to humiliate me, to have me at your beck and call. You could sit back smugly and think, there goes Mary Helbren's child, and she's completely under my control. I can shape her life any way I want. Did you know about Lester and me?'

'Of course.' Julia slipped off her rings and dropped them over the branches of a little Dresden china tree especially designed for the purpose.

'Did you also know your son had a bet with him? The stakes were five hundred guineas which Lester won when he seduced me.'

'I didn't bother myself with the sordid details. You can just thank your lucky stars that it wasn't Roderick who put that baby in you, or you might have produced a freak.'

'And you wouldn't have felt the smallest twinge of conscience?'

'None whatever. Why should I? "The sins of the fathers", you know.'

'I've never met anyone as evil as you, Lady Julia.'

Julia's eyes flashed and she rose slowly, as upright and stately as an empress. She gestured toward the door. 'Get out of here! You're just like your slut of a mother!'

'Don't worry. I'm going.'

'Pack your things and leave first thing in the morning. See Mrs Colby and she will settle your wages. If you make any attempt to contact this family again, I'll have the law on you.'

Chapter 12

'What will you do?' Anna asked anxiously as she came into Margaret's room to say goodbye.

'I don't know.' She looked up from fastening the straps round the Pilgrim basket. 'Find another post, I suppose.'

The bride-chest stood ready, and two large suitcases. Whatever else may have transpired, Margaret thought, I've more belongings than when I arrived at Roslan Manor at fifteen years old.

'Do you want to talk about it? All I've heard is that you're leaving.'

'There's nothing to say.'

Margaret was ready, checking one last time to make sure she had left nothing behind. Anna's concern made her want to break down but there was no place in her life for sentiment now. Her love for Lester was dead, and during a sleepless night she had planned to be revenged, not only on him, but on the whole pack of Auberts as well. She wanted to root them out, expose them, smash them. Unsure as yet how to accomplish this, she vowed to do it even if it took her the rest of her life.

'Take care, *chérie*.' Anna's expressive dark eyes spoke volumes.

'I'll write when I've a settled address.'

'Are you going back to Cornwall?'

'Oh, no! One place I'm not going is Cornwall. I'd not give my aunts the satisfaction of gloating over my dismissal.'

It was still early and two footmen came to carry her luggage down to the waiting hansom. They did not speak or meet her eyes. When the cabby enquired her destination, she said, 'The Midland Agency. Carmichael Street.'

She had studied the Situations Vacant columns in the newspapers before she knew she was pregnant. Her conversation with Peter, followed by the quarrel with Lester, had made her seriously consider leaving Lady Julia's service. She had put this on hold when she found

213

out about the baby, but now she needed a job urgently and had underlined the address of an agency who advertised for women seeking posts as domestics.

A live-in position was best, for the thought of lodging in some squalid boarding house in a row of mean streets horrified her after her experience in Soho. But close on this came the depressing thought: how long can I remain in employment? I'm pregnant and single. The shame of it burned her like a brand.

Even if she lied, saying she was a widow or her husband away, would she be believed? Yet work she must for as long as she was able. Her money would not last for ever and she dreaded ending up in the workhouse, her child coming into the world in harsh surroundings, cold as charity. Circumstances would force her to have it put up for adoption, and she would be for ever scarred, never forgetting that someone else was rearing it while she faced a bleak future with little alternative but prostitution.

No, that precious hoard must be saved against the time when the baby arrived, then, with careful management, they could survive while she decided on her next move. Now was the most difficult stage of the game, for Julia had refused her a reference and without it her chances of finding a decent, well-paid position were slim.

It was raining again and Carmichael Street was crowded, with nothing to commend the dingy building from which the Midland Agency operated. Margaret's spirits were at a low ebb, faced with no alternative but to go in.

'Wait here,' she said to the cabby, and lifting her skirt to keep the hem away from the filthy pavement, she pushed open a shabby door and mounted a rickety staircase to where a dog-eared notice told her she had reached her destination.

She rapped on the glass panel and a voice called to enter. The office was cluttered. A harassed-looking woman sat behind a large black Imperial typewriter. Another occupied a chair at a desk, a hard-eyed creature with pepper-and-salt hair pulled into a bun.

'Yes?' she asked ungraciously as Margaret closed the door.

'I'm looking for work.' She held out the folded newspaper with their advertisement. 'Can you help me?'

The women waved a hand in her direction. 'Take a seat,' she said, eyeing her up and down. 'What's your name and former occupation?'

'Mrs Helbren, and I'm a lady's maid. My husband is in the navy and abroad at present.' She took the wooden chair on the far side of the desk and suppressed a shudder. It was an unprepossessing place.

'I see. I'm Mrs Midland. I've a number of applicants on my books, and enquiries for servants coming in every day. We've a sound

214

reputation, Mrs Helbren, and have to be careful who we recommend.'
She sifted through some papers, found the form she sought and
spread it out, pen poised. 'First of all, tell me your full name and that
of your former employer.'

'Margaret Elinor Helbren, and all I'm prepared to say is that she's a
titled lady, but we parted after a disagreement. It's no good asking me
for a reference.'

Mrs Midland pursed her lips, then tapped them thoughtfully with
her pen. 'This poses a problem. You seem respectable, but my clients
like to know the background of the people we send along. You might
be dishonest, insane or immoral. Perhaps you were dismissed for stealing, or corrupting the footmen.'

Her tone was mocking, faintly insulting, and this interview was
proving more difficult than Margaret had supposed. 'Nothing like
that, I promise you,' she replied stiffly. 'I'll be frank. My husband and
I have decided to separate, and her ladyship disapproves. She thinks
one should remain married, no matter what. A deeply religious
person.'

It was impossible to tell if Mrs Midland swallowed this story or
no, but she was undoubtedly impressed by Margaret's well-cut costume, tasteful hat and fur tippet. Her eyes narrowed as she said, 'I'm
inclined to accept this, Mrs Helbren, and will add you to our
register.'

'I need work now.' Margaret tried to keep the desperation from her
voice.

Mrs Midland raised an eyebrow. 'That urgent, is it? There's no post
available like your last one.'

'That doesn't matter. I'll take anything.'

'You do realise there's a fee?'

Margaret didn't but, 'Naturally,' she replied, and tightened her grip
on her handbag wherein lay the remainder of Lester's money and the
wages Mrs Colby had paid her before she left.

'Give me three sovereigns and we'll say no more about the
reference,' Mrs Midland concluded. 'I'll put you in touch with a
respectable family who need a maid. I'm afraid it won't be the kind
of work you're used to, but under the circumstances—'

'I'm sure it will be fine.'

Beggars can't be choosers, Margaret thought, remembering the
nursery adage. This woman is a charlatan, greedy, avaricious, un-
scrupulous. I can tell by her eyes. How horrid people are, so quick to
profit by the misfortune of others. She had never felt more alone, not
even after her mother died. In those days there had been a glimmer of
hope in the darkness. Now there was none.

She left the office shortly after, three pounds poorer but in possession of an address and a covering note.

The hackney bowled away from London's centre and into the outlying districts, eventually stopping in an avenue of villas, each one identical to the next. Small balconies, bay windows, lace curtains, a tiny oblong garden leading from pavement to front step.

Once again Margaret had to ask the driver to wait. More expense, but she had too much luggage to risk being turned away by her prospective employer. The bride-chest was the most bulky article, but she refused to be parted from it. To make matters worse the rain was falling more heavily, the dreary, polluted rain that drops from the skies over big cities.

Heaping maledictions on Lester's head and cursing her own gullibility, Margaret marched up the path and knocked on the door. It stood under a porch and had panels decorated with etched glass.

Dragging footsteps answered this summons, accompanied by a muttered string of complaints. The door swung inwards revealing a large woman. She was fat, slovenly and wafted an unpleasant odour.

'Well?' she asked truculently.

'I'm looking for Mrs Hutton.'

'And who might you be?'

'I was sent by the Midland Agency.'

'You better come in.'

A dim hall, with dingy terrazzo tiles and a chocolate-brown dado; a flight of stairs covered in dusty carpet held in place with tarnished brass rods; a long passage disappearing into darkness.

The woman tapped on the parlour door, shouting, 'There's a gal to see you, Mrs Hutton. Says she's from the agency.'

'Show her in,' answered a woman's voice, a flat voice, origin uncertain. From the North? Margaret wondered in the brief moment before she went into the parlour.

In common with the entrance hall, it was in need of a thorough spring-clean. Nothing like the grand apartments to which Margaret was accustomed but in keeping with the house, one of many built during the last quarter of the old queen's reign to accommodate the ever-increasing army of white-collar workers and tradesmen who ran their own modest businesses.

A coal fire smouldered fitfully in the iron grate surrounded by black marble. The mantelshelf was hung with a green velvet cloth, the scolloped edge of which trembled in the draught. The gas-lamps each side of the central mirror burned dimly from behind smutty glass shades, supplementing the wintery daylight. It shone on the what-not with a circular top supporting a drooping plant. There were reproduction

216

Chippendale chairs, and gaudy knick-knacks on the sideboard below an engraving of *The Last Supper* by Leonardo da Vinci, and another of the late Prince Albert.

Mrs Hutton reclined on a sofa by the fire. Two boot-button eyes in a puffy, pallid face stared at Margaret, a woman of uncertain age, probably in her late thirties, but so overweight she looked older. Her faded hair was dressed high, but ineptly, long wisps straggling across her short neck.

A rustling black taffeta skirt flowed over her broad hips. Her thick waist was encased in a boned bodice, bosom heaving under the restriction, the sleeves full to the elbow, then narrowing to the wrists and fastening with a row of jet buttons. She wore a long gold chain and a brooch pinned in the centre of a high, tight collar, over which her double chin flowed.

This was an ensemble suitable for the afternoon, not the morning. Like the room, its mistress lacked taste.

'So, you want to work for me, do you?' she said, and her stubby hands settled in her ample lap.

Margaret stood in the middle of the carpet, holding her bag and wondering how on earth she was going to cope. Resent and hate the Auberts though she might, she had to admit they had provided her with an existence in elegant surroundings and she had known no other, apart from Hazel Cottage. The narrow confines of this establishment were already closing in on her like a coffin lid. The fat woman, her blowzy servant, the atmosphere of false gentility, revolted her more than the smells of must and dirt and stale cooking.

'I'm Mrs Helbren. The Midland Agency sent me,' she said steadily.

'Married, eh? Where's your hubby?'

'In Gibraltar at present. He's a seaman. Doesn't get home often.'

'He won't be wanting to stay here, then?'

'No, madam. We make other arrangements when he's on leave.'

'When can you start?'

'Now, if you wish, madam.' Margaret was all too aware of the hackney carriage outside and the cabby's fare mounting by the minute.

'Good, good. I've been without a maid for some time, with only Freda to help me, and she's really the cook. Isn't that so, Freda?'

'Yes, missus.' The woman glared at Margaret, shapeless, paunchy, frumpishly clad in a faded dress with half-moon stains at the armpits.

The idea of her preparing food made Margaret feel even more unwell. She seemed hostile, too, as if resenting a stranger in the house. Does very well for herself, I imagine, Margaret thought. That lazy slummock, Mrs Hutton, won't notice what's going on.

'You're well dressed for a servant,' Mrs Hutton observed, taking in every detail of Margaret's attire.

'My last position was that of lady's maid,' she answered.

'Excellent!' Mrs Hutton cried, beaming. 'I've always wanted someone to help me dress and look after my clothes. But, of course, this won't be all. There's Mr Hutton and my son and daughter who'll need attending.'

God preserve me if they're anything like her, Margaret thought. 'And the general management of the house?' she asked, wishing she could sit but Mrs Hutton was enjoying the feeling of superiority.

'I see to the ordering of food,' she explained. 'With Freda's help, of course. But you'll have to do the rest. I don't employ more than one maid at a time. We haven't the room.'

Or the wherewithal, Margaret wanted to say, but kept quiet. She had to have this post, degrading though it was. 'Very well,' she agreed. 'And the terms of employment?'

Mrs Hutton named a wage that was a pittance compared to the Auberts' rates, but Margaret could do no other than accept. She had to have a place to sleep that night. But when later she met Mr Hutton and their offspring, she regretted her decision.

By that time she had settled her belongings in the tiny, cheerless upstairs backroom. An iron bedstead and lumpy mattress, coarse patched sheets and thin blankets; a washstand with china jug and basin, for the villa lacked a bathroom. A deal cupboard held her garments, and ripped curtains hung at the small window. She looked out at the endless vista of identical streets, too tired even to cry.

'Have you heard anything about Margaret while I've been away?' Peter asked Lillian, striding into her parlour on his return from Cornwall.

'I've not seen hide nor hair of her since that night she left Lord Lester's rooms weeks ago, and I told you about that,' Lillian said seriously, pausing in her bookwork.

'Where the hell is she?' He took up a stance on the hearth rug, hands locked behind his back. 'I've been down to Roslan Manor and searched Porthross, then tried Upper Grosvenor Street again, but she's vanished into thin air.'

'What about asking Lester?'

'It means calling on him at the Auberts, or catching him in one of the clubs. Awkward, him leaving here.'

'He was in a hurry to move out.'

'Avoiding her?'

'It looks that way.'

Peter's expression was grim. 'I won't give up. I'll find her if it's the last thing I do.'

Lillian blotted the ledger and closed it, then reached for the decanter, poured two tots of brandy and gave one to him. 'Your best bet is Lester – or Roderick,' she said, wishing she could have found someone so gallant and devoted in her younger days instead of always falling for rogues.

His blue eyes were fierce, and the hand holding the glass shook slightly. 'I wouldn't trust myself, Lillian, and that's the truth. If I see Lester and he gives me any of his arrogance, I'll probably end up punching him. Will you come and visit me in prison?'

'Of course I will! I'll even smuggle in a file hidden in a cake, in traditional style.'

And they touched glasses, united in their concern about the girl who, though entering their lives briefly, could not be forgotten.

Mrs Hutton expected her pound of flesh. It took every reserve of strength Margaret possessed to carry on, weakened as she was by tiredness and discomfort as her body adjusted to pregnancy and such heavy work.

There was so much to do, everything in that disorganised household heaped on her. Mrs Hutton nagged, always finding fault; nothing Margaret did pleased her. As for her husband, he was a small, lantern-chested man, half the size of his wife and completely dominated by her. He had relinquished any authority over his family long ago, confining his activities to his backstreet hardware shop.

The first time Margaret met Nelda, the eighteen-year-old daughter, she recognised an enemy, familiar with her brand of spite and envy, and had sensed danger from the son, Graham, who was twenty. He swaggered, thought himself a dandy though his suits were off-the-peg, was made much of by his mother, sandy-haired, like her, with pale protuberant eyes. Despite his pimples and sour breath he was convinced he was the answer to every maiden's prayer. He could not keep his hands to himself and Margaret had a job avoiding him, unable to yield to her longing to slap him across the face.

It was a soul-destroying experience, her day beginning at half past five. Mrs Hutton expected her to have cleaned the house and lit the fires before she went to help her dress at eight-thirty. Nelda, too, as lazy as her dam, used her as a personal maid. Fortunately, Mr Hutton and Graham were long gone by that time, Freda seeing to their breakfast.

Graham worked with his father in the shop, but Nelda, whose head had been stuffed with illusions of grandeur, was required to do

219

nothing but doll herself up and lure a man of means into the fold. A butcher, maybe, or grocer, who would marry her, aid the family financially and keep her in idleness.

Jesus Christ! Margaret would mutter, exasperated after a session trying to please the girl who was never satisified with her appearance, I've met some uncouth people in my time but these take the biscuit. My aunts, Mrs Broom, no one has been quite as nasty as the Huttons. How much longer can I put up with it? And how much longer before one or other of them notices that I don't receive letters from my sailor husband?

So far, her figure was trim, though she was aware of a slight bump below her waist. The morning sickness had stopped, but even so she was always on the alert for any signs which might betray her condition.

She took her meals in the kitchen where Freda ruled, a dark place dominated by a massive, smoky range that needed polishing regularly. The family were served in the dining room with Margaret waiting at table. Mrs Hutton had provided her with a brown dress for housework and a black one for the afternoons, when she sometimes entertained female friends as ignorant and small-minded as herself.

I can't stand it, Margaret would think, listening to their silly, often malicious chatter.

'And how is Helbren settling in?' they would ask Mrs Hutton, as if Margaret was a deaf-mute or simple-minded.

'Very well, aren't you, Helbren?' she would reply with a pleased smirk. 'Do you like the way she's done my hair? Clever with her fingers. Does lovely sewing. It's nice to have my own maid, and she sees to Nelda, too. Doesn't she, my pet?'

'She's married, you say? Just as well, for she's a pretty girl and you don't want no bother with followers at the back door, do you?'

'She's all right, I suppose, if you like those sort of quiet, dull looks,' Nelda would butt in, never losing the opportunity to add her pennyworth. Margaret could do nothing but subjected her to a blistering glare.

Even the gloomy kitchen and the company of the dour Freda was preferable to these humilating tea parties. She was finding it increasingly hard to recall that she had ever been to Monte Carlo, walked the palm-fringed esplanades and stayed in magnificent hotels. Harder still to believe a lord had made love to her on a golden beach under a Mediterranean sun. Now there was nothing but rain and grey skies, cold winds and endless toil. She contemplated suicide.

One morning in November she awoke from a dream when she was back in Marseilles. It had been amazingly vivid – Lester and herself in the café again. Her room was dark, freezing, and she lit the lamp, went

220

to the bride-chest and lifted out Mignonette, needing to hold this beautiful thing. The poetry book was there, too, and the empty chocolate-box Lester had given her when they went to see *La Traviata*. Margaret's tears dripped down, wetting the doll's silk dress, and she sat on the bare boards and rocked her.

She permitted herself five minutes' indulgence, then packed Mignonette away and splashed her face with cold water. She dressed, put on a hession apron, tied up her hair, went downstairs and turned up the gas-jet. The fire still smouldered in the range and she added more coal, setting the kettle on the hob before going into the scullery.

How she hated Monday morning. Washday, slave day, when piles of whites had to be boiled and blued, then starched and dried, ironed and put away. The Huttons were too mean to use a laundry. Why should they when they had Margaret? Colours, too: socks, stockings and underwear, both male and female. Mrs Hutton's and Nelda's drawers and chemises; Mr Hutton's combinations; Graham's shirts, underpants and vests.

In a mood of black depression she struggled with the wash-house boiler situated under the copper in the corner. She raked out the dead ashes, then relaid it with newspaper and kindling before filling the copper from the stone sink, carrying across buckets of water.

Backwards and forwards she trudged until the correct level had been reached, then, dropping on her hunkers before the furnace door, added a few knubs of coal and applied a match. The flames roared, sucked back towards the flu. She let it blaze, spreading her hands to the warmth, then moved the damper across a fraction so the lively flames settled down to a steady glow.

The copper simmered, and the white flakes were ready, grated from a bar of household soap. They cascaded down in a snowy stream, hitting the surface, and she stirred them in with a pair of wooden tongs which would later be used to lift the scalding linen.

These actions were second nature. This was how she had done the washing at home, but had not dreamed it would ever be her job again. She was sweating by the time she had sorted out the first batch and dunked it, but her feet remained stone cold. She could feel chilblains forming on her toes, a discomfort she had not suffered for years. She heaved the heavy circular wooden lid across the top of the copper to retain the heat and speed up the process.

Her work had only just begun for, apart from anything else, Mrs Hutton had a bee in her bonnet about rinsing in rainwater, so Margaret had to brave the cold and dip pails in the water butt standing under the drainpipe in the yard.

221

'Damn the bitch!' she muttered. 'Why can't I simply turn on the tap? Would she know the difference?'

The blue bag lay in an azure puddle on an enamel saucer. Margaret added it to one of the baths. The water began to swirl, changing to the colour of summer. Blue as the seas of Monty – blue as Peter Newark's eyes. She could have gone to him for help. No doubt he still had a room at the Warwick Hotel, but pride stopped her. She could not face him with her tale of woe. He had feared this would happen, and had been right about Lester.

'I'd rather die,' she whispered, straightening up and pressing her hands against the ache in the small of her back. What would he think of me now? And she glanced down at her coal-smeared hands.

She mixed the starch from the packet with a robin printed on the side. A tablespoonful added to a measure of cold water resulted in a blue-tinged paste. She scraped this into a further basin to be poured into the final rinsing water. There was no way she could skimp on the job. Her mother had trained her too well.

By now the water was hot enough for the coloureds, and Margaret transferred some to an empty tub, setting to work with barsoap, scrubbing board and brush. Her pent-up rage was relieved by such vigorous action, murderous thoughts like a swarm of angry hornets in her head. She imagined Lady Julia's face beneath the bristles, the skin peeling away under the scourge, becoming nothing more than a piece of meat on a butcher's slab.

Later she raked at the cinders and fed the fire, rinsed the clothes and wedged them between the hardwood rollers of the mangle. If she arranged them evenly, the pressure as they passed through would make ironing easier.

She finished one batch and rested for a moment. The harsh soap stung the chaps that split her fingers and reddened her arms to the elbows. But there was no real let-up till she had arranged all the washing on a clotheshorse round the kitchen fire and draped the rest on a Manchester, that trellis-like arrangement which was then hauled up to the ceiling on pulleys.

It was noon and the house quiet. Freda had gone to the market with Mrs Hutton and Nelda. Taking off her soggy apron and hanging it close to the fire, Margaret made herself a cup of tea and carried it upstairs. She was extremely tired and intended to snatch half an hour under the blankets.

She stopped dead on the threshold. Graham was sitting on her bed.

'Do you want something, sir?' she asked coldly. 'I thought you were at work.'

222

'I slipped home during my lunch break.' He flipped back a lock of greasy hair and stared at her insolently.

'Why are you in my room?' Margaret's already irritated temper was rising.

'Why not? You got something to hide?' he sneered.

'I'm entitled to privacy. Please leave at once or I'll complain to your mother.' She took a pace back, very aware that no one would hear her if she screamed. The cup trembled against the saucer and she set it on the washstand.

Graham laughed, and made no attempt to rise. It was not the first time he had tampered with one of the maids. Usually they had been too frightened to deny him. Despite his assertions otherwise, he was not successful with the opposite sex, paying prostitutes to pander to his lust.

He had wanted Margaret from the start, putting her under seige, inflamed by her aloofness and the warning look in her eyes. Totally without principles, he had resorted to another method. Blackmail usually worked.

'You should know by now that I'm Ma's blue-eyed boy,' he said with that nasal twang Margaret found particularly repellent. 'In any case, you've been lying. You ain't married, no more than the man in the moon.'

'Mr Graham, get out of here before I throw you out.' Margaret was shaking, but more in anger than fear. 'You know nothing about me.'

'Don't I?' He lifted an eyebrow at her and his smile deepened. 'That's what you think, deary. While you were down in the scullery, I've been taking a little look at your things. Nice dresses you've got. Too bloody good for a skivvy, if you ask me. And that dolly in the chest. Where did she come from?'

'How dare you pry into my possessions? Who d'you think you are?'

'Naughty, naughty,' he mocked. 'No need to get on your high horse. Not a girl like you who's got a bun in the oven, put there by a gentleman who don't mean to do the right thing by you.'

Her diary! Margaret's eyes flew to the bride-chest. She kept it there, right at the bottom under the baby clothes. Too late she regretted the impulse which had impelled her to write down her deepest feelings. This debased creature had read her most secret thoughts. Had he found her money as well, and her mother's book? She prayed not, for she had stitched them into the lining.

'Leave. Now. Before I hit you,' she snarled, her hands bunched into fists.

He rose slowly and came towards her. 'Don't be silly, Margaret. We'll say no more about it, eh? Just you be nice to me and I'll keep it

223

from Ma as long as I can. You don't want to be flung out in this weather, do you? You've nowhere to go, and she hasn't paid your wages yet.'

He put out a hand and touched her breasts. Margaret knocked it aside and sprang for the cupboard, hauling out her clothes and stuffing them into the suitcases and chest, checking the lining hurriedly. It was still intact. He came after her, pulling her into his arms and trying to plant his wet lips on hers. Margaret gave him a smack that rocked him on his heels.

'Get off me!'

'What are you doing?' he massaged his stinging cheek, angry and offended.

'Leaving. I can't stay in this house a moment longer. You thought I'd be afraid to go? You've never been more wrong. Get out of my way.'

Graham let out a strangled roar and threw himself on her, bearing her backwards on to the bed. He was thin but strong, pushing her down, legs tangling with hers as he tried to jerk her skirts up. He was grinning, his mouth seeking hers. She threshed beneath him, twisting her head from side to side, then suddenly freed one thigh, brought up her knee with all the force she could muster and rammed it in his groin.

He yelled, doubled up in agony, hands clasping his testicles.

Margaret flung on her coat, grabbed her hat and lugged her two suitcases on to the landing, then returned to drag out the chest. She was panting heavily, beside herself with rage and disgust. This gave her the almost superhuman strength needed to get them downstairs and into the hall.

Mrs Hutton was coming in at the front door. 'Whatever are you doing, Helbren?' she asked, astounded, Freda's heavy face at her back and Nelda peering across her shoulder.

'I'm leaving. I'd like my wages now.' Margaret stood her ground, white-faced but awesome in her fury.

'You can't. How am I going to manage? Why are you leaving?' Mrs Hutton put down her parcels and glared at her.

'Ask your son.' Margaret held out her hand, palm up. 'My money, if you please.'

'Money? Money! You've got a nerve, leaving me in the lurch.'

'Don't give her anything, Ma,' Graham shouted, leaning over the banisters. 'She's a whore.'

'Graham! What a thing to say in front of your sister!'

'It's true.' He limped down the stairs, still clasping himself between the legs, his face greenish.

224

'Whatever has been going on? I can't go out for five minutes within the whole house falling apart.'

'I came home to get something for Pa and she started to come on strong. She's not married, Mother, and she wants a father for her baby. Can't you see she's carrying? Thought she could trap me into taking responsibility.'

'You bloody liar!' Margaret shouted. 'It wasn't like that. You tried to rape me. Went through my personal belongings – poked your nose into things that were not your business.'

'Well, really! Is this true? Aren't you married? I'm sure my boy would never – you'd not, would you, Graham?'

'Of course not, Ma.' He put an arm round her and she was beguiled by his innocent expression.

'Give me my wages,' Margaret repeated, wearily. Every muscle in her body seemed to have its own particular ache.

'Wages? You've got a cheek! You don't deserve anything after the way you've behaved! Betrayed our kindness, that's what you've done.'

'My wages!' Margaret held out an insistent hand, the look on her face terrifying.

Mrs Hutton fumbled in her reticule. 'Oh, very well – but only half. You've not earned the rest. Should have given me proper notice. It's not right. I'll be complaining to the Midland Agency. Oh, yes, they shall hear about this.'

Margaret pocketed the few shillings, and went out the front door, saying, 'I shan't be a moment.'

Finding a boy playing in the road, she gave him a penny to fetch her a hackney, then went back to wait. The hall was deserted, but she could hear Mrs Hutton's complaining voice somewhere in the background.

The cabby helped her load her things and, 'Can you take me to a boarding house?' she asked, standing in the gutter and looking up into his red, kindly face.

'Sure, missus. Cheap and cheerful, I suppose.'

It was not until he pulled up at a tall thin house in Paddington that she fully realised what she had done, so shocked that she was working with the top of her mind only. That shock helped her through the next hour, when she saw the obese, beery-breathed proprietor, agreed on a rent and was shown into a room on the second floor.

She sat down on the dirty mattress when he had gone, and realised this was the kind of place she had wanted so badly to avoid. Dirty, bleak, and cheap. The sort of dwelling where no questions were asked, just as long as one paid the landlord. A fine residence indeed for Lord Lester's trollop and his illegitimate baby.

*

Resilient, above all, Margaret learned to survive the cold, the meagre rations, and the loneliness of her new way of life. She tramped the streets looking for employment. Without a reference, only the meanest positions were available, worse even than the Huttons.

She served as a barmaid for a while, but the late hours, the coarse company and the danger to a woman living alone made her give it up. Also, her condition was becoming noticeable. No one wanted a pregnant woman doing barwork. The punters expected someone lively, willing to step out the back and earn a few extra coins by copulating against the wall.

Too tired, and suffering from a streaming cold and hacking cough, she gave up trying, staying in her wretched room, huddled in bed to keep warm, reading books borrowed from the lending library, or writing her diary by candlelight, afraid to use the gas for fear of the shilling metre running out. It was bad enough that she had to ignite the single ring to boil the kettle or heat food.

There was no peace in this overcrowded house; harridans screaming; babies wailing; men coming in drunk, beating their wives or getting into fights. Scruffy children haunted the passageways. There was one tap on the landing and a single lavatory shared by twenty people. Pails of garbage stood in corners; the doorways and corridors were deathtraps, and the whole place would have gone up like a tinderbox had there been a fire.

Margaret's only comfort was the baby, kicking strongly inside her, yet even this brought terror. She could not spare the money to visit a doctor or midwife. What would happen to her when she started labour? The women in the lodging house seemed to help one another when their time came, but she kept to herself, alarmed by their strident voices and rough ways.

Her money was disappearing fast, though she had eeked it out as best she could. She put off pawning her dresses. These represented the better life to which she had aspired. Once they went she might as well throw herself in the river.

The thought of ending it all was becoming obsessional. Early one morning, coughing and feverish, she crept through the murky streets and stood on the Embankment, watching the brown waters flow quickly past. The memory of Lester festered in her mind. How different the Thames had seemed in his company, the lights sparkling from the bridge as he talked of how they would visit Dublin.

'Liar and cheat!' she muttered, crouching near the stone pillars. 'Why do I go on living?'

Barges moved downstream, their sirens loud and imperative and a part of Margaret responded to the smell of tar and the sight of masts rising into the sky. They reminded her of home. I need to go there, she thought, nostalgia sweeping up, to stand on the shore and visit the Weeping Maids, though they've not helped. But Porthross is forbidden me. I can't kneel by my mother's grave or walk down to the harbour. I'm a pariah, unmarried and big with child. The women would drag their children indoors out of my path, the men eye me as if I was a whore.

You've done this to me, Lester.

A policeman paced towards her with measured tread. She returned his smile, pulled her shawl around her and tried to look as if she was simply admiring the view. At five in the morning? Hardly. Human contact. She missed that. Someone to talk with – no chance with the strumpets in the flats.

'Bitter cold,' the constable said, stopping.

'It is,' she answered.

'You going somewhere, missus?'

He probably takes me for a prostitute or thief, she thought. 'To the market.'

'Best time for prices, eh?'

'That's right.'

'Good morning, missus.' He touched his helmet and turned away.

'Good morning, officer.'

The fog swirled over the river and the thought of seeking a suicide's watery grave dismayed her. As if in agreement, the baby heaved, drumming against her bladder with its tiny heels. I can't kill it, she realised. Take my own life, perhaps, but not my unborn's.

She found a public convenience, and then made her way to the market. If one went very early, before the fresh produce came in, it was possible to pick over the crates of yesterday's vegetables, scrag ends of mutton discarded by the butcher and stale loaves thrown out by the baker.

It was there that Peter found her when he went to buy beef for the Warwick Hotel at Lillian's behest. He did a double take, staring at the grubby waif sorting through a noisome bin of bones.

'Margaret? Is that you?' he said, coming up behind her.

Her eyes were those of an animal in a trap, shifting from side to side, her first impulse to flee. This elegant gentleman in his woollen coat with the fur collar would have only one motive: that of buying her services for sexual gratification.

'Don't you remember me?' His gloved hand was on her arm, and she looked into his face.

'Mr Newark,' she mumbled, and the shame of him seeing her like that made her dizzy.

'I've been searching for you everywhere,' he exclaimed, and his smile dazzled her, so wide and sincere in that handsome face, the blue eyes gleaming like jewels.

He saw at once that she was pregnant, was horrified by her sickly appearance, yet wanted to shout aloud with joyous relief. She was alive!

She tried to shake him off, her eyes filling up with tears, starting to cough as she struggled to say, 'What d'you want?'

'To care for you,' he said, alarmed to find a lump in his throat. 'My dear girl, you're ill. Let me take you somewhere warm.'

'It's a cold – nothing really. I can't come with you. Look at the state of me.'

Her clothes were worn, a black shawl dragged over her shabby coat. She was painfully thin, and this served to emphasise the roundness of her belly, yet in his eyes she was beautiful.

'It doesn't matter,' he said, pity flooding through him. 'You can't stay here in the street.'

'I'm all right. I've somewhere to live,' she muttered, wishing the pavement would open and swallow her up.

'Margaret, hush. We'll eat and then talk about this. Come along.'

It was wonderful to cling to his arm, to feel the warmth of his concern and know that she was not alone any longer. Tears wetted her cheeks and she feared that if she let go she would never stop crying.

'I presume Lester knows about this?' He rested a gentle hand on her bulge.

'It's nothing to do with him.' She lifted her chin defiantly.

'Isn't it his child?'

'Yes, but I can manage.'

Peter decided not to question her further for the moment, squashing down his rage against the Irishman and saying, 'You look as if you could do with some breakfast. Let's go to the Warwick and have bacon and eggs and coffee.'

'I can't face Mrs Glynn, not in this state.'

'She's not up yet. She hasn't been well and the doctor says she is to rest, but we've the devil's own job making her stay put.'

Feeling that she looked like a vagrant, Margaret allowed him to help her into a cab and was soon walking across the hotel's lobby. Painful memories welled up and she almost turned tail and ran. The first person she saw was Jenkins. His eyebrows shot skywards as he recognised her, but Peter silenced him with a brisk, 'Breakfast for two, Jenkins, if you please.'

In the dining room, Joe was setting a tray with a plate of triangular-shaped toast, a pat of butter, marmalade in a glass dish and a pot of tea. He was about to add a rose when they entered.

'Morning, Joe,' Peter called out cheerily. 'How is she today?'

'She didn't have too bad a night, sir, thank you,' Joe replied, eyeing Margaret as he placed a folded napkin over one arm, bandbox fresh in his dark uniform and white shirt, clean-shaven, handsome, radiating a kind of boyish innocence.

'Try to keep her off the booze. The doctor's told me that it isn't doing her any favours. Her heart's not as strong as it might be. Apparently she had rheumatic fever when she was a nipper.'

'I know, sir, and I do my best, but she's stubborn.' A shadow passed over Joe's sunny face. 'I'd better get this to her.'

'He's a capital young chap,' Peter remarked conversationally, determined not to press Margaret. Get some food inside her, take away that hunted look and maybe she would tell him what had been happening to her, and Lester's part in it.

He pulled out her chair before seating himself opposite, adding to keep the atmosphere light, 'I can't remember the last time I entertained a young lady to breakfast.'

A waiter took their order, and when the liver, bacon, sausages and eggs arrived, Margaret set upon it like a starving animal. But it was too much for her, and before long she rose, hand pressed to her lips.

She found the lavatory, coughing and vomiting, clinging to the porcelain rim until the spasm passed. She blew her sore, reddened nose, washed her hands and face and straightened her hat, then returned to where Peter waited.

'I carried on without you,' he said, a large damask napkin spread across his knees. 'I take it you won't feel like eating any more.'

'No, thank you. I'll try a cup of tea. I'm not used to so much food.'

He shot her a concerned glance. 'You should see a doctor about that cough.'

'Doctors cost money.'

'Have you seen one about the baby?'

'Not since I had the pregnancy confirmed.'

'And Lester refused to help you, I suppose.' Still attempting to be matter of fact when dealing with a situation that was tragic, he spread butter on a slice of toast, bit a deep crescent into it and chewed vigorously. Eliciting no response, he said, 'Please forgive me for tucking in like this. I'm no use to man nor beast till I've had my breakfast. Can't think properly.'

'Does he still stay here?' she asked at last, grateful because Peter neither questioned nor condemned. It would have been so easy for him to tell her that he had predicted this.

229

'No.' He wiped his mouth on the napkin and ordered a fresh pot of coffee for himself and one of tea for her.

'That's because of me,' she said quietly.

'Ah, yes. Just so. He did a bunk, in the time-honoured tradition of the cad.' Those keen eyes met hers, caught and held them.

'Not exactly.' She was feeling better now. 'He offered me two alternatives.'

'I'll stake my life that one of them wasn't marriage.'

'Correct. Not to him at any rate. To Luke Watson, the chauffeur.'

'How very noble. I always said Lester Kealan had a heart of pure granite.' His lips still smiled, but there was a tightness about them now and a fierce glint in his eyes. 'And you refused?'

'Not at first.' Suddenly Margaret could no longer control her emotions, tears welling up.

'We can't talk here,' Peter said, rising from the table. 'Come upstairs. You've nothing to fear from me, I promise. We'll leave the door of my room open, if you like.'

Margaret was too distraught to make a rational judgement concerning his sincerity. She did not know him well, had once been angry with him for criticising Lester, but now had no option but to trust him. There was no one else prepared to offer a helping hand.

Peter was nothing like as calm as he appeared, seething with fury. He had not given up the search and had, on one occasion, met Lester in the foyer of the Albert Hall with India on his arm. He had tried to broach the subject of Margaret's whereabouts, but Lester had merely smiled and walked away.

Now in his plain, strictly masculine room, filled with books and papers, with a typewriter in the middle of the flat-topped desk, the dam burst and Margaret talked and cried till she was exhausted. She kept nothing back, telling him about her mother and Lord Henry, Lady Julia's cruelty, the backstreet abortionist, Lester's wager with Roderick, her experience with the Huttons, and what had taken place since leaving their house.

Peter, long limbs stretched out in a cushioned club-chair, listened without comment, handing her a succession of fresh white hand-kerchiefs while his need to fight Lester and give Roderick the thrashing of his life grew stronger by the second.

Her beauty tore him apart, this waifish, pregnant girl with the tear-stained face and swollen nose. Her heaving shoulders were as thin as a child's, her lovely hands red with chilblains. Many might have turned aside from her in disgust. Peter wanted to undress her, tenderly bathe away the dirt, smooth perfumed oils into her skin, and lay her between satin sheets, holding her close to him during the night.

Eventually when she stopped long enough for him to speak, he said, 'What are your plans?' and linked his hands behind his head, looking at her with thoughtful scrutiny.

'I haven't any. My money's nearly gone.'

'Don't worry about that. I'll see you don't starve. But you must think of the future. A child costs a fearsome amount to rear. I think it might be wise to see a lawyer who'll insist that Lester pay maintenance.'

'Impossible,' she cried. 'Who would listen to me? I'm just a stupid maidservant who allowed herself to be seduced. It's an old story, isn't it? Either that, or I'll be painted as a scheming hussy who thought she could trap him. Lawyers work for the gentry, and look after their interests.'

He ran his fingers through his tousled hair and leaned towards her. 'Not necessarily. I know a fellow keen on fighting for justice. I'll take you to see him. You have one powerful weapon.'

'I have?'

'Lord Henry, and what you know about him. You're his daughter, God dammit. He should be made to assist you.'

The face turned to his was a small white mask of hopelessness. 'You don't know Lady Julia. She's capable of anything.'

'I've no doubt she is, but I can be ruthless, too.'

'It isn't your fight,' she reminded.

'There's nothing I enjoy more than tilting at windmills,' he rejoined with a grin, resisting the urge to place his arms round her and hug her to his chest. 'Oh, come on, Margaret! Let me play at knight errant.'

He intended to make her laugh, and succeeded. She could feel the first faint ray of hope. Now, gradually and cautiously, she began to consider the possibility of challenging those arrogant people who had ruined not only herself, but her mother. She wanted vengeance, didn't she? Maybe this was the way to achieve it.

She suddenly saw Peter in a new light, her defender, tall, strong and forceful. 'Will you really help me?' she asked.

'I'm at your service, fair damsel,' he declaimed, hand on heart.

'Be serious for a moment, please. What do you advise I do?'

'First, we'll see Lillian and get you fixed up.'

'With a job? Will she let me work here, an expectant mother?'

'She's been worried about you, too.'

He stood up, towering over her but not in the least intimidating. She had learned to fear and distrust men, but found herself wanting to nestle against him, and rest her head on his broad shoulder like a tired child coming home at last.

*

231

Lillian hated being ill. She had no time for the weakness that had taken over lately, a series of minor complaints, colds, bronchitis, difficulty in breathing. She despised herself and fought to carry on, but a particularly unpleasant episode when her heart had felt as if it was about to burst through her ribcage had forced her to slow down.

'I can't stay in bed,' she had shouted. 'Damn it! What about my business?'

'It won't be any use to you if you're pushing up the daisies,' Dr Robert Manson had replied, a tow-headed, untidy, talented young man who had set up in practice two streets away.

'Stop fussing!' Lillian had grumbled, knowing him well enough to argue. He often dropped into the Warwick for dinner.

But he had been insistent, and the medicine he prescribed had made her sleepy, compelling her to rest. Biddy had nursed her, and Joe had proved invaluable, along with Monsieur Philippe and Jenkins. Peter had jumped at the chance to get involved in the running of the hotel.

Now she was better, but still taking it easy, reclining on the sofa in her bedroom while Manson listened to her chest and back, then returned his stethoscope to his bag. 'The rest has worked wonders,' he pronounced. 'Keep it up.'

'I'm feeling fit as a flea. Can I go downstairs?' She swung her legs over the side of the couch. With a surge of her old energy she had applied cosmetics that morning, but left her hair tumbling about her shoulders in a riot of Titian curls. She was wearing a long red velvet robe, the deep V at the neck bordered by a band of black fur.

Manson, smiling, laid a restraining hand on her shoulder. 'Not so fast. I know you. Once I permit a resumption of activites, you won't know when to stop. Have you taken my advice and given up drinking and cigarettes?'

'Yes – well, not entirely. I didn't feel like smoking to begin with, and that medicine was beautifully soothing. I had the most amazing dreams. What was in it? Laudanum?'

'Among other things. Seriously, Lillian, I don't want you to drink alcohol.'

'I thought you medical men considered it good for one.'

'In moderation, like everything else. But just for now, I'd like you to give it up completely.' He turned to Biddy who stood behind her mistress. 'See that she behaves.'

'I will, sir.'

Lillian was just about to open her lips in protest when Peter knocked on the door. He came in smiling from ear to ear, shouting jubilantly, 'See who I found in the market!'

'My goodness! Miss Helbren!' Lillian's eyes widened. 'Where have

232

you been hiding yourself?' One look at Margaret's wan face and big belly told her most of the story.

'I'm sorry you've been ill,' Margaret said huskily. 'I've a cold. Perhaps I shouldn't come too close.'

'Nonsense, my dear,' Lillian answered, regarding her from under thick lashes, half reclining, her head propped on one hand and her wide sleeve falling back to leave her arm bare to the elbow.

'Not too much excitement,' Manson warned. 'I'll be back to see you in the morning.'

'Now then, tell me all about it,' she said when the doctor had gone. She patted the space beside her. Margaret sat down and began to talk.

'Men!' Lillian exploded once or twice during the recital. 'They're like creatures from another planet! Not you, Peter, you're an exception and so is Joe, but on the whole I wouldn't give any of 'em spit.'

'Can you find Margaret a place on your staff?' Peter said.

'I'm sure I can.'

'Thank you, Mrs Glynn.' Margaret was overwhelmed. 'I'll work hard.'

'I'm not a slave-driver,' Lillian laughed. 'But I expect work to be done properly. I guess you don't know the first thing about hotels. There's a lot to learn. I need an assistant as Dr Manson says I'm not to do too much, but when your baby comes, we'll have to think again.'

'Shall we go and fetch your belongings?' Peter asked Margaret, knowing he would not feel secure until every item she possessed was beneath the Warwick's roof. She might vanish again like a will-o'-the-wisp. He did not think he could bear it if that happened.

Fear sprang into her eyes. 'The landlord may not let me have them. I owe two weeks' rent.'

'I'll come with you and sort him out.' Peter was already on his feet, ready to explode into action. It was so much better to have a visible opponent rather than boxing with shadows.

'Take Joe along,' Lillian advised. Ill she might be, but she had not lost her powers of observation and could see how it was with him, moved by the tenderness he showed towards Margaret. 'He'll back you up if there's any trouble.'

Chapter 13

Margaret's room at the Warwick was painted in eggshell blue. It had a high ceiling, dimity curtains and a brass bedstead. A radiator supplied heat, although there was a tiled fireplace.

I've died and gone to heaven, she thought, and the first thing she did on returning from the lodging house was strip off her soiled clothes and sink into a tub of hot, scented water in the adjacent bathroom. The meeting with the landlord had not been pleasant, but Peter had taken over, and she had indulged in the comforting sensation of being supported by two strong men.

What price independence when faced with an unreasonable bully? Especially one who had seen Margaret as a potential source of income, envisaging making a handsome profit by permitting her to take men to her room when, in desperation, she went on the game. Peter had demolished him with a few well-chosen words, and settled her account.

Cleaner than she had been since leaving Upper Grosvenor Street, she arranged her possessions, the bride-chest under the window, her garments in the antique tallboy and wardrobe. Mignonette was stashed on the top shelf, along with *The Rubáiyát of Omar Khayyám*, and the chocolate-box, mementoes she would look at in the future when she had succeeded in putting the past firmly behind her.

Biddy arrived with a cup of herbal mixture she had made, swearing it was the best thing to cure a cold, advising that she stay put, but though Margaret drank it, she wanted to find Peter and express her thanks all over again. Fate had brought them together. Like the knights of old he aspired to emulate, he had rescued her from Castle Despair and carried her to safety and the hotel. She owed him a debt impossible to repay.

Kindness, warmth and friendship worked quicker than Biddy's potion and, determined to prove worthy of Lillian's trust, Margaret worked hard and learned fast, having admirable teachers in Mr Grist and Monsieur Philippe.

'I've missed a woman about the place. Biddy's a treasure, but not too bright up top,' Lillian said a few days after Margaret had moved in. 'You and me are going to get on just fine.'

She took a lot of interest in Margaret's story and in the coming baby, but when she was shown the layette her eyes filled with tears. 'I was pregnant years ago,' she confessed, sinking down in a froth of silk skirts beside the bride-chest. 'I had it removed, and nearly died. My inside was so badly damaged that doctors say I'll never conceive again.'

'I'm so sorry . . .' Margaret put an arm round her.

Lillian wiped her eyes with a scrap of lacy handkerchief. 'That's the price I paid for falling in love with a toff. I can't forgive Lester for leaving you in the lurch, it brings it all back to me. As for Roderick! He needn't show his face in my hotel again. I'll help you with the child. You can live here as long as you like, if I get to cuddle it now and again.'

'I'm worried, Lillian. I've told you that I worked in the Aubert nursery, but I didn't have much to do with the baby, William. I find the idea of looking after one of my own daunting.'

'I think you'll make a lovely mother.'

Margaret's cheeks went pink with pleasure. 'Do you? That's reassuring. There's something I wanted to ask you.'

'Fire away.' Lillian's capable hands were rewrapping the tiny clothes in tissue paper.

'Will you stand as godmother?'

'Try and stop me! Heavens! Isn't this exciting? The Warwick's first baby!'

No longer physically depleted and having locked up her emotions and thrown away the key, Margaret began to bloom, the colour returning to her face, her body filling out with advancing pregnancy and Philippe's superb cooking. She was busy from dawn till dusk, overseeing the charwomen and chambermaids, organising the linen, shopping with Peter, making sure the silver was polished and the tables up to standard, taking bookings and acting as chief cook and bottle-washer. She did her best to shield Lillian from stress, learning diplomacy and the cardinal rule that the customer was always right.

But she quickly discovered that no one could protect Lillian from herself. She drank and she smoked, one cigarette after another plugged into her jade holder. She stayed up late, playing poker. She was not happy to delegate, needing to control. She was caretaker to innumerable friends, involving herself with their problems. It was too much for her, but she could not let go.

Joe was utterly devoted to her. She loved him with a woman's passion and a mother's tenderness. But, too much the realist to imagine that he would stay with her for ever, she used this as another excuse to drink.

'I won't ever leave you,' he declared for the umpteenth time, lying by the fire with her on a night in late November. 'I love you, Lilly.'

She rested on her elbow, replete with loving, the firelight moulding the deep hollows and peaks of her smooth flesh, the sable wrap which cushioned them and the silk of her négligé forming a luxurious carpet for their naked bodies.

'Ah, you say you love me now,' she said, swirling the brandy in a balloon-shaped goblet. 'But how long will it be before you fancy some younger women, eh?'

'It won't happen,' he swore, and took the bottle from her as she was about to add more. 'It's you and me for all time, Lilly. But I wish you'd look after yourself. The doctor says—'

'Damn the doctor! What does he know?'

'I'm here, the hotel's flourishing, Margaret's a find, and there's a baby to look forward to. You can't be unhappy, can you?'

'You don't understand,' she sighed and sat up, arms round her knees as she stared into the peaks and caverns of the fire.

'I'm trying to.'

'I know, darling. Take no notice of me. I'm just a cantankerous bitch.' She turned to him, ran her fingers over his face, loving the feel of his skin, the soft stubble on his chin, the odour of fresh sweat, forgetting for a moment the fear of abandonment that for ever lurked on the edge of consciousness.

A peasouper blanketed London. Margaret and Peter went out in it, the city mysteriously changed into an incredible underworld. Passersby resembled silhouettes cut out of black paper. Motorcars, cabs, omnibuses, carts, were shadows that nosed their way along painfully like blind beasts. The streetlights hung, unripe oranges in the murk. Peter flagged down a hackney. It crawled towards Marble Arch.

'The fog tastes like melons,' he said, glancing sideways at her in the near-blackness of the interior.

'More like soot,' she answered, huddling into her collar. The fog gripped her throat and made her eyes water.

'Maybe you should have stayed at home.'

He was as concerned as if he was her mother, or the infant's natural father. He had never lived close to a pregnant woman before and was in turn proud to be her right arm, awed by her condition, frightened for her and, above all, regretful that it was not his.

236

'Oh, no. You've been promising me this treat for ages. A bit of weather isn't going to put me off,' she said, smiling up at him.

Her real reason for going was curiosity. She longed to learn everything about him. He was always surprising her with some new aspect of his diverse personality. She had been mystified by his regular absences from the hotel on two afternoons a week, wondering at first if he had a mistress and finding the idea distasteful.

'Ask him,' Lillian had suggested, her eyes twinkling.

Margaret had taken her advice, and he had told her that one of his hobbies was swordsmanship. 'I practise on Wednesdays and Fridays,' he had explained.

'I expect you're good at it,' she had said.

'I came first in the officers' Sabre Competition and won the Foils Competition at the Military Tournament held in the Agricultural Hall.'

'But you're not an officer, are you?'

'Not the regular army, but I belong to the Inns of Court Volunteers, and gave a display at their last Assault at Arms.'

'Can I watch you fight, oh knight, "alone and palely loitering"?'

'You certainly can. I'll take you with me next time I go to the fencing academy. It's run by a fiery little Italian called Signor Tabaldi. He has the most fearsome moustache. You're not to giggle.'

Now they left the cab, the fog putting out clammy fingers and touching their ears and noses. Before them loomed a large building, once the town house of a duke but recently transformed into a gymnasium. The hall was high and echoing, the wide stairs uncarpeted. Peter conducted her to the erstwhile drawing room, now a studio for the refined art of sword play.

Several couples were already engaged in combat, their feet stamping on the cork matting. The room was bare, except for a row of chairs against one wall, and racks containing foils, protective clothing and face masks.

Margaret thrilled to the clash of steel on steel, the footwork of the protagonists as graceful as ballet dancers. She took a seat while Peter went off to the changing room, returning in a while wearing a white padded jacket, canvas breeches and pumps. Signor Tabaldi, energetic and voluble, came across to greet him.

'Ah, Mr Newark, what a day! This climate! Most dank. But now you have brought the sunshine in the shape of your so charming companion,' and he bowed elaborately to Margaret, rolling his soulful brown eyes and smiling beneath a truly magnificent black moustache.

'This is Mrs Helbren,' Peter said, amused. Wherever they went, Margaret attracted male attention, even more so since her pregnancy

237

had become obvious, the sight of this beautiful young mother-to-be rousing their dormant chivalry.

The Italian sighed, winked, expressed by his gestures that he understood, his romantic imagination suggesting she might be Peter's inamorata. The room was brightly lit, in contrast to the gloom outside, and she was content to rest and watch Peter as he skilfully disposed of one opponent after another, while Tabaldi instructed and criticised.

Peter's performance was impressive. His strength and endurance, his agile movements, the way he seemed relaxed yet ever alert, parrying his adversary's lunges, giving him no chance to pierce his guard, made Margaret's heart thump with excitement. Point after point was conceded to him, and eventually he retired, the winner.

'I shan't be long,' he said, taking off his mask and mopping over his sweating face with a towel. 'A quick shower, and then I'll take you out to tea. How does the idea of hot buttered crumpets and cream cakes appeal?'

'Delightful,' she said, thinking how lucky she was to have him as her champion. He really was a splendid man, personable and gallant, his behaviour towards her impeccable.

She was stiff from sitting, the baby, ever active, had been kicking vigorously and her ribs were sore. Walking round the studio, admiring the trophies, the diplomas, the evidence of Tabaldi's claims as a master, she suddenly heard a voice that chilled her blood and set her pulse racing.

'Good God! Margaret!' Lester exclaimed, his overcoat swinging from his shoulders like a cloak, sparkling with foggy droplets. He looked sleek and prosperous in a dark blue suit, a black silk tie and a damask waistcoat. Gold-crested cufflinks and a ruby signet ring flashed at every movement.

She backed away till she could feel the wall behind her. Adrenaline pumped through her veins, urging her to run away. But her wayward senses rushed into life, breaking the chains with which she had bound them – memories smashing open the locks of her mind, springing out like the contents of Pandora's box.

She trembled, stared into that handsome face and wanted to weep. His eyes went down over her, pausing momentarily at her thickened waist, then lifting to her face again, one black brow raised in a question mark. She dared not trust herself to speak and went to pass him, longing for Peter to appear.

Lester's hand shot out and gripped her. 'Aren't you going to say hello?' he said, his voice softened by that Irish lilt.

She tugged on her arm, amazed at his affrontery. That was the measure of the man. He was like it through and through, unfeeling,

238

selfish, a law unto himself. She recognised these flaws, yet knew the cure was not yet complete. He had treated her shabbily, but part of her still responded to him. The shock of this revelation was devastating, all her carefully constructed defences smashed by a single glance from his steel-grey eyes.

She stumbled, but the hand clamped round her wrist supported her. They stood, locked together as if in mortal conflict. She could smell him, feel his power, almost see the fiery aura that surrounded him. The only man who had known her body, the father of her child. Of what use was common sense when such things were remembered by the nerves, blood and central core of being?

'Where are you living?' He demanded more than asked.

'The Warwick Hotel.' It would have taken the resolution of a saint to deny him.

'I thought you might go there, that's why I moved.'

'It wasn't that easy,' she whispered. 'I've been through hell.'

'It needn't have been like that. You disobeyed me.'

'I had to.'

'There's no one else? No man who is providing for you?'

'No. I'm working for Lillian.'

He laughed. 'What a do-gooder that woman is!'

'What do you know about good deeds?' She flashed with sudden vehemence. 'I've never met anyone so self-centred. Nothing matters, does it? It's all for the entertainment of my Lord High-and-Mighty Lester. I hate you!'

His eyes darkened and his lips curved, full and sensual, ready to feed on hers. 'Hate me? You love me. You'll never be free of me. Here's the proof,' and he rested a hand on her belly wherein lay the child created from their passion. 'If you truly hated me you would have killed it.'

'Are you ready, Margaret?' said Peter, stalking towards them, his face grim.

A hot tide of anger swirled through his entire being. The sight of Lester standing so close to Margaret urged him to desperate deeds – he wanted to take the Irishman by the throat and choke the life out of him.

Lester let her go, saying, with a mocking lift of one dark brow, 'Ah, I see you've found a new protector, my dear. Congratulations.'

A vein throbbed in the centre of Peter's forehead and his eyes were like blue spears. 'Leave her alone. Haven't you done enough damage, Kealan?'

Lester flicked him a disdainful glance. 'I don't recall asking your opinion. This is between my mistress and myself.'

239

'Your ex-mistress. She's made a fresh start. The last thing she needs is interference from you.'

Tabaldi was dithering in the background, plucking drama out of the air, seeing the angry faces of the two men and Margaret's anguished expression. This was the stuff from which duels were made.

'Are you fencing today, my lord?' He addressed Lester.

'I am. I'll be with you in a moment.'

'Shall we leave?' Peter held out his arm to Margaret. She placed her icy fingers on it and he covered them with his warm ones.

'What a charming picture,' Lester mocked, his eyes scornful. 'So domesticated. Speaking of which, I'm getting married when we return from America towards the end of next year. It's to be a double wedding. Roderick will be marrying Fay and I'll be marrying India. It will take place at St Martin's, and the reception is to be held at Clariges. You'll get an official invitation, Peter.'

'I shall be otherwise engaged.'

'Pity,' Lester drawled. 'It's to be a very grand affair. Lord Edward and Lady Ethel insist on nothing but the best for their daughters.'

'Then they've made a grave error with regard to the bridegrooms. Someone should warn them,' Peter said in clipped, furious tones.

'It wouldn't be wise to try anything like that, old boy,' Lester purred menacingly. 'Pointless, actually. The young ladies are beside themselves with joy and anticipation.' He inclined his head towards Margaret, adding ironically, 'I'm sorry you can't be included on the guest list, my dear, but I'm sure you understand. You'll be hearing from me now I know where you are. Perhaps later, when you've had the baby, we can carry on where we left off.'

'Never, never!' she cried, her heart throbbing with all the agony and rage of the strong-willed woman who has been savagely wronged by the man she once adored.

It was not until Margaret was seated in the cosy atmosphere of a busy café in Regent Street that she stopped shaking.

'Now will you see a solicitor?' Peter demanded, his face tense, his eyes dark and stormy. 'Kealan should be horsewhipped! I've a good mind to see Lord Edward.'

'He's right when he said it wouldn't make any difference,' she whispered. 'You don't know what it's like to be under his spell. I do. India loves and wants him. She wouldn't listen, and her father will do as she wishes.'

'Then at least get the legal ball rolling. You must, Margaret. Why should he get away with it? He's responsible for your baby.'

A waitress in a black dress, white cap and apron appeared, pencil

240

and pad at the ready. Peter ordered, but absently, still wrestling with his own violent reaction.

Margaret was lost, her hard-won calm shattered within a split second of seeing Lester. She could hear Peter going on about lawyers and justice, and around her the buzz of this select tea shop where ladies took refuge from the rigours of shopping. They were as pale and insubstantial as ghosts, her sight blinded by the vision of Lester's face, her ears attuned to his voice, her body fired by memories of physical passion.

Peter poured the tea and pushed a cup towards her. A plate of crumpets arrived, emitting little wisps of steam. Eclairs glistened under the glass cake dome. All she could do was murmur, 'He's marrying India.'

Peter riveted her with his eyes. 'And it matters to you?'

'I'm not being sensible about this, but yes, it does. I can't help it.' She begged him to understand, her hands fluttering helplessly as if seeking an anchor. He took them in his, gripping them so fiercely that it hurt, wanting to kiss them, to press them to his hot face.

'You can. You will. He's worthless and you know it,' he said forcefully.

In the background a girl was describing a ball gown; another was talking about her mother; a third had just discovered the novels of H. Ryder Haggard. Cups rattled and saucers clinked. The tea shop was a secure oasis, but Margaret was in purgatory.

She withdrew her hands and Peter damned Lester and all like him, adventurers who swept women off their feet, robbed them of their honour and then discarded them, leaving wounds that never healed. 'I suppose I'll have to chain you to the bedpost for your own good, to stop you going back to him,' he said, with a bleak smile.

'No. It was just the shock of seeing him. You'll find I'm more rational tomorrow,' she said tremulously. 'I can't let my friends down, can I?'

'To the devil with that,' he shouted, and people looked in their direction. 'You must think of yourself. My God, Margaret, if there was only a pill one could take to cure unrequited love.'

Even as he spoke a thought struck him like a blow between the eyes: if there was such a cure, then he should apply for it himself.

He had fallen deeply in love with Margaret, probably from the first moment he clapped eyes on her. Oh yes, he felt compassion, exasperation, tenderness, care, all those things, but admitted to overwhelming desire, willing to lay his heart, his life's blood and devotion at her feet and to fight any man for the possession of her, body, mind and soul.

And now he had a piece of unfinished business to complete.

He delivered her back to Lillian and after dinner left the Warwick, went out into the fog and walked briskly towards Mayfair. He could have taken a cab but needed to clear his head. The darkness, the sinister hazy light seen through patches of drifting mist suited his mood.

The Connaught in Alderman Street was a club that had flourished since the eighteenth century. In its pillared halls gentlemen met to dine, drink and gamble. Ladies were excluded. Peter walked up the wide stone steps and was greeted by a liveried flunky.

'You're a member, sir?'

'I'm a guest of Lord Kealan.'

'Very well, sir. I'll just check with him,' and the man bowed and disappeared into an inner room.

In a moment he returned to murmur, 'Will you join him in the salon, sir?' And he took the black opera cloak, white silk scarf and top hat Peter handed to him.

Peter smiled grimly, counting on the fact that Lester would not have been able to resist seeing him, to gloat, probably, confident that he had only to crook his little finger and Margaret would be his again. He followed the footman across the velvety carpet and into the hushed, cathedral-like atmosphere of the smoking room where members could enjoy a brandy and relax before chancing their arm at the card tables.

Lester was sunk in the depths of a leather armchair, immaculate in white tie and tails. He looked up as Peter approached, his lips curved in a tigerish smile, his eyes watchful. 'You wanted to see me? Can I offer you a drink? After all, I owe you for looking after Margaret. I don't mind if you use her, old chap. I'm not the jealous sort.'

Peter flexed the hands held stiffly at his sides, saying, very quietly, 'I suggest you take that back, Kealan.'

Lester chuckled. 'My dear fellow, it was only a joke.' He swung to his feet and reached for the handbell. 'Have a drink. You're too damn serious, always have been. What's one woman, more or less.'

'I'm not drinking with you.' Peter's blood was up, a red haze dancing before his eyes. 'I came here for a purpose.'

'And what is that?' Lester paused, stared at him. Several gentleman glanced across at the raised voices. Newspapers rustled.

'Just this.' Peter stepped forward and landed him a right hook to the nose, hearing the satisfying crunch as the bone broke.

The gentlemen leapt to their feet. Footmen came running. Lester crumpled, eyes watering, blood streaming down his face to crimson his shirt front. Peter stood over him, massaging his bruised knuckles.

'I'm warning you,' he said, low and menacing. 'Don't come anywhere near Margaret again.'

He glared round the room, strode into the vestibule, picked up his

242

things from the dumbstruck footman, and left. He did not tell Margaret what he had done, but Lillian was pleased.

Always hospitable, the Warwick Hotel excelled itself at Christmas. Margaret remembered the activity in Mrs Frith's kitchen at the festive season. Monsieur Philippe's domain rivalled even this.

She was swept along by the excitement, helping shop for provisions at Covent Garden Market where all was pre-Christmas bustle. She was always accompanied by Peter and Gino, Monsieur's apprentice and protégé. A lively lad with sloe-eyes and olive skin inherited from parents who had once lived on the slopes of Tuscany, his accent was pure Cockney. Philippe doted on him, though they sometimes screamed at one another in a shrill mixture of French, Italian and East End English. Gino was learning to be a chef, and showed a rare aptitude.

Peter, grinning as he and Margaret escaped from the kitchen during one of their stormy outbursts, exclaimed, 'It's only a lovers' tiff.'

'What d'you mean?'

'Don't you know? Dear me, is this another fact of life I have to explain to you? Have you heard of Oscar Wilde?

'Yes. He wrote plays, didn't he?'

'Plays and poems and novels. A brilliant man, unjustly treated by a prejudiced society.'

'What has he to do with Philippe and Gino? You talk in riddles sometimes, Peter.'

'I'll tell you later. We've to "deck the halls" and all that nonsense.'

Her arms were full of ivy, while he carried the holly. They had haggled for it at the market, along with oranges, lemons, vegetables, four monumentally large turkeys, half a dozen capons, three geese and six hens, all dead, of course, and about to be plucked by underlings, then stuffed and prepared by Philippe. The hotel was filled to capacity, and the evenings leading up to Christmas, besides the day itself, were fully booked for dinner.

For days the most amazing odours wafted upwards as mince pies browned in the oven and puddings steamed on the hotplates. The gargantuan fruit cake had been baked in October, wrapped in grease-proof paper and sealed in a tin. It now waited the final touch of glory; covered in marzipan and iced by the master craftsman.

The Warwick was ablaze with tinsel, glass balls and colourful crêpe streamers. Jenkins and Joe had undertaken the task of blowing up balloons. A resinous-smelling fir tree dominated the vestibule where it could be seen by those passing in the street. This year it twinkled with miniature coloured electric bulbs in place of candles.

243

Lillian had sweets made and handed them out to the urchins and beggars when she went shopping, while those who turned up on the back doorstep were each given a parcel of fruit, pies and a handful of small change. She sorted through cupboards around this time and distributed clothing and blankets to the needy.

Margaret sent cards to Susan, Thora and Anna with whom she had been in touch, telling them about her work at the hotel, but not that she was pregnant. Susan had abandoned the idea of marrying someone in service and, after a whirlwind romance, had become the bride of a grocer who had borne her off to live over his flourishing shop in Battersea, to which Margaret's letters had been forwarded.

She learned that Fenella had become engaged to an officer in the Life Guards who was related to the Royal Family. Anna was to stay with her till the wedding, after which she would take up her post as governess to Jane and also teach William. Thora remained their nanny. Later Anna planned to return to France, there to prepare her trousseau and household linen, twelve of everything as was the custom.

Evelyn had yielded to parental pressure and gone to the finishing school in Paris. Natalie Toner had blotted her copybook with her outspoken comments on this, and had been dismissed as an undesirable influence. She had joined an artists' colony in St Ives. Anna gave Margaret her address.

When she wrote enquiring after Luke, Anna informed her that he had left the country, heading for America and the Detroit motor trade. This saddened Margaret, and she felt guilty about that loving man who had been willing to give her his name.

Somehow, and for this she had to thank Peter, she had survived the meeting with Lester, though the memory of him was as close to her as the baby in her womb. Nothing more had been heard of him and it was only at night, when she lay alone in the brass bed, that she would allow herself to remember, her hands resting on the lump within her, lively when she was trying to rest. Sometimes she ached with desire, remembering so much, wanting so much, doubting she would ever be able to respond to another man.

She had let out her skirts and bought dresses that flowed from the yoke, rich in fabric and trimmings and with billowing sleeves, ideal for concealing an ever-expanding girth.

'It's a boy!' Lillian declared triumphantly one day having, under Biddy's instructions, plucked a hair from Margaret's head and threaded it through the wedding ring she always wore to convince people that she was indeed 'Mrs' Helbren.

Next she had made Margaret lie flat on the couch and held the

244

makeshift pendulum over her stomach. Whether it swung backwards and forwards or formed a circular motion was said to be an indication of the baby's sex.

'A boy, right enough,' Biddy agreed, nodding her head sagely.

'How strange,' Margaret gasped, struggling into a sitting position. A boy, Lester's son, but never his heir.

'Why d'you listen to that old wives' tale? How can it possibly work?' Peter teased Lillian from an armchair by the fire, feet propped against the overmantel, a bowl of Brazil nuts to hand. He smiled at Margaret, never tired of looking at her and thanking heaven that he had her in safe keeping.

'It never fails,' Lillian answered firmly. 'This girl is going to give birth to one of your kind – more's the pity!'

'Man-hater!' Peter mocked, but gently. 'Though you're not when it comes to Joe.'

'That's different. They broke the mould once they'd made him.'

'Ah, as old Omar says, "I watched the Potter thumping his wet Clay—"'

'Don't!' Margaret shouted angrily.

Peter's smile vanished, and his eyes hardened. 'What's the matter?'

'Lester used to quote him. He bought me *The Rubáiyát*.'

Peter gave vent to a violent expletive, threw down the nutcrackers and stormed from the room.

Lillian shook her head. 'Oh, dear, now you've upset him. He hates to be reminded that you were Lester's mistress.'

'Why does it bother him so much?' Margaret lumbered to her feet, and as dusk had descended early, went over to pull the crimson damask portière across the window.

'He's in love with you. Hadn't you noticed?'

Margaret turned sharply, facing her across the cheerful room filled with evidence of the Yuletide festival. 'He's my friend,' she replied defensively, indignation in her eyes, in the uplift of her chin, in her clenched fists.

'So? Does that bar him from a deeper emotion? You couldn't find a better bloke in a month of Sundays.'

'I know,' Margaret answered quietly.

She wished Lillian had not suggested Peter cared for her in any other way than as a friend. He was an attractive man, but just for now her heart was closed. They encouraged and supported each other. He was always there when she needed him, and she made sure he was kept supplied with coffee when he worked late on his books or newspaper articles. He was like the brother she had never had, or what she imagined a brother should be, though the Auberts had not been an

245

inspiring example of sibling devotion. But as a lover? She shivered, nowhere near ready for another commitment.

Lillian revelled in the festive season, queen of the Warwick, wearing costly, elaborate gowns, moving among her clientele graciously as if they were her subjects. Margaret could not keep up with her; the extra work was enough without an endless succession of late nights. Peter embarrassed her by buying her a gramophone and records as a Christmas present. She had not been able to get him anything expensive, only rising to a dictionary he wanted. He shared her love of music, but deliberately avoided the opera, taking her instead to performances of ballet, and introducing her to *avant-garde* composers. She was prepared to listen to anything that had no association with Lester.

The advance of pregacy was so slow a process that she had become gradually accustomed to her unwieldy body, making allowances for the decrease in speed, the backache and puffy ankles. Sometimes it seemed she had always been that shape and could not visualise the day when she would revert to normal proportions. She was slowly slipping into complacency, when nothing mattered but her unborn, maternal thoughts turned inward – a vegetable, or rather an animal preparing its nest.

By resting in the afternoon she usually had enough energy to enjoy Lillian's evening parties, providing she was in bed by ten o'clock. The company was stimulating, a noisy crowd who loved, above all things, to talk. Their common fund of intellectual interests made their conversation exhilarating. No one seemed to give a jot that Margaret was residing there under somewhat questionable circumstances.

'You'd make an ideal hotelier,' Lillian remarked, kissing her as they exchanged gifts on Christmas morning. 'You have the knack of putting folk at ease. Stay with me, dear. I couldn't bear you to go. You're like a sister.'

Though she had had several, the family had broken up when Gran died, never to meet again. She had no idea what had happened to them and no desire to find out. Lately, her world had been complete, with Joe and Margaret, and soon would come the little bundle of joy.

'And we'll "wet" the baby's head when he arrives, the darling,' she promised as she whisked off to the boudoir with Joe to try on the lace nightgown he had bought her. He was wearing his present from her, a flamboyant East India dressing robe with a huge sable collar and cuffs.

Baby, dear baby, Margaret thought as the New Year dawned and the days slipped from January into a cold and snowy February. Hurry, baby, I want to see you.

She was apprehensive of the ordeal ahead, though Dr Manson had accepted her as his patient and recommended a midwife who called in regularly to see her. Different again from that debased and greedy creature Margaret had encountered in Nelson Place, this was a clean, bright-faced Scottish woman by the name of Mrs Macguire.

Peter insisted Margaret exercise, so they stumped off through the slush together once it had stopped snowing. It was a fine, crisp day with a sparkle in the air. High overhead in the pale sky the white clouds drifted before the breeze. She wore a long wrapover coat and a matching toque. He was dressed like a Cossack in an enormous fur hat and wolfskin overcoat. They had both donned galoshes, and she had not felt so full of energy for ages, almost dragging him along.

'Steady on!' he gasped, slipping and sliding in her wake, stopping where a frozen pond lay grey among the alders. 'Good Lord, have pity on an aged cripple. You know I crashed the toboggan the other day. Barked my shins and gave myself lumbago.'

'Serves you right for showing off,' she answered, eyes dancing, cheeks pink with exertion. 'You wouldn't let me have a go on it.'

'I should think not. Supposing you'd given birth in the snow? I don't know the first thing about midwifery.'

She sobered, a shadow passing over her face as the wintery sun fell on the stark bare trees of the park. 'I'm scared, Peter. Will you be there when I'm in labour?'

His eyes widened, terrified of what lay ahead. 'Oh, God – d'you really want that? I should probably faint or do something equally pathetic.'

Her gloved hand found his. 'Please. I shall feel so alone.'

'You won't be. Lillian has already decided that she'll be the one to mop your brow and hold your hand. And old Biddy will be around with her spells and potions. Besides, I don't think the redoubtable Mrs Macguire would take kindly to a man being present. She frightens the living daylights out of me.'

'Please, Peter,' she pleaded, and her face took on such a look of woe that he forgot his dread of witnessing her suffering.

'All right, if Dr Manson and the dragon will allow it.'

She slid her hand into his arm, but as they turned back towards the road there, on a bare bough, sat a magpie, his chest as white as if someone had been snowballing him. Margaret stopped, staring at the bird in alarm.

'One for sorrow,' she whispered. 'It's unlucky to see only one.'

'Oh, darling, come into the twentieth century do,' Peter exclaimed. 'You and Lillian and Biddy encourage each other in these superstitions.' He clapped his hands and the magpie lifted itself into the air and made off. 'There. It's gone now. Does that make you feel better?

Were you always so jumpy, or is it just your condition? I'll be glad when it's over and I can get to know the real Margaret.'

'I'm not sure who she is,' she said, her lower lip trembling, so full and red that he ached to kiss her. 'I've never been sure, even less now that I know I'm part aristocrat. What is to become of me, Peter?'

'We'll run off together, over the hills and far away, to a magic land where the sun never sets,' he joked, but his eyes were grave, his hands enfolding hers, afraid to show too much, yet wanting her to somehow know he was hers for the asking. 'Margaret, darling—' he whispered, his lips touching hers.

She leaned into him and accepted his salute, liking it, enjoying it, wanting more. And he held her within the circle of his arms, cradling both her and her baby, exalted by the sheer beauty of the moment.

The days seemed to be gathering speed, and Margaret was worried that she would never have everything ready in time. In a panic lest the two dozen towelling napkins stored in the chest along with matinée jackets, bootees and gowns should prove inadequate, she boarded a bus one blustery, rain-swept afternoon.

It was a horse-drawn vehicle, brightly varished and with enamelled signs advertising Rowntree's Cocoa and Pear's Soap fastened to its sides. She climbed the step, helped by the conductor, a fatherly individual in a rusty black uniform, rather shiny at seat and elbows. A peaked cap was set at an angle on his head, and he was small, wiry, and chirpy as a London sparrow.

He clanged the bell and the driver, seated at the front of the unprotected top deck, clicked his tongue and jerked the reins. The patient horses started forward, no doubt fretting after dry stables and full nosebags. Margaret slid along the slatted wooden bench.

'Where to, ducks?' the conductor asked.

'Regent Street.'

He whistled between his teeth as he punched a pink ticket and handed it to her. 'That'll be a penny.'

'Thank you,' she said and settled back, looking out of the window at the grey, wet streets.

'You safe to be out, missus?' he enquired cheekily.

Margaret blushed. Though she wore the wedding ring, she always had the uneasy feeling that people could see straight through this fabrication, somehow sensing she was a fake. 'I've another two weeks to go yet.'

'I got four of me own back home. This your first?' He was bored, part of his mind streaking ahead to the bus depot, warmed by banter and the companionship of other operators, the air thick with tobacco smoke, steaming mugs of dark brown tea and bacon sandwiches waiting to be consumed. But it lightened his day to talk with this pretty young woman.

'Yes,' she murmured shyly, wishing he would leave her alone, relieved when he moved to the open doorway of the bus, hanging on with one arm, and still whistling under his breath.

They joined the traffic streaming through the West End and eventually rumbled to a halt outside the stores. Margaret alighted, but not without a final quip from the conductor. 'Mind how you go, ducks. Straight back home when you've done your shopping, and no calling in at the pub. Good luck.'

Embarrassing man! she thought crossly, and hurried through the revolving doors into Harrods. Up in the lift to the children's department, and a leisurely stroll round. She looked longingly at the muslin-draped rocking cradles and magnificent perambulators, then examined the price tags and decided she would have to settle for something more modest. To start with she would use half of her wicker Pilgrim basket as a crib.

She bought the napkins and the black-gowned assistant smiled at her. Everyone seemed to shyly appreciate the sight of an expectant mother, for many women refused to be seen in public after the sixth month. This healthy lady in her voluminous panne velvet gown and purple cape roused their admiration and she received a flattering amount of attention, even though her purchases were small.

It was with uplifted spirits and a strengthened belief in the innate goodness of the human race that she idled through the store, considering the possibility of venturing into the restaurant on the upper floor and having a cup of tea before the return journey. She had never done this alone, but felt bold that afternoon. Arriving by lift at her destination, she was about to enter the tearoom when she heard an American voice drawling, 'If I ever looked like that, I'd never go out of the house.'

Margaret turned her head and saw India in the distance, staring straight at her with disgust on her face. The person to whom she was addressing this remark was Lester. It was obvious India did not recognise her. She had probably never even registered Lady Julia's maid, but there was no doubt that Lester knew who she was.

After stabbing one look at Margaret, he guided his fiancée in the opposite direction, saying, 'Darling, even you will lose your shape when we have children.'

A gale of poisonous rage swept over Margaret. He knew her. Cut her dead. Allowed that silly, vapid creature to insult her. Her lips were

249

silent but inside she shrieked, I hope you'll never have a baby, India! I hope you're barren!

She was borne on the wings of fury and ill-wishing, remembering the old Cornish superstition that a mothering woman's curse carries. She hoped it was true. Dear God, how much she prayed for that! India didn't deserve to produce children. If she did they'd grow up as nasty as herself.

Unaware of what she was doing, she tottered to the lift, entered its cage, like a prison now, too full of people. Were they staring at her? Condemning her? Was she indeed too hideous to be seen? Her body swollen with the bastard she carried. A bantling. A child born from the mist – with a father who didn't want to know.

The rain poured over her as she waited for a bus. Her legs ached, her back ached, she wanted to crawl into a corner and die. It came at last, crowded, stuffy. A labourer gave up his seat to her, standing swaying, his fist locked round an overhead strap. He was reading a sporting paper held in his other hand. On either side were strings of lighted lamps; long avenues of amber mellowness from which ascended a dull, uniform roar of traffic. Down Regent Street into Piccadilly Circus, past lines of coaches, wagons, hansoms and tradesmen's vans.

Horses steamed, motorcars honked, wheels churned up mud and piles of dung. Crossing-sweepers dodged between them, with spades and buckets. On the pavements people hurried by, coat collars up, umbrellas aloft, braving the drizzle.

Margaret crept into the Warwick Hotel where Jenkins dozed in the porter's chair, and dragged her way to her room, hauling herself up by the banisters. Once there she collapsed an the bed, buried her face in the pillow and howled like a dog. She stuffed the sheet into her mouth to stifle her cries, wanting no one to find her in this state. Such anguish must be endured alone.

In her mind's eye she saw India vividly, her elaborate, toffee-coloured coiffeur under an outrageous hat, her thin, spiteful lips and silly, grape-shaped eyes. And Lester holding her arm, guiding her away from the spectacle of his mistress whose pregnancy revolted her.

When the storm of weeping had passed, she took off her damp cloak and, untying the string from her parcel, removed the brown paper and put the napkins away. The room was darkening and she switched on the bedside lamp, undressed and slipped into a night robe, then huddled under the quilt. She was drained, all the optimism of earlier on destroyed.

Sleep evaded her at first, back aching persistently, miserable thoughts giving her no peace, then, 'You should have read my diary earlier,' her mother said, shaking her head sadly as she sponged the leaves of her castor-oil plant. 'I hoped you would. Forewarned is fore-armed, my dear, and I didn't want you to follow in my footsteps.'

'She's a wicked girl, born into sin,' snapped Aunt Prudence, taking up an egg whisk and beating yolks furiously in a big china mixing bowl. 'We always said she'd come to a bad end. Didn't we, Mercy?'

'We did, sister, we did,' Aunt Mercy agreed, and it was strange to see them both on the seashore, white legs bare, skirts lifted as they waded in the waves.

'She's a hussy. Tried to have her way with my Graham,' nodded Mrs Hutton, folding her little fat hands over her stomach.

India and Fay stood on the cliffs above, gaudy fuchsia parasols arching over their heads. 'I'm having a baby,' India declared. 'But there's something wrong. The doctors say I shall miscarry. She cursed me, you know.'

'She's a witch,' shouted Aunt Prudence, whisking faster. 'Witches and liars never prosper.'

Margaret woke to find herself in a pool of water. The noise was louder now, coming from outside the bedroom where one of the maids was wielding a broom. The aunts, her mother, Mrs Hutton and the Americans faded and she forgot the dream instantly.

Mrs Macguire had advised her to spread a rubber sheet across the mattress in case the waters broke. This had happened, and she lay there for a moment as pain washed over her in a giant wave, gathering momentum, then dying away.

Not an unfamiliar pain, the ache in the lower back, the dull throbbing across her belly all reminiscent of the discomforts of menstruation. When she got up to find a towel and fix it between her thighs, she discovered that she was bleeding. During the lull between contractions she changed into a clean nightgown, then, keeping fear at bay, went to the door and called for help. The maid, flustered, dropped her brush and dashed away. Lillian was there in next to no time, Joe and Biddy at her heels.

'Have you started?' she asked excitedly.

'I think so,' Margaret said, anxious, pleased, mostly terrified.

'I'll go and get me things,' Biddy said. 'Charms and that, what'll make it easier.'

'Joe, ring for Dr Manson,' Lillian instructed, taking charge. 'If you can't get through, then run round with a message. Tell him it's urgent and send someone to fetch Mrs Macguire.'

'It's coming, isn't it? I'm going to die. I deserve to die. I cursed her,' Margaret whimpered, gripping the bedpost till her wrists ached as the next pain seized her like a relentless beast, gripping her vitals in its teeth and then slowly letting go.

251

'No, you're not. You'll be right as ninepence,' Lillian exclaimed as she started to change the sheet and plump up the pillows. 'Cursed who, for God's sake? Curse that bugger Lester, if you want to curse anyone. Walk around if it helps, but the bed's ready when you are. My sisters squatted to have their babies. Funny, I haven't thought of that for years, but I remember now. Gran always delivered them. We kids used to stand around and watch.'

'So you know what to do?' This was a comfort of sorts, though nothing could take away the fear and agony.

'Kind of, but I hope the doctor gets here soon.'

'I didn't know it would be so bad.' Margaret, doubled over, could think of nothing but pain. Every part of her was focused on it.

Joe came tapping at the door. 'The doctor's out, but his house-keeper's going to tell him soon as he comes in, Lilly.'

'Right. Now make a pot of strong tea, there's a lamb, and hold the fort downstairs, will you?'

'Oh.– ah—' Margaret groaned, clinging to the post like grim death. 'I want my mother!'

'I know, pet, but your mother's in heaven. Hang on to me. That's it. There, there – brave girl – it will soon be over.'

'Will it?' Margaret had heard that labour could go on for days.

'Of course.' But Lillian was not sure, sifting back through memory to the instances when girlfriends or relatives had produced their children. Unfortunately, the most dramatic cases sprang to mind – stillbirths, haemorrhages, Caesarean sections, maternal deaths.

Biddy returned, hobbling round the room and loosening every knot, saying, 'Can't have anything tied tightly. It'll make the birth difficult.' She approached the bed and tucked a pebble with a hole bored through it under the mattress. 'There, that'll make it come quick and easy.'

Would it? Margaret was willing to embrace any witchcraft if only the pain would stop. This was a time of primitive magic and her thoughts were irrational as she warned Biddy, 'Watch out for sprig-gans when it's born. They may snatch it and leave one of their own instead, an ugly little changeling.'

Biddy nodded solemnly. 'Don't you fret. I knows all about the fairies, deary. Not a one of 'em will get anywhere near our precious. I've got charms ready to hang round his neck.'

The chambermaid clanked in with the coal bucket and stirred the fire, staring at the labouring woman with round eyes. 'Is she going to be all right, Mrs Glynn? My sister lost her babby only last week. They had to cut her to get it out. She had twenty-four stitches.'

'Yes, yes, Maisie. That will do, thank you. I'll ring if you're needed. Is that tea ready yet? Go and hurry it up.'

Words floated round Margaret in meaningless sequences. Death – maybe she would die and the child with her. The peace of unutterable blackness, alluring and desirable. No more pain. No more shame and hurt. An endless nothingness.

'Mother,' she sobbed, unaware of saying it aloud.

But it was Mrs Macguire who answered, not her mother. Mrs Macguire who hung her navy-blue cape on a hook and came over to examine her.

'You're doing well, my dear,' she said reassuringly, consulting the fob-watch pinned to the left breast of her pristine apron. 'I want to time the pains. Tell me when you have another.'

There were plenty of them, of a grinding persistency, inexorable as fate, leaving no room for any other thought. A pause, relief, then another starting, rising, gathering force, digging in with fierce talons, flinging Margaret high then letting her drop down.

'Humm, every three minutes,' the nurse murmured, satisfied. 'You should have it before midnight.'

'Where's the doctor?' Lillian asked agitatedly, taking the tray of tea things from Joe, then shooing him out of the room, though Biddy remained, crouched by the fire, staring into the flames as if reading the future, muttering as she ran a string of strangely shaped beads through her fingers like a rosary.

'He was called away to attend an urgent case at the hospital. Don't worry, Mrs Glynn. It won't happen yet, but if it does, I can deal with it. I've brought dozens of babies into the world.'

When Peter arrived he wished he had finished Lester off instead of merely breaking his nose. Kneeling by the bed, he clasped Margaret's hands in his. 'My sweet girl, is it very terrible?'

She hated to see him so worried. 'No. I can bear it, but I want you to stay.'

'He can't,' said Mrs Macguire firmly. 'Even the father wouldn't be allowed in.'

'I wouldn't want him!' Margaret shouted, heaving herself up and clinging to Peter's shoulders.

'Now, be a good girl or Mr Newark will have to leave at once.'

'I'm not a child. Don't treat me like one.'

She yelled as pain leapt on her again and Peter glowered at the nurse. The woman he loved was in agony and he was helpless to aid her.

'Can't you do something?' he roared. 'God, if anything happens to her! Where's Manson?'

'Nature takes her time, sir,' Mrs Macguire said calmly, brow raised at his agitation. Really, this was one of the oddest deliveries she had ever attended. A man who wasn't the baby's father. A cripple mouthing spells. An ex-actress wearing rouge and the most unsuitable attire who seemed to be on close terms with one of the footmen. Not that it was any of her business. Her job was the safety of mother and child.

'There's no cause for alarm, sir,' she continued. 'The doctor will be coming presently. I suggest you go down and have a few drinks. You can't be of any help here and it will only upset you and, more importantly, the mother. We don't like our mothers upset. It's bad for baby.'

'Go on, Peter,' Lillian urged, giving him a reassuring hug. 'I'll let you know the moment it arrives.'

'No,' Margaret sobbed, trapped in that vulnerable, helpless position of having to obey when she needed Peter so desperately.

'I've got to go, sweetheart,' he murmured, pressing her hands to his lips. 'I love you,' he added, so low that he was not sure if she heard. He had not meant to say it, not then, but it slipped out. With a reluctant, backward glance he left her.

'Try walking,' Mrs Macguire suggested, helping Margaret to stand.

The pains were coming heavy and fast. They just gave her time to walk round the bed before they caught her again. Sweat was tricking down her body as they paced the room, with her leaning heavily on the midwife's arm.

'He loves me,' she said, words tumbling from her lips uncontrollably.

'That's nice, dear,' the nurse answered, humouring her.

'He loves me but Lester doesn't, and I'm the slave of pain,' Margaret kept saying. The rain beat a tattoo on the windows, and the wind thrashed the trees, howling and moaning, becoming the song of her agony.

Back in bed again, and time passed. Mrs Macguire, Lillian and Biddy sat by the fire and drank cup after cup of tea. Margaret tried one but brought it back up.

'Sick labour, safe labour,' Biddy proclaimed, as she cleaned up the mess and replaced the sheets and pillowcases.

Margaret lay and watched them, sleepy between contractions. The midwife was knitting, fingers flying over four steel needles as she turned the heel of a sock. Did she have a life beyond nursing?

'Are you married?' Margaret asked, startling them. Three pairs of eyes looked at her.

'Oh, yes. Married for twenty years, dear. I have two children.'

'Two,' Margaret groaned, biting her lips as pain rolled up and over her. 'I can't imagine anyone going through this twice.'

'People do,' Lillian said. 'A dozen times.'

'You'll forget the pain once it's over,' the nurse promised. 'All mothers do.'

Later, Margaret glanced at the gilt carriage clock on the bedside table. The hands pointed to eleven-thirty. Had it really been that long since she saw India with Lester? Somehow, it didn't matter any more, nothing mattered – Peter's love, Lester's betrayal – all were as naught compared to pain.

Dr Manson strode into the room, nodded to the nurse and Lillian, peeled off his jacket and rolled up his shirtsleeves. He carried with him the fresh smell of night air and rain and antiseptic and had come straight from the hospital.

'An emergency, doctor?' Mrs Macguire had done part of her training at Guy's, and showed a professional interest.

'Accident at the docks. A stevedore's leg mangled, trapped by a davit during unloading. I administered the anaesthetic while the surgeon amputated,' he answered from the bathroom where he was scrubbing his hands. 'Is that tea I spy there?'

Lillian poured some for him. 'You must be tired.'

He grinned at her, a strong, outdoor kind of man, who played rugby as a hobby. 'Tired? What's that, Lillian? You can see why I'm a bachelor. I'd not inflict my way of life on any woman. Never home, and when I am, sleeping like the dead. And don't you do too much during this crisis,' he added warningly. 'I saw you at Christmas, tearing around like something possessed.'

He moved over to the bed, one bushy eyebrow shooting up as he said, 'Good evening, Margaret. Getting busy, I see. I'm going to take a look.' He lifted her nightgown, competent hands moving over her bullet-hard belly. 'Fine, fine. You're doing well.'

'Can't you hurry it?' she whined, the pains of an agonising intensity, giving no quarter.

'Don't worry. Matters are proceeding normally.' To the nurse at his elbow, he said, 'She's at the second stage.'

'You got here just in time.'

'Will someone tell me what's happening?' Margaret shouted, red shafts of anger cutting across the pain. 'Why are you talking about me as if I'm not here? I'm not a bloody idiot! Mrs Hutton used to do that, the old bitch!'

Manson smiled and took this outburst in his stride. 'Lie on your back. That's right. Raise your legs, hold them under the knees, take a deep breath and push.'

This was nothing like that hard table of destruction in Soho. No one was going to harm her baby. Now she could do something to help herself escape the pain. Push – push. The midwife was holding her legs, Lillian behind her, supporting her shoulders.

'And again. Take a deep breath first. Don't push without a pain.'

Margaret collapsed till the next onslaught. Lillian wiped away the sweat that trickled back across her temples. Cool flannel. Cool water bathing her lips. Her nails dug into one of Lillian's hands as the battle started again. This was better. That grinding torture had changed into something productive. She felt herself to be a warrior using the pain to fight for her life.

It was the beginning of a fierce, primeval battle. The nurse looped a towel round the foot-post and thrust it into Margaret's hands, giving her something to pull on as she strained to expel the baby from her body. She grunted, low in her throat, teeth locked together.

A pad of cotton wool was held over her face. 'Breathe deeply, Margaret. Come on now.'

The smell of chloroform in her nostrils and throat, not enough to make her lose consciousness, but sufficient to separate her mind from reality. She forgot she was tired, forgot to push, though nature had taken over and she was doing it anyway. She was shooting upwards, bumping against the ceiling, looking down at herself on the bed, legs raised by the midwife, the doctor busy between them, Lillian watching intently, Biddy, too.

Laughing, Margaret observed the scene – and laughing she felt her physical self being disembowled, but she no longer cared. If this was death, then death was superb. Free, she twisted, turned and dived in the air. But not quite free. She could see a long, thin silver cord attaching her to her body, an umbilical anchoring her to existence. I must go back, she thought. It isn't time for me to leave the earth for ever.

She returned with a jolt, plunged into agony and brightness and a cracking, splitting sensation. She heard a cry – her own – and another, a shrill, angry squall.

'It's a boy,' Lillian shouted.

Eyes still closed, Margaret felt something warm and wet placed on her flat naked stomach. She lifted her lids and looked down at her long, red, skinny son, took his tiny fist in hers and gave him her heart in exchange.

Chapter 14

'I saw her again today,' Lester said, as Roderick paid the cab driver who then tipped his rain-sodden bowler and gave a tug at the reins.

The hackney rolled off into the darkness and the two evening-suited young men ducked down a side street towards a building behind Piccadilly Circus.

'Saw who?' Roderick asked disinterestedly, hoping that gorgeous redhead was available, with her black stockinged legs, red leather basque and high-buttoned boots. Heaviness spread through his loins at the recollection of her whip stinging his naked buttocks.

It was after midnight, and they had done their duty by their fiancées during a soirée given by Edward and Ethel in their new Mayfair establishment situated in the same prestigious district as the ones they had bought as wedding presents for their daughters. Mere town houses, of course. Edward had agents scouring the property market for estates where his girls could join the country set once they were married.

'Margaret, of course,' Lester snapped, eyes hooded under the curved brim of his top hat. 'Surely you've not forgotten the girl in the mirror?' His sarcasm coiled snakelike from his lips.

'No chance. Her seduction cost me a packet. Lovely breasts, though. God, just to think of them makes me hard. You're a lucky dog.'

'She's trouble,' Lester said sombrely as they reached a door and rang the bell. 'Last time it happened Newark bust my nose. It's not back in shape yet. Doubt it ever will be. I had to tell India a couple of ruffians set on me in a dark alley, trying to steal my wallet.'

'Does that mean we've to be on the lookout for him tonight?' Roderick asked nervously. Peter had made a mess of Lester's nose and he did not fancy having his own treated in a like manner.

'Maybe. India was with me and I thought Margaret was going to give the game away. It was a nasty moment. Fortunately, India's so thick-witted she didn't twig.'

257

'Then there's nothing to worry about.' Roderick, slightly tipsy, pushed his hat to the back of his head as the door was opened by the hulking ex-prize fighter who guarded the domain.

The madam lolled behind a knee-hole desk in the hall. It was there that business was done, a case of pay first, sample the goods later. No one could get past her, each client telling her what he wanted, how much he was prepared to spend and how long he intended staying. The rates varied accordingly.

'Good evening, sirs,' she called as Lester and Roderick entered.

Of Junoesque build, she had a shadowy upper lip, carmined cheeks and an auburn wig. Her gown, cut exceedingly low, displayed a broad expanse of mottled skin and a cleavage like a canyon.

This was a disreputable house, different to the luxurious bordellos Lester and Roderick usually frequented. Both had felt the desire for raw sex after being incarcerated with their mother-in-law-to-be and her vapid daughters, who were as alike as two peas in a pod.

As Lester had said to Roderick after the engagements had been announced, 'I shall close my eyes and think of India's millions, or I'll never be able to perform.'

Now he sought a magnificent piece of flesh, nothing more, though Roderick's requirements were more complicated. The house provided a flagellation parlour for those who needed this form of stimulation. Music filtered through the reception room, a tango played on a gramophone, redolent of Paris dives where apache dancers went through their routine, presenting a vicious parody of passion.

Girls wandered in and out in various stages of undress; silk stockings upheld by garters, stilt-heeled shoes, some with knickers, some without; satin corsets, transparent pegnoirs, curls, powder and make-up, white thighs and bare breasts. A few were dressed as schoolgirls. All wore expressions of acute boredom. The air was thick with the smell of cheap perfume and the underlying feral odour of coition.

The men, mostly in evening clothes, waited on little chairs and sofas, smoking cigars, drinking, and avoiding the eyes of their fellow lechers. The furniture, as overblown and tawdry as the proprietress, had a pinchbeck glitter. There were a number of prints on the walls, their subjects pornographic.

Lester, downing a brandy purchased at an exorbitant price, was haunted by Margaret's reproachful eyes. He had thought himself immune, steeled his heart to feel nothing, sense nothing, crushed the faintest flicker of regret. He had not listened to music properly since they parted. It was irritating to sit through an opera with India at his side, fretting for the interval when she could show off her new gown.

He had missed Margaret's appreciation of the music, her tears, her empathy, but had told himself he was a fool. India's fortune offered him everything he had always imagined he wanted.

The madam sidled up, flirting an enormous ostrich-feather fan and saying with heavy coquetry, 'I hear you're getting married, my lord.'

'Not yet. We're visiting America with our fiancées first. Next week, as a matter of fact,' Lester answered, despising the fat old bawd.

'Have a good trip. Will you be coming here on your stag night? Both of you, it being a double wedding?' She winked at them archly.

'We certainly shall,' Roderick promised. 'Got to limber up for breaking maidenheads, what?'

She cackled, her mountainous bosom shaking. 'Oh, that's a good one, that is. You're not used to virgins, are you? Don't find many of them round here.'

The girl whom Lester chose had large, firm breasts and flawless skin. Her features were fine, her eyes blue, her hair blonde, but her laugh was offensive and loud. When they were alone in her small room with its basic requirements – a washbasin, a towel, a bed – she shivered and heaved voluptuously, almost convincing him that she was enjoying his possession.

And he was remembering soft hands and genuine love, a girl giving herself to him with eager passion because she wanted him, adored him, was his for ever. The whore was skilled at her job and satisfied him physically, but that was all. He was sick of the sight of her directly their bodies separated.

Mrs Macguire was booked for a month, and Margaret ordered to stay in bed for at least three weeks of that time. Then, all things being equal, she would be permitted to put a foot to the floor, but only to go to the bathroom.

The thought of this inactivity was galling, particularly since she felt perfectly well. A short sleep after the delivery and she was convinced she could have ploughed a field if need be, though she was aware of being bruised and sore, her jaw stiff where she had clenched her teeth so hard with the effort required to give birth.

'Why do I have to stay in bed?' she complained on waking, her voice hoarse through screaming. This was now forgotten as she basked in that rosy, euphoric glow which graces the new mother. 'It isn't an illness. Having a baby is natural, surely?'

'Be that as it may,' the midwife declared, handing her the swaddled bundle, 'but you're not some native who has her child behind a bush and then goes back to the paddy fields. White women have more delicate constitutions. We must watch out for post-parturition fever.'

'I don't feel in the least feverish,' Margaret declared, gazing down, enchanted by her little son.

She thought him the most beautiful baby ever born. A thick thatch of black hair curled round a perfect face that had lost its first redness and was now the translucent pink of a cameo. Tiny starfish hands with long fingers and minute nails gripped hers with astonishing strength, while he stared back at her with slate-grey eyes, uncannily like Lester's.

'Hello, you,' she murmured, the feel of him in her arms the first real solace she had known since her break with his sire. Ignoring the nurse's disapproving glance, she unwrapped the shawl, lifted his gown, took off one bootee and gloried in his little toes.

His legs were bowed, the skin velvety soft. His nappy, folded twice, reached his knees, and she wanted to remove it and look at the rest of him. This miracle, this man-child to whom she had given birth so cleverly.

'Cover him up again, dear,' Mrs Macguire said. 'We don't want him to get a chill, now do we?'

Peter, hovering over the bed, was uncertain of his feelings. He, too, was achingly aware of the child's likeness to Lester, though usually he lumped babies together as resembling wrinkled old men. Uppermost in his mind was relief that Margaret had survived; the rest could wait.

When Lillian had dashed downstairs and told him the news, he had gone out into the night and later appeared at Margaret's bedroom door half hidden behind a massive bouquet that had cost a king's ransom. Most of the blooms were out of season, and he had knocked up a florist to supply them, an inconvenience that had been added to the bill. He didn't care. Nothing was too good for her.

'What are you going to call him?' he asked.

'Dominic,' she said, and he thought he had never seen anyone more lovely, her hair brushed loosely about her shoulders, her eyes pure amethyst as she cradled her child in her arms.

'I want to hold him,' Lillian said, flushed with champagne, having been toasting the arrival of the little stranger.

'Now, now – not too much disturbance. He's still very new.' The midwife had an almost proprietorial regard for her charges. 'And Mrs Helbren mustn't get overtired either. Time for visitors to go.'

'I'm not tired,' Margaret protested, but she was. It had come upon her quite suddenly. She wanted to be alone with Dominic. They had to get to know one another.

'You'll do as I say,' said the nurse, and Margaret was glad to hand everything over to her. 'Besides, we've to put Master Dominic to the breast.'

Over the next few days Margaret grudgingly admitted that Mrs Macguire was right. The milk came in with a vengeance, her breasts engorged, almost too much for the hungry baby who choked and spluttered as it gushed into his mouth. Every time his jaws clamped round her nipple, her womb contracted, bringing her out in a cold sweat and making her toes curl. She was weepy and could not stop brooding, having crazy ideas about sending Lester a telegram announcing the arrival of their fine son who had weighed in at seven pounds twelve ounces.

'I want to tell him,' she sobbed when Lillian glided into the bedroom wearing a satin and velvet evening gown the colour of ripe raspberries. Mrs Macguire was having her dinner, so Margaret could cry without restraint.

'Don't upset yourself, sweetheart,' Lillian said. 'Where's the fighting spirit that made Boudicca defy the Romans? What right has he to know? None whatever. All he did towards it was supply the seed. You carried the baby, suffered to have him. Forget Lester.'

'I know, but it's hard.' How lucky I am to have found such a friend, Margaret thought, remembering her kindness during those dragging hours of labour.

'You'll feel better when you're in charge of the baby yourself, though you'll have to be firm with Biddy or she'll interfere. Mrs Macguire is having a running battle with her about putting amulets on him.'

Dominic stirred in the crib and began to whimper. Lillian had been waiting for an excuse to hold him, lifting him against her shoulder, patting his back, saying, 'Hush, my darling – there, there. Has he a nasty pain, then?' Her voice was a deep, maternal croon, and she leaned her cheek against his elongated head.

'Mind he doesn't posset over your dress,' Margaret warned.

'I don't care about that,' Lillian murmured. 'D'you realise how lucky you are to be able to have children?'

There was such a wealth of sorrow in her voice that Margaret stared at her. 'You want a baby so much?'

Tears sparkled in Lillian's eyes. 'I'd give ten years of my life to be able to have one. But I told you what happened to me. There's no chance, and now they tell me my heart wouldn't stand the strain anyway. I'm doomed to be an auntie or a godmother.'

She replaced the now sleeping infant in the beautiful cradle she had insisted on buying him. Made of fancy ironwork, it swung at a touch, draped in white muslin, lace and bows of blue ribbon, with a canopy at the head.

Margaret repeated her first remark made when Joe had carried it

261

proudly into the bedroom. 'You shouldn't have gone to the expense. It's fit for a prince.'

'Well, isn't that exactly what he is – our little prince? The Prince of Warwick. If you think this is grand, just you wait till you get downstairs.' Lillian, in control of herself again, smiled mysteriously, for she had sailed into Harrods ordering not only the crib but the grandest perambulator they had in the store.

'I'm longing to go out,' Margaret complained.

'You won't be able to till you've been churched,' Lillian reminded, adding solemnly, 'It would be courting bad luck to do so before giving thanks to God for your safe delivery. Leave the arrangements to me. It's a grand excuse for ordering a new dress. Then, of course, we must think about the christening.'

'His father should be there,' Margaret muttered.

'I expect we can manage without him,' Lillian said sarcastically. 'But don't worry about anything, or you'll upset the milk and Dominic is doing so well.'

'You're right. I must build up my strength. I have him to fight for now.'

There was something in her tone of voice that bothered Lillian, and she voiced her fears to Joe later. 'I must have a go at Peter. Margaret's not been to see a solicitor yet and this has to be done. No use her thinking she can expect anything from that swine unless she puts pressure on him.'

A nursemaid had been found to take over from the midwife. Lillian helped interview several applicants, even more particular than Margaret when it came to selecting someone clean, efficient, devoted and loving for the important task. Nancy Sterling had these qualities; eighteen years old, experienced, good-humoured and energetic. She took one look at Dominic and fell instantly in love. Now he had four women doting on him.

Margaret was churched and the christening took place, with a party organised at the hotel and an iced cake supplied by Philippe. Dominic was a placid infant, growing plump and contented on her rich milk and sleeping most of the time, though occasionally Margaret, peeping into the cradle, would find him staring about him with wide eyes as he if viewed the world with wonder.

She could not quite believe he was hers and shed tears of weakness, wishing her mother was alive, despondent because she had no relatives to be with her during this crucial period. She recognised this as a fantasy, for Aunt Mercy and Aunt Prudence would have felt nothing but shame at his birth, besides which they were not kin – Lord Henry was, and she could not imagine him receiving this illegitimate sprig of the House of Aubert with anything but dismay.

Peter had bought himself a car, a brightly painted Rover, with a hood that could be erected over the occupants in wet weather. He placed himself at Margaret's disposal, ready to drive her anywhere she wanted, and on a sunny morning in the middle of April, she dressed herself smartly in a beige wool ensemble, kissed the baby, handed him over to Nancy and stepped into the Rover. She had an appointment to see Mathew Unwin, one of Peter's friends in the legal profession.

The car eventually pulled up in a square with a green at its centre. The trees were tipped with sticky buds, the sky misty blue, the first breath of spring warming the air. The lawyer's chambers were in a terrace of Regency houses. With his hand lightly cupping her elbow, Peter took her up a short flight of stone steps and pressed the brass bell to one side of the central door. A servant answered, conducting them across the entrance hall and into an office.

Sunlight cast golden pools over the polished floorboards and rugs. Coals glowed in the fireplace. The room smelled of the dusty papers, files and documents piled on shelves and the tops of cupboards. There were a pair of upholstered armchairs, and four of uncompromising hardness, a bureau, a side-table, and a vast desk with a green leather surface and metal trim.

A man rose from behind it, formal in dress with the obligatory frock coat and pearl tiepin, but informal in manner. He was of medium height, his face dominated by a jutting chin and hooked nose. His full moustache drooped downwards, and he looked more like a piratical sea captain than a lawyer.

After he had shaken him by the hand, Peter introduced Margaret. 'This is Miss Helbren. As I explained briefly over the telephone, she has been grievously wronged on two counts.'

'Please sit down, Miss Helbren.' The lawyer waved her into a chair, adding kindly, 'Tell me about it.'

Hard to put into words to a strange man – too personal, too painful, and Margaret stumbled at the start. Gradually, however, she warmed to her theme, sparing no detail. Unwin listened without comment, picking up a gold pencil and tapping it lightly against the edge of the desk.

'Well, well, here's an unfortunate chapter of events,' he said when she had finished, putting the pencil aside, rising and pacing slowly to the window, gazing across the square. 'You have no proof with which to substantiate your accusation that Lord Lester promised you marriage? Love letters, for example?'

Margaret, who was staring at her gloved hands locked in her lap, shook her head. 'He never wrote to me.'

'He wouldn't, would he?' Peter growled angrily. 'Too canny to compromise himself.'

Unwin turned back to them, face folded into serious lines. 'Without such evidence, I don't see we have much of a case, Miss Helbren. It's your word against his, I'm afraid. Who knew of your association with him?'

'Lord Roderick. His valet, Rigby – no one else. He was careful not to take me anywhere he might be recognised.'

'Except for the Warwick Hotel. I saw you with him and so did Mrs Glynn,' Peter put in, seated with his legs apart, feet planted firmly on the carpet, broad hands placed on tweed-covered knees. He was anxious to get the matter settled, to free Margaret from Lester for good. Only then might he be able to court her with any hope of success.

Unwin shook his head. 'Lord Roderick won't speak out, he's too deeply implicated – neither will the manservant for fear of losing his job. As for your visits to the hotel? You could have gone there for perfectly innocent purposes, even though you were unchaperoned. These matters are deuced difficult to prove.'

Her eyes were like violet pools, tearless but holding a cold, clear fury. 'So you're saying there's nothing I can do – no recompense or financial support for my child?'

He spread his hands wide and lifted his shoulders in an apologetic gesture. 'I'm afraid not. I prefer that you know the truth. It wouldn't be fair to give you false hope.'

'What about my mother's diary? Can't I sue Lord Henry?' She was grasping at straws, for the law protected the male animal, particularly if he happened to come from the right side of the track.

'Again, it would be her written word against his, and from what you've told me, I'm sure Lady Julia would back him up. Why, if all men were suddenly forced to pay for their unlawful children half the male population of England would be bankrupt.'

'How grossly unjust!' Margaret shouted, rising to her feet.

'I agree,' Unwin said. 'If you had the smallest shred of evidence proving breach of promise that could be brought against Lord Lester, I wouldn't hesitate to fight your case. But it's hopeless, Miss Helbren.'

'Thank you, Mr Unwin,' she replied dully. 'I'm not surprised. I suspected this is how it would be.'

'You did the right thing in coming to see me,' he assured her as he walked them to the door. 'If you can think of anything we might use, anything at all, then don't hesitate to let me know. I'd like to help you very much indeed. These men should be brought to justice. That they're able to get away with it is a disgrace and a scandal. I hope to see the day when women are treated fairly, but I shall probably be in my dotage. It's going to take years.'

'Centuries, more like,' she said bitterly.

'If ever,' Peter added glumly, depressed by her continued obsession with Lester. Loving or hating him, he was for ever in her thoughts.

Margaret's days were filled with Dominic, and the Warwick for which she and Peter now took more responsibility. She packed every moment. This way she rarely had the opportunity to brood, and guarded her emotions zealously, building a mile-high wall around herself. But it was not always possible to avoid pain, as when she picked up a copy of *The Tatler* and saw photographs of Lester and India, Roderick and Fay, and a piece about their engagements and absence in America.

She showed it to Lillian who said, 'I hate to admit it, but Dominic's the spitting image of his father.'

'I know,' Margaret replied quietly. 'I can only pray that he hasn't inherited his nature.'

'I shouldn't think so,' Lillian answered as she wheeled the pram through the hall. She liked to be at the helm of this elegant vessel, and for passers-by to mistake her for Dominic's mother. 'He has enough of us around to turn him into a more pleasant human being.'

'I sincerely hope you're right,' Margaret said as she went up the stairs, her arms piled with clean linen, her face set and cold. Lester and India. It was like a wound inside her that refused to heal.

'Come along, Jenkins. Get your nose out of that racing paper and give us a lift down the steps,' Lillian commanded, though glancing after Margaret, worried. Pretend though she might, she was convinced that she was not yet over Lester Kealan.

Clad in pastel pink, with a draped skirt and picture hat, she set off for the park, one gloved hand holding her parasol aloft, the other gripping the porcelain handle of the shining black baby carriage. It took the bumps smoothly, beautifully sprung on leather straps slung between large, thin, spoked wheels, the front ones overlocking smaller ones at the back. Dominic, warmly wrapped in bonnet, cape and shawl, was propped up against lace-frilled pillows, the leatherette hood folded down and a fringed canopy, lined with bottle-green, protecting him from the sun.

'I wish you were mine, honey-bunny,' Lillian declared, and he gurgling serenely as she pointed out the birds, the flowers, and dogs being walked by proud owners.

She found a quiet spot near the pond, brushed a handkerchief over a bench to ensure its cleanliness, then seated herself. After glancing round to make certain she was unobserved, she took a hip flask from her handbag, flipped up the lid and raised it to her lips.

'Good health, Dominic,' she said, and he granted her a radiant, toothless beam. 'You won't tell anybody, will you? This is our little secret. You see, Biddy and Joe are too fussy. They think I'm making myself ill.'

He stared at her unblinkingly from those enormous, dark-lashed eyes, then grabbed up a fistful of lacy coverlet and started to suck it. Lillian took another swig, popped a bull's-eye in her mouth and replaced the flask in her bag. She sat there thinking, her mind crystal clear. Margaret's self-control bothered her, and the romance she had hoped to see blossoming between her and Peter was slow getting off the ground. Lillian decided it needed a kick.

On returning to the hotel, she lifted the baby out of the pram and gave him to Nancy, then peeled off her gloves, unpinned her hat and strolled into the parlour.

'It's a lovely day out there. You need a holiday, Margaret,' she announced without preamble.

'How can I go anywhere?' she protested, glancing up from the secretaire where she was working her way through the lastest crop of bills and receipts.

Lillian leaned over the back of her chair, confident in the deodorising properties of peppermint. 'You're going, and that's the end of it. Buy Dominic a bucket and spade and take him to the seaside.'

Margaret pushed a strand of hair away from her eyes, suddenly tired. The idea of seeing the ocean and inhaling its salt tang was immeasureably appealing. She glanced at Peter who was perched on a corner of the table, one leg swinging, the other braced on the floor. Her dear friend, though she was becoming increasingly aware of him as a man, plagued by dreams of passionate kisses and heated caresses during those balmy nights when a young sickle moon, balanced on its horn, sailed across the sky.

'I'll drive you,' he offered, as worried as Lillian about her. She was too fine-drawn, like to crack and, with a lover's perception, he knew the reason behind this. He clapped himself on the brow in mock alarm, adding dramatically, 'But what of your reputation? A young, comely woman travelling with a bachelor who isn't related?'

'Rather late in the day to worry about that,' Margaret said briskly. 'Anyhow, we'll be chaperoned by Dominic and Nancy.'

'Then it's settled,' Lillian announced, recognising that here were two people made for each other and, while he was fully aware, Margaret was denying it stubbornly.

'Well, if you're sure, Lillian,' Margaret said dubiously, and eased out of the chair. 'Not Porthross, though it must be Cornwall. I'll write to Natalie. She keeps inviting me down. Between them, she and her friends have bought an old manor house. They grow their own vegetables, make their own bread, lead a back-to-nature existence.'

Lillian's eyebrows shot up. 'It sounds ghastly, darling. You're going for a rest, remember?'

'I think it sounds tremendous fun,' Peter said, and his eyes locked with Lillian's, reading her approval of anything he might have in mind with regard to the wooing of Margaret Helbren.

My God, the preparations are more tiring than staying put, Margaret concluded by the time the departure day dawned and a heap of luggage occupied the lobby. It seemed impossible that the car would hold it, although Peter had bought a larger model, with plenty of space for a growing family.

They left London far behind, trundling through the countryside at twenty-two miles an hour, putting up at charming inns en route, and arriving at St Minver Grange several days later. The sun was setting when, stiff and weary, they clambered out, landing in the squelching mixture of mud, manure and straw that littered the courtyard.

'Jesus!' Peter exclaimed, looking ruefully at his boots.

'Help!' Margaret countered. 'I knew I should have worn my overshoes.'

'Hello, everyone!' Natalie carolled, appearing at the back door, sleeves rolled up, arms powdered with flour. 'How grand to see you!'

'Where's the loo?' Margaret asked, *sotto voce.*

'Over there, dear,' and Natalie pointed across to a huddle of tumbledown stone buildings with purple toadflax growing in their crannies.

It was wonderful to be breathing Cornish air again, and to see that peculiar lightness in the sky which was like nowhere else on earth, but the privy left much to be desired. Margaret had begun to take modern sanitation for granted, forgetting primitive rural conditions.

The yard was deserted, except for two liver-and-white spaniels who sniffed at her and tried to poke their noses up under her skirt. She walked into the big kitchen. Stone-flagged, with blackened beams, it was old as the hills and had hardly changed since the day it was added to the original 'hall-house'. Hung with bunches of herbs, dried flowers and strings of onions, it smelled strongly of grilled chops. A man lounged at the refectory table, a huge mug of coffee balanced on his knee. In his great, grimy hand was a slice of meat hidden between two paving stones of bread.

'Jock, meet Margaret,' Natalie said casually, kneading dough on a floured board, greased loaf tins at the ready. The man grunted and nodded, continuing to chew as he stared up from a heavily bearded face.

'You've fine bone structure,' he said, crumbs spattering from between his lips. 'Ever done any posing?'

'No.'

Margaret slid along the bench at the table where Nancy sat with Dominic on her lap. His feeding bottle had been filled and he was guzzling greedily. Recently, he had begun to need more than breast milk and had accepted the bottle with no trouble. This gave Margaret more freedom, but she missed the close bond.

'Care to pose for me?' Jock's eyes were washed-out blue, mild for such a hirsute giant.

'I don't know. Just for now I want to laze on the beach and swim in the sea.'

'D'you bathe nude?' he asked, as he helped himself to apple pie and a generous dollop of cream.

'Sometimes.' Margaret was almost overpowered by the barrage of pungent odours, spices, vegetables and hot bread.

Peter lounged on a sagging sofa, legs stretched out to the inglenook fireplace where blackened pots hung over the flames. He was listening, intrigued, to the girl curled at his side whose straight hair fell to her waist in one unbroken sweep of gold. A willowy female, clad in a long smock of muted hues. She had heavy-lidded eyes and wafted a faintly exotic perfume.

'Making him feel at home, are you, Fiona? Watch out for her, Peter, she eats men for breakfast, then spits out their bones,' Natalie warned.

Margaret, alerted, said, 'You must tell me what you want me to do,' as she indicated the piles of dirty dishes and saucepans stacked on the wooden draining board by the stone sink.

'Don't worry. We've a woman who comes in and "does" for us, but we share the cooking, don't we, troops?' And Natalie grinned at Jock and swept a glance over Fiona whose impractical looks threw doubts on her usefulness.

'I paint. Do you paint, Peter?' she drawled, moving closer. He could feel the warmth of her body through the thin smock.

'Only walls,' he joked, amused by the blatant invitation in her eyes.

Margaret, watching them while pretending otherwise, was aware of an ugly feeling deep inside her as Fiona's silvery laugh rang out. It was an emotion she recognised. This was terrible. She did not want to feel like that again, tortured, losing confidence, reduced to nothing by jealousy.

Footsteps in the yard, and more people tramped into the kitchen, sandy and windswept, dumping easels into corners, along with cricket bats and deck chairs. The lamps were lit, the kitchen transformed into the life, eloquence, bombast and wit of a student café.

268

Natalie introduced them to her visitors. There was an athletic lady who rushed away to change out of her soggy bathing dress, a dark individual of foreign extraction whose eyes smouldered as they rested on Margaret, and a rather effete youth with shaggy blond curls.

'Is it all right for me to sit with you, Mrs Helbren?' Nancy whispered, ill at ease. 'Or shall I take my food up to the nursery?'

'Is there a nursery? I'll have to find out what the sleeping arrangements are. Join us, Nancy. There's no formality here.'

Natalie managed to get everyone seated round the table, blue and white willow-pattern plates set before them, wineglasses and two bottles of Burgundy, cold meats, rolls and baked potatoes in their jackets, well smothered in salt, pepper and butter.

Later Natalie showed Margaret to the upper rooms. 'It's a rambling old place,' she explained, 'but we got it for a song. I love it, though some think it too quiet.'

'Are there just the six of you?'

'It fluctuates. We have had as many as two dozen. They come flocking down during the summer, eating us out of house and home, though we make them earn their keep digging the garden and milking the goats.'

They arrived at a central lobby from which rose a staircase lit by a skylight. 'It's very grand,' Margaret murmured.

'It was – once. There are heaps of rooms, mostly mouldering away and unused. Home for mice and spiders. I hope you're not afraid of ghosts?'

'Ghosts!' Nancy piped up. 'It's not haunted, is it, Miss Toner?'

'Oh, I expect so. We'd be disappointed if we couldn't offer you at least one Headless Apparition, Grey Lady or Mad Jester.'

'Don't be nervous, Nancy,' Margaret comforted, wishing Natalie would be quiet.

'I'm not, ma'am,' Nancy declared bravely.

They mounted the stairs and went down a dark passage and Natalie opened a door at the end. 'This is the Rose Room,' she said. 'It's one of the finest in the house. D'you like it?'

'Makes me feel like a princess,' Margaret commented. Like it? She knew at once that she never would.

The light of the single lamp cast huge shadows on the panelling; their own, grown to grotesque dimensions. The figures on the tapestries became animated – couples caught in some long-ago minuet, riders whose mounts appeared to charge across a storm-racked landscape. The atmosphere had damp undertones. Heavily carved furniture of Elizabethan vintage crouched like hungry beasts in the corners. And the whole was dominated by a canopied bed with bulbous posts at head and foot, and a solid oak tester from which hung faded crimson velvet curtains.

'Nancy and Dominic will be in the next room,' Natalie said. 'And I'll get the men to light the fires.'

'Is it possible to have a bath?'

'Sorry. We use the sea mostly, in the summer anyway. Or else it's the hip bath, I fear.'

'No bathroom. No running water. This will be a challenge, won't it, Nancy?' Margaret tried to sound encouraging, for the nursemaid was about to dissolve in tears.

'How am I to manage, Mrs Helbren?' Her voice was an anguished wail. 'What about baby's nappies?'

'You can use the tub in the yard, with cold water from the well and hot from the kettle in the kitchen. That's how we clean our clothes, my girl,' Natalie said sternly.

'I'll help you, Nancy,' Margaret assured her. 'Take off Dominic's things when he's on the beach. That will save on napkins.'

'Never, begging your pardon, madam!' Nancy's head went up, the light of battle in her eyes. 'Expose him to the sun and that harsh air! He'll catch his death!'

There followed an hour of activity during which Peter and Jock brought up logs and kindling and kettles and water, getting fires going in both bedrooms and filling washbasins and jugs. Natalie arranged flowers in vases and lit candles everywhere, but Margaret could not shake off the awareness that darkness waited beyond the golden aureoles.

Dominic, crotchety, needed his bed, and Natalie unearthed an old oak rocking cradle from one of the deserted rooms. Nancy insisted on polishing it, then made a cosy nest for him within, quite taken with the beautiful crib with a family crest carved on its hood. Margaret sat down to cuddle him and gave him a final bottle, and by the time he had finished, Nancy was ready for bed, a fire glowed on the hearth and the kettle was singing.

Peter could feel the tension leaving him. The homebrew was potent, the company stimulating, and Margaret happier now Dominic was settled. It was late when they took up their lamps and walked through the dark house to their respective rooms.

'Will you be all right?' he asked, leaning a shoulder against the wall, watching the play of lamplight over her features and wishing she was his wife and Dominic their son.

'Of course!' she replied sharply. He must not know she was uneasy and in need of a man's arms round her during the dark hours.

270

'Then I'll say good night,' he said, making no attempt to move.

She wanted to cling to him, to beg him not to go, but wariness forbade it, spiked with pride. For all she knew he might have made arrangements to sleep in Fiona's bed.

'Good night, Peter. I'll see you in the morning.'

'Down to the beach, is it?'

'Yes.'

Checking before retiring, Margaret saw, by firelight and lamplight, Nancy sleeping soundly and Dominic, too. He would not wake till dawn when his little stomach would tell him it was empty.

He lay on his back in the rocker, and the air of fragility and innocence about him made her feel afraid. She bent and kissed his brow, trailing a finger over the petal-soft skin, delaying the moment of leaving, oddly reluctant.

This is silly, she scolded herself and, closing the door resolutely behind her, covered the short distance to her room. She resisted the temptation to look over her shoulder, straining her ears to catch the reassuring sounds from other areas. The silence was thick, as if this part of the house was enclosed in a vacuum.

The tapestries were motionless, and she went round lighting the candles and placing the lamp on the bedside table. 'Well, Rose Room,' she addressed it out loud. 'Seems like we're stuck with each other for a week at least. You'd better get used to me, and me to you.'

The logs collapsed in a shower of sparks, making her jump. She pushed the embers back with the poker, then brushed her hair and put on her nightgown.

The four-poster was of great age, and Margaret was sure it had a faint smell bequeathed by generations of sleepers. It was impossible to lie there and not speculate as to who they might have been and if happy or sad, successful or failed. Like hers, their hearts had once beat a steady tattoo, the blood pumping through their veins, heads filled with hopes, dreams and ambitions. But the Grim Reaper had claimed them, as he claimed all.

One candle remained burning on the bedside table, along with the lamp and a box of matches. Margaret wished she had brought a book, tired but wakeful, thinking about Peter. Fiona had taken a liking to him and she supposed she should be glad. It was high time he found someone, but the idea brought her no satisfaction.

Her eyelids grew heavy and she welcomed that drift towards sleep, caught in the hypnagogic net where voices, faces and situations vanished instantly when she spoke out loud and woke herself with a jolt. Diving back through the billowing waves of dreams, she heard Lester saying India had refused to marry him. She looked at him and saw his

271

clothing alter as if he was attending a fancy-dress ball, his hair longer, his face masked. The wind rose, shrieking so loudly that she could not hear his voice, but he held a sword and his hands were covered in blood.

Somewhere a child was crying, a shrill little voice rising above the tumult. Margaret sat bolt upright up in bed. The noise ceased aruptly as if a door had slammed shut. She was blanketed by layers of dreadful dark depression. Had Dominic cried out in his sleep? Before this thought clarified, she was gone again, acting out parts in restless, violent fantasies.

Sun-drenched days and ensorcelled nights: Peter wished they could go on for ever. The house seemed to be enchanted, or maybe it was just that Margaret was a different woman to the one he knew in London. She had shed years, a child again, proud of her county and of the mystical Celtic blood that flowed in her veins, courtesy of Lord Henry.

Fiona's interest was flattering, and part of Peter responded. It was reassuring to have a beautiful woman make no secret of her desire for him, and the animal within toyed with the idea of taking her up on her offer and spending himself between her thighs. Had it not been for Margaret and the bitter-sweet torment of loving her, he would have enjoyed a brief fling with Fiona.

He thought about this as he carried Dominic through the overgrown garden towards the shore, the path lined with Spanish chestnut and silver birch trees and clumps of Scotch firs. Nancy and Margaret followed, loaded with necessities as they pushed through bracken and passed sandy rabbit holes pocking the turf, then went down a winding track to where rocks made natural steps to the cove.

The view was spectacular, the curved beach two miles long, the mighty ocean sending white-crested waves thundering over the sand, sucking it up and spewing it out again as it had done for millenniums, crushing shells of prehistoric molluscs till they were nothing but infinitesimal grains.

Dominic lay on his shawl, a naked cherub, much to Nancy's vexation. Peter watched over him fondly, this little miracle of creation busy mapping out his world. He wondered if there was any chance a child might be born to him and Margaret one day, yet she still seemed remote, self-contained – afraid of admitting to emotions.

'He's happy here,' she said, wrapping Dominic in a bath towel when she brought him back after dabbling his toes in the shallows.

'So am I,' Peter answered, resting on one elbow on the rug. 'I can't remember being so happy since my childhood in India when we were looked after by a loving ayah, mostly left to simply grow, principles taught gently, not forced.'

'She was your nanny?'

'That's right.'

'Let me have him, ma'am.' Nancy, jauntily attired in a striped blouse, a linen skirt and straw hat, received the child in her arms.

Margaret lay against the cushions, an arm shading her eyes, allowing the heat of the sun to penetrate every corner of her being, even though it brought back memories of Monte Carlo.

She peered at Peter from under lowered lids. He was wearing a black wool knitted *maillot* that fitted his muscular body closely and left his arms, chest and legs bare. His wet hair was smoothed back from his forehead and dripped down his neck. She watched the droplets trickling over his smooth skin, his eyes bright blue in that nut-brown face. It was obvious why Fiona found him so attractive, and had Margaret not had her fingers burned so badly she might have wanted him for herself. Even so, she did not like him paying attention to Fiona.

This thought recurred at dinner, a meal partaken beneath an elderly cedar tree, while the stars came out one by one and pipistrilles swooped and dived. Moths fluttered and blundered round the lamps, and there was a large quantity of wine on offer. Several other persons had arrived during the course of the day, and Natalie presided over supper wearing a bright green silk tea gown.

A musician had turned up on his motorcycle with a fluffy-haired Irish girl in tweed breeches riding pillion, and two Canadians had been delivered in a gig from the station. The musician strummed on a mandoline, and Fiona attempted to monopolise Peter, trailing chiffon scarves and throwing back lace ruffles from her beautifully shaped hands.

The gramophone was carried out, and a selection of ragtime music rang across the unkempt garden. The musician materialised at Margaret's side, asking her to dance. He was a hearty man wearing a Norfolk jacket and corduroys.

'Care to come for a ride on the bike?' he asked, pumping her arm up and down as they went through the motions of the quickstep.

'No, thank you.'

'No harm in asking. Maybe tomorrow?'

'Maybe.'

There were others eager to court her, but she was not interested. She sat quietly in a basket chair, watching the dancers, watching Fiona, listening to the chatter, withdrawn and pensive. Because she was not frantically busy, as in London, Lester loomed large in her thoughts, and her dreams were becoming increasingly hag-ridden. She had

273

contemplated asking Natalie if she could move to a different room, but this seemed foolish.

Every night she woke to hear a child crying. It wasn't Dominic, for she had gone to the nursery and found him fast asleep. Besides which, the sobbing was too close, within the Rose Room itself. Was it haunted? The alternative was even worse, pointing to derangement.

The party did not break up till two o'clock, and then Margaret could delay the moment no longer. Though she fought sleep it eventually triumphed, and she was lost in the untamed forests of her dreams. A dell, shrouded in hanging vines and Spanish moss; flowers with vast waxen trumpets of a livid hue, and thick fleshy leaves. One lashed out as she passed and pricked her hand. Three bright drops of blood glistened in the sombre light. A little way ahead a child was crying.

Margaret lifted weighted lids. Beyond the thick bedpost she could see the remnants of the dying fire, glowing like a red eye. The child cried close to her. She could hear its inhalations of breath, feel them fanning her cheek. A tear splashed down, wetting her mouth. She gathered her shaking limbs and sprang out of bed. The matches. She fumbled, found them, struck one against the side of the box. It caught the wick of the candle though she was shaking so much she nearly dropped it. A glimmer of light. An empty room. The continuing sound of crying, so loud now, screaming in her ears, waves of distress buffetting her.

'No, no! Go away!' Margaret ran for the door, the candle streaming, lying almost flat.

She pelted down the passage, past Nancy's door – skidding on a rug, crashing to the floor, the blessed candle still held aloft. Then she was inside Peter's room. She leaned against the door, her heart leaping and pounding, knees buckling with terror.

He sat up in bed, eyes wide open. 'What's the matter?'

She could not speak and he came to her and prised the candlestick from her paralysed fingers and led her to the bed, sitting her down, whipping off the quilt and wrapping it round her. His arms, too, drawing her into the warmth he had just left, under the covers where he had lain. Still she said nothing, and he simply held her and waited.

When she quietened a little, only occasional spasms shaking her body, he said, very gently, 'Did you have a bad dream?'

'It wasn't a dream,' she whispered, the terror flooding back.

'Care to tell me about it?' His lips were against her temple, and his fingers pressed the hair back tenderly.

'You'll think I'm insane.'

'Try me.'

'Someone cries there in the middle of the night.'

'I won't insult you by asking if you've made sure it isn't Dominic.'

'It was my first reaction.'

'Let's take a look.' He pulled his dressing gown over his nightshirt, then lit one of the lamps. 'Are you coming?'

'I can't stay here on my own!'

Back down the corridor, but this time his warm hand held her cold one and the lamp challenged the darkness, stronger than a feeble candle. Even so, terror weighted her limbs as he pushed open the bedroom door. The only sound was the settling of ash in the hearth.

'It's gone,' Margaret said.

'So it seems.' Peter explored the room, looking behind curtains and under the valance.

'Can I sleep in your room?'

'Yes.'

On their return he poured two stiff brandies. She drank, staring blankly ahead of her, while he suffered the sweet agony of having the woman he desired in his bed. Gradually fear abated, and she became conscious of the hard firm shape of him, the strength of his arms, the musky odour she associated with the male. Something came to life within her, a feeling she had long suppressed, the need for a naked body pressed close to her. His warmth penetrated her, even though she wore her nightdress and he had retained the shirt and dressing gown.

'Thank you, Peter,' she said. 'You're always so good to me.'

'Darling, no one as beautiful as you ought to look so sad.'

'It's been awful.'

'I know – the last straw – this little presence or whatever – tugging at your heartstrings.'

'You believe me, then?'

'Why shouldn't I?' He would hardly credit that the unattainable might be within his grasp. He drew his hand down the length of her hair and the emotion he felt transcended anything he had ever experienced.

'You think me beautiful? I thought you liked Fiona.' Her voice was soft, filled with that need to talk of normal things to drown out the unexplained.

'Fiona?' He was surprised that she had noticed, still afraid of expressing his feelings. 'She amusing, that's all.'

'You don't mind me being here?' There were smudges under her eyes, her lids drooping with a heaviness she was unable to control.

'Oh, Margaret, don't you know? Can't you understand? Forget Lester and have me instead.'

The challenge of his words roused her. He was offering reality, not a sad and fruitless dream. Lillian was right. This big, good-looking man wanted her, had been waiting patiently, giving her time to heal. Why shouldn't she at least try to accept him?

Slowly she sat up and, equally slowly, unfastened the ribbon ties of her nightgown and pulled it over her head. Then, naked, she looked into his eyes as she lifted his broad hands and extended them towards her. Sucking in a harsh breath, he turned his wrists so his palms cupped each rounded breast.

He groaned and pulled her closer, his lips meeting hers as her head tipped back against his arm. He kissed her, long, strong and deep, but she was aware that it was not right. She was too afraid of being betrayed again. How could she love and trust him? She had put a seal on her emotions, and without that subtle blending of spirit and flesh there could be no satisfaction.

He knew, lifting his head, still holding her, but lightly now. 'It's no use, Margaret.' His voice was sad. 'I'll not take you wondering if you're thinking about him. I'm not prepared to play second fiddle.'

'I'm sorry,' she whispered, throat swollen with tears.

'You need an exorcist, my love.' He smiled wryly, and reached for his cigarette case. 'You're as haunted as the Rose Room – haunted by what-might-have-been. Don't waste your life in empty regrets. Do something about it and when you're free we may have a chance of happiness.'

Margaret wrapped a blanket round herself and left the bed. She spent the remainder of the night sitting by the window, her thoughts locked in combat within her.

'Have you visited the Round House yet?' Natalie asked next morning as they idled over breakfast in the kitchen. The others had already left for the beach, but Peter had suggested Margaret lie on. He and Nancy would look after Dominic.

She had returned to the Rose Room at dawn, ashamed of the way she had treated him. In daylight the bedchamber always smiled at her, as innocently peaceful as could be. It was only after dark that its ambience altered. Even then it was tolerable till the depths of night.

'No. Should I visit it?'

'It's by the spinney, the playhouse of Little Charlie.'

'Little Charlie? Who is he?'

'Rather, who *was* he?' Natalie concentrated on dribbling single cream over her spoon till it lay, a thick blanket, covering the surface of her coffee. 'He lived here once, years ago, but died of some childhood ailment.'

Margaret went cold. 'Does he haunt the house?'

Natalie pulled a face. 'I've never seen anything. I'm glad he hasn't

276

singled me out, for the story goes that a visitation from him foretells illness, even death.'

'Why didn't you tell me before?'

'It's not important, is it?'

With the dogs nosing about in the undergrowth, they walked along a path shadowed by trees and rhododendrons, coming to an iron swing-gate near the paddock. Squirrels played hide-and seek among the branches, and birds were busily engaged in nesting. A straight, pebble-covered track led to a small, circular, thatched building, with leaded windows and overhanging eaves.

There was a porch with seats each side, and the door was decorated with cord nailed into spiral patterns. Natalie produced a key and they stepped into dimness. Margaret kept close to her, aware of the chill striking home after the sunshine outside.

'Who built this?' Margaret asked, weighed down by depression.

'Little Charlie's father, as a play place for his son. D'you want to see Little Charlie? He's in here.'

Natalie opened a door and Margaret looked in. There on a plinth in the greenish-yellow light, lay the life-sized statue of a sleeping boy – a sweet-faced child of around five years old.

'The story goes that his Papa was heartbroken when this beloved child died, in pain, it seems, subject to crying fits before the end,' Natalie said, then glanced at Margaret sharply. 'I say, are you all right? You're as white as a sheet.'

When they arrived back at the house, a telegram was waiting. It read:

'Lilly ill. Serious. Come home at once. Joe.'

Chapter 15

Lillian drifted in and out of consciousness. Sometimes it was daylight, sometimes not. Faces appeared, hanging over her – Joe's, Biddy's, Dr Manson's, and now a new face – round and scrubbed, surmounted by a stiff white cap. At times she thought she heard Gran's voice. And the most wonderful thing of all – there was no pain.

No pain, no gain – over and over the words wheeled in her head like birds winging towards heaven. My dear old hotel. Who will care for it now? But it didn't really matter. She was too tired. All she wanted was sleep – endless oceans of it. Not Joe – no one – her soul reaching out across the universe to those vast realms of space, borne there on the strong, syrupy draught prescribed by her good friend, Robert Manson. If it meant coming back to the agony that had felled her like an ox, then she was content never to return.

As soon as Margaret arrived at the Warwick she was met by Joe who hurried her upstairs.

'When did this happen?' she asked, pulling off her gloves as they went. There was an unnatural hush about the place, even though it was very late.

'Last night.' He was close to tears, young to be presented with this emergency, though working through it manfully. 'I telegraphed you first thing.'

'How bad is she?'

'Pretty bad.'

I won't let it happen, Margaret vowed. She's my best friend. I owe her my life. Take me, gods, if you must have a blood sacrifice. I can be sinful, selfish, unworthy of mercy. I cursed India, didn't I?

The bedroom was quiet, a night breeze wafting in at the windows. Flowers breathed out their scent, and Margaret stood by the bed, gazing down at the sleeping face within, the sunken eyes, the blue-tinged

278

lips. Lillian without cosmetics looked older in some respects, younger in others, her red hair spread across the pillow. Someone, she guessed it to be Joe, had brushed it carefully.

Biddy was on guard over her mistress and a uniformed nurse stood in the background. 'What does the doctor say?' Margaret asked, her spirits dropping like stones.

'It's her heart,' Joe replied, in that low, almost reverent tone reserved for the sickroom. 'But worse than last time.'

'I shouldn't have gone away.' Margaret was riven with guilt.

'Don't blame yourself. We were getting on well. Mr Grist and me – we did it all – wouldn't let her tax herself, but you know Lilly. She insisted on throwing a party.'

'I told her not to, but she wouldn't listen,' Biddy grated harshly, but there were tears in her eyes.

'There were some actors she knows, come from up North, playing at the Alhambra Palace. 'Course, nothing would please her but that we had a "do" in their honour. Got herself overtired.' Joe sank to his knees at the bedside, his hands resting on Lillian's limp ones.

Margaret took off her hat and coat and addressed the nurse. 'Let me know if anything is required.'

'Yes, madam. I'm Nurse Fielding. Dr Manson has instructed me.'

'I shall be in charge from now on. My name's Mrs Helbren.'

'I'm glad you came,' Biddy said, and her face crumpled. 'She's going to get over it, ain't she? I've prayed and prayed.'

'Of course, Biddy.' Margaret spoke with a confidence she was far from feeling.

It was down to her, it seemed, to buoy up their hopes and keep the hotel afloat. It will be better when Peter comes, she told herself resolutely, going to Dominic's nursery. Nancy had put him to bed and was unpacking the two suitcases which were all they had brought with them.

'Leave it till the morning. Get some sleep, my dear,' Margaret advised, hanging over her son, the marble image of Little Charlie haunting her. How did parents survive losing a child?

'And you, ma'am. You looks worn out. How is Mrs Glynn?'

'In a stable condition.'

'She won't die, will she?' Nancy's freckled face was concerned beneath the brim of the boater she had not yet had time to remove.

'It's in the lap of the gods.'

Margaret prowled to the window and drew the curtains aside. The gas-lamps etched yellowish circles on the pavement and, in the distance, she could hear the throbbing heart of London that never slept. Paddington Station had been buzzing when the Plymouth train pulled in and there had been no difficulty in obtaining a cab. Peter was following on in the car, bringing the remainder of the luggage.

Will he come right away? she wondered. Or will he dawdle in the company of the ravishing Fiona? He has every right to do so after the way I've behaved towards him.

A great dark swathe of loneliness enmeshed her. That phantom child. Had he tried to warn her of Lillian's sudden seizure? Cold fingers crawled down her spine. All day she had been unable to get warm, even during the rush and panic to reach Penzance and board a train with Dominic and Nancy. Such a tedious journey, with changes and delays – Dominic fretful as if he sensed tragedy in the air, Nancy coping brilliantly.

I must give her a raise in salary, Margaret decided. She's worth her weight in gold and her workload is bound to increase during this crisis. But I need Peter – his calm, his strength and organising abilities. I can't manage alone.

She closed her eyes and saw again his lean face and anxious eyes as he held on to her hand when she had leaned from the carriage window before the stationmaster blew his whistle.

'I'll get there as soon as I can,' he had promised, his grip tightening. 'Don't worry, Margaret.'

Believing him to be sincere, she had yet been beset by doubts throughout the journey. Fiona was an enchantress, and experienced, or so Natalie maintained. Many lovers had fallen by the wayside, lured to their doom by the glamorous young painter. Even someone as sensible as Peter might not be invulnerable.

Margaret undressed and went to bed, but was too tired to sleep, her mind whirling. She heard the steeple clock strike four. A solitary thrush gave vent to full-throated song, awakening other birds who joined in a hymn to the sun. An omnibus clanked in the distance. It was officially tomorrow.

This tomorrow and two more passed before Peter dumped his valise in the vestibule and enlisted Jenkin's aid to unload the car. Margaret was unaware of his arrival, in consultation with Grist and Philippe. He came clattering down to find her.

Her heart leapt as his broad-shouldered form appeared in the kitchen doorway. She dropped the menu notes on the table and rushed towards him. 'You're here!'

'Large as life and twice as ugly,' he laughed, and though they did not touch it was as if he held her. 'Right. What d'you want me to do first?'

There was plenty: she hardly knew where to start. Never before had the entire responsibility for the hotel rested on her. Lillian had always had the last word. Now she must not be bothered with the tiniest detail.

For a week, she hovered between life and death, but the drugs administered helped her damaged heart and Dr Manson cautiously pronounced her recovery satisfactory. He would not, however, permit her to move a muscle. Helpless as a new-born babe, everything was done for her, and Margaret took her turn with the sick-nursing. Then she vividly recalled the time when she had looked after her mother single-handedly, a baptism of fire for one so young.

Unlike the inconvenient Hazel Cottage, facilities were to hand, and Nurse Fielding and Biddy on call, with Joe insisting on sleeping on the chaise longue close to his beloved. His adoration went a long way towards restoring Margaret's faith in men, and she began to open up to Peter, tentatively at first, but with growing confidence.

He seemed unusually reserved which she attributed to her own behaviour, but on going through the daily cache of letters she saw one with a Cornish postmark addressed to him in a flowing, feminine hand.

'This is for you, I believe,' she said, giving it to him, her tone of voice indicating curiosity, and something else, too.

'So it is.' He opened it on the spot, scanned the contents as he leaned against the reception desk, and glanced at her face, testing the air. 'It's from Fiona. Remember her?'

'How could I forget? She's the one who avoided doing any of the work at the manor,' she replied uncharitably, and briskly slotted the rest of the mail into pigeonholes labelled with the names of the residents, then could not help adding, 'What does she want?'

Peter rubbed a hand across his chin. 'Oh, nothing much. We promised to keep in touch. She'll visit me when she comes to town.'

For some reason which Margaret refused to accept, this information needled her. The memory of it came back to her unbidden, even when she was in the midst of much more important things, at Lillian's bedside, presiding over the dining room or snatching a moment with Dominic.

She made sure she was the first person down in the mornings to peruse the incoming letters and, sure enough, two more came from Fiona. Her attitude towards Peter was now positively frosty.

'Why aren't you talking to me?' he asked, deliberately blocking her path as she made to escape across the hall one morning.

'Don't be ridiculous!' she answered grittily. 'We talk all the time.'

'Only of hotel matters – that's not real talk.' He stood near her, and she was very aware of the solidity of his body, the light sparking coppery glints from his curly hair, his mesmeric blue eyes.

'What do you expect? There's so much to do and I'm worried about Lillian.' She was defensive, refusing to allow herself to be hurt again, and squeezed past him. He followed her into the parlour.

'We're all worried. Joe must be beside himself. But there's something wrong between you and me. I want to know what it is.'

She tried to laugh it off. 'You're imagining things.'

'No, I'm not. We had something special. It's gone.'

'I don't know what you mean.' Her slim fingers were nervously toying with the tea roses whose heavy petals spilled over from the vase on to the polished mahogany surface of the table.

She was wearing black, relieved by touches of white at throat and wrists, and it made her look even more slender. Her hair was drawn back into a chignon, and its severity emphasised the delicate cheek-bones as pronounced as a ballerina's.

Peter was torn between the longing to sweep her into his arms and common sense that advised he leave her to her strange, disconcerting mood. He hazarded a guess as to the cause of this, but could hardly believe it was the obvious one. It threw him off kilter to think that she might be jealous, and of Fiona of all people. That forward minx had tried to take advantage when Margaret had left the grange, but he had packed the car and departed, though not before she had managed to wheedle his address from him.

Perhaps this is not such a bad thing, he thought. Sadly Margaret, like most women, was excited by the unattainable. This was part of the hold men of Lester's type had over them. Yet he did not want to add to her worries.

He walked across to the table and seized her restless hands in his. 'Take the night off and come to a concert with me.'

'We can't both be absent at the same time,' she countered, feeling herself blushing, unsure in his presence.

'I'll arrange it with Joe. Say you'll come.'

'I'm afraid to leave the hotel, sure that if I do disaster will overtake it.'

He chuckled. 'My dear girl, if we alert the fire brigade and police force – not forgetting Dr Manson and the whole staff of Guy's – the Warwick will survive for a few hours without you.'

'You're poking fun at me!' She knew she was being unreasonable, unable to contend with her jumbled emotions.

'Ever so respectfully,' he murmured, and lifted her hands to his mouth, his breath brushing over them like a caress.

'So, I've allowed you to sit out for short spells, and permitted one or two visitors. How do you feel?' the doctor said, thumbs hooked in his waistcoat pockets.

'Well enough to wish I felt better,' Lillian sighed, resting on the sofa by the window, looking out wistfully at the garden filled with the colour, scents and vibrancy of summer. 'You can have no idea how tired I am of this room.'

'I can imagine,' he said and, drawing up a chair, seated himself beside her. 'I've suggested to Joe that he take you away for a while.'

'I can't leave my hotel!' Her eyes, huge in that ashen triangle of a face, stared up at him reproachfully.

'Yes, you can. Margaret and Peter will hold the fort. You must listen to reason, Lillian. You'll never be able to indulge your old lifestyle again. With care, rest, proper food and no stimulants, you can live to a ripe old age. Disregard these simple rules and I don't give you more than a year.'

'But the Warwick? I can't give it up. It's my home.' She was becoming agitated, a bright spot of colour flaring on each cheek.

'Have I said anything about giving it up? There will have to be alterations, that's all. A suite on the ground floor, for example, to avoid you climbing stairs. Time to think about this later. For the moment, Joe will take you to some peaceful spot to recuperate. Talk it over with him, there's a good girl.'

'What d'you think about it, Joe?' Lillian asked him when they were alone in the bedroom. She was well enough now to have dispensed with Nurse Fielding. Biddy and Margaret washed and dressed her, and Joe carried her from the bed to the couch or bathroom and back again.

She lay curled in the circle of his arm and he wanted nothing more than to look at her and marvel that she was still alive. 'I think it's a grand idea,' he enthused. 'I've been wanting to ask you if we can get a car. Can we, Lilly, so I can drive you about?'

'No problem there, love.' Lillian smiled up into his eager face, admiring the fair moustache sprouting on his upper lip. A recent addition, it gave an added maturity. 'Where d'you propose we go?'

'Let's find some nice little town not too far from London. You don't want a long, exhausting journey. What about Chichester? It's a pretty place near the sea.'

'Chichester it is,' she replied sleepily, her head buried against his shoulder, willing to let him take command.

'Tell you what, Lilly – how about if you and me got spliced? It'll make it easier all round. We shan't have to book separate rooms. Regular mister and missus. What d'you say?'

The bedroom glowed in the light of the pink petal-shaped lamps, and Lillian's worn heart glowed too. 'Are you sure, love?' she whispered, her hands playing with his hair. 'D'you really want to take on an old, sick woman like me?'

'You're not old, and you're getting better. I love you, Lil. I don't want anyone but you.'

She was moved by the sincerity in his eyes. 'You know I can't have children.'

He shrugged this off. 'That don't matter. There's Dominic, and we can adopt a few, if that's what you want, and nursemaids to go with 'em.' He kissed her lips and squeezed her tight, though remembering halfway through that she was still classed as an invalid. 'Say yes, Lilly. Go on. Say it.'

Tears coursed down her face. She cried easily these days, as if the grief bottled up within her for years had burst the banks of reserve. 'Yes. Oh, yes! I'll marry you, Joe. When?'

'Soon as may be. Don't you worry about a thing. I'll do all the worrying from now on.'

The wedding was announced, the day decided upon. Not too much stress, so Lillian was carried downstairs by her bridegroom, placed in the new car as tenderly as if she was made of glass, wrapped in furs over her bridal gown, and conveyed to the church on the corner where Dominic had been christened. It was a day of great joy, with a reception prepared by Monsieur Philippe and his assistants.

'Pity I can't drink bubbly at my own wedding,' Lillian grumbled, but was grateful for this second chance, seated by Joe as the triple-tiered cake was sliced and handed round.

He had booked rooms for them in a private hotel in Bosham, a fishing village in Chichester Harbour. It was little more than sixty miles from London and they reached it by nightfall. Exhausted though she was, Lillian was prepared to criticise the management. The hotel, however, proved to be faultlessly run by a Miss Herbert, a brisk, kindly lady of uncertain age who made much of the newly-weds.

Biddy had accompanied them and she immediately struck up a rapport with Miss Herbert, leaving the honeymooners alone, and they needed no one else, absorbed in one another.

'It's funny,' Lillian remarked when they were settled in their big bedroom where honeysuckle nodded in at the windows. 'I feel sort of different somehow. We've been living over the brush for ages, and you'd think a ring wouldn't make any odds, but it does. I'm Mrs Joseph Talbot. Can you believe that? I suppose every woman wants to be married, deep down.' She held out her hand, admiring the gold band on her thin finger.

She wore a fragile silk negligé, black and lacy, sick and tired of sensible night attire, her hair, freshly hennaed for the occasion, flowing over her bare shoulders. Joe picked her up and deposited her on the

284

large brass bedstead. 'Mrs Talbot,' he said, grinning. 'I like the sound of that.'

'I'm going to enjoy my wedding night,' she vowed, nestling close to his hot body, while he opened her gown, his mouth seeking her nipples which rose to the touch of his lips.

'I don't want to harm you,' he whispered, face buried in the silken smoothness of her flesh.

'You won't. I'm strong now, darling, strong for you – strong for our love. Don't be afraid,' she whispered.

A month passed, and Lillian was content. Bosham entranced her, with its pebbly beach and harbour. Miss Herbert spoiled her; Biddy had told her all about the illness. And Lillian considered their lodgings a bargain at twenty-five shillings a week per person, all in.

'Maybe we should buy a place down here and open up,' she mused, reclining in a hammock on the lawn that faced the sea.

Joe, seated on the grass, groped for and found one of her hands. 'We'll do no such thing. Think of the work. Won't you ever stop scheming?'

'Might as well ask the waves to stop pounding the beach down there. I don't like being idle.' Her eyes were heavy-lidded, mouth drooping slightly.

'Aren't you enjoying it here?'

She brushed back a lock of hair that fell forward across his sun-tanned brow. 'Yes, I'm loving every moment. I was just wondering – that's all. How does Miss Herbert feed us so well on the money? She must be a wizard.'

They had both put on weight, the breakfasts substantial, the midday meal consisting of two vegetables, beef or a chicken off the farm. Lillian had begged the recipe for the creamy sauce Miss Herbert served, garnished with chopped eggs and parsley. Tea-time, and more food, homemade jam, toasted teacakes, cream and scones and a variety of fancies.

'I shall be as fat as a workhouse pudding by the time we get home,' Lillian moaned, tucking into dinner at seven-thirty. 'Of course, Monsieur Philippe would have a fit! D'you realise we haven't had a single foreign dish since we've been here? All good English fare, and isn't it delicious?'

'I like this,' Peter remarked, five weeks into Lillian's absence.

'So do I,' Margaret agreed.

It was dawn at Billingsgate Market. They were not the only ones meandering between fishy corpses. Others wandered, too – merchants, hoteliers like themselves – prodding, examining, comparing, now and then tasting a shrimp or cracking an experimental mussel.

'Just think, there was a time when I didn't know one end of a whiting from the other,' Peter remarked, staring at the dead codfish, skate, red-eyed herrings and white-bellied plaice, strewn in rich profusion between gleaming lumps of ice.

'I can't get over the smell,' she said, unable to decide between lobster or crab for tonight's hors d'oeuvre. 'Get a whiff of those bloaters.'

'It must be heaven for cats,' he agreed. 'And the ozone which exudes from prostrate cod seems to have a singular effect on the traders' lungs. They find it necessary to shout, and the auctioneers are positively vociferous. Close your ears, my darling girl! Their language is picturesque, to put it mildly.'

'I'm used to it by now,' she laughed, revelling in the bustle and noise of the market where the porters weaved between the crowd, wearing leather helmets and balancing crates on their heads.

After much haggling and bargaining, they left the colourful invective and ripe tang of the market and stowed their purchases in the car. They paused for a while on Billingsgate Wharf.

'This is probably the oldest in London,' he said, lighting up a cigarette. 'It's supposed to take its name from Belin, King of the Britans, though others say it was once owned by a man called Biling. The Romans landed their furs and wine here.'

'I'm beginning to feel I belong in the city,' Margaret replied, leaning against the car, the wind lifting tendrils of her hair.

August and hot, the water sparkling, a haze hanging over the rooftops. She could see the bluish shadow of Tower Bridge, and the brown Thames licking the broad hulls of fishing trawlers.

Herrings. How well she remembered them from Porthross, but now she had met many other fascinating denizens of the deep. I've come far, she thought, learned much, become a different person from the green girl who had worked under Nanny Broom.

Neither were in a hurry to return to the Warwick Hotel. They drove further into town and found a café, continuing their conversation over coffee. 'I'd like my own establishment,' Peter said reflectively. 'It's all very well writing books and articles about hotels, but nothing to owning one.'

'You won't leave the Warwick, will you?' she asked, stabbing a glance at him, the sunlight falling across the Liberty-print tablecloth and polished steel coffeepot, the scent of wallflowers wafting from a nearby window box.

'I haven't any definite plans. There are several options. Fiona wants me to go back to Cornwall.' Let Margaret mull that over, he thought, though having no intention of going.

'Does she, indeed? Why?'

'Something about starting a gallery in St Ives.'

'You'd like that?' she asked casually over her shoulder, seemingly absorbed in a glass case with stuffed birds of gorgeous plumage.

'Not as much as having a hotel, but I can't do it alone. I need a partner. At best – a wife.'

'I can't see Fiona as a landlady,' she said in honeyed tones.

'I'm not thinking of Fiona.' He was serious now, all attempt at flippancy banished. 'What d'you say? Will you join me?'

'I can't abandon Lillian. She's going to need me when she returns.'

'She might retire.'

'Can you imagine her retiring?'

'Damn it, Margaret, I'm not talking about Lillian. I'm talking about us. I wasn't going to say this but I can't stop myself. Will you marry me?'

'I don't know,' she faltered, but Peter would have none of this.

He swivelled round in his chair, almost knocking his cup flying with his elbow. Capturing her knees between his so that she could not move, he stared directly into her face.

'I love you, Margaret. I want you. But the question is – do you love me?'

'I'm not sure what love is any more.'

He let her go abruptly. 'Then it won't work. It's Lester, isn't it?' His eyes had gone black as midnight and she had never seen him so angry.

'No, it isn't. I'm not stupid!' This was better. By whipping up an answering rage she could forget that she was hurting him, hurting herself.

With an exasperated snort he pushed back his chair and stood up, snapping his fingers for the bill. The waiter brought it over and Peter tossed a handful of coins on the table, then strode out.

Margaret followed, the lovely morning quite ruined. She had quarrelled with the one man who mattered. Catching up with him, she touched his arm tentatively. 'Oh, Peter, forgive me. Lester means nothing to me. I'm proud that you've asked me to be your wife, and I accept.'

He stopped dead in the middle of the pavement, and passing pedestrians stared curiously at the handsome man and lovely woman looking at each other so intently. 'If I could only believe that,' he growled, his throat dry, hardly daring to blink, sure that the slighest flicker of an eyelid would make this dream disappear.

'It's true. I do love you, but it's not the mad passion I felt for Lester. I doubt I'll ever feel like that again. I'm too afraid of being hurt.'

'I won't hurt you. I'll never hurt you.' Careless of spectators, he drew her into his embrace. 'I'm willing to take a chance, if you are.'

287

'Yes,' she whispered, thrilled by the way he looked at her, by the feel of his arms about her, by the security he represented.

'I'll take you to meet my mother,' he exclaimed, grinning like a boy, while he wondered if he dare make plans. He wanted to, was prepared to give her time, yet there lingered the fear that one day, maybe not yet, maybe far in the future, she might meet Lester again.

'Is that a good idea? I'm sure she won't be impressed by her son marrying a servant. What about Dominic? How are you going to explain him?' Already practical issues were impinging on the happiness Margaret was allowing herself to feel.

He laughed, suddenly reckless. 'She gave up trying to understand me years ago. I offended her by refusing to take a commission in the army. Father's more indulgent. I'm sure he'll like you, and so will she after you've met once or twice. In any case, I don't need their blessing. I'm nearly thirty and have been independent for a long time. My grandfather left me an inheritance. He admired free spirits, and so does Uncle John. My brother Stewart will eventually have Stanford Orcas, but I'll have Martock Hall.'

Margaret realised how little she knew about him. He rarely mentioned his family or gave any indication of his financial state, though it was apparent that he was a man of means. With her fingers linked in his she looked up at him and said, 'Where does your mother live?'

'In a mansion in Park Lane, when she's in town,' he replied. 'There's the estate in Suffolk, and other houses dotted about all over. She likes to move around, and my father goes along with it for a quiet life. He should have been an Oxford don, it would have suited him much better than the army, but he didn't have the choice I had and ended up in India. That's how I came to spend my early years in Bengal.'

Margaret was concerned with the difficulties ahead. His family were bound to disapprove of her. Once she had imagined such things were of little importance, fully prepared, in her ignorance, to face Lester's father, earldom and all. Now she knew better.

Peter was unconcerned. He had escaped the family influence years past, deciding in adolescence that this was his life and he was going to live it how he pleased.

'Let's go to Hatton Garden and buy a ring – now,' he urged, needing to see this symbol of commitment on her finger.

'We can't,' she said, face serious as she looked at this broad, quiet man who was offering her his world and everything in it.

'Why not?'

'Because, my dear, that fish in the car must be dispatched to Monsieur Philippe post-haste.' Then she added with a smile, 'Besides, I'd rather like you to choose it and present it to me at some more romantic moment.'

'On bended knee?'

'Of course.'

'It shall be done. Anything you say, sweetheart.'

'That's wonderful news. I'm so glad,' Lillian said when they told her.

She was tired from the journey but her features lit up with a radiant smile as Joe carried her into the lobby where the staff waited to greet her. Even Monsieur Philippe had consented to leave his kitchen for the occasion, and Lillian asked Biddy to hand him a bundle of papers – recipes she had begged from Miss Harvey.

He stared at them, and his long face became longer. 'English recipes, madame? You expect me to use these?'

'We'll discuss it later,' she replied with a mischievous smile, waving to the others as Joe bore her into the parlour. She did not betray her exhaustion, had not been Lilybelle Lucerne for nothing, those years as an actress standing her in good stead.

'You look so well,' Margaret cried, face alight with pleasure.

'You must tell me everything that's been happening while I've been away,' Lillian commanded from the sofa. 'And I want to have another look at that ring, Margaret.'

It was an amethyst set in diamonds, an ostentatious, sparkling stone. 'She should always wear amethysts,' Peter declared. 'They match her eyes.'

'I'm happy for you both,' Lillian said sincerely. 'Have you any plans for the future?'

'I've a proposition to put to you and Joe,' Peter began, needing a cigarette but restraining himself for her sake. 'The house next door is for sale. It's the same size as this one. What would you say to my buying it, going into partnership with you and expanding the Warwick?'

'Whew!' Joe whistled.

'Hang on a minute,' said Lillian. 'Let me get this straight. You're saying you'd put up the money for an adjoining property and we'd divide the profits down the middle?'

'It'll have to be legally drawn up, but yes, that's the rough idea. You've got the expertise. I've got the cash. You need a bigger place because part of the ground floor has to be turned into an apartment for you. Margaret and I want our own business, so this seems to be the answer.' Peter had gone into it carefully before she arrived back, viewing next door and consulting Mathew Unwin.

'It sounds good to me,' Lillian replied slowly. 'We'll go into it more fully tomorrow. Can you get hold of the keys so I can see it?'

'That's easily arranged. I've already put in a tentative offer, knocking the owner down from the asking price, of course.'

'Of course!' she agreed, liking this thrifty touch. 'I think it would work out fine. Are you happy about this, Margaret?'

'Very happy.'

Everything fell into place so smoothly that Peter was suspicious, knowing fate had an unpleasant habit of keeping nasty little tricks up its sleeve. The house was purchased, and workmen moved in, knocking through doorways and adding more bathrooms, and this done with the Warwick staying open for business. Because Lillian could not go to the furnishing emporiums, Margaret brought home swatches of material, samples of carpet, books of wallpapers and paint schemes over which they pored. Every aspect came under discussion and it was an exciting, productive time.

Peter and Margaret planned to marry after the grand opening. The church had been booked, her wedding gown, beige not white as she made no claim to be a virgin, lay in readiness at the couturière and a honeymoon had been arranged in Bournemouth. The meeting with Peter's parents had gone remarkably well, far better than Margaret had imagined.

She had tried not to be overawed by the magnificent eighteenth-century salon in which they had been received. His mother was a sharp-witted, handsome lady, well read and a great traveller. After initial skirmishes with Peter, she had accepted his future bride, and graciously agreed to attend the ceremony.

The opening of the annexe had been advertised in the newspapers. Enquiries were flooding in. The expanded Warwick Hotel looked all set to be a huge success.

'Can you manage, darling?' Peter asked Margaret one morning in late autumn. 'The carpet fitters will be in, but they know what to do. I want to go off and do some shopping. I've not bought myself a morning suit yet, and I need new shirts and I don't know what-all. Can't be eclipsed by my bride.'

'Don't worry. Joe and I can will see to it,' she smiled, elegant in a black velvet dress with a cream lace bolero and jabot.

She was glad of a moment to herself, wandering through the orderly Warwick where the day's work was underway. Lillian was already installed in her downstairs suite. Popping her head round the door, she found her friend resting on a splendid new couch of lemon brocade, surrounded by her treasures.

'D'you like it?' Margaret asked, admiring the spacious room where once guests had dined.

'Like it? I adore it!' Lillian enthused, clad in flowing crimson, quite taking to the role of beautiful invalid.

Next Margaret checked on the workmen. The extension was still chaotic even though they were due to open in a few days. Plumbers tapped pipes and checked water supplies; electricians adjusted wiring; carpenters added a final sheen with beeswax and elbow grease; acres of carpet were rolled out and stretched and tacked into place; floors sanded and polished, but—

'It'll be ready. Don't you fret, missus,' the foreman assured her, frock-coated and bowler-hatted, a stern taskmaster for his workforce.

She went through into the enlarged kitchen. This had been completed first in order to prevent Monsieur Philippe having a nervous breakdown. He was well satisfied and had personally overseen the arrangements, pleased as a cat who has been at the cream by the sets of gleaming copper pans, an additional gas stove of the latest design, and many other improvements.

My hotel, she thought and ran her hands over the banister rails as she went aloft. Well, not entirely mine, but at one time I never dreamed of even partly owning anything so grand. I've come far, Mother. I hope you're pleased with me. Your little grandson will now have a future. There will be money for his education. He can go to the very best schools, proud of his name – a Newark, legally adopted by Peter.

Her heart lifted and her body warmed as she thought about him. Peter, who offered her everything. They worked together, played together, but were not yet lovers.

'I want us to wait,' he had said when he had placed the ring on her finger. 'This must be done properly. No hole-in-the-corner affair for you this time. When we come together in love it will be on our wedding day. Do you agree?'

'I do. We'll wait. You are right,' she had said, curbing her longing to experience his passion, and they had waited, keeping themselves fully occupied, too busy with the amalgamation of the two houses to permit time for temptation.

But now their part of the work was all but completed. Now she was counting the hours till their love could be fulfilled. Not long, a week, no more . . .

The original lobby had been retained, though freshly decorated. Lillian's parlour had been incorporated in her apartment, and a different, more businesslike office had been designed in the next building, leading from the foyer where Jenkins still reigned at his reception desk. Margaret liked this place, feeling it to be her domain where all the paperwork pertaining to the hotel was done. She opened the door, intending to check on the menus, then stopped to pick up the mail and chat with Jenkins. He gave her the newspapers and she stood there idly scanning *The Times*.

Then her attention sharpened. The day darkened and a shaft of ice penetrated her heart. She put out a hand and rested it on the desk, needing the feel of something solid.

There, glaring up at her as if written in letters of fire, was an announcement: *The marriage of Roderick, Viscount Stanmore to Lady Fay Culverhay, and that of Lord Lester Kealan of Treleen Towers, Ireland, to Lady India Culverhay, will take place at St Martin's Church on October 31st.*

That's tomorrow, she thought. He's marrying India tomorrow.

Chapter 16

'This will be the wedding of the year,' Julia pronounced as she and Ethel floated into the ballroom.

She was entertaining the brides' parents and sundry of Ethel's relatives from Boston, Philadelphia and Florida who had steamed across the Atlantic to be in at the kill. Parkside Mansion, the Culverhay residence, was full, the overspill lodged in various hotels nearby. The house on Upper Grosvenor Street also resembled a pension, for the Auberts had not lagged behind in their distribution of invitations.

'It's like a dream come true,' Ethel gushed. 'My own wedding to Teddy was perfect and I so much wanted the same for my girls – marriage to English gentlemen.'

'And you have it, Ethel dear.' Julia could afford to be gracious, though wondered just how much of a gentleman Edward had turned out to be. Was he, like Henry, consistently unfaithful, carrying on his own secret life in which Ethel had no part?

These things were never spoken of in their circles. They were ladies and, as such, slaves to convention and to the men they had accepted as husbands. But sometimes Julia wondered what had happened to Margaret Helbren, that spawn of Henry's lust. Was she now a street-walker? Had her child died, or ended up in a foundling home? The thought of the girl's destruction gave her a warm, contented feeling.

It was in order that Julia patronise her cousin's American wife. She had a perfect pedigree. Ethel did not. She was the product of generations of women trained to be decorative, pliant and gracious. By no stretch of the imagination could Ethel fall into this category. Though she might adopt a grand manner, her small eyes and round face put Julia in mind of Mrs Colby, the housekeeper. Even so, this alliance was already proving beneficial.

Roderick appeared to have changed since coming under Fay's influence. At one time Julia had thought him promiscuous, but it seemed he had merely been doing what all young men did – sowing a few wild oats. She was pleased with him, and showed it. Everything he asked for was granted these days – clothes, cars, horses. Julia and Henry could afford to be generous, knowing he would soon be someone else's problem. The visit to America had proved a spectacular success. They had been treated like visiting royalty.

The ballroom was dazzling, and the visitors impressed. These large, rangy men in their tuxedos, the chattering women in gorgeous gowns ordered from French fashion houses, were descended from original settlers, almost America's aristocracy, proud to boast that their ancestors had sailed for the New World from British shores.

The English gentry received them with cool British aplomb, smugly secure in their family trees which went straight back to the Norman conquest. They might not be as wealthy, the ancestral homes mortgaged to the hilt, the jewels in hock, the portraits, porcelain and priceless libraries mere frozen assets, but they had something that could never be taken from them – centuries of rule and governorship.

'Oh, I'm so thrilled to think I'll be a Kealan tomorrow,' said India, seated with Lester in the shadowy, humid conservatory.

He leaned back against the stone bench and drew out his cigarettes. She tolerated his smoking habits, though lectured him on endangering his health, keen on exercise, playing tennis and croquet and being a champion archer. Unlike English débutantes, but in common with the other girls he had met in the States, she talked a lot, supposedly open and frank, yet not, of course. He was sure she had been given no instruction regarding her wedding night.

He stubbed out his cigarette and, slipping an arm round her waist, drew her towards him and kissed her, a chaste kiss with closed lips. She responded eagerly, yet with innocence. It was as if she kissed a cousin or her father. Her body, too, covered by that girlish white tulle ball gown, remained stiff in his embrace.

She sat up and rearranged the lilies of the valley adorning her hair. 'I suppose it's all right for us to be alone like this, Lester. We're nearly married, aren't we?'

Mocking, careless because there was no turning back, cruel because he was hurting inside, he gave her an oblique, flinty glance from under half-closed lids. 'That's true, my dear. What would you say if I asked you to sleep with me tonight, instead of waiting till after the ceremony?'

'The ideas you have, Lester!' she murmured, in love with the wonderful good looks he possessed, his arrogant manner and sartorial elegance, bewitched by his title and soft brogue. Even his little scar and that slightly crooked nose added to his glamour, hinting that he could use his fists in an emergency.

Though she and her girlfriends might whisper and titter about their beaux, take surreptitious peeps at the naked male statues in art galleries or glance at paintings of classical subjects, they had only the vaguest notion of what took place when a man and woman were in bed together. Veiled in mystery, she anticipated something wonderful, frightening, maybe painful, but was not sure what to expect. Among other misconceptions, she firmly believed that when she had a baby it would be born through her navel.

He found her reticence amusing and irritating, 'You do love me, don't you, India?'

'Of course, and I'd do it, if you really wanted, Lester,' she answered unhappily, her lace-gloved hands and rounded arms clasped about her body as if protecting it from a ravisher. 'Though it wouldn't seem right. I'm surprised you've asked me.'

His dark face was unsmiling. 'Supposing I said that I can't wait, want to make wild, passionate love to you?'

'Oh, Lester – please don't talk that way.'

She cast a worried look towards the double glass doors leading into the ballroom, wanting to be back there, amid the music, the flashing jewels, the highly glazed shirt fronts and fresh kid gloves of the dancers, so safe and normal. She could simper and flirt in Lester's arms as they twirled in the waltz – his hand pressed decorously to her back, hers resting on his shoulder, the other clasped in his. This was love as she visualised it, romance incarnate. She did not want to think about tomorrow and endless nights to follow when he could claim his marital rights any time he wanted.

Still smiling, he leaned over, took her hand in his and laid it against his groin. India started back as if scalded, but he would not release her, keeping her hand trapped there. He allowed the daemon to rule, as he had done when he seduced Margaret. This simpleton wanted to own him, didn't she? Her father had bought him for her, just as if he was purchasing a stallion to service a favourite mare. He was angry, resentful, recognising her inexperience and taking twisted pleasure in showing her the evidence of his arousal.

'You see how much I want you?' he murmured, his eyes boring into hers. 'This is reality, India. I'm no storybook prince. I'm flesh and blood, with a man's needs. Do you know what I mean by that?'

'I don't understand.' She had never been more embarrassed, and the look in his eyes was frightening. What sort of a person was she marrying? She realised that, after all these months, she still did not know him. He was a stranger with strange ways. Above all, he was a man.

295

For a moment she imagined him naked – muscular, hairy, and with that large, foreign something between his thighs which, she did not know how, would make her pregnant.

'You'll have to be patient with me, Lester,' she said, and the bewilderment in her eyes deepened as he forced her hand closer to the heat and hardness of his body. 'Oh dear, I'm not sure I want to get married.'

'Too late, darling,' he chuckled unpleasantly. 'It's all arranged.' Then, with a complete change of mood, he subjected her to his charming smile, letting her go and merely kissing her cheek in his usual gentle manner. 'Don't worry. I was only teasing. I'll let you keep your virginity till the ring is on your finger. It won't be so bad, you know. You might even get to like it.'

'I've quite made up my mind. No one knows, not even Peter,' Margaret wrote in her diary while early morning light crept into the bedroom. 'He can't help me, neither can the lawyer, so I'll take the matter into my own hands. It may not do any good, but at least I shall feel I've struck a blow for women like me who have been betrayed.'

She washed and dressed, coiling her hair into a knot fastened low at the nape and choosing a black velvet dress decorated with art nouveau appliqué work. It was one of her favourites and she always felt more confident when wearing it. She selected a matching coat and unadorned hat with a concealing brim. Nothing too eye-catching for she did not want to draw attention to herself until the time was ripe.

Planning carefully, she had given Nancy the night off, and she would not be back till afternoon. Margaret woke Dominic, fed him, got him into his clothes, then picked him up and let herself out of the quiet house where only the kitchen staff were stirring. The traffic was just beginning to build, public transport and milk floats drawn by horses, postmen and paper boys doing their rounds on bicycles.

Because she had time to kill Margaret went on foot, though Dominic was heavy. She hung around for a while, drinking tea at a stall near the river, then sitting on an iron bench, cuddling Dominic close. She watched the water unseeingly, lost in thought, while sparrows hopped at her feet, little brown scavengers quarrelling over scraps with the grey and white pigeons.

Eventually she got up and plodded on. There were few sightseers at this time of the year, the season closed, but a large crowd had already gathered outside the red and white awning leading to St Martin's church.

A narrow strip of scarlet carpet ran from kerb to porch. Policemen held back the throng, mostly women. Some of them had been diverted from shopping by the excitement, but others were professionals who made a hobby of waiting in all weathers to see events like this one, often selecting their pitches at daybreak to ensure the best vantage point.

'A double wedding and the brides are Yankees,' Margaret heard one of them say, a middle-aged, shabby woman. Her hat had seen better days.

'How d'you know?' answered her friend, scraggy, tired-eyed, hefting two bulging carrier bags.

'Read it in the paper. Their father's an English lord, but he married into money – an American heiress.'

'Go on!'

'It's true.'

Yes, it's true, Margaret wanted to shout, standing tensely behind them. One of them is marrying my lover. Bigamy, as Peter once said long ago in Monte Carlo, for by the laws of nature, he's already my husband. I've lain down with him and this is our child. And now he's waiting to exchange vows with another woman.

The crowd thickened, a swarming, heaving mass of women, eager to look at the brides. Carriages and automobiles arrived in a steady stream to disgorge their splendidly attired passengers. This gave the spectators more food for talk.

''Cor, look at 'er 'at! It's like a bleedin' cushion. Did you ever see so many feathers? Some poor bloody bird's feeling the draught up its backside!'

'And those furs! They didn't come from Petticoat Lane, I know.'

'Wonder what she did to get 'em?'

'Same as you and me, Vi, when our old men come in pissed of a Saturday night. 'Cept she gets paid for it in furs and jewels and we don't.'

'All we can expect is a smack in the eye. Watch out, 'ere come some more. Every toff in London's 'ere, by the looks of things.'

The dark arch of the church was busy. There was an anticipatory liveliness. Young men in morning clothes, white gardenias in their buttonholes, were acting as ushers. Though they had been rehearsed, there seemed to be a hold-up. They were coping with several arrivals at once, checking the guest list, asking each other whispered questions, pointing, hesitating.

Margaret worked her way closer and, under cover of the confusion, slipped unnoticed past the flustered young men, through the shadowy porch and into the back of the church, melding into the dimness behind a pillar topped by a circle of grinning stone grotesques. Black

297

as the shadows – black shot with red, like the murderous fury scalding through her blood.

The smell peculiar to places of worship assailed her nostrils, that feeling of fear and guilt making her heart pound. She looked up the aisle and saw the group at the altar through a blur of scarlet, blue and orange as light poured from the arched windows. Stained glass images of Christ, of the Annunciation and the Virgin Mary, saints and martyrs, sacrifice and death. Her attention focused, sharpened, centred on Lester, resplendent in morning dress and a silk waistcoat.

Music drifted under the Norman arches, the organist filling in till the given signal. The atmosphere tingled with anticipation. The packed congregation fidgeted but very discreetly, too well bred to show impatience. The relatives and friends of the respective families occupied opposite sides of the aisle, and each lady there had striven to outdo the others. Heads in huge-brimmed hats occasionally craned round to snatch a glimpse of the entrance where the bridesmaids stood waiting. The tension seemed to stretch out endlessly, like a protracted, silent yawn.

With a tumultuous burst of sound the organist broke into the triumphant Bridal March from Wagner's *Lohengrin* as Lord Edward, leonine head held high, paced solemnly in with a daughter on each arm. The audience rose. A sigh rippled round the nave, breathed from the throats of a hundred females as they saw themselves as brides, either in the past or in the future.

The whisper of silk, the slither of satin, the overpowering scent of orange blossom – like funerals, like graveyards. Margaret, who had sworn not to look, glanced up.

India passed close by her, a vision in white gauze and chiffon, carrying a cascade of flowers. Like Fay, she wore a full court train of silver tissue that brushed the ground for yards behind her. At a suitable distance walked six bridesmaids in pink taffeta and six in blue, each carrying posies and crowned with floral wreaths. Both brides were veiled in exquisite Brussels lace, their head-dresses sparkling with diamond clusters set among wax roses. The procession halted at the candle-bright altar where the priest, glittering like an icon, waited to begin the ceremony.

The music ceased, the congregation hushed and grew still, the vicar's voice rang out, accentuated by the acoustics of the vaulted ceiling. Words, hymns, more words: 'This man, this woman – united in holy wedlock – forsaking all others—'

Forsaking! Lester forsook me. Margaret was as if turned to stone.

The vicar got into his stride. Here was a wedding worth performing, a double wedding with double responses and a double gift for himself.

He came to the passage where the congregation was advised to speak if they knew of any impediment to these couples being joined in matrimony.

The church seemed suspended in silence. Everyone held their breath, though sure nothing would happen. It was impossible in their well-structured circles. The vicar had been years in office, and had conducted many marriage services. He was confident there would be no interruption.

Margaret stepped into the aisle, the slumbering child in her arms, her voice echoing loudly as she said, 'I know a reason why Lord Lester shouldn't be married.'

There was a horrified gasp and all eyes switched to her as she advanced towards the altar, passing the bridesmaids, ignoring the bestmen, the brides and Roderick and the flabbergasted priest, bearing straight down on Lester.

She lifted Dominic high, pronouncing in ringing tones. 'This is his son. He promised to marry me but broke his word.'

The stunned silence broke. A roar rose to the heavens, the church thrown into pandemonium.

'Is this true?' India was staring at Margaret from behind her veil, as stunned as if the roof had caved in.

'What the devil's going on?' Her father shouted, springing forward, an arm round her protectively. 'Is she telling the truth, Lester?'

'It's no use asking him. He'll lie. He's the Prince of Liars! Aren't you, Lester?' Margaret cried, but Lester remained silent, averting his gaze. She directed her rage at Roderick. 'And you were in on this, weren't you? You want him, Lady Fay? D'you know he's a pervert? He watched while Lester seduced me – watched through a trick mirror while he made love to his fist! You'll be fools, both of you, if you go on with this. These men are libertines!'

'What have you been up to, son?' demanded the Earl of Treleen, a large man with a shock of greying hair and weather-beaten face.

His countess was gazing at their boy in horror, a faded beauty in a feather-loaded hat and matching boa. 'Lester – how could you?' she gasped.

Lester ignored his parents, staring straight ahead, only the twitch of a muscle beside his mouth betraying any emotion.

'Please keep calm, ladies and gentlemen, stay in your seats,' the vicar implored, striving to salvage the situation. His cold pebble eyes glared into Margaret's as he said, 'Can you substantiate these claims?'

'She has no proof. Absolutely none!' Roderick exclaimed, grabbing at Fay's hand. 'Don't believe a word of it, darling. She's mad.'

Dominic, frightened by the hubbub, began to cry lustily. Margaret jogged him as she struggled to make herself heard above the din. 'I'm not mad. I'm telling the truth. You know it, Roderick. So do you, Lester.'

He turned his shoulder away from her, and placed his arm round India who was trembling and crying. Margaret shoved her aside and pounded on his back with her free fist, yelling, 'Look at your son! He's yours – *yours!*'

Then he met her eyes and his were stormy dark, the sea in winter, grey and cold. Little shocks, like prickles of ice crawled under her skin. She was trembling so hard it was difficult to stand. His gaze dropped to Dominic, and stayed there for a fraction of a second, then he spoke, but not to Margaret.

'Take no notice of her, India,' he said coolly. 'She was Lady Julia's maid but was dismissed because she was expecting a child by the chauffeur. She's a troublemaker. I suppose she hoped to get money out of me.'

'Liar! Liar!' Margaret screamed, while Dominic bawled and the spectators stared. It was the most thrillingly scandalous event they had ever attended and the tale would buzz round their dinner tables for months to come.

'Get her out of here!' Lord Edward's face was beet-red, a vein pulsing on his brow, furious to see his girls in floods of tears, humiliated in public, their wedding day ruined. 'If it's money she's after, then give it to her!'

The two scarlet-jacketed guardsmen who had been acting as best-men, seized her by the arms. 'Come on. No more trouble or we'll call the police,' they said sternly, trying to hustle her to the door while she kicked and struggled and hung back.

'Is that really your baby, Helbren?' asked Fenella, from among the round-eyed bridesmaids.

'But you're not married, are you?' Jane piped up, a plump pink angel in frills and laces.

'I believe Helbren,' Evelyn declared stoutly, flinging her posy to the floor and stamping on it. 'There's no justice for women. I'm going to tell Natalie about this.'

'Be quiet at once, Evelyn.' Her mother descended on her, face a rigid mask of controlled rage.

'Why should I be quiet? I'm sick of being quiet. I never wanted to go to that stupid French academy, and I'm never going to marry some pimply, chinless wonder like Fenella's fiancé. Never! Never! Never!'

'Good heavens! Do something with her, Mam'zelle. Take her away. The child's hysterical!' Everything was slipping out of Julia's control and she was mortified. The wedding of the year? More likely, the fiasco of all time!

Rebellion was contagious, sweeping through the younger members of the congregation like a forest fire. Anna placed her hand on Margaret's, her thin face expressing deepest concern. 'You are so brave,' she whispered.

'This is disgraceful!' Julia breathed, the egret plumes in her hat quivering. 'How dare you come here and make this disturbance, Helbren? After all we did for you!'

Margaret broke free from the soldiers, turning on her with spitfire fury. 'And what did you do? You satisfied your revenge. Now I'm taking mine!' She glared at Henry who seemed to be struck dumb. 'You know who I am, don't you, Father? How could you do it? Abandoning my mother, insisting she wed Tom Helbren.'

She had captured his attention. He was staring at her, and at the baby in her arms. She held his eyes, shouting, 'History repeating itself! My mother with her bantling – and me with mine! Are you proud of yourself, Father?'

Just for one glorious moment she had them – Lester and her father. They froze, exposed before the whole company. Then, like globules of mercury running together, so the nobility closed ranks.

'It's preposterous!' Henry said crisply. 'Get rid of her! The woman's insane! She needs locking up!'

Undismayed, Evelyn said, 'If you're Helbren's father, Papa, that means we're half-sisters.'

'Be quiet! The whole thing is a monstrous lie!' Julia stepped in, answering quickly.

Evelyn refused to be silent. 'That makes me the baby's aunt, Fenella and Jane, too, while Harry and William are uncles.'

'Evelyn, if you don't stop this instant, I'll—' Julia was within a hair's breath of smacking her daughter's face.

'Roderick, you must be the baby's uncle, too,' Evelyn continued. 'And Fay will be his aunt, when you two are married. You are still going to be married, aren't you?'

Obeying Julia's frantic signals, the guardsmen gripped Margaret forcefully and frogmarched her down the isle.

The church entrance was blocked by blue uniforms, and a beefy police sergeant loomed over her. 'What's all this, my girl? You'd better come outside quietly or I'll have to take you to Bow Street and charge you with causing an affray.'

'But don't you see? He made me pregnant. This is his child.' Margaret flung up her head, stretched out her arm and pointed towards Lester like some vengeance-inspired Megaera.

301

'We can't have you upsetting the wedding, can we?' The sergeant nodded to the guardsmen. 'That's all right, sirs. I'll take over. You get back to the service. She won't give you no more trouble.'

'Trouble?' Margaret thundered, her aspect deadly. 'I haven't even started!'

Then Peter pushed through the crowd, saying calmly, 'There's no need to take this any further, officer. I'll vouch for the young lady. She's my fiancée.'

'Ah, I see, sir. Well, that throws a different light on the matter.'

'I'm telling the truth,' Margaret insisted, her eyes blazing.

The policeman had spent years pounding the beat and there was nothing that shocked or surprised him. He had used his truncheon to quell brawls in the East End, taken the wounded to hospital, witnessed the victims of grisly murders, and helped the river police drag soggy bodies on to the pier under Waterloo Bridge, known as Suicide Station. Mostly women, many pregnant. He believed Margaret but now was neither the time nor place to discuss it. He had his duty to perform.

'So you know where she lives, sir?' he asked Peter, sending his men back to their posts controlling the agitated crowd.

'Of course,' Peter said, eyeing them warily. They could turn either way, for Margaret or against her. She could become their heroine or they might want to lynch her.

'Then I suggest you get her home as quick as you can.'

'Thank you, officer.'

With Dominic held in one arm and the other locked in hers, Peter used his elbow to wedge a path through the solid wall of human flesh to where his car stood. The people watched silently, but just as he handed Dominic in and was closing the passenger door behind her, a man materialised. A ferrety little man with a shifty expression and greasy hair, flourishing a notepad.

'I'm a reporter from the *Evening Star*,' he said, leaning in at the window. 'I'd like to talk to the young lady.'

'Go away!' Peter growled and, having turned the engine over, climbed into the driver's seat.

'Just a few words for my column,' the man insisted. 'Can you tell me how you met Lord Lester, miss? Jilted you, did he? What's your name?'

'Get lost!' Peter raised his fist threateningly and the reporter darted nimbly away.

Peter did not speak a word throughout the drive from St Martin's, but when they drew up at the Warwick he got out to assist Margaret, then returned to the driver's seat. The engine was still running.

302

'Aren't you coming in?' she asked, alarmed by the cold, distant look in his eyes.

'Not just yet. I need to think,' he said levelly, and slipped the gears into place. The car sped off down the road.

Margaret walked into the lobby of the hotel, the baby clasped close. Jenkins raised his grizzled head and looked at her, his usual cheery greeting dying on his lips.

Her mind was whirling with pictures of the scene in the church – Lester's coldness, her father's refusal to acknowledge her. This hurt her most of all. He could have vindicated her, stood at her side, accepted his grandchild. Instead he had humiliated her. So be it. She had proved to herself that they were heartless. No more illusions.

Jenkins stared after her, and asked, 'Is there anything wrong, Mrs Helbren?'

'No,' she lied. 'Everything is fine.'

But inside she was possessed of terrible anxiety, and quickly carried Dominic upstairs to where Nancy was waiting for him. Once in her own room, Margaret opened the wardrobe and lifted Mignonette from the shelf, along with the leather-bound book of poems. She tested her reaction as she handled these relics, but was aware of nothing but relief, and laid them in the packing case ready for transference to the magnificent double bedroom in the extension which would be awaiting her and Peter on their return from their honeymoon.

If there was a honeymoon.

Oh, he couldn't be so disgusted by her action that he no longer wanted to marry her, could he? Maybe he had gone for good, furious at her behaviour, taking it as a sign that she still loved Lester. Perhaps he was already heading for Cornwall and Fiona. Her footsteps quickened as she left the room, her heart pounding as she remembered his love and support, the plans they had made.

I can't lose him, she thought frantically. I love him, my partner, my future husband. She ran out into the garden and across to the mews at the back which was used as a garage. It was deserted. She waited for a while, praying to hear the rumble of wheels, longing to see him. The light was beginning to fade, the afternoon cold, and that chill seemed to penetrate her heart as she visualised a future without Peter.

Seriously worried now, she went inside and searched the house and annexe, trying to conceal her anxiety from the staff. I've been such a fool! she thought. I should have told him where I was going, but then he would have stopped me and I had to do it. At last she went towards her new office, hoping against all hope that he might be there. She pushed open the door.

But it was Lester who rose from the swivel chair before the desk –

Lester in his morning suit, a black overcoat swinging from his shoulders, sprinkled with little flakes of confetti.

'What do you want?' she said, closing the door and leaning against it.

'To see you, and our son,' he said in that half-amused, partly contemptuous drawl. 'I've slipped away from the reception. The cake has been cut and they're all drunk on champagne. India's gone to get changed as we're off on our honeymoon. She's cross with me, but I'll make sure we consummate the marriage tonight.'

'How could you, after what she's been through today? That poor girl.'

'I'm her husband. She'll do as she's told. You've got guts, my dear, walking into the lion's den as you did. I've always wanted to hear someone interrupt a wedding ceremony.'

'Don't you care that it was your own?'

'It hasn't made any difference, just given tongues the chance to wag. Not only about me, either. So, Lord Henry's your father, eh? I knew you had a drop of blue blood in your veins. Now I want to have another look at my boy.'

'How dare you?' She was shaking with fury. 'You denied he was yours – there, in front of them all. You have no right. None! Go away.'

'Margaret, darling. I'm sorry if I hurt you, but I promise we can be together again in a while. I'd like to make amends.'

'You have a wife now. You can't get out of that.'

'She'll do what I want. She's besotted with me. And later, if she wants a divorce, I'm sure her papa will buy me off with a handsome settlement.'

'This has nothing to do with me,' she hissed, her face hard, her eyes like daggers. 'I'm finished with you, and am marrying Peter in a few days.' But am I? she thought.

'Really?' he sneered. 'Are you sure that's what you want? You don't love him. You love me. I can see it in your eyes, feel it in your body. You're flesh of my flesh, Margaret, bone of my bone. You belong to me. Give me time, and then I'll fetch you and the child. Set you up in a house somewhere. Say yes. You know you want to.'

'I don't. You're mistaken.'

'Yes, you do.' He touched her hair, ran a hand down the side of her cheek. 'We can have fun, darling. You don't want to be stuck in this hotel for the rest of your life, do you? I know all about it, have read of it in the newspapers. You and Lillian and Peter, business partners. Dearest girl, you're worth more than that.'

'You'd never be able to marry me.'

'No. This was always impossible. It's a question of the inheritance, you see. I hope India will give me a couple of sons.'

'So I'd be your mistress, and Dominic your bastard?' Cold as ice but fire inside, Margaret faced him.

He spread his hands in an almost apologetic gesture. 'Whatever I do, he'll never be legitimate.'

'And whose fault is that?'

A knock on the door startled them. Margaret opened it, admitting Nancy with the baby in her arms. She looked from one face to the other, mistaking Lester for a client. 'Sorry, madam. I didn't know you were busy. It's nothing important. I'll come back later.'

'Leave him,' Lester said, using his captivating smile. 'I've yet to meet Mrs Helbren's boy.'

'Is that all right, madam?' Nancy was unsure, something in Margaret's expression alarming her.

'Yes. I'll bring him up directly. Oh, and Nancy – have you seen Mr Newark?'

'No, madam.'

'Thank you, Nancy. That will be all.'

There was a dangerous fascination about seeing Dominic and Lester together, a situation Margaret had once longed for. Her sturdy son and his handsome father. Unmistakably related, the same nose, the same eyes, the same olive skin and dark hair.

'He's beautiful,' Lester murmured, and his smile was soft.

'He is indeed. My son, not yours,' she answered, holding Dominic tightly. 'Peter is going to adopt him. He'll be his father – has been since the day of his birth.'

'But he's mine. You can't get away from it. He looks like me. He'll grow up like me,' Lester insisted, and there was no longer mockery in his eyes. It had been replaced by a desperate hunger.

'Not if I can help it,' she said quietly.

'Won't you change your mind?' This was the first time ever that Lester had been denied something he wanted.

'No, Lester.'

'You'll not reconsider?'

'It's no use.'

He stood there silent, then said, 'May I hold him? Just once before I go.'

She hesitated. What was to stop him striding off with the boy before anyone could prevent him? He was crazy enough to do it, and his money and influence would help him. She'd never get her child back.

'Please, Margaret,' he said humbly.

She had wanted revenge and now it was sweet. She had never

305

expected to have him begging her for a favour. But her triumph was short-lived, turning to dust in her mouth. Hurting him gave her no pleasure, this man whom she had once loved more than life. She held Dominic out to him and he scooped him into his arms.

'Hello, little one. I'm your papa,' Lester said gently.

Dominic, usually suspicious of strangers, stared at him unblinkingly, answering his smile with one of his own. Then he looked towards Margaret for reassurance, his mouth quivering.

She took him and, from this safe vantage point, he continued to subject Lester to that clear, steady stare.

'You mean it then? You'll never come to me?' he said slowly.

'No.'

'Very well. I must go back to the reception before questions are asked.' He fumbled in his pocket. 'I've money here. Will you take it for Dominic?'

'No. I want nothing from you.'

'So, I've lost you both.'

'Yes.'

'You are without mercy, Margaret.'

'I've been taught by experts.'

He let himself out of the office very quietly, and Margaret waited until she was sure he had gone and then took Dominic to Nancy. After this, she continued her search for Peter.

She found him, leaning against a tree, his hands stuffed deep in his pockets. He looked up as she came out of the side door.

'Well?' he said, calm outside, churning within. 'Has he gone?'

'You knew he was here?'

'I saw him leave his car.'

'Why didn't you interrupt us?'

'It was for you to sort out, my dear. I read about the wedding, but didn't mention it hoping you'd let the matter rest, but when you weren't here for breakfast, I knew you'd gone to St Martin's.'

'Oh, Peter,' she whispered.

'Even after I'd saved you from the police, I still wasn't sure. Even less so, when I saw Lester come here. I can't go on like this, Margaret.'

'It's finished, I promise you.' Her face was white and pinched.

He got out a cigarette and had trouble with the matches. Then he threw her a hard glance. 'Why did you go to the church? That was a bloody silly thing to do.'

'I had to see with my own eyes, face him and my father—'

'What good did it do?' His voice was chilly.

'It cauterised the pain in my soul. And even though the wedding went ahead, I'll guarantee they'll never be happy. Lester came here to ask me to be his mistress later on. He'll not change, and they will have a miserable existence.'

'You refused him?'

'Peter, how can you ask me that? It's insulting!'

'Is it? Can I be sure of you after this?'

'There's no question of it.'

'But you still seek revenge? You won't allow him contact with Dominic?'

'Never!'

'"Hell hath no fury",' he said and his mouth turned down at the corners. 'Such vehemence makes it sound as if he still affects you deeply.'

'You're wrong. There's something I want to say, Peter.' This is so difficult, she thought. I've led him such a dance and don't deserve him.

'Go ahead.' He looked directly at her and held her gaze.

'I came here to say that I love you.'

Silence. Margaret twisted her hands together in desperation. He was so very still.

His face changed subtly. Was it softening? Or was this wishful thinking on her part?

'You already told me that,' he said, the cigarette to his lips.

'I know, and I meant it then, but this is different.' She was determined to have this out, no matter what. 'Lester was my first love, and I went into it madly, giving everything, expecting everything in return. All right, so I deceived myself – I accept that. I fell in love with love, if you like. I needed so much to be wanted, and he was very convincing. Now I've come through the fire and realise the meaning of *love* – not infatuation or obsession, but the solid bedrock foundation that lasts a lifetime.'

'You make it sound very dull,' he said, but he had moved a little closer. She could smell his cologne and the fresh scent of his hair and skin.

Lights sprang on in the house, and Philippe had fixed up pumpkins with candles inside. They grinned like hobgoblins. Halloween Night, a suitable choice for Lester's wedding, Margaret thought grimly. The bare branches rustled overhead and the kitchen cat came up from the basement to wind round her skirts. She bent to rub him in that ticklish place behind the ears that made his yellow eyes slit with ecstasy.

'It's not dull, Peter. It's lovely,' she said. 'I'm mature now. I can give you so much more. We're friends, aren't we? And I want to know you even better, to be closer to you than anyone else. You're handsome, charming and I want you, but it's romantic, too – the way you woo me,

307

care for me, laugh with me, love me. And I'm free to return that love in full now. The spell was finally broken today.'

Peter was silent again and she could feel herself disintegrating. She wanted to reach out for him and touch him, but they were standing close and not moving. And she could not, dare not be the first one to touch. Supposing he rejected her? This would be a blow from which she would never recover.

'I've been such a fool,' she whispered, and wanted to cry, the episode in the church, her father's denial, the meeting with Lester just now, and the fact that she may have lost Peter, coming upon her like a tidal wave.

'Margaret.' He breathed her name caressingly, so close she could see the fineness of his skin, the tiny lines radiating from his eyes.

'I'm yours, Peter,' she said, and rested her head against his chest, feeling his hands moving over her hair.

'He's out of your life for good?'

'Yes.'

'Are you quite, quite certain? I can't marry you looking over my shoulder the whole time, wondering if he's going to turn up.'

'All I feel for him is scorn.'

He opened his greatcoat and wrapped it round them both, but still she could not get close enough. 'Come inside, Peter,' she whispered urgently. 'Take me to bed.'

His hands were shaking, but his grip on her tightened. 'We said we'd wait,' he reminded her.

'I need to belong to you – now. To feel you with me, you alone – no ghosts of the past, no one else – just you.'

'Margaret,' he repeated before his lips closed over hers, and now his kiss was possessive, confident in her response, his hands moving over her body, learning to know the gentle curves and angles, wanting to push away the clothing and experience her in every way.

They stood there in the advancing twilight, locked in an embrace, almost afraid to let go, then slowly, still pressed close, they went back into the hotel and climbed the stairs.

Lillian, standing in the doorway of her apartment, saw them go, though they were oblivious to everything. There was something different about them that moved her deeply – a radiant, blissful aura. She sighed, giving a satisfied little nod as she offered up a silent prayer that it would remain thus for them, for always.